10|17

J

LONG JOHN SILVER

Also by Björn Larsson in English translation

THE CELTIC RING

Björn Larsson

LONG JOHN SILVER

*The true and eventful History
of my Life of Liberty and Adventure
as a Gentleman of Fortune & Enemy to Mankind*

*Translated from the Swedish
by Tom Geddes*

THE HARVILL PRESS
LONDON

First published in Sweden with the title
Long John Silver by Norstedts Förlag, Stockholm 1995

First published in Great Britain in 1999 by
The Harvill Press
2 Aztec Row
Berners Road
London N1 0PW

www.harvill.com

3 5 7 9 8 6 4

Copyright © Björn Larsson, 1995
English translation copyright © Tom Geddes, 1999

This edition has been translated with the financial assistance
of the Swedish Institute

Björn Larsson asserts the moral right
to be identified as the author of this work

A CIP catalogue record for this book
is available from the British Library

ISBN 1 86046 694 X (hbk)
ISBN 1 86046 539 0 (pbk)

Designed and typeset in Miller Text at
Libanus Press, Marlborough, Wiltshire

Printed and Bound by Butler and Tanner Ltd
at Selwood Printing, Burgess Hill

To Janne and to Torben,
rebels who submit to nothing,
other than to love

If there are some Incidents and Turns in the Stories of the Pyratical Captains, which may give them a little of the Air of a Novel, they are not invented or contrived for that Purpose; it is a kind of Reading this Author is but little acquainted with, but as he himself was exceedingly diverted with them, when they were related to him, he thought they might have the same Effect upon the Reader.

(Captain Johnson, alias Daniel Defoe: *A General History of the Pyrates*, 1724)

In an honest Service, there is thin Commons, low Wages, and hard Labour; in this, Plenty and Satiety, Pleasure and Ease, Liberty and Power; and who would not ballance the Creditor on this Side, when all the Hazard that is run for it, at worst, is only a sour Look or two at choaking. No, a merry Life and a short one, shall be my Motto.

(Captain Bartholomew Roberts, elected Pirate Captain
by the grace of the Crew, 1721)

Says William, very seriously, "I must tell thee, Friend, I am sorry to hear thee talk so; they that never think of dying, often dye without thinking of it."

I carried on the jesting way a while farther, and said, "Prithee do not talk of dying: how do we know we shall ever dye?" and began to laugh.

"I need not answer thee to that," says William, "it is not in my Place to reprove thee who art Commander over me, but I had rather thou wouldst talk otherwise of Death, 'tis a coarse Thing."

"Say any Thing to me, William," said I, "I will take it kindly."

I began now to be very much moved at his Discourse.

Says William, tears running down his Face, "It is because Men live as if they were never to dye, that so many dye before they know how to live."

(Captain Singleton, Pirate Captain by the grace of Daniel Defoe, 1720)

He's no common man, Barbecue. He had a good schooling in his young days, and can speak like a book when so minded; and brave – a lion's nothing alongside of Long John!

(Israel Hands, coxswain to Teach, called Blackbeard,
afterwards in Flint's company)

Everybody know'd you was a kind of a chapling, John; but there's others as could hand and steer as well as you. They liked a bit o' fun, they did. They wasn't so high and dry, nohow, but took their fling, like jolly companions every one.

(Israel Hands to John Silver)

I had, by this time, taken such a horror of his cruelty, duplicity, and power, that I could scarce conceal a shudder when he laid his hand upon my arm.

(Jim Hawkins, on John Silver)

Gentlemen of fortune usually trusts little among themselves, and right they are, you may lay to it. But I have a way with me, I have. When a mate brings a slip on his cable – one as knows me, I mean – it won't be in the same world with old John. There was some that was feared of Pew, and some that was feared of Flint; but Flint his own self was feared of me. Feared he was, and proud.

(Long John Silver, called Barbecue, quartermaster to
Captains England, Taylor and Flint)

Of Silver we have heard no more. That formidable seafaring man with one leg has at last gone clean out of my life; but I dare say he met his old negress, and perhaps still lives in comfort with her and Captain Flint. It is to be hoped so, I suppose, for his chances of comfort in another world are very small.

(Jim Hawkins)

LONG JOHN SILVER

The true and eventful History
of my Life of Liberty and Adventure
as a Gentleman of Fortune & Enemy to Mankind

One

T HE YEAR IS 1742. I have lived a long life. No one can take that away from me. Everyone I have known is dead. Some of them I have myself despatched to the next world, if there be one – but why should there be? In any case my fervent hope is that there is not, for we would meet again in Hell, Blind Pew, Israel Hands, Billy Bones, that dolt Morgan who dared to tip me the black spot, and all the others, even Flint, God preserve him, if there be a God. And they would bid me welcome, bowing and scraping, telling me that everything would be like the old days. But at the same time they would be radiating fear like a burning sun on a calm sea. Fear of what? I ask myself. In Hell they can hardly be in fear of death. How would that look?

No, they were never afraid of death, for by and large it was all one to them whether they lived or died. But even in Hell they would be in fear of me. Why? I ask. All of them, even Flint, who in every other respect was the most courageous man I ever saw or met, were afraid of me.

Despite everything, I thank my lucky stars that we never salvaged Flint's treasure. Because I know how it would have been. The others would have squandered every shilling in a few days. And then they would have sought out old Long John Silver, the only conscience they could ever boast, to wheedle and beg for more. That is how it always was. They never learned.

But there is one thing I am sure of. There are folk who do not know they are alive. It is as if they did not know they even existed. That may be the difference. I was always anxious to save what little skin I had left. Better condemned to death than hanged by your own hand, say I, if we have to choose. The vilest thing in the world is a noose.

Was that why I was like no other man? Because I knew how to live?

Because I knew, better than anyone else, that we only have one chance to live our lives this side of the grave? Was that why I frightened them out of their wits, the best and the worst of them? Because I cared not a jot for the life to come?

Maybe. But one thing is certain: I did not make it easy for anybody to be my equal or my companion. Barbecue is the name I have been called ever since the day I lost my leg, and there was reason enough for it. Ay, if there is anything I remember in this life, it is how I lost my leg and got my name. How could I not? I am reminded of it every time I stand up.

Two

I CAN STILL FEEL the surgeon's knife slicing into my flesh as if it were butter. Four men were given the task of holding me down, but I ordered them about their business. I would see to mine. Their eyes widened and they looked to the surgeon, but not even then did they dare defy me. The surgeon exchanged his knife for a bone-saw.

"You're not human," he said to me when he had finished, having sawn off the leg without a sound passing my lips.

"No?" said I, gathering my last strength for a smile that must have frightened him more than any of the rest. "What am I then?"

On the morrow I hauled myself up on deck. I wanted to live. I had seen too many perish in the foam of the keel, from choking on their own vomit, from gangrene or from loss of blood. I can still vividly picture the scene when I poked my head up over the fo'c's'le. All work came to a standstill as if Flint had bellowed out an order in his hoarse, penetrating voice. Not being stupid, I knew full well that some of them had hoped I would die. I glowered at them particularly, until they averted their eyes or slunk away. Charlie Hangshaft, so called for having by far the longest member on the ship, took to his heels at such a speed that he collided with the rail and toppled overboard, his arms flailing like a windmill. Then I let out a guffaw that even to my own ears sounded as if it came from the underworld or from beyond the grave. I laughed till the tears ran. They say a good laugh prolongs life. Maybe. But if so, then by the powers you should laugh before things come to such a pretty pass. When you are lying on a bench having your leg sawn off it is too late.

Then I observed that nobody but myself was laughing. Thirty fearful pirates were standing like statues about the deck staring as if their eyes would pop out of their sockets.

"Laugh, you lily-livered cowards!" I roared, and all thirty did so.

It sounded as if that many mouths were all trying to outdo one another. It was so preposterous that it set me off laughing again myself. It may have been in some ways the most comical moment in my whole life. But in the end their cackling began to irk me.

"Belay there, or the devil take ye!" I cried, and their jaws clamped shut so fast, you could hear their teeth rattle.

At that moment Flint came down from the poop deck. He had stood watching the whole thing without betraying a flicker of emotion. He walked over to me now with a pleased but respectful grin on his face.

"Good to see you again, Silver," said he.

I made no reply. It was never good to see Flint. He turned to the crew and said, "We've a need of real men aboard."

And bending down, he took hold of the end of my stump and squeezed it hard for everyone to see.

All went black before my eyes, but I did not faint, nor did a sound issue from my lips.

Flint straightened up again and looked at his men, whose countenances and attitudes were grotesquely distorted with horror.

"As you can see," said Flint dispassionately, "Silver is a real man."

That was the closest Flint could get to friendship and human warmth.

I sat the whole day long in the sun and roasted myself. The pain ebbed and flowed like a throbbing heart. But I was alive.

Nothing else counted but the fact that I still lived. Israel Hands had put out a bottle of rum, as if grog were the fountain of life, but I did not touch it all day. I have never had need of rum, even less so on that occasion.

Later in the evening I asked John, the ship's boy, to fetch a lamp and sit down beside me. I have always had a weakness for young boys. Not to touch them. Not at all. I am not drawn to skin and flesh, no matter who may be wearing it. Perhaps because I have so little of it left myself. When I have lain with women – because we must if we are not to go mad – I have done it as fast as it came, in a manner of speaking. Young boys are a different matter. They are as clean as a new-scraped hull, as smooth as polished brass, more innocent than nuns. It is as if nothing affects them, not even the worst. Take Jim, Jim Hawkins of the *Hispaniola*. He shot Israel Hands, and it was well that he did; he stood by while men were dying and shrieking in agony; yet it was as if nothing had really happened when we left that accursed island. He believed he still had his whole life before him.

John was the same. He did not draw away when I put my arm round his shoulders like an old friend in the mild night air of the Caribbean. He even asked, "Do it hurt, Mr Silver?"

Thank'ee kindly for the enquiry, I thought. I did not know what to reply. I could hardly assert that I had pain in the foot that was no longer there and that was presumably floating around somewhere in the vicinity of the old *Walrus*. If the sharks had not already eaten it. I regretted not having asked the surgeon to keep my amputated limb. I could have cleaned off the flesh and had it as a keepsake: that is what I should have done. Now I could imagine instead some negro finding it on the beach with no idea that it had belonged to none other than myself, Long John Silver.

"No," was all I said, "John Silver don't never feel pain. How would it look? Who'd have any respect for me if I whimpered for having lost a leg? Who, I asks?"

He looked at me with eyes full to the brim with admiration. I'll be hanged if he didn't believe me.

"Now, tell me about the battle," said I.

"But you was there yourself, Mr Silver."

"Ay, that I was. But I wants to hear 'bout it from you. I didn't have time to follow all that was a-goin' on. I had my hands full, so to speak."

John seemed to accept that. He had no inkling of what I was after.

"We took pris'ners," said he. "Ten on 'em. There were a woman too."

"Where is she now?"

"I think Flint's got her."

That was more than likely. Flint was crazy for women and could never keep his hands off them. I have met many a captain, and sailed with a goodly few, each one worse than the last. But none of them, save Flint, would allow himself to appropriate a prisoner for his own account. There were many who had been deposed for trying to keep a woman for their own pleasure. I have myself been responsible for writing it into articles that no one was to lay hands on a woman. Unless everyone could. But Flint could do it. I don't even remember what was in the articles on the *Walrus*. Probably nothing. Flint had his own articles, and that was an end to it.

"So, he has, has he?" said I to John. "And what's Captain Flint a-doin' with her then, thinks you?"

The poor boy blushed. It was almost touching.

"What about the battle?" I added, to divert his mind to other things. "You was a-goin' to tell me how it went."

"Where d'you want me to begin, Mr Silver?"

"At the beginning. A story always begins at the beginning."

I wanted him to learn. All young men must be able to spin a yarn if they are to look after themselves in life. Otherwise they can be led by the nose, time after time.

"The look-out sighted a ship at daybreak," began John. "The weather were fine, so he could see a fair distance. We set full sail, but even so it were eight bells afore we drew level. The second mate hoisted the red flag."

"What do that mean?" I asked.

"That no mercy'll be shown," replied John in a flash.

"And what do that mean, d'you think?"

He looked confused.

"I ain't rightly sure," said he at last in some perplexity.

"Well, I'll tell you. It means we intends to fight for life or death. And the victor decides whether the others live or die. Do you understand?"

"Ay, Mr Silver."

"On you goes, then!"

"Israel Hands said Flint were a wily cap'n. He said as how Cap'n Flint had made sure the enemy had the sun in their eyes an' lay to leeward behind us. Hands said they hadn't a chance, they should've surrendered instead o' defying the likes of us. We sailed 'neath their stern first of all an' fired off a broadside. Then we turned athwart the wind an' fired again, this time with all our cannon at once. Their sails was riddled with holes an' one o' their masts come tumbling down."

"Tumbling down?"

This was hardly good enough. A cannon-ball hit the mainmast straight on, and it splintered like matchwood and came crashing down and plunged overboard with an ear-splitting din. The mainsail sounded like the crack of a whip as it tore. Many of their musketeers screamed their last as they were dragged down into the sea.

"Well, snapped off then," said John, as if that were an improvement.

"And then?" I prompted.

"Then the whole crew of the *Walrus* lined up at the rail. They all had muskets, sabres an' grapplin' irons. An' they was all shrieking."

"And why was they shrieking?"

"To frighten 'em," said John confidently.

That was something he was sure he knew.

"Right!" I replied. "Or maybe they was screamin' like stuck pigs because they was afeared they was a-fillin' of their breeches."

John looked at me in amazement.

"Ain't everybody on the *Walrus* brave?" he asked.

I did not answer. He would also have to learn to think for himself.

"And then?" I asked again. "What happened next?"

John hesitated.

"I don't rightly know what happened next. The other ship suddenly swung round afore we had time to board her. Someone said as it was their broken mast in the water as pulled the bow round. So then they fired a broadside too. Some of our men died. And you, Mr Silver, was hit in the leg. But then we rammed into 'em an' all our crew jumped aboard to fight. It weren't long afore they struck their flag."

"Stay a minute," I interrupted him. "This is important, so listen closely. You said everyone on the *Walrus* was standing along the rail. Are you certain it was everyone?"

"Not the second mate, Mr Bones. He were a-standing at the wheel steering all the time."

"'Tis so, he was. But apart from Bones on the bridge, was there no one else standing on deck, somewhere amidships, behind the rest of us? Think carefully!"

"No," began John, but then stopped himself. "Oh, ay, there were actually one man not standing at the rail."

"Who was it?" I asked, trying not to show what I was feeling.

"Deval, the Frenchman."

"Are you sure?" I asked, though I already knew he was right.

The boy must have heard something in my voice, for he hesitated, but then said, "Ay, I'm sure."

I drew a deep breath and put my arm round John and hugged him.

"Just between real men," said I, and he glowed with pride.

"That were a fine account," I continued, letting go of him. "Now, a word o' good advice from ol' Silver, who's been through a lot, he has. Learn how to tell stories. Learn how to invent and how to lie. That way you'll always do well enough. Keeping silent and at a loss for an answer is the worst that can happen to a man, says I. If you wants to be a man, o' course. If not, it don't matter so much."

John nodded.

"Now I'd like to be alone for a while," I went on, "to sit here on my own and look at the moon and the stars. You can turn in. You've done a good day's work, as sure as my name's Silver."

"Thank'ee, sir," said John, without really knowing what it was he was thanking me for.

I watched him go and leaned back. He had saved my life, I have a mind to believe. I am not certain I could have borne for long not knowing who it was who had tried to murther me from the rear. Everyone thought it was the enemy's broadside that shattered my leg. I was the only one who knew that the ball struck me after their broadside. Only by seconds, perhaps, but after. Deval, the cowardly rat, who once upon a time had wanted to be my friend, had shot me from behind. It was lucky for Long John Silver that the old *Walrus* had taken a lurch as the broadside hit us, otherwise I would have been dead and my story at an end, just like so many others in our profession, all for nothing.

I closed my eyes to await the coming day.

The next morning I hobbled up to Flint's cabin and went in without knocking. He was lying in bed with the woman.

"Well, if it ain't Silver," said he. "Out for a walk?" he jeered, with his customary gallows humour.

"Doing my best, Flint," was all I said.

He managed a wry smile and gave the woman at his side a meaning-ful look.

"Silver," said he, "is the only man on board who's worth anything. He can't navigate, which is my good fortune, or he would've been cap'n and myself quartermaster. Ain't that so, Silver?"

"Mebbe. But I'm here now on other business than my own qualities."

Flint saw that I was serious, and sat up in bed. His hairy chest put me in mind of fox fur. I explained calmly what had happened, taking care to show no anger. Flint listened equally calmly, while the woman could not take her eyes off the stump of my leg, a-muck with the red blood that had already seeped through the new bandage the doctor had applied that morning.

"I mean to punish him myself," said I. "With your permission, o' course."

"Of course," said Flint without any hesitation, which was by no means unusual for him. "Of course," he repeated. "But how? That's what I'd like to know."

I saw a smile of anticipation playing on his lips.

"With that leg," he added doubtfully.

"Don't let that trouble you! I could handle a craven coward like him with no legs and only one arm if need be."

"I'm sure you could," said Flint, and meant it.

For him there was nothing unnatural about the idea that a person could live and fight without arms or legs.

"We're going ashore this afternoon as planned?" I asked, more by way of stating a fact than asking a question.

"Ay," said Flint, "as we agreed at the fo'c's'le council. We'll go ashore with all the victuals and rum we took from the *Rose*. Then we'll eat and drink till we drop. As we always do. No change."

"Good. Then I'll take care of the entertainment."

"You won't be disappointed," said he to the woman, nudging her thin, naked body, "I promise you that. I know my Silver."

She was still staring at my leg. But I was surprised she was not scared witless from having spent the night with Flint. Perhaps he had one virtue after all. If so, it was the only one, apart from the fact that he could navigate and lead a boarding party like no other man. I still cannot understand how he could have learned navigation. Flint was shrewd, that he was, but he was not a man who could think, unless it were a matter of life or death.

We went ashore in the late afternoon, three gigs and the jolly-boat. Everyone went. I had lain on deck all day while it was being swabbed, gathering my strength. The blood from the previous day had been swilled away; the corpses had already been cast overboard. A party of men was unloading the booty from the *Rose* to the *Walrus*. There were cries and huzzas for each gold coin and each jewel that came aboard. I lay with half-closed eyes watching every movement. Deval went by several times without vouchsafing me even a glance.

"Deval," I called out as he passed on one of these occasions.

He stopped and looked at me with eyes full of loathing. But there was fear too, not unusual in those who lack the courage to stand on their own two feet.

"Fine booty, Deval," said I, giving him one of my warmest smiles that would melt butter in the sun.

He made no reply, but just continued on his way.

The *Rose* was a good prize, one of the best, that she was, but just then doubloons and gold were the last things on my mind. No, not even her precious stones, my weakness, could throw me off course.

I made sure I climbed aboard the same boat as Deval. I think it was Pew who aided me, though he had lost his sight when a fuse exploded in his face as we boarded the *Rose*. Not that it seemed to affect him in the least. He was just as bloody-minded as he had always been. He stood on deck and dropped me down like a sack of potatoes. He threw the stick the carpenter had cut me that morning haphazard after me like a spear. For all Pew cared it could have pierced the skull of one of the men. Blind or not, it was his idea of amusement. People had to die before he thought life worth living. But I stretched to my limit and caught the stick in flight. Putting a spoke, or stick, in Pew's wheel, so to speak, was something I always tried to do when I had the chance. Yet he harboured no grudge against me. It was probably beyond his simple understanding.

Taking the stick in my right hand I gave Deval, who was for'ard of me, a gentle tap on the shoulder.

"That were close to the mark, Deval," said I. "It could've hit home. But 'tis a grand day, Deval, ain't it? We couldn't have had a better one."

He grunted something inaudible in reply without turning round. He probably did not dare look me in the eyes for fear I might guess what had really happened when my leg was shot to shreds.

"A good prize and plenty o' grog," I went on cheerily. "Shiver my timbers, that's all we needs to make the day for a gentleman o' fortune. What else should we need? Women, says you. Ay, mebbe. But gold an' grog are easier to divide up. Among friends, that is."

A murmur of approval could be heard from the men. They were all happy and expectant. Life was a game for them. On shore there was never any semblance of discipline. They were a law unto themselves entirely, and not even Flint could do anything about it. It was where they could demonstrate that they had a right to live like other people. It was the same sorry tale every time. One long infernal melée of endless grog, bawling and brawling, squabbling and squalling, gaming and grog, and yet more grog.

I looked across to Flint's boat a cable length for'ard of us. He himself was standing at the stern in his big blood-red hat roaring out his orders. In a boat with a crew Flint had only one tone of voice. It mattered not whether it was a jolly-boat or a frigate. Flint had a mouth like a foghorn. He had left the prisoner behind on board after all, which indicated that he meant to keep her to himself for a few more days. I looked around for the surgeon. Ay, he was there too, his bald pate visible two thwarts in front of Flint, standing out like a fresh-plucked turkey.

I have never understood ships' surgeons, and our own on the *Walrus* perhaps least of all. What was it that made them try to keep the likes of us alive when we did not exactly seem to concern ourselves too much about it, and on top of that detested them like the plague? I have never met a sailor who had any time for doctors. A life spent with blood, to what avail? They were certainly not religious. Nor yet merciful Samaritans. So why? I did not understand it then, and still do not understand. They were often educated fellows, as well. Apart from myself, the surgeon of the *Walrus* was more or less the only one who had read a proper book. And I don't mean the Bible. Not that it would have helped him overmuch. He was a miserable devil. But today he would at least do something useful for his share of the booty. And he had saved my life, after all. I might even bring myself to express some gratitude. For a change.

We sailed half a sea mile the length of the island till we came to the north-east point, and then hauled up the boats on the south side of the headland. It was not the first time we had been there. The remains of our old fires were still on the beach. Empty rum bottles, too. The sand was white and glittering like the diamonds that had been crushed into a thousand pieces by the madmen on the *Cassandra* just so they could share the stones out equally. The crowns of the palm trees cast big black star-shaped shadows that fluttered when the wind rustled through the branches above. From time to time a coconut would drop like a cannon-ball. When we were here before, one of the crew was hit on the head by a coconut and died on the spot. To everyone's delight. None of us had believed you could die of such a thing. But now no one would sit near the trunks of palm trees. It was not that comical.

The headland was not a random choice. Flint was a careful captain when his own skin was at risk, at least until he went completely out of his mind in the last year of his life. He had discovered the advantages of the place long ago. The point jutted out a couple of hundred ells from land like a slender crooked finger. From the top of the crook there was an uninterrupted view both to the north and to the south, allowing sight of any vessel on its way to the island. And the passage through the reef was so far out that we would always have time to go aboard the *Walrus* and make the ship ready for battle. Assuming we were not blind drunk, naturally.

We had hardly got ashore before a few of the men had broached a barrel of rum. Others were not in such a great hurry. They flung themselves down on the beach with their arms beneath their heads and just lay there as if dead. I hopped around on my one leg as well as I could, and spoke to all of them like the genial comrade I could be when the need arose. I spread as much good humour as possible, so that no one would forget that Long John Silver had a kind heart, and that whatever he did, he had his reasons.

Some of them began to boast at the tops of their voices about their exploits, as if they sounded better if you bayed like a wolf. Morgan, who could not count much beyond six, had brought out his dice and was tempting each and every one of them to gamble for their share of the spoils. That was the sort of man Morgan was. He risked his life to be able to play dice. I once suggested to him that we should just roll the dice for our lives instead. It would be quicker, said I. But Morgan didn't understand the joke.

Pew wandered about as always picking quarrels, though rather more confusedly than usual. Black Dog prowled round some of the newer, younger members of the crew. The first to fall in a drunken stupor would be dragged off into the bushes. What enjoyment he had from it the gods alone knew. Flint, befitting his reputation, sat with his own keg of rum. He would have drunk it all before the evening was at an end. Flint could drink rum like no other man. When all the rest had toppled over Flint would still be sitting upright, eyes glazed and staring into the fire. The more he drank, the quieter he became. In the end not a sound would pass his lips, he would just sit and stare. And believe it or not, I have seen him on nights like this weep tears that were far from crocodile. For what? I once asked him.

"For all the good seamen that have died to no avail," he answered sentimentally.

"But you and I are alive, and hale an' hearty," I protested, to cheer him.

"What satisfaction is that to me?" he asked, staring into space.

That was the only time, I think, that I did not understand Flint. Deuce knows whether he did himself.

That evening I observed that he was holding back on the rum. I knew what he was waiting for, but I was in no hurry. Let the food be served first. It arrived straight after nightfall. Job, Johnny and Dirk came back dragging two goats they had managed to shoot before the sun went down. This caused some excitement, with much cheering and other signs of approval. It suited me well, for it would give extra spice to what I had in mind, I reckoned.

"Deval!" yelled Dirk, "you old goat-butcher, you can be grillmaster."

That was exactly what I had been hoping for and counting on. Simply because he was a Frenchman he was still regarded as something of a buccaneer of the old days. That was why he was the one to roast the goats on the spit, what the French called *barbe-au-cul*, instead of what it really was, *barbacoa*, in the language of the Indians. But it was not so strange that the French had misheard, because the method was to cut off the goat's tail and push a pointed stake up its backside right through to the other end. And by the powers, it sometimes looked as if the goat, with its tiny residual stump of tail, had acquired a beard on its hind quarters, *barbe-au-cul* in the French language. Ay, that's the reason, though 'tis forgot now. There are not many who know that my name, Barbecue, means beard on the arse.

Deval smiled his best sneering, scornful grin, as only he could. It was the only one he had, for that matter. Then he took up his knife and cut off the tails in the proper way. Dirk gave him the sharpened stakes and Deval pierced the beasts with a single thrust from stern to stem. That was the way it should be done, and the men whooped in excitement like the connoisseurs they were. Meanwhile Johnny had erected tripods on either side of the fire, and it was not long before the air was filled with the smell of roasting goat flesh. I saw some of the men salivating like dogs. It was hardly to be wondered at, after all. It was the first fresh meat they had scented for many a week.

I bided my time till they were all feasting and the fat was running down their chins. I had taken up position directly behind Deval with my musket at the ready.

"Shipmates!" I cried, "May I crave your attention for a kindly soul who wishes to say a few words?"

I think they all looked up, but none of them stopped their guzzling and gobbling.

"You're eating good meat," I went on, "you're in fine fettle, you are. There's rum enough for a whole navy. You've a smart cap'n who can make you rich men if you've a mind to it. I propose a toast to Flint!"

They threw themselves heart and soul into a huzza. They knew that without Flint they were not worth a brass farthing.

"'Tis naught but your doos," I continued. "It were a fine prize you took yest'day. Every man did his dooty."

I fell silent for a moment, and then said, "You can be proud o' yourselves. All of you."

There I paused again, but briefly.

"All of you save one."

I saw with the tail of my eye that Flint had put his hand on his cutlass. He probably reckoned there might be a skirmish if the man I was out to get was one who had the confidence of the crew. A rattlesnake like Deval, however, had never enjoyed the confidence of anyone.

But it was evident that there were many who did not consider their consciences to be clear, the way they squirmed and averted their eyes.

"I lost a leg in the battle yest'day. 'Tis the sort o' thing that happens when you fight for a good cause. I can even think myself lucky, since I'm alive and can still stand with one leg on the ground, leastways. Imagine if it'd been both that'd been docked. What would that have looked like, d'you think?"

Think they obviously did, and several burst into uncontrollable laughter. I have to admit that a legless Long John Silver speechifying by the fire and stuck down direct on the sand would have been quite a diverting sight – for everyone else, that is. Because that was exactly the picture the men had in their mind's eye. That was the limit of their imagination.

"I propose a toast to the surgeon!" I shouted amidst all the hubbub, and they all cheered again from the bottom of their hearts.

The surgeon's face did not light up – it never did – he just wiped the sweat off his bald pate with his hand. I wondered if he thought I was playing a trick and about to accuse him of not saving my leg. Well, it would do no harm.

"So our surgeon shall have a new honour. He shall saw off another leg, with the same skill and dexterity he displayed on mine."

His eyes suddenly glistened with fear. Now he certainly believed that I was going to force him to saw off his own, that I was displeased with his medical abilities. But at that same instant I raised my double-barrelled musket and pressed it to Deval's skull.

"Here sits our worthy grillmaster feigning innocence," said I in a voice that brought even their guzzling to a halt. "We gentlemen o' fortune are free partners. We shares our spoils and perils accordin' to the rules. We've wrote into the art'cles how much 'tis worth to lose a leg or an arm or a thumb in battle. We 'lects our cap'ns. We reaches agreements. If there are any dissenters, they can demand a council in the custom'ry manner. If anyone has a pers'nal grudge, 'tis settled ashore. We has our faults and shortcomings, we has, but on board is on board, wet or dry. Ain't that so, messmates?"

There were mutters of assent here and there. They were a rough and disorderly bunch, that they were, but they had their rules so that no one could take liberties or set himself up above others.

"Howsomever," I continued in the same tone of voice, "this cowardly rat alongside o' me here, Deval by name, tried to shoot me from behind as we was on the p'int o' boarding the *Rose*. What d'ye say to that, messmates?"

Murmurings again, but no more than that. I knew that nobody would be bursting with anger or sympathy for me, but on the other hand nobody would want to be shot in the back either.

"Proof!"

It was Flint's foghorn voice that cut through the air.

"What proof do you have?"

That was just like Flint. When anything serious was at stake he always had his head screwed on the right way. If I had not had proof, there would have been doubts and discussions.

"The *Rose* fired a broadside of grapeshot and case-shot," said I. "But blest if I ever seen any shot turn in the air and fly back the way it comed. Ain't you of the same mind, Doctor? Tell 'em how the ball went into my leg from the back!"

The surgeon uttered something that was scarcely audible. He was still terror-stricken.

"Pipe up, pipe up! Did the ball go in from the back, ay or nay?"

"Ay," the surgeon croaked. "Ay, it did, without a doubt."

"What d'you say now? Is that proof enough?"

Many of the men yelled ay, and shouted out that Deval could die as far as they were concerned. It would not spoil their appetite, it seemed.

"How do we know Mr Silver didn't have his back to the *Rose*?"

"Who said that?" I bellowed in rage. "Is there any man here who's ever seen Long John Silver present his stern to the en'my?"

There was silence. They were all convinced it was impossible. I turned to Deval.

"What've you to say for yourself?" I asked contemptuously.

Hatred blazed in his eyes. Never in my wildest dreams could I have imagined that anyone could hate with such passion. Not even if I was the object of it.

"That it was a confounded pity I only got your leg!" replied Deval, without seeming to see what a fool he was making of himself.

He could simply have asked how I could be so sure it was him and nobody else who had fired the shot. He could not have known I would never have called on John as a witness. Because that would have signed John's death warrant, sooner or later, you may lay to it.

"A pity for you, I reck'n," said I to Deval with a laugh. "But not for the rest on us. Doctor, come here!"

He approached me with reluctance.

"Now, my dear Surgeon," said I, "you can show the entire crew of the *Walrus* and Cap'n Flint how you ampytates a leg. All accordin' to the rules."

"No, not that!" shrieked Deval, as white as a corpse.

"Ay, no more, no less. A leg for a leg squares the count. Dirk and George, come over here and hold the swab down till he loses his senses. He ain't famous for his brav'ry, you may take your affy-davy on't."

Dirk and George came running over. I pulled the bone-saw out of my jacket where I had stowed it away since taking it while the surgeon slumbered.

"There you are, Doctor! Prove your skill. Once could've been luck. But let's hope not, for Deval's sake."

"But my good Mr Silver, I can't do it. The man isn't wounded. I'm a doctor, not a butcher."

The sweat was pouring off him.

"But my good Doctor," I replied, "was not I in fine health when Deval shot me from behind? Accordin' to the rules I've a right to settle his hash, like the dog he is. But I don't go round a-murth'ring people unnecessarily. No one benefits from that. Not even myself. What use is a corpse? Anyhow, my good Doctor, you have no choice."

Deval screamed as the Surgeon tightened the blade. But I think he fainted before the Doctor had even managed to make a start.

"By thunder," I heard Black Dog say behind me. "He's a-sp'ilin' all the fun."

I also observed that the Surgeon seemed to have a marked distaste for his work. He obviously had a squeamish spot in his murky conscience. That was a discovery that might come in useful some day.

When Deval's leg was off I picked it up and went across to the fire. There was complete silence, except for the sobbing of the surgeon. I took down one of the grill spits and pierced Deval's leg from top to toe with a single thrust, in the proper way. But this time none of the men rejoiced, despite their epicurean tastes. Then I hung the stump over the flames.

"We'll call this Barbecue!" I shouted.

Nobody said anything for a moment, but then I heard Pew's cracked voice again, who else's, when he apprehended what I had done. His sense of smell, at all events, had not suffered any harm from his misfortune.

"Huzza for Silver!" he roared elatedly. "Huzza for Barbecue!"

A few weak cheers came from various directions. But there was no real spirit in them. Fear, if anything. Abject terror. And was that not the intention? What did I care about Deval? I could equally well have shot him on the spot. Truth to tell, I might have preferred to put a bullet in him there and then. That would have been more merciful, after all, for Deval. But now at least I could be sure that no one else would set themselves up against me for a good while, not even behind my back. I would be left in peace. It was as simple as that.

I cast a glance at Flint. He was sitting gazing rigidly at the charred leg. Then he looked at me long and hard and nodded silently. With all due respect.

Since that day Barbecue has been my name. And just to think that Trelawney, Livesey, Smollett and their cronies imagined it was for my culinary skills.

I sat myself down heavily on the beach, and when I finally fell asleep it was to the stench of burned human flesh and roasted shoe leather.

Just the one.

Three

T HE SUN IS coming up over the horizon and makes the sea in Ranter Bay glint and shimmer like all of Madagascar's precious stones at once. It is what passes for beauty, but what good is that to me? I am not grumbling, but I have to say that life has little left to offer me.

I came here in 1737 with Dolores, and my parrot, and Jack and the other ransomed slaves from the unsubmissive Sakalava tribe. I fled here, to Plantain's old refuge, after the wretched bungle of the expedition for Flint's treasure. Here, on the main island, the former Paradise for gentlemen of fortune, I have run aground as the last of my ilk and calling. Here I shall live till the time comes for me to go to the breaker's yard. I have started writing my log-book, and that is about all. I have told many a yarn, and led many by the nose. That was how I got on in the world. I always had an answer. No one else would have answered for me.

Now there is nobody to lead by the nose. Not my parrot, that I called Flint, nor my wife, whose name I did not even know. I named her Dolores, because she had to be called something. Dolores and Flint died at almost the same time. Dolores first, without a sound, without the slightest warning, without leaving the slightest trace of life behind her, like the wake of a ship or the morning dew. All of a sudden she was simply gone, just as though she had never existed. And I was left alone, like a numskull, no longer knowing the meaning of anything.

Flint went the next day, but she did it in style. I don't know how old she can have been; nobody knows. Maybe an hundred. She had sailed with all the great captains, with Morgan, with L'Olonnais, called the Bloody, for obvious reasons, with Roberts, England and La Bouche. But Flint was the parrot's last captain and so her name, since I don't count that buffoon Smollett on the *Hispaniola*. All her life the parrot had been in the habit of keeping her beak shut, in a manner of speaking, when it was too hot in the middle of the day. But on this particular day she hooted and squawked from early in the morning to late in the evening. She came out with all the rigmarole and insults she knew – no small amount. She enumerated all the strange coins there are in the world, hardly few in number either. Then she looked at me, with her head on one side, and her eyes so sorrowful that I burst into tears. I, Long John Silver, started to weep for a wretched parrot! Finally, with her last remaining strength, she straightened her head and whispered, if a parrot can whisper:

"Fifteen men on the dead man's chest. Yo-ho-ho and a bottle of rum!"

And then it was over. A parrot that had lived an hundred years or more consigned to the grave as if none of the adventures she had taken part in had ever happened. And I, alone, was left. Alone with a few ransomed slaves, a body-guard with scarce anything to guard but a leaky hull full of riches. Shameful, but true. I, who all my life had been my own man and sufficient unto myself, I no longer knew what the point of it had been!

I counted my coins without knowing what use it was. I bedded the native girls, but the sap had long ago dried up in me for ever. I rambled on about one thing and another, but nobody listened. Not even myself.

But then one day I began to tell my story, just as it came to mind, about my leg and how I came to be given my nickname, with due cause. Who would have believed this was how it would all turn out? The true and eventful account of Long John Silver, called Barbecue by his friends, if he had any, and by his foes, of which he had many. An end to foolery and fantasy. An end to humbug and deceit. Cards on the table for the first time. Nothing but the truth, straight to the point, without tricks or evasions. How it really was and nothing more. That was what was needed! That was what was needed to keep me sane for a while longer!

Four

IT IS NOT impossible that I was born in 1685, if, as I believe, I have lived for fifty-six years. It was in Bristol, that much is certain, in a room with a view of the sea, or at least of the arm of the Atlantic called the Bristol Channel, that contained more smugglers' haunts than any other inlet in the whole world. But anyone who thinks I went to sea because of the view is mistaken. Everyone in Bristol went to sea sooner or later, including myself, though it was not my intention.

It was said that my old man had a mind of his own, and it may well have been true. The only thing I know for certain is that he would have very little in his head when he came home from the tavern. Nor on it, for that matter: it sometimes even looked as if he had been hauled home by his feet with his head in the dirt like a plough. He had as much difficulty distinguishing right from left as he did standing on his feet, and I have always been inclined to think this was my good fortune as well as his. His good fortune in that he died, and mine for the same reason.

One night on the way home from the tavern, he turned left instead of right, and fell straight into the harbour. They found him two days later, washed up by the tide on a rocky islet, for once with his head in the air, to the extent that it was still intact. His face was smashed and swollen like a toad. I saw him as the coffin was about to be nailed up. He might have had a mind of his own, as they said of him, but not at that moment, and never as far as I recollect. It was a good thing he went off to die, quite literally. I thought so then, and I think so now. If there is one thing we could do without here on earth, it is fathers, both God the Father Himself and all His puffed-up likenesses. Let them beget and then drink themselves to death. Is that not what they do in any case?

Things were neither better nor worse because my own creator was an Irishman. Nor because my mother was a Scot from the Islands. I have no idea how they ended up in Bristol, but there can be no doubt that it was the seafaring life that brought them together and caused him to ram and board her.

My mother was my mother, and that is the most important thing. She did the best she could, and what was the result? – Long John Silver, quartermaster on the *Walrus*, a man of means and much feared, whose words carried weight wheresoever he steered his course; educated to boot, who knew how to deport himself and speak Latin, if the need arose. Should she not have been content? Was this not the same as could be said of many great men who sat at Westminster or on their estates?

My mother really did do the best she could, perhaps even for me, but at any rate for herself. I came to understand that she was a woman of quite prepossessing appearance, with her head firmly on her shoulders. That went a long way, or too far, depending on how you look at it, but it served her well until she married again, this time a prosperous merchant. He hated me, but he was a Scotsman and so I had to go to school and at least learn Latin and the Bible. That would always come in useful, he said. Strangely enough, he was right. Amongst gentlemen of fortune I often enjoyed and profited by the reputation of being an educated man. It was said of me that I had received a good education in my youth and that I could speak like a book. But on the other hand the simple reputation would have been sufficient. In that respect my *de facto* knowledge of Latin was neither here nor there. After all, who would I speak it with?

I do not know how it is nowadays, but when I was young it was only in Scotland that everyone had to go to school. That was why there were so many Scottish ship's doctors among us jolly buccaneers. It was a good thing for us, you could say, since we thus escaped having to make do with incompetent drunkards dismissed from the navy. There were so many unemployed doctors in Glasgow that they signed on with the likes of us for an ordinary wage, at any rate until they discovered that no contract in the world could save them from the gallows when the time came. Then they also began to sail for prize money, and the only difference was that they sullied themselves with blood with an easy conscience, while most of us had no conscience at all.

But I knew even before I went to school that I would not be a surgeon. Blood was never my favourite repast, however unlikely that may appear. So what else was there to choose: priest or lawyer? Either would have been fitting for me. They were professions that gave plenty of scope for lying and leading folk by the nose; indeed, that was by and large the whole point of them. But gradually I comprehended that it would involve singing the same tedious tune over and over again. You had to say what was already said, written and prescribed, not a single syllable more nor less. That was probably the reason why, in the end, they were convinced they were speaking the truth.

Either would thus have been ill-suited to me, since for as long as I can remember I have made things up, exaggerated and embellished. My head was always full of secret doors, and the grass was always greener on the other side. My mother called me imaginative, my step-father called me a liar, especially after I spread it around the city that he was a pimp, though I did not know what it meant at the time, just that it was bad.

So I stayed on that tack. I never concerned myself about who had the right of passage or windward position in the world of words. At school I twisted and turned the landlubbers' rules and articles and made up new ones. I juggled with the Bible till in the end no one knew whether it was up or down, backwards or forwards.

I made progress in law and was much praised. No one had read the law in its entirety, and the laws I created in my chamber were at least as good as the others. But I fared less well with God, in Whose name I was always getting my ears boxed and whippings galore.

When I was tired of spouting His words to the point of blasphemy, I would turn them upside down and shift the ballast to the bridge, so to speak. I let Judas set the course and sent Jesus before the mast, where, by His own admission, he belonged. I transposed Adam and Eve, changed all the men into women, and vice versa. I put the Holy Spirit into a corked bottle, where spirits belong, and hey-ho there was no one to say who would be Pope. I made Moses stumble on the mountain and all the stone tablets shatter into a thousand pieces, and yo-ho we lost the Commandments and our consciences. And so on and so forth, in one interminable hotch-potch.

Until the day I stood up in the refectory to read from the Bible at evening prayers, as was the custom on Sundays. I opened the Holy Book and read out the Commandments as they came into my head. There was not much to be done with the first, of course, it had always struck me as good enough as it was, with one little correction, just to be sure: "I shall have no other gods before me."

What I did with the others I cannot now recall, except that it was in the same spirit, and certainly not the Holy one. But I like to think that the eighth, the last I managed to read, expressed the way I lived: "Thou shalt always bear false witness."

I got no further. When I looked up momentarily from the Bible that I thought I had been reading, I was not aware of what I had done. But seldom have I experienced such a silence. I assumed that I was the one who had silenced them. I had triumphed. I thought.

But then the headmaster stood up very slowly and came towards me. I can still hear his footsteps echoing on the flagstones. Without saying anything he snatched God's words out of my hands and looked long and hard at the open page. When he had seen enough he turned to me.

"Can't you read, John Silver?" he asked in a menacing tone of voice.

"Yes, certainly, sir," I replied cheerfully.

I don't know whether it was this cheery and impudent answer that made him fly into a passion, but within seconds he was as red as a turkey-cock and screaming like a stuck pig.

"If you think you can do just as you please, Silver, you are wrong. If you imagine you can make fun of people and blaspheme with impunity, you are equally mistaken. Out, damn you! If ever I see you here again, I will sew up your mouth, as sure as my name is Nutsford!"

I was rigid with fear, and not just from the thought of never being able to open my mouth again. I had never seen Nutsford lose control of himself. He had always been a courteous and uncommunicative man, especially when he had the pleasure of beating us black and blue with the cane. I was so benumbed that Nutsford was compelled to chase me out of the refectory with vicious heavy kicks that landed on my posteriors with the unerring precision only acquired through long and dedicated practice.

For the first and last time in my life I was really afraid. I learned once and for all how it felt to fear for your life and have to save your skin. The kicking was nothing. Kicks were quite usual for anything and everything. It was the headmaster's white-hot fury that filled me with terror. I was convinced, perhaps with reason, that he would kill me if I stayed. I have seen Taylor lose his temper, I have seen England do so, although he was always regarded as merciful, and I have been present when Flint's rage blossomed forth. But, upon my soul, Nutsford was worse than they, because all he did, he did in the name of salvation and the conviction of his faith. And there are no better credentials for an executioner, life has taught me, than that.

I was saved by the fact that the headmaster returned to the refectory first to lead his flock back into the fold before they came to any harm. That allowed me time to throw together my few belongings, some coins that I had been given by my mother, and even my books. But I left the Bible behind. And I have never missed it since. My own Commandments were more than adequate. At least they were something you could live by.

But it was not until later that same night, as I was running through fields and hedgerows making my way to Glasgow, that I fully understood what I had done, that I had led myself by the nose. It taught me one lesson, I like to believe, although maybe it was something I thought of later. If you are going to lead people by the nose, you must keep your mouth shut. And it is better to find your own words than to try to make use of others'.

Five

ODAY WHEN I awoke soon after sunrise I could not stop looking at my hands and was unable to remember what I was using them for. My hands have always been as soft and white as the thighs of a woman. The inside, that is, nearest the groin.

It was in Glasgow, in an ale-house in the seamen's district of Greenock, where I found myself after my headlong flight from school, that I began to understand the ways of the world. That, for example, there was not a single sailor who could not be recognised by his hands.

By the time I reached Glasgow I had already decided to go to sea. At sea I would be liberated from the folk on land; that, I thought, I could be sure of. No one would take the Commandments particularly seriously there. At sea I would escape raging headmasters and step-fathers who wielded the whip at the slightest provocation. At sea there was life and excitement, and you travelled round the world to places where no one knew you, and where whatever happened it was better than being here. That was what I thought, for what did I know of the world and the sea? Not one jot.

But I had no intention of going aboard the first vessel I came to. I had hung around enough with sailors and dockers in Bristol to have learned that there were captains who hated sailors and captains who hated people, and it was those who hated people that had to be avoided like the plague. For captains to hate sailors was only right and proper. Because sailors hated captains in equal measure. It was their privilege and their duty.

I had hardly put my foot over the threshold of the tavern in question before I heard a grating voice hack out at me like a labourer's pick.

"Sit ye down here, boy. I wouldn't hurt a fly, but I've lived too long and could use a tankard of ale. On someone else's account, as you might guess. I don't think I can add up aright myself any more."

It took me a few seconds to turn round, peer into the gloom and make out a creased, burnished face on a pair of broad but sunken shoulders. Two huge hands – I think I had never seen such hands, and riddled with scars they were – thrust themselves forward as if to demonstrate how things stood, what he looked like and what had become of him, and that that was all there was to say. But the eyes seemed kindly enough amongst all the wizened wrinkles.

"A bit o' company wouldn't harm, neither," he went on, "with the ale."

I had nothing to fear, I reasoned. At fifteen, with a body to match my years, I could stand up to a weary old man if need be. I was not scared of anything, as I have said. Nutsford, the headmaster, was the only one, the first and the last, who ever made me go weak at the knees, apart from a few women, of course. Besides, I thought to myself, I needed to talk to someone who knew about seafaring life in Glasgow.

"So, what's your name, then?" asked he as soon as I had sat down and put my knapsack on the bench.

"John, John Silver," I replied simply and truthfully, and not without a certain pride.

"Silver," he repeated slowly, savouring each letter as if it were a quid of tobacco, "no, I never know'd anyone o' that name. Where are you from?"

"Bristol," said I.

"And your father, what does he do in life?"

"He doesn't do anything in life any more. In the after-life, maybe. He went and drowned in the harbour, and a good thing too."

"Good?" said he enquiringly. "Why?"

"I don't know. It just was." And then I added by way of explanation, "We didn't have a lot of time for one another."

"A'right, John," said he, "We won't go into that. You knows best. But you'll treat me to an ale in any case?

"William Squier!" he cried, without waiting for an answer, in a voice that resounded through the whole establishment. "Ale for two thirsty seamen!"

A shrewd sharp face with thin lips hove into view as a curtain was pulled aside.

"Ale doesna' come free," said the innkeeper.

"I knows that, you ol' skinflint. I ain't never lived on alms, you mind. But we, my friend and I, are in funds."

The landlord inspected me closely, turned on his heel and disappeared into the back room.

"We are, I hopes?" asked the old man in a lower voice.

"What?"

"In funds enough for two ales?"

Certainly, thought I, and plenty more. I had eleven pounds and ten shillings that I had received from my mother when I went to Scotland, without my stepfather's knowledge. "'Tis your inheritance," she had said, "from your real father." But I was not to tell anyone that I had it, nor that it even existed. "Your father didn't actually possess any money," she'd added by way of explanation. It was only later that it occurred to me that there is money that does not exist, and that there is no better money in this world to procure than the invisible kind. I am in no doubt that my money came from smuggling and other questionable dealings on Lundy Island. I was not aware of that then, in Glasgow, but I took my mother at her word. The money was not to be seen, and so I had stitched ten of the pounds into my trouser lining and the rest was distributed loose in small coins in every possible pocket.

"Yes," I replied, "I've enough for a couple of ales, but no more. That's why I'm here. I want to go to sea."

"You?" said he, as if he could not believe his ears. "In them clothes? They're school clothes, if my eyes don't deceive me and I ain't viewing things awry. Why should you go to sea? Ain't you heard what they say? Those who take to the sea for pleasure might as well look for their diversions in Hell."

"I'm not thinking of going to sea for pleasure," I objected.

"No? That's good then. Else I'd 've had to think you wasn't altogether right in the head. But you looks a'right. So why've you thought o' going to sea? Not for the money, surely?"

He looked at me cannily. Did he not believe that my funds were limited?

"Yes," I replied carefully, "for the money I haven't got."

He burst out laughing and banged his great fist on the table.

"That were a smart answer," said he. "Like a royal envoy, that were. You'll go a long way in life."

The landlord came back and slammed down two tankards of ale so that the froth splashed over.

"So ye've had a bit o' guid fortune, then?" said he in a surly tone to my companion, "findin' someone to fleece."

"Have a care!" replied the old man, in a voice that would stand no nonsense. "Watch your step, Squier. Old and tired I may be, but you just look at my hands!"

Involuntarily the landlord glanced down at them, and in a brace of shakes, so fast that I did not even see how it happened, the old man had grabbed his neck with one hand in a grip of iron. With one hand! The landlord's scornful mockery gave way to terror.

"I could break your neck as easy as kill a fly," said he calmly. "But I'm a peaceable fellow. At my age I just wants a quiet life. But not at any price. Get that into your thick skull. Cap'n Barlow ain't a man to push around while he yet lives."

As he spoke he slowly released his grip on the landlord.

"You sees, John," said the old man who called himself a captain, turning to me, "I ain't no envoy like you. Straight to the point has been my motto. I hadn't intended to fleece you, had I? Didn't I say from the very start how things were? Straight to the point."

I nodded. The innkeeper was rubbing his neck and coughing to try and get his breath back.

"I think our dear landlord needs heartening," said Captain Barlow. "You, John Silver, as purser for the both on us, can perhaps reimburse Mr Squier for his civility and trouble in serving us two tankards of ale."

I looked on wide-eyed as I dug a couple of shillings out of my pocket and laid them on the table. But Captain Barlow took hold of one and pushed it back across the table to me.

"There ain't no need for tips here, eh, Squier?"

The landlord shook his head, snatched up what we owed him and hastily left the room.

"You has to do what's right an' proper," said Captain Barlow, "but no more'n that."

I listened and learned. All my life, if I recollect rightly, I have always been eager to learn. Nothing went in one ear and out of the other. Everything, as far as I can tell, everything I might have a use for, was stored inside. What I learned from Captain Barlow was never to believe that people were useless until they proved to be so. And to think that I had been confident that with my fifteen-year-old frame I could easily overpower him if need be!

"Are you a genuine captain?" I asked my new-found companion.

"What d'ye reck'n yourself?" he responded, as amiably as before his threat to break the landlord's neck.

"I can't tell," I answered honestly.

"You know, John Silver, I've took to you. I might be able to teach you a thing or two. I sailed the seas for twenty years, longer'n most. There ain't many seamen who've been out so long and can sit in a tavern and drink a glass of ale in the comp'ny o' good friends, if they has any left, you can take your affy-davy on it. You can write, I assume? Ay, I thought so. And read? Reading's the most important, you may lay to that. I'll tell you one thing, there ain't many sailors who can read, and that's bad, for they'll sign any contract they're offered. If they're told they'll be carrying tobacco from Charleston, they'll believe it, and no one tells 'em they'll be fetching slaves from Africa first. Then they lies at anchor an' moulders in Accra or Calabar. It can take six months to load a slave ship. The slave run is the worst, John, never forget that. Desert, turn pirate, scupper the cap'n, do anything to avoid it. Else you'll have been played false and you'll be leaving this earthly life ere you knows it. I knows, because I've had to throw dead sailors to the sharks on a slave ship. With no hymns nor amen. Slaves by day and sailors by night, so the slaves wouldn't discover that the crew was dying off, one after another, till we was so few that we wouldn't 've been able to hold our own if the negroes had decided to revolt. That's how it is, believe you me: just as many sailors dies on the slave runs as does slaves. No one talks about that, do they?"

I shook my head uncertainly. Partly because I had never met a sea captain before at such close quarters, and partly because I had never heard of one who would defend the welfare of sailors.

"And are you really a captain?" I asked again, cautiously and with a touch of respect, I imagine.

"In the heat o' battle," replied he, "in the heat o' battle there were never one so much of a cap'n as I were. The rest o' the time I were never superior to any other man on board."

I was none the wiser for that answer.

"I were one as was elected," he added.

"That cannot be," I exclaimed. "You can't choose who's to be God, can you?"

Everyone knew that captains were gods on board, or God and the Devil combined, if there was any difference. At sea God did not seem to be any more bothered about sailors than did Old Nick.

"Ay," replied Captain Barlow, "certainly you can choose. If you knew how many gods there were, you wouldn't know whether you're a-comin' or a-goin'. Every corner of the earth is crawling with 'em."

"Then I'd like to be elected a god," said I.

Captain Barlow laid his rough hand on my shoulder and looked deep into my eyes.

"O' course," said he, "o' course you might think it'd be a fine thing to be a god when times are bad. But if you'll take a word of advice from me, John Silver, a man who's been through a bit of everything, it ain't nothing to aspire to. Anyhow, you has to sail for prize money if you wants to be voted cap'n, and I ain't so sure as that's what you wants."

"For prize money?" I asked. "What's that?"

"Gentleman o' fortune, pirate, sea rover, buccaneer, freebooter, corsair, privateer, filibuster, picaroon, adventurer, man of honour, call 'em what you will, but they're the on'y ones who decide themselves who's to be god on board. And who depose that god when the spirit moves 'em. And it do, I can attest to that."

Light dawned upon me. Captain Barlow was a pirate captain, no more and no less. I became even more goggle-eyed. But the strange thing was, I thought then, that he did not look the way I felt pirate captains should look. For example, I was not afraid of him, other than of his hands perhaps.

He saw, naturally, that my deadlights were as wide as saucers, like a man o' war opening its cannon-ports for action.

"Ay, John," he began, "that's how it is and how it was, a long time ago. But I'll tell you one thing, I'm no worse a person than the next man for all that. Mebbe, when all's said an' done, a mite better. Ay, that's how it is. I've done what I could to lead a reasonable life here on earth, an' things jus' turned out the way they did. I ain't dissembling and I ain't ashamed. I sailed on the good ship *Onslow* without knowing what I were a-doin' of. On the voyage carpenters suddenly started building huts for the crew on deck, and as soon as they was ready we got orders to move in. The ones who'd been around a few years knew what was a-goin' on. Space was being made for slaves. Myself, young, foolish and inexperienced, goes up to the cap'n and asks straight out what the idea was. Our destination was Charleston, not Whydah in the Bight o' Benin or any other godforsaken pestilential place, like Madagascar. The cap'n simply looks at me as if he ain't heard what I've said, and then suddenly asks whether there was others on board who thought as I did. O' course there was, but I didn't want to drag the others into it. That was stupid of me, for as soon as I'd said 'No sir, I'm just speaking my own mind', he picks up a big block of wood and gives me a colossal blow on the side of the head that knocks me to the deck. I were dizzy for weeks a'terwards and spewed when I had to go up the mainmast. I dunno how many times I stood on the yard-arm, my limbs quivering like leaves, my head about to burst, and cramps everywhere so I didn't know whether I were a-comin' or a-goin'. If there's a Hell in the hereafter, John, I tell you, it couldn't be any worse than that. And if there's a God, He's as deaf and blind and helpless as flat, piss-warm ale. The mate were below me yelling the moment I paused to draw breath. I survived, as you see. Thanks to my hands – and you've seen what they looks like and what they can do – and because I wanted to live to be able to teach the cap'n a lesson he wouldn't forget. And that's what happened: I threw the cap'n overboard, as easy as pie, one night in a raging storm. What would you have done, I asks?"

I made no answer. How could I have known what I would have done in his place?

"And so things turned out the way they did. I got the others on my side. Even the second mate, though not willingly, needless to say. It was us or the plank. He taught me how to navigate later on and I was voted in as cap'n. That's my story. What d'you say to it, my lad?"

I croaked out something inaudible. I was both overwhelmed and not a little flattered. I knew a real pirate captain and was sitting supping ale with him and chatting as if we were two old friends.

"But, by thunder, be on your guard, my boy. You're like me, I could see that from the beginning. It ain't as easy as it sounds. Once you've been a freebooter there ain't no going back as a rule, however much you wants it, and especially not for a former pirate cap'n. It's like walking a tightrope over an abyss, with the gallows waiting at one end of the rope and a knife in the back at the other, if you ain't bloodthirsty enough. Ay, I've been there when 'lected cap'ns has been murthered by the crew because they wouldn't agree to the decision of the fo'c's'le council, absurd as it was. And there was other 'lected cap'ns, the clever ones, who resigned the honour afore time because their willingness to serve brought 'em naught but hostility and criticism. That's how people are, I can lay to it, pirates and ordinary folk alike. They can't live nor stand on their own two feet without scapegoats. So take my advice, young friend, and never be a cap'n, not even an elected one."

"But you're alive," I protested.

"Ay, that I am. To the extent you can call it living. But we can reck'n I was lucky. I accepted Morgan's amnesty. I was afeared for my skin, when all's said an' done. And now here I am sitting here. I took a job as a longshoreman. I would never go to sea again. For I'll tell you one thing, once you been your own free man at sea – and as a gentleman o' fortune you are free – it would be a fate worse than death to be a serf and a slave a'terwards. And life as a sailor in the merchant fleet or the navy ain't no better'n that."

Captain Barlow said nothing for a while. I could see in his eyes that he was day-dreaming, and perhaps as happy as the likes of him could be. It was that, I think, that made the profoundest impression on me. I may not have known what freedom was – who does? – but I knew what servitude was, and to be free of that, if such were possible, I would gladly give my life. That was what I thought, though it was not completely worked out in my head at the time. Had I not seen Captain Barlow with my own eyes losing himself in fond memories, I might have lent greater weight to his words about the miserable conditions of a life at sea, and the brief time it was apt to last.

It would be a falsehood – and now I am writing the truth, leastways as I see it – to claim that I decided to be a man of honour, a gentleman of fortune, or whatever pirates and privateers are wont to be called. But the mere thought of being able to live my life at liberty, and yet still able to live, made my heart beat faster.

For if there be anything here in life that gives it rhyme and reason, I came to understand later, then it must be not having to obey any laws, not being bound hand and foot. It matters not what the rope looks like, nor who has tied the knot. It is the bonds themselves that are evil. They are what eventually lead you to tie the knot yourself or be hanged. That is my belief, and I am still very much alive.

Suddenly, Captain Barlow's dreams were rudely shattered, as the tavern door was kicked open, to admit three well-built men with a peacock of an officer strutting ahead of them.

"Make way for the navy's men!" shouted the officer. "We've come to apprehend deserters."

"'Tis a press-gang," whispered Captain Barlow. "Let me take care o' this, else you'll be in the navy afore you knows where you are."

The officer stood in the middle of the room looking round in surprise, but without observing us where we sat in our dark corner.

"Devil take it!" said he to his men. "It's empty in here. Someone must have told them we were coming."

At that moment Squier's face appeared from behind the curtain.

"Where the deuce is everyone, landlord? It's as silent as the grave in here. The whole of Greenock seems to be clean out of sailors."

We waited in a state of tension, as quiet as mice, as they say, though in my experience mice are anything but quiet.

Squier said nothing about us, not daring to for fear of Captain Barlow, but stared meaningfully in our direction.

"Business cu'd be better," said he. "The day before yesterday we were full, but yesterday the earth seemed to have opened up and swallowed them all. I thought everyone must hae gane doon to the docks to admire the navy's ships."

"Hardly likely," said the officer sourly.

"But business hasna' been its usual self today, neither," Squier went on in an ingratiating tone. "We've anely had auld men and bairns in here."

Saying which, he glared so intently over the officer's shoulder that the latter finally turned and saw us. His face brightened and I saw Squier behind him grinning with malicious pleasure. It was revenge, he must have thought, and I learned that it is of no small consequence to watch your back when among the vengeful. And there are plenty of them.

"And who may you be?" asked the officer with a confident grin, absolutely certain that it would not be long before both Captain Barlow and I were tramping the deck on one of His Majesty's vessels riding at anchor in the Glasgow Roads.

"Captain Barlow, at your service," said my friend in a voice that must have carried right out on to the street.

The officer blinked, but lost none of his arrogance.

"What ship, sir?" he demanded.

"None, for the moment. I've reached the respectable age when room has to be made on the ladder for younger talents, such as yourself."

The flattery seemed not to have its intended effect, because the officer still regarded Captain Barlow with overt suspicion, seeming to weigh up how much harm a superannuated captain on half pay could do if he should happen to misjudge Captain Barlow's position, patrons and career. In the end he must have decided that the risk was non-existent, in view of Captain Barlow's appearance and his presence in such an ale-house.

"That's all well and good, Captain," said he, looking at me. "We've no quarrel with you, none at all. But you've landed up in bad company. Your companion is one of the very deserters we're seeking."

I stared at the officer in amazement. Here was a man trying to lead people by the nose without so much as a by your leave or the flicker of an eyelid. Had I not had Captain Barlow at my side, I might well have gone along with what the officer said, simply to see how it would develop. Perhaps my life would have turned out quite differently if I had followed my inclination, just on the basis of a simple yes, because life is like that. The watch dozes at the helm, maybe for only a minute, dreaming of the Kate he met in the last port, and a minute later the ship has run aground and life is altered out of all recognition. But I said nothing, held my tongue on Barlow's advice, despite, it has to be admitted, being somewhat indignant that the officer was lying about me to my face, when he could simply have asked me and got an answer, even though it might not have been completely truthful.

"My dear Lieutenant," said Captain Barlow, as if speaking to a cabin-boy, "anyone can make a mistake, but I didn't think the navy's men were as blind as bats. Look at the boy's hands! Have they ever seen a hint of sun or salt or block an' tackle? Well? And look at his clothes! Since when did the navy dress its sailors like scarecrows on their way to school or church?"

But the officer refused to give ground or back down. He was obviously afraid of being discredited in front of his men, who were hovering inquisitively in the background.

"With all due respect, Captain, if only you knew what ruses deserters stoop to in order to get off. I've seen them burn themselves with vitriol to look like scurvy, I've seen them sever their tendons and break their limbs to put themselves *hors de combat.*"

"And ain't you never, Lieutenant," Captain Barlow interrupted him, "ain't you never wondered at all about the reason?"

The lieutenant raised his eyebrows. Captain Barlow had once again gone straight to the point, that much I understood, despite my youth and innocence, without perceiving that what he had said was a defence of deserters as much as anything.

"I'll stand guarantee for the boy here," continued Barlow, "as if he were my only son."

Even I could see that Captain Barlow failed to understand human nature, and I prepared myself for the worst. Why had he not just said that I was his son? Falsehoods were obviously not for him, not even when they were needed most. Straight to the point was his motto, but was it wise and where was the advantage in it for us?

"Captain," said the lieutenant, his confidence restored, "the one does not preclude the other. If you'll stand guarantee for the boy, he must be an excellent candidate for the navy, methinks."

Captain Barlow stood up to his full height. Perhaps he knew he had been outmanoeuvred and had lost his windward position because of his blunder. I could distinctly see his anger welling up through all his wrinkles and tightening the skin around his mouth and chin. The lieutenant made the mistake of assuming that the rest was a mere formality. He reached out towards me, but before his hand even touched me his wrist was caught fast in Captain Barlow's vice-like grip, and in an instant his arm was hanging limp at his side. It was snapped in twain and a bone must have been protruding, since his sleeve had a tent-like appearance. His face was a sight for the gods: astonishment, pain, incredulity, fury, humiliation, fear, all in one single grimace.

"Men," said Captain Barlow to the sailors, who had not really had a chance to see or take in what had occurred, "the lieutenant has had an accident. He was careless as he tried to lean against the table. Unfortunately things like that can happen when you ain't watching what you're doing."

At last! Captain Barlow was no worse than anyone else. He could also make things up when he had to.

"I think it would be best to get the surgeon to take a look at the lieutenant's arm. Who knows whether it might not have to be ampytated?"

The lieutenant's countenance turned even whiter, if that were possible.

"Captain Barlow," he forced out between his bloodless lips, "I shall make a report."

"Do so," said Captain Barlow pleasantly. "I only hope you can write with your left hand. Very few people have the gift. And don't forget to mention that you took an unfortunate tumble when you were going to shake hands with an elderly gentleman and a slip of a boy."

Did I glimpse the trace of a grin on the sailors' lips as they led the lieutenant out? Sailors in a press-gang were no doubt carefully selected, but it was no less likely that they would relish the humiliation and defeat of a superior.

"That were a narrow escape," said Captain Barlow when they had departed. "It could've gone very badly. I has my hands to thank for a lot – more'n my brain, which ain't up to much."

"Shouldn't we run for it?" I asked in some agitation. "Won't they be coming back?"

"I ain't so sure as they will. What would the poor lieutenant put forward in his defence? That he was overpowered by an old man like me, and with one hand? No, that would never do. And let's suppose his commanding officer investigated the matter anyhow, and found you and me here. He would have to prove that you were a deserter. And how would he do that, with your hands?"

I looked down at my hands. What was so strange about them? Captain Barlow saw the direction of my gaze and chuckled.

"Your hands is as white as a lamb, as soft as a baby's bottom. Not a scar, not a scratch, not even a callous from all the books you might've carried. No sailor's hands look like that, not even a cabin-boy's. Look at mine!"

He put them on the table for inspection. And how I stared. His hands were a complete mesh of scars, large and small, intersecting one another in curious patterns and forming cracks and rents, hills and mountains. The colour, copper-brown like new varnish, looked as if it had been burned in with a branding-iron.

"This," said he, "is the mark of a sailor, that you can never hide or rid yourself of. In India they has marks on their foreheads to show their caste, where they belongs and what rights they has. We don't need that. We've got our hands. The press-gangs know that. They can always recognise a sailor. So, my friend, if you don't happen to have Cap'n Barlow along of you when you're a sailor – and you won't always have – there's only one thing to do. Never get drunk when the fleet is in, and keep well out of the way. As a sailor you're marked, don't forget that, not for life but for death, even if some do survive, like myself."

All this came flooding into my mind that day when I started looking at my hands and forgot what they were for. Only when I had recollected everything did I commit it to paper, in the light from the *Walrus'* old hanging oil lamp. And only afterwards, having written down Captain

Barlow's last words, did I understand what it was I had also learned, more important than anything else: that I was going to be marked for life, not for death. That was why I decided that my hands, at any rate, should never give me away. I went to sea with leather gloves that I had smeared with grease. I was ridiculed, until I was feared, but when I went ashore, I was the one who remained at liberty. When all the others were followed, chased and tricked by runners, crimps and press-gangs, I was the one who sat calmly supping my ale. No one would fathom John Silver, you may lay to it. And I believe, by God, as the saying goes, that no one ever has.

Six

S O I ESCAPED the navy's press-gang, and a good thing too. Half of the men pressed into service with the fleet never came back. They died as if they had never lived. The rest spent their whole lives under the command of others, and that must be even worse than death. If you want to live, that is. Otherwise 'tis all one.

I left Captain Barlow to what folk would call his fate: a few ales in a tavern, old memories, happy ones for the most part, and his big scarred hands that would slowly but surely lose their strength. I left him without having questioned him, as I meant to, about which captains in Glasgow extended their hatred not simply to all people but contented themselves with hating sailors. That, I thought, was something I could find out for myself anyhow.

But once again I was mistaken, and there is no greater sin than deceiving yourself in the face of all the evidence. For if there is one lesson that life has knocked into my head, it is never to take anything on trust, especially not human beings, and very particularly not yourself.

I wandered the streets and alleys of Greenock for hours. Greenock, like all harbour cities, stank of tar, excrement and refuse. The whole of my life, until now, has been permeated by smells: tar, corpses, blood, foul water and putrid meat, rank wool and mouldy sailcloth, filth in every shape and form, sweat, rancid fat, rum and more besides. The tar was worst, because it clung in the memory and became a surrogate for all the rest. No doubt about it. It was thanks to tar, its fault rather than its merit, that seamen, no matter how drunk, insensible, distressed or battered they might be, found their way back to the harbour and to their ships, whether they wanted to, which was as good as never, or whether it was what they were forced to, which was the general rule. Their nose was their compass, and there was never any variance: the smell was their north pole.

I fled the fumes of the seamen's quarter of Greenock and, human affairs being so ordered, found myself, as the smell faded, in the more fashionable heart of Glasgow. I thought that there, among shipowners, pot-bellied merchants and other self-important personages, I might find reliable advice on suitable vessels and fair captains who could have need of the likes of me.

But whom should I approach among all these faces that did not deign even to glance at me, as if I did not exist? I took up position near grand men with brass buttons, tricorn hats and gold-tipped walking sticks to hear whether they were talking about ships that were due to sail. But as soon as I came within earshot someone would always aim a blow at me and cast a few oaths in my direction as though I was a cur.

"On your way, boy! You've no business here."

Why not? thought I, feeling resentment of a kind I had not experienced before. What did these fine gentlemen know of my business, I could well ask? In their bloodshot eyes I was nothing more than a louse, a fly, a cockroach, a weevil in a ship's biscuit. What were they themselves? Puffed-up toads who might burst with their own magnificence at any moment. But I was too young and green and foolish to know that I was worth at least as much as them. Instead, my sense of impotence grew every time I was rebuffed without being heard, until finally I stood my ground in front of three men who likewise had no time for me; one of them with epaulettes that seemed to glint as he sunned himself in his own radiance.

"Are you deaf?" asked this man of rank after having told me to go to Hell. "Be off with you!"

"Don't stand there like a thief listening to the conversations of honest men," said one of the others.

"I beg pardon, sir," said I, "but I can't be deaf and eavesdrop at the same time, can I?"

They fell silent. I thought I had given the gentlemen as good as I got. But again I was mistaken. An arm adorned with an epaulette shot through the air like the sail of a windmill and gave me a smack on the face that made me go red with pain up to my ears.

"Have you no shame, you insolent scoundrel?"

"No," I answered with one hand on my stinging cheek. "I just said what I thought."

"Exactly," he replied in a threatening voice. "And you think you can do that with impunity?"

That time I kept my mouth shut, wishing I had Captain Barlow's hands and not just my own words. Lessons were tumbling down upon me like ripe apples. I had spoken the truth for a change, by saying what I thought, but all I got was naught but smarting temples.

"Well, well," said the only one of the three men who had not spoken before, in a milder, more indulgent tone, "tell us what you want, and then take yourself off. We have more important things to attend to."

"I want to go to sea," I explained. "I'm looking for a good ship and a just captain."

The three men exchanged glances that should have warned me, but I was all too intent on my own concerns to be on my guard.

"Well, you've certainly come to the right people," said the man with the gentler voice. "I can be at your service on both counts, with satisfaction guaranteed for all parties. Meet me in an hour at the Anchor down by the tobacco dock, and I'm sure we can come to an agreement and sign a contract. I represent the respectable firm of Messrs Johnson, who ship tobacco from Virginia. I'm responsible for manning their vessels."

I bowed and scraped and accepted, thanking them for their kindness. But, despite my delight in being taken seriously, I had the sense to ask how I should know when an hour had passed.

The man looked at me with interest.

"That's true," said he. "Who bears a pocket-watch at your age? You have a head on your shoulders, I can see. Perhaps you can read as well?"

"Latin," said I, with some pride.

"Devil take me!" he exclaimed, turning to the others. "Did you hear that, gentlemen? The boy can read Latin. Don't you think Captain Wilkinson would appreciate a ship's boy who knows Latin?"

They laughed.

"Indeed," said the one in uniform. "He needs all the men he can get. And somebody who can read the Bible to him would not be a bad notion, either."

"Your fortune is as good as made," said the first, gravely. "Just run along to the Anchor, now, and await me there. Say that Ned sent you and you shall have something to quench your thirst until I come."

So off went I along the River Clyde, in the full belief that my fortune was indeed made, looking with longing at all the ships that were making ready to bring back tobacco – the Indians' revenge, as sailors called it – from Virginia to Scotland and England. Chesapeake and Charleston, I repeated over and over again to myself. That was where the tobacco barons of Glasgow sent their ships, that much I knew.

I was going out into the world, I thought; I would be as free as a bird, my own master, subject to none. I was as happy as a lark and life was good, as we say without thinking. But I had not forgotten Captain Barlow, and on the way to The Anchor I bought two pairs of leather gloves.

And what next? It was the same old story. It was new for me, of course, but what help was that?

I walked into the Anchor, mentioned Ned's name, and was given a noggin of rum, which I drained at once so as not to lose face, the way you do when you are young and brash. As soon as it was empty I was immediately presented with another, charged to the house, as the landlord said, since he had been a sailor himself once; and I durst do naught else but swig it down in one. As was intended, the rum went straight to my head and addled my wits.

When Ned came striding in across the threshold I greeted him like an old friend, and a whole bottle was put on the table.

I awoke the next morning on board the good ship *Lady Mary*, without the slightest idea of how I got there. Ned, of course, as I found out later amidst peals of mirth from my brothers in misfortune, who had also once been his victims, was one of Glasgow's most notorious crimps, providing captains with seamen, willy-nilly. The method varied, but the outcome was always the same – the captains got their men and the crimps received the sailors' pay for a couple of months. The sailors, the captain would say if anyone took it upon himself to object, had employed an agent to sign them on. And there was always a contract, with an irrefutable fingerprint or signature, provided when drunk, that formalised the agreement between the seaman and the agent to the full satisfaction of both parties, as Ned had expressed it. But all the seaman got out of it was to know that he was alive and kicking. If he had enough gumption to be aware of it.

I at least came off fairly lightly. They drank me under the table, that was all. I signed a piece of paper in my intoxicated state giving away three months' wages, and payment, of course, for the rum I had imbibed. But it could have been far worse. Some were carried on board half dead from beatings. There were some who knew even when they came on board that they were in debt up to their ears to the crimp, and would not get a shilling when they signed off a year, or even two years, later. And there were the contracted men, who had signed themselves up for serfdom on the plantations for five years before they would be set on their own feet again. If they could even stand by that time.

And to think that there are folk ashore writing page after page asking in all seriousness how it is that the profession of piracy constantly attracts new and willing recruits! Being able to write is no antidote to stupidity, you may lay to it. A fact, it has to be said, confirmed by my own signature on the contract that Ned must have pushed under my nose when the rum had done its work.

I was brought back to life by a bucket of seawater and a hefty kick on the backside from the first mate's boot. My head ached fit to burst, I was in a cold sweat all over my body, my hands were shaking and I could see stars dancing before my eyes when I turned my head. In short, I was suffering from the effects of the liquor, and, if anybody had enquired of me, at that moment I would rather have died than lived, for the one and only time in my life, if my recollections do not play me false.

I was thrust up a ladder, out on deck, and in through a door at the stern, though I hardly knew which was the front and which was the back, and suddenly came eyeball to eyeball with the ship's god.

"Sir," said the first mate respectfully, "this is John Silver, the ship's boy, who came aboard with Ned last night."

The captain inspected me from top to toe, as if I were a horse at auction.

"I have a contract here," said he, "saying that John Silver undertakes to sail as an apprentice seaman from Glasgow to Chesapeake and back, for a wage of two-and-twenty shillings a month. This is signed by yourself in the presence of a witness. Are we agreed?"

I think I must have nodded.

"Good."

The captain stood up, walked round the table and looked at me as if bent on scaring me out of my senses.

"I understand, Silver, that you've never set foot on board a ship before. So there's something I have to tell you. There's no justice or injustice on board a ship, as there's reckoned to be on land. On a ship there are only two things: duty and mutiny. Everything you're bidden to do is duty. Everything you refuse or neglect to do is mutiny. And mutiny is punishable by death. Please commit that to memory."

"Yes, sir," I stammered, as if in a trance, without knowing what I had said or done.

So that is how John Silver began his illustrious career as a sailor. I had gone to sea to have my hands free, with leather gloves at that, and discovered myself to be bound hand and foot. I was set to work without further ado in a world that was totally incomprehensible to me. I was benumbed and speechless. I obeyed order after order in endless succession. I never said what I thought, because I had learned that honesty is never the best policy. If I opened my mouth, it was to say what others wanted to hear, no more and no less. I convinced myself that it was the only way to survive until I knew better, if I ever did.

But worst of all was the fact that at the beginning I hardly understood a word that was said before the mast. It was English, of course, but many of the words were new to me, and the rest were jargon. I, who thought I really had the gift of the gab and could make words twist and turn until they did not know whether they were coming or going, I, who could even speak Latin, was left on the outside like an imbecile, glassy-eyed, a figure of fun. One day, I remember, Morris, a much-travelled man, said that Robert Mayor, the new young first mate, had crawled aboard through the hawse-hole. And I, blockhead that I was, went off to the cable housing, came back and asked Morris how in the world anyone except a rat could crawl in through there.

Morris and the whole of the off-duty watch laughed till the tears ran. And the merriment, otherwise in such short supply on board, was unrestrained, thanks to me, when I heard in Chesapeake that the carpenter, Cuthbert, had swallowed the anchor.

"Cuthbert," said I, "certainly had a prodigious mouth, but as far as I could see it weren't even big enough to swallow the grappling iron from the gig."

And so things continued on this tack. But slowly and surely I was learning. I soon discovered that there was one language for the ship, short and sweet, and another among the sailors off watch, consisting of songs, yarns and idle chat. I was accepted and eventually liked, for in just a year I had learned to spin a yarn and compose a sea-song as well as the next man, maybe even better. It was a custom before the mast that nobody troubled about what was true or false. A good story was the main thing, and so it was perhaps not surprising if I won respect. And maybe it was also because of that – the respect, I mean – that I could put up with obeying the orders issuing from the poop deck. At all events, I never drowned myself in rum to make myself forget that I was a sailor and not a human being, neither alive nor dead. And for a long time, for as long as I knew no better, Captain Wilkinson's threat echoed in my troubled mind, that obedience was the way to save my skin, the best way and the only way.

Seven

I SAILED UNDER Captain Wilkinson for ten years. He was a
tyrant, one of the worst without a shadow of doubt, but he
knew how to sail, that he did. During the whole time I spent
on board I never saw him make a single decision that was not seamanlike. When he finally lost the *Lady Mary* it was neither his fault nor
hers, though he had much else on his conscience – if he had one. For the
gods must know, if they bother to hearken to us, that being seamanlike
was the only thing Captain Wilkinson was capable of here on earth.

As time went by I achieved a place, not in Captain Wilkinson's heart,
for he had not been endowed with one, but in the world he recognised,
the ship and naught beyond. I came to be for him a self-evident part
of the equipment that he had grown accustomed to having at hand. In
the end I was the only one left of the crew who had signed on, willy-
nilly, in Glasgow ten years earlier. Even the officers deserted and signed
on with other captains when we came into port. Captain Wilkinson
drove his men harder than any other; harder but also without the
slightest hint of favouritism. Everyone was treated equally badly. I have
seen experienced old sea-dogs collapse in utter exhaustion the moment
Lady Mary's anchor cable rattled out through the hawse-hole. The
fact that they took the first opportunity to run off as fast as their legs
would carry them, if they could run at all, seemed to trouble Captain
Wilkinson not one jot, provided that the ship was safely at its destination. He was not even concerned about the unloading of the cargo; the
shipowners and agents could take care of that. He detested, I am sure,
the thought of even setting foot on land. He certainly had no need
to remember the captain's rule that intimacy with the crew breeds
contempt. It was as if he had bidden farewell to his own humanity the
day he went to sea.

And I, John Silver, remained under his command for ten years! I became a fully-fledged seaman, AB master mariner, promoted to boat-swain and all. I went to school in Old Nick's Academy and became proficient in the sailors' seven subjects: swearing, drinking, stealing, whoring, fighting, lying and backbiting. I grew as strong as an ox, and in the end could do every job on the ship. I acquired a greater under-standing of human nature and survived Hell. But ten years!

Not that there was very much choice at my age. Once a sailor, always a sailor until you died, that was the rule. No one ashore wanted to know us, unmarked hands or not. Docker or drunkard, that was the only future on land. Escaping from the ship, a few happy days in tavern and brothel, then signing on again in the hope of better treatment and better wages, that was all that most of them desired. But I stayed with Captain Wilkinson and showed him and everyone else that I was not the sort to whinge at the slightest excuse. I wanted to become a man first, before I adopted any tone of superiority.

"Silver," said Captain Wilkinson to me one day, in what might almost have seemed a confiding manner, "we ought to be able to insure the likes of you."

"Insure, sir?"

"Ay. You see, no insurance company, not the Royal Exchange and not the London, will insure people. Cargoes and ships, ay, but not crew. But what would a ship be without her crew? Masts and rigging can be insured, but not the sailors who climb them like monkeys to reef and brace. Can that be right?"

"No, sir," I replied, because that was the answer expected.

"But that's the way it is," he went on. "There's no difference between you, Silver, and the yard-arm up there. I can't do without either."

I nodded and tried to conceal my emotions, the feelings of rebellion that were finally stirring in my breast like bolting horses, after my ten years of obedience. I suddenly knew that this was to be my last voyage with the *Lady Mary*. Captain Wilkinson had turned me into a master mariner as no other man could have done, but turning me into a yard-arm was another matter altogether.

He saw no sign of what was fermenting within me, of course. A piece of wood has no feelings. It creaks and groans when it is pressed too hard, that is all, and it can be put right. Like a sailor. But I kept quiet. Joy was what would have issued from my lips, joy at the rebelliousness that made me a man, the equal of anyone. Captain Wilkinson needed me and his yard-arm, but I for my part had no need of him.

"The companies should at least insure against death," said he, without looking at me. "The shipowners ought to get compensation, that's what I think."

"Sir," said I, "if you'll permit me?"

Captain Wilkinson gave a start and looked at me in surprise.

"What is it?" he asked.

"Ain't the risks too great, sir? Sailors die like flies, that's a well-known fact. They desert in the first port they come to. No shipowner could afford the premiums, I shouldn't think."

"You're quite right, Silver. That's exactly what they say. But what use is that to me? Sailors still perish."

He was silent for a moment and then stared at me again, for the first time, I think, as if I was something other than block and tackle.

"And who told you, Silver, that that was the way of it?"

"Nobody. It was something I thought out for myself."

"I see."

He gave me a look that was meant to fill me with fear, but I returned it without ceremony.

"No one thinks for himself on board my ship, Silver," said he. "*Lady Mary* has only one captain, and that's me. Eh, Silver?"

"Ay, ay, sir," said I, as respectfully as I knew how.

"Back to your duties, Silver."

Right you are, thought I, right you are. Till we get to the next harbour.

On the morning of the following day we sighted the red sandstone of Ireland in bright, calm weather. To port rose Cape Clear, to starboard Fastnet Rock. The day was strangely still. The sky was covered in fluffy balls of cotton that would bring no harm to any seafarer. Visibility was so good that the look-out could see four points, Toe Head, Galley Head, Seven Heads and Old Head of Kinsale. The off-duty watch were all lined up and hanging longingly over the port rail. I knew it irritated Captain Wilkinson to see inactive seamen, whether on or off duty, but not even he could have called all hands on deck to set the sails and brace the yards in the gentle breeze that was barely ruffling the water.

I myself was standing on the poop deck, in the lee of Captain Wilkinson as was the rule, and I was as lighthearted as the time I was searching for a fair captain and a good ship to make me as free as a bird. But everything was different now. I knew what I was talking about on those rare occasions when I opened my mouth. I no longer stood spouting Commandments, no matter what sort, to anyone. I did not boast of knowing Latin to all and sundry. I did not go round asking about just and equitable captains, a subject it was not always fitting to broach. I no longer said what I really thought in my heart, because it would only be used against me.

But I had learned that there are always words that everyone is keen to hear, even the simplest sailor, and that I had the ability to fulfil their wishes. So no one got the better of me, while I seemed increasingly to get the better of others. And at the same time, such is the way of the world, I was liked and regarded as a good shipmate.

I even had money, clever and thrifty as I was in that respect. I still had my father's smuggler inheritance in my trouser lining, and on top of that about three years' wages and the profits from a little trade of the kind that every sailor has a right to. I was good for sixty pounds, all of it stitched into my clothes. Who would have believed it? None of my messmates, leastways, you may lay to that.

Almost absent-mindedly I noticed the first mate come running up to Captain Wilkinson and point animatedly astern. I turned round, since like all the others I had only had eyes for the cliffs and the pure green inviting hills ahead. I will never forget the sight that met my eyes. Rapidly and all unnoticed the sky had darkened to the blackness of pitch spreading like tentacles across the clear blue heavens that still surrounded the *Lady Mary*. The horizon had been transformed into a foaming frenzy of breakers rushing towards us like a landslip. No one aboard, I am sure, not even the weatherbeaten old salts who had spent their entire lives at sea, had ever seen anything like it. I saw fear and terror on many a countenance when we turned as one to Captain Wilkinson. We all knew what to expect: a battle for life and death with sail and rope.

But the order to head round into the wind did not come. Captain Wilkinson cast another quick glance astern and then turned to the crew.

"Men," said he, in his usual whiplash voice, "in a few minutes we'll have the worst storm over us you've ever seen. If you do as I say we may be able to save the ship. If you don't obey orders, you'll be shot on the spot for mutiny. Have I made myself plain?"

There came no answer, save from me. I raised my voice for the first time, the voice that was later to become so notorious for shouting out what no one else had the imagination or calculation to express.

"A cheer for Cap'n Wilkinson!" I yelled to the skies.

And the men, at first listlessly, then under my direction more vociferously, powerfully and all together, gave a huzza for Captain Wilkinson, the last person in the world to deserve one.

For a second Captain Wilkinson was on the point of losing control of his temper. He took a step backwards, as if someone had struck him, but in an instant he was himself again and bellowing at the top of his voice.

"Silence!"

All went quiet as the grave – naturally enough, because we already had one foot in it.

"Now is not the time for cheering," he went on. "You might wonder why we're not facing into the wind. For one good reason: the wind behind us would rip our sails to shreds before you'd had time to tie half your reef knots. And a goodly number of you would be tossed into the sea when the sails filled. So . . ." he looked over his shoulder one last time, "let's have the port watch on the pumps. Starboard watch slack all the sails and let out all the sheets you can. All helmsmen take your turn together, and make sure you're lashed to the ship. When the sails are slack half the starboard watch can tie lifelines. The other half make ready storm sails and we'll see if there are any masts left to hang them from by then. I don't need to say you're to do it as fast as the very Devil. Even you can work that out."

The mate spat out his orders with showers of saliva. The sails flapped and banged as the sheets were let out. I, as the ship's boatswain and not belonging to any watch, always ready to lend a hand where needed, had time to turn round and peer astern. This, I told myself in dread, was not just a white squall, strong gusts from a clear sky. This was a raging tempest that would do its best to put an end to all of us and to me. I knew when I caught sight of Bowles, the oldest sea-dog on board, whose memory was the measure of storms and waves for all of us. I saw him fall to his knees and pray! A man who had never said a prayer in his life. Who had always sworn that his only credo was the compass. Who had taught us all that the best way to let a ship sink was to waste time appealing to the Heavenly Father for help! And now he was praying!

At that moment Captain Wilkinson left the starboard side and made his way with steady measured steps over to me.

"Silver," said he in an icy voice, "why did you call for a cheer? Why did the men cheer?"

"I dunno, sir," said I. "But mebbe because they needed some courage and hope instilling into them."

"Courage and hope? Isn't it enough to be under threat of death?"

"Begging your pardon, sir, not when they think they're going to die anyhow."

Captain Wilkinson looked me straight in the eye.

"You're sure they didn't cheer for me?"

"Ay, sir, I'm sure. See for yourself!"

I pointed at Bowles, who was still on his knees praying.

"They say," I declared, "that when a sailor prays, all hope is gone."

Captain Wilkinson looked at Bowles as if he were a coward without equal.

"And what about you, Silver, why don't you pray?"

"Who should I pray to?" I asked. "Yourself?"

He gave a sharp laugh that sounded like the bark of a dog, the first laughter I had ever heard issue from his mouth.

"Silver," said he, cutting short the laugh as abruptly as the report of a cannon, "you ought to be insured, as I said. I'd never find your like again."

Then he leaned down towards the deck and yelled, "Bowles! I hope for the sake of your soul that you're praying to me and nobody else."

Bowles jumped and looked up with a terrified face.

"Ay, ay, sir," he said. "Ay, ay."

"Silver," said Captain Wilkinson to me, "I think you'd better help me at the helm when the storm hits us. Devil knows it doesn't look as if the others are much troubled whether the *Lady Mary* floats or founders."

With that the storm was upon us. It ripped apart the flapping sails like lace handkerchiefs. The foremast was next to go, with a crack that no one could hear against the shrieking of the wind. On deck all activity ceased. The crew were on their knees, not before God, but before the wind. All eyes were fixed on the mainmast, the top of which was already bent over like a willow and the foot quivering like the string of a lute. That was the ship's life support, they and I were thinking in horror.

Captain Wilkinson was rushing around amongst the kneeling and prostrate sailors like a Fury. Whether he would prevail now he could no longer threaten with death, and unable as he was to tempt with life, I did not know. But in the midst of the rain that was whipping everyone like a cat o' nine tails, in the midst of the thunder, the screeching and the wailing of the wind that was deafening us, on a deck that was swinging like a pendulum and forcing everyone to the rail, in the midst of the spray and salt that was blowing around like hail and snow, in the midst of all this Captain Wilkinson was kicking and punching, cursing and screaming, and managed to chase half the port watch below deck to man the pumps and the other half, creeping, crawling and swearing, to rig up lifelines and replace the stays where they had snapped.

Seeing Captain Wilkinson rushing hither and thither in an attempt to save his vessel broke the spell of my terror-stricken numbness. If he could spit in the face of death and mock it for the sake of a collection of old planks, then I was a blot upon this earth if I could not do likewise to save my own skin. After all, only moments earlier I had been thinking it would be time to start living as soon as I got ashore.

From that instant I was everywhere on the ship, lending a hand and encouraging the men. My will to live turned to burning rage, so that even Captain Wilkinson took several paces back when our paths crossed.

The grey-black seas were now breaking continuously over the deck and the heavy waves were smashing against the planking like broadsides from a man o' war. The land had disappeared from view in the rain that was lashing our faces like hail, and it was not long before the inevitable occurred. On the way down into the bottomless pit of the trough between waves, the rudder lost its grip and the *Lady Mary* was thrown on to her side. We heeled over more and more, further than any vessel could withstand, and through the banging and booming, the crashing and clatter we could hear the first dull rumble of the ballast shifting to the lee side.

Bowles, that wretched prophet of doom, cried out that all was lost and fell to his knees again with his hands clasped before him. I was already on my way to the mainmast, clambering along the windward rail like a monkey, when I saw Captain Wilkinson doing the same on the lee side with an axe in his hand raised to strike. And I saw him take his time to straighten up and give Bowles a blow with the axe that sent him overboard with his hands still clasped. It was, to my mind, no more than he deserved, and I could see the others thought so too. It cannot be right that those who have given up should be able to pull down with them into the void those who are fighting for their lives, especially not in the name of God.

Captain Wilkinson and I reached the mainmast simultaneously and made our sharp-bladed axe heads fly through the air like flashes of lightning.

"Faster!" he yelled in the midst of it all. "The ship must be saved!"

Not even then did he think of his own, or my, skin.

We had soon opened a gaping wound half way into the wooden flesh of the mast and I could see a split slowly opening upwards.

"Now!" he shouted. "One more blow – and get back!"

I raised my axe, brought it down with a crash, and threw myself backwards so that I fell headlong into the scuppers, with water up to my ears. This time I heard the crack as the mainmast splintered and I could feel the *Lady Mary* beginning to right herself again, infinitely slowly. But the ship was still caught in the rigging, and the mast hanging over the side was a dangerous drag-anchor that could destroy us at any moment.

"Free the shrouds!" I heard Captain Wilkinson bellow like a foghorn, and the cry went from mouth to mouth, since no voice carried more than arm's length, whether with or against the wind.

It seemed as if new hope was born, and the rigging disappeared overboard before I had even found my axe again. The helmsmen, made fast to the helm so as not to be hurled across the deck when the wheel span in a lurch, pulled her back on the only course we could steer. We were waterlogged and drifting, but, for the time being, still afloat.

"Heave the log, lead-lines at the bow and relieve the pumps!" ordered Captain Wilkinson, once again at his post on the starboard side of the poop deck.

At that moment I saw him, as doubtless did the others, as more than human, standing eternally on the poop deck of the *Lady Mary* like the oak he seemed to have been carved from.

Then the carpenter emerged and declared that the water was up to the cargo hold and that the ballast must have smashed a hole below the water line. Captain Wilkinson told him to order more hands to the pumps and shorter stints.

By that stage I had recovered myself and was able to make myself useful again. I went to the slate and picked up a piece of chalk, half dissolved and stuck fast to the deck.

I climbed down into the hold and crawled forward in the dark with the water up to my waist. Above me I could hear the men trying to instil courage and hope into themselves by singing, but it was no more than a breathless raucity that would deceive nobody. I attained the ladder up to the pump room, and, groping around with my hand where the wood was still dry, I took out the chalk and drew a thick white line. Then I pulled myself up, opened the hatch and was confronted by ten half-naked men, their bodies sweating and scarlet under the strain, and with the fear of death in their glazed and haunted eyes. They stared at me as if I was Charon himself, with good reason perhaps, although my intentions were the opposite. But I also saw something else: respect, I think, of a new quality, which must have been occasioned by the way I had wielded the axe at the mainmast.

"Messmates," I began, "this ship ain't got long to go. She's a-goin' down. But if you asks me, there ain't no cause for us to strike our flag with her."

"Cap'n Wilkinson's mad," Winterbourne yelled in my face. "We'll die at these pumps to save his old hull."

"Not if he needs you to save that very same hull!" I shouted back. "I reck'n I knows what's in his mind. He's a-goin' to try to make Old Head of Kinsale and anchor behind the point till this damn wind dies down. Then we can be towed into Kinsale."

"What'll happen if it don't work?" asked Winterbourne.

"The same as if you stops pumping. We'll be in Davy Jones's locker, and that's all there is to it. So heark'ee, messmates! I'm not of a mind to strike flag this time, you may lay to that. And you know I'm a man that keeps to his word, I am. If you pumps for your lives, as if your last hour was come, which it is if you don't do as I says, I promise I'll do my bit."

"And what's that?" asked Winterbourne, a little less truculently now.

"If we can't make Old Head, I swear I'll run the ship aground on a beach where you can walk ashore with dry shoes. If you had any shoes on, that is."

"And what do Wilkinson have to say about that?"

It was Balthorpe, one of the English sailors, who unlike the rest of us, Welshmen, Irishmen and Scots, had an inclination towards obedience.

"When it comes down to it," said I, off the top of my head, so to speak, "it'll be Cap'n Wilkinson doin' as I say."

There was a muttering, but there were enough of them prepared to take me at my word – even myself, for I still had not learned my lesson.

"An' don't forget one thing. If the ship runs aground, we're in our full rights to help ourselves to the cargo. We'll be free men and in duff. What d'you say to that, eh, my hearties?"

"Count me in," said Winterbourne, who besides being obstinate and pugnacious was also greed incarnate.

"Me too."

More voices spoke up, including finally the servile Balthorpe. I opened the hatch.

"Messmates," said I, "down there on the ladder you can see a line where the wood is still dry. If the water rises above that mark, we'll be dead and strikin' our flags. Understood?"

They all nodded. They were not stupid. They did not know why it was good to live, and as seamen they did not have much to live for, but they knew how to fight for life if they just had a little encouragement from the likes of me.

To show that I was serious, I fell upon one of the pumps and began to work it at a speed that little Curwen, the youngest and slightest, found hard to keep up with. I think the rest of us lifted him right off the deck. But eventually he found the rhythm and contributed the strength of the invisible muscles he must have had in his body just to stay on his feet. Block'n'tackle Harry, so called because his enormous frame gave him twice the power of the rest of us, started up a song that doubled the tempo. It was a joy to see. And to think that men like these needed captains and whips to urge them on!

After half an hour, measured by the glass, ere the strength of all of us was exhausted, save for little Curwen who was already nigh on half dead, I called a halt.

"Next!"

The four men I had been pumping with flung themselves panting to the deck. I fetched a barrel of water and doled it out. Then I climbed down the ladder, anxious and uneasy – I was no more than human after all – and checked the mark. I stood there for some time before I was sure: the water was washing back and forth in time with the *Lady Mary*'s rolling. But I was certain. It was subsiding.

I was up the ladder in three bounds.

"Mates," I yelled, "'tis down an inch! The Reaper can look for other corn to cut than us, an' Devil take him!"

There was an almighty cheer. I looked around. They would be all right now to reach Old Head, and no mistake.

"If you can keep going," said I, "the carpenter'll soon be able to make good the leaks. But 'twill be a longer job if you sweat as much as Curwen here. 'Tis enough to make another half inch for each o' the teams to pump."

The others laughed, but not at Curwen, who gave me a broad grin. Gratefully, I think, as if I had done him good, and there was I intent only on saving my own skin.

By the time I returned to the deck I had almost forgotten how bad things were. The waves were one great seething, lashing, thundering mass breaking high over the deck. On the backs of the waves I could see a jagged spume of foam forcing its way to the top where it held fast for an instant before losing its grip and racing down again.

"Cap'n," said I as I came up on to the poop deck where Wilkinson still stood as I had left him. "We ain't going to sink. The men are pumping for their lives."

"Good man, Silver," he replied with an empty voice that frightened me more than his threats and curses. "You're a real marvel. I'd have liked to make you first mate straight away if you'd had any inkling of how to navigate. Look at that scum. It's beyond my comprehension that men like him should be allowed to sail a vessel at all."

I followed his gaze and saw Hardwood, the first mate, clinging on to the rail, soiled by his own vomit and scared out of his wits, certainly not living up to his name.

"He's afeared, sir," said I.

"Do you think I can't see that? Afraid, ay, for himself. What use is that to the *Lady Mary*? Answer me that!"

I could not, and would not, for when all was said and done I did not give a damn for the *Lady Mary*, her fittings, fixtures or crew, from her keel to the tops of the masts that were no longer there.

"They're pumping for their lives, did you say?" Captain Wilkinson went on presently. "Well and good, it'll keep 'em busy. But it won't be enough. We're not going to make Old Head. In half an hour the farmers are going to get new stocks of timber for their winter fires. And I'm going to lose my vessel and my good name."

"Sir?" said I.

"What do you want?" he answered, with the stress on the 'you' as if he had never seen me before.

"There might be a way."

"Silver, if you didn't know before, for a captain there's only one way to Hell and that's to survive his wrecked ship."

"I actually meant to save the ship, sir."

"And how would you do that?" he asked angrily. "Can you, Silver, a simple seaman, have seen a possibility that I haven't already considered?"

"I don't think so, sir, not at all. But if I remember rightly, there's a sandy beach in the cove, Lispatrick Lower. We could sail her up on to it."

"Indeed we could," said he sarcastically. "And do you think that *Lady Mary* could go to sea again after that?"

"No," said I, "but you and I might, sir. And some of the crew too. And we'd be able to save a few spars and some of the cargo."

"Sea-soaked tobacco," said Captain Wilkinson. "Who d'you think would buy that, Silver? Who?"

"And the crew, sir? And myself?"

Captain Wilkinson did not even vouchsafe me a reply. He was totally uninterested. I looked across at the helmsmen. If *Lady Mary* were to end her days on Lispatrick Lower, they would have to shift the helm now, before it was too late.

Why did I not just fetch an axe and cleave Captain Wilkinson in twain, from top to toe, like the timber he was intent on turning the *Lady Mary* into along with his good reputation? Why did I not do what Captain Barlow had said? But no, I did not lift a finger. By the time I finally sped into action we were steering a course directly towards the cliffs of West Holeopen Bay. I hurtled down to the pumps and told the men there what was happening, that Captain Wilkinson cared as little for their lives as for mine, that they could save their energies for getting themselves ashore, and that Captain Wilknson intended to drive the ship right into the cliffs, sacrifice her to Neptune, as if that would be some confounded penance for the shame of losing his vessel.

"What did I say?" shouted Winterbourne threateningly. "The man's mad, stark starin' mad. An' to think we was relyin' on you, John, on your word. Go to the Devil! Here's what I think of your word."

He aimed a hefty gob of spittle at my feet.

"You can think what the Hell you likes, Winterbourne, and spit an' splutter as much as you please," said I calmly. "I'm minded to go up on deck right now, seize the helm and throw Wilkinson overboard if I have to. There may still be some little bit of beach we can steer for."

"I'll gladly throw him in," said Block'n'tackle Harry, clenching his fists, "if it's the last thing I do in life."

"Me too," said little Curwen, and nobody as much as grinned.

"It's mut'ny," said I, "just so's to remind you. But there's no time for round robins or swearin' of oaths. On my head be it."

So up we sped to tell the others, and then entered the poop deck with me in the lead. I advanced upon Captain Wilkinson.

"Cap'n," said I, "I'm taking over the *Lady Mary*. If there's the slightest chance of getting her round the cliffs and on to the sand I'm a-goin' for it."

Captain Wilkinson did not answer at first, as if he had not understood what I had said. I turned my back on him and went towards the helmsmen. I had not gone far before I heard a frenzied bellow and then Winterbourne, of all people, yelling out a warning. It came too late, because before I knew what was happening I felt a violent blow across my shoulders that, combined with the rolling of the ship, sent me flying across the deck, smashing into the rail. Then I felt hands grabbing hold of my clothes and in the next instant I was in mid-air plummeting towards the boiling, heaving waves.

That I survived is obvious, since I am writing this. But as I was falling I reckoned myself a dead man, an uncomfortable sensation when you do not believe in having anywhere to go after that. But I knew how to keep afloat and I could swim. I had been taught how, as something that would always be useful, by an old Indian in Norfolk, Virginia, where we were loading tobacco. The others had laughed and shaken their heads when they saw me going under, coughing like a consumptive, and spitting out seawater. For a sailor to be able to swim invited ridicule. But they were not laughing now with the *Lady Mary* only a few cable-lengths from the sheer cliffs of Old Head of Kinsale.

As I floated to the top of a wave like a half-empty bottle I caught a glimpse of Wilkinson back on the poop deck gazing resolutely for'ard, towards his doom. The crew, the brave mutineers with whom I was planning common cause, stood terror-stricken, huddled together on the deck, still even at that moment in the lee of their captain, as the rules demanded. All of them were staring straight ahead, all except one. Little Curwen had turned round and was looking astern, for me.

The next time I reached the crest of a wave I saw the men on deck drop down, as if to order. Only Captain Wilkinson remained standing; he seemed fixed to the deck. Only then did I hear the crashing sound, the noise of timber cracking, breaking, twisting and splintering. And the screams of the men about to meet their death, ebbing and flowing in time with the waves on which I rose and fell. *Lady Mary* was thrown up and tossed abeam on to the nearest jagged reef.

Now that she was no longer making headway I found myself drifting inexorably closer to her. I did what I could to get round the side of her, but the current was too strong and I only had energy enough to gasp for breath in the turbulent foam. Yet it was my salvation, I am sure, because I was near the end of my tether when I managed to grab hold of a broken piece of rail, heave myself on to it and clasp it tightly to my body. I struggled for breath and held on. That was all I could do.

The last I saw or heard of the *Lady Mary* before I was hurled in towards the cliffs was Captain Wilkinson's immobile figure on the poop deck as it broke in two, and a death scream from little Curwen.

"Silver, John Silver!" he shrieked. "Help me!"

But I could do nothing in that Hell. Once again, upon my soul, Long John Silver's big mouth had done him no good. I could feel myself being lifted higher and higher on the last precipitous wave, lying across the top of it as if suspended betwixt Heaven and earth, before the wave tumbled over itself, smashing down in surging cascades with me and my rail somewhere in the middle of it all. And I remember more clearly than anything else that I had time to experience a feeling of resentful, abhorrent bitterness and gall at having to die, I who wanted to live so much more than anyone I had ever known.

When I opened my eyes again – because I must have closed them rather than stare death straight in the face – I could not at first believe what I saw. I was on my piece of rail in a kind of tunnel, moving towards the light of an opening that could only be on the other side of Old Head of Kinsale. But was I alive or dead? This was the question I was considering in full earnest until I heard, like an echo in the tunnel, the muffled boom of the waves hitting the west side of the cliffs, and the cries, already fading into the distance, of those yet to die. Comprehending that I was still alive, I tried to give voice to some form of joy, but my throat was constricted by an invisible noose so that not even the slightest sound would emerge. Alive, I thought before I blacked out, and felt a sense of even greater horror: alive, but dumb.

Eight

WHEN I CAME back to life again I saw a tangled beard, two troubled but benevolent eyes and a cascade of ginger hair against a background of grey cloudy sky.

"Easy there," said a voice from within the beard. "To be sure an' you're goin' to be all right."

I raised myself with difficulty to a half-lying position and supported myself on one elbow. My whole body hurt, from the soles of my feet to the top of my head. I was naught but a wreck, like the *Lady Mary*, fit only for tinder.

The man put a flask to my lips and I felt the rum searing my dry throat and spreading through my body. I could feel it progressing along my limbs to the outermost points, and the pain was excruciating as the warmth seeped back into my fingers and toes.

"Where am I?" I asked.

"Hangman's Point," replied he.

Only then did I remember everything and know that at least I had not lost the power of speech. But gradually the man's words penetrated my fuddled brain and consciousness.

"Hangman's Point!" I repeated. "I ain't done nothing wrong!"

Devil take me if the man did not laugh right in my face, distressed and half dead as I was.

"You must have done," said he, "if you can be so afeared of the hangman after what you must have been t'rough. Don't you worry! There's never been a gallows here, as far as I'm aware."

He whistled a signal and two burly men immediately appeared. I was laid on a blanket and carried like a child. To starboard I could see wooded hills, and to port I could hear the noise of breakers that diminished as we went on. The men were speaking some unintelligible lingo, but the one who had found me explained from time to time in English where we were and whither we were heading.

"This, my good fellow," said he after a while, "this is Tobar na Dan, the Poet's Spring. This is where one of our bards used to sit playin' the harp an' tellin' stories. He traversed the whole country with his stories, but always came back to his source, so to speak. Even to hang himself. That's how Hangman's Point got its name. Not because ordinary folk like you and me are hanged here."

"Hanged himself?" I gasped, having just risen from the dead myself. "Why the Devil should anyone strike their flag voluntarily?"

"No one knows, but his memory was starting to play tricks on him. He'd begun to forget his stories, tellin' them wrongly and havin' to keep goin' back to the beginning again. Someone had seen him hackin' off a great tuft of hair, an' wringin' his hands in furious desperation until they bled. The stories were more than a t'ousand years old, word for word the same since time immemorial. The object of the bard's existence was to remember them, so what could he do if he forgot? Tell different stories? Invent new ones? Nobody would ever forgive him."

A little later he said, "Over there is Eastern Point, the entrance to Kinsale. Beyond lies Bulman Rock, a foul reef. Away opposite you can see Sandy Cove Island, and behind that Sandy Cove itself, one of the finest hidden bays, easy to sail into, even at night."

"At night?" I asked.

"For sure, the best cargoes spoil in the light o' day," said he, laughing with the others.

I slipped into unconsciousness again and did not open my eyes until the next morning, to find myself lying on a bed of straw, even clad in a coarse nightshirt, near a roaring fire that was warming my stiff and aching body. I have never been haunted by memories in my life, let alone fed on them, but if there is anything apart from my leg that comes into my mind from time to time, it is probably that moment. Cheating death like that must be the nearest to Paradise you can get.

What made it even better was that one of the first things I saw when I opened my deadlights fully was a soft and delightful female face. The woman said nothing, but smiled and disappeared out of a doorway where the sun streamed in and shone through her white cotton blouse and long skirt, so that I could make out the contours of her body. After a while she returned with food and drink, followed immediately by the man who had saved my life, for indeed he had done no less.

"Thank'ee kindly," were the first words that passed my cracked lips.

He just shook his head, as if it was not important, and asked how I was feeling. I told him: I was alive, and that was enough.

"My name's Dunn," said he. "This is me daughter Eliza, and you're in Lazy Cove, not many miles from Kinsale."

I nodded and was within an ace of giving my name when I suddenly saw myself telling Captain Wilkinson that I was taking over his ship, and recognised that I was a mutineer, to my shame, and that you could be hanged for less.

"You're welcome to stay here for as long as you want or need," said Dunn.

"I can pay my way," said I, reaching for my belt.

It was gone.

"Your belt is under the bed," said Dunn, "what was left of it when we fished you out."

"That's what my old father bequeathed to me," I explained with relief. "Smuggler's inheritance, I shouldn't wonder. And ten years' hard-earned dues from the *Lady Mary*."

"To be sure, 'tis not'in' to do with me where your money's from," said Dunn. "You can put in a shillin' for food if you t'ink it matters. But we'll speak no more about it."

No, and it was just as well, because I was having trouble finding words. I had been welcomed with no other credentials than that I had been half dead and incapable of looking after myself. They had seen the sum of my wealth, or what remained of it, but I could see that it was not for their own profit that they were treating me so decently, so humanely.

"*Lady Mary*?" he continued. "Doesn't she ship tobacco from Charleston?"

"Did," said I. "She went down off the Old Head of Kinsale yesterday, with all hands, except for me, I imagine. I was thrown overboard afore she struck the rocks and split asunder."

"That was what we feared. We saw a number of boats go out today from Sandy Cove. It was impossible to go out in the storm yesterday, even for us who're used to the waters hereabouts. I've never seen such a sudden and violent gale. It was lucky for you that you got round Old Head. There may be more who've survived."

"We didn't," said I quietly, "we ran aground in West Holeopen."

"In West Holeopen?" repeated Dunn. "How the blazes could I have fished you out at Hangman's Point, then?"

I closed my eyes and saw myself again being driven like a piece of flotsam through the tunnel in the cliffs, with the echo of the others' death-cries just audible behind me. Then to my horror I saw an image of little Curwen and heard his scream. What was he doing there, inside my head? He was gone, according to all the rules of the game. Dead ere he had even had a chance to find out whether there was any point in being alive.

"Has there been any news from any o' the boats?" I asked.

"Not as far as I know," said Dunn. "We live a mite off the beaten track in Lazy Cove. We have to sail round to Kinsale for news an' necessities. But I'll go in this evenin' to see what I can find out, an' will be back in the mornin'."

"I'll come with you," said I.

Dunn shook his head.

"The best t'ing for you is to stay where you are. Give your body and your mind some rest."

I accepted this, because I was still weak and exhausted. But time hung heavily. My one diversion was seeing the profile of Eliza's sun-flecked body as she went in and out of the door. She kept coming in and asking if there was anything I needed, or just to straighten my blankets. She washed and shaved me with hands that caressed, our eyes met and were just as quickly averted. Ay, I became more and more disturbed and my behaviour more unpredictable as the day advanced. I put it down to my enfeebled state, for how could I have known that there were women who could bring the likes of me to his knees for something other than their inviting haunches?

As dusk fell Eliza entered and sat by my bed. Without saying a word she took my hand and held it until I did not know whether I was coming or going. I lay absolutely motionless, as rigid as a poker.

"How do you feel now?" she enquired.

"Better," I replied. "Much better."

"'Tis lucky you were. If my father hadn't found you, you would probably be dead by now. It must be Providence that brought you here. You can thank God for the fact that you're alive."

"Why should He help the likes o' me when He didn't lift a finger for the others?" said I. "No, I'd rather thank myself and an Indian in Norfolk, Virginia, who taught me how to swim. And your father, who picked me up. And you, who're tending me."

"Perhaps that was the idea behind it all. That you should come here."

"What do you mean?"

In response she gave me a look that seemed to suck me in like a leech. It was the very Devil that I was lying here, having got a new life, and I ought to be thinking of nothing else; yet instead, my head was being turned by a skirt, enough to make me giddy. Could that have been what was in my mind when I determined to start living as soon as the *Lady Mary* reached harbour?

"Have you been at sea for many weeks?" asked Eliza, with the same enticing look in her eyes.

I reckoned up.

"Four months or thereabouts."

"And all that time without having a woman?"

"Ay," I managed to utter.

"And would you be wanting a woman now?"

I may have nodded in reply, but truth to tell I almost swooned and hardly knew what I was doing after Eliza undressed, crept in under the bedclothes and pressed her body against mine. My head emptied of all thoughts, and John Silver ceased to exist as the person he was and wanted to be, Devil take him.

When I regained my senses Eliza was lying by my side with a playful and contented smile on her face.

"You could make a woman very happy," said she. "You're not like the others. You're soft and smooth."

She took my hand.

"Never have I seen a sailor with hands like these."

"Nor I," I must have replied.

"Are you really a sailor?" she asked.

"Ay, that I am, what else would I be?"

"I've had sailors before, some of those who sail with my father, some in France when I've sailed there with him. But their hands have all been rough and calloused and covered in scars. Not soft like yours. Is it so you can caress your woman better? I've never met anyone who could touch me the way you do."

I stared at her. What had I done? Touched her? My memory was a blank. For a while I had not been my own master, and that discovery sent cold shivers down my spine. I had had women before, many women in fact, as sailors tend to have in port, but I had simply taken them, from the back, from the front, from above or below, however it went, without any frills or niceties, neither before nor after. How and where could I have learned how to touch a woman? I was a sailor, an AB master mariner. I could splice and sew, tie knots and sheets; but to be dexterous with women too, that was something new and quite different.

I tried to tell Eliza that and more besides, but did she understand what I said? In all honesty, I just talked because I did not know what to say.

"I've never met anyone like you," said she when I stopped. "And not just because of your hands."

She took my hand again and put it between her warm thighs. I swear by the little I hold sacred that I tried to withdraw it, but the cold shivers seemed to have been blown away, so things took their course, in a manner of speaking. John Silver completely lost the use of his brain, and turned into a lump of wax that in Eliza's hands melted into pure unalloyed sensuality and then, perhaps – why not? – happiness. What else might it consist of, for the likes of me, may I ask?

Eliza curled up afterwards and I held her in my arms all night long as if she were Flint's whole treasure chest and more. When she awoke at sunrise, stretched herself and was a woman again, I shouted out loud, cold shivers or not, "Nor, by the powers, have I ever met anyone like you, as true as my name's John Silver."

Eliza smiled.

"John Silver," said she, "'tis a fine name, to be sure."

I could have bitten out my tongue. Without thinking I had not only severed my own line of retreat as deceased and signed off. On top of that, and far worse, I had heedlessly delivered myself into the power of another person.

Dunn returned at about noon.

Eliza threw herself round his neck as if she had not seen him for years, or as if she had not been sure she would ever see him again. Then she whispered something in his ear with a meaningful glance at me as she slipped out of his arms.

Dunn brightened up.

"I'm glad to see you're improvin'," said he.

I looked across at Eliza.

"It's entirely thanks to her," I managed to say.

"Yes," said he, with a look that was both devilish and understanding, "so I gather."

I looked in surprise at Eliza's innocent face.

"My daughter," said Dunn, "is a grown woman, self-sufficient an' aware of it. There's not a lot I can do about it, even if I wanted to."

"His name's John Silver," said Eliza.

"Is it, now?"

His voice took on a different tone, and he looked at me as if he were not certain what to think or do.

"What's amiss?" asked Eliza anxiously when she saw her father's countenance.

"It depends," answered Dunn.

"Depends on what?" I asked.

"On who you are an' who you want to be. If you've a wish to be John Silver for the rest o' your life, 'tis not as good as it could be."

Dunn looked me straight in the eye.

"Only one survivor's been found from the *Lady Mary*," said he.

[72]

"Captain Wilkinson is his name. He maintains that the ship went down because the crew mutinied. An' that the leader o' the mutineers was a certain John Silver."

That's what he was saying, was it, the damned lying swine! That was how he thought he would protect his wretched reputation and pride, by seeing me swing if he could and if I were alive. Or by dragging my good name into the dirt if I was dead. And he had not lifted a finger to save my precious life!

I cannot have been a pretty sight, because both Eliza and Dunn shrank back. But then Eliza came forward and laid her hand on my cheek. Something snapped inside me and I, who was later to be so feared and detested, burst into tears like a stripling. But what choice did I have? It was either that or rushing off in search of Wilkinson to kill him with my bare hands – which by that stage could have challenged Captain Barlow's reputation – only then to be hanged.

With the tears came the thought of little Curwen standing on the poop deck, the only one looking astern to see what had become of the John Silver who in his own words gave not a damn for the *Lady Mary*, nor her crew and fittings, from her keel right up to the tops of the masts that were no longer there, including little Curwen himself.

"'Tis so diabolically unjust," exclaimed Dunn, "that tyrants like Wilkinson can live while sailors die! Wilkinson, one o' the most infernal of all who sail the seas, b'Jesus!"

Dunn's outburst sobered me.

"D'you know Wilkinson?" I asked.

"Who doesn't?" he asked rhetorically. "Every sailor has heard that Wilkinson is a worse captain than Old Nick himself, if Old Nick took it into his head to go to sea."

He gave a bitter laugh.

"But why should Old Nick trouble himself? With Wilkinson an' others already holding his colours high."

He put his arm round my shoulder.

"We have a lot to talk about: first of all how we're going to put together a new life for John Silver, who if I understand aright went to his grave the day before yesterday an' for a goodly time to come."

We went in and sat down by the fire. Dunn asked me to tell him about myself, from the beginning to the end, which now really was the end, if I was to be consigned to the grave. I told him everything, just as it was, except for my miraculous ride through the tunnel in the cliff, for who would have believed that?

"Was it Curwen you were weeping for?" asked Eliza when I had finished.

"Why should I do that?" said I. "Sailors die on every voyage, you may lay to it; 'tis sad, I dare say, but no more for one than another."

"You don't need to defend yourself," said Dunn. "Anyhow, we've had enough o' misfortune for today. 'Tis John Silver who matters now."

"He's staying here," said Eliza unhesitatingly.

I gaped at her.

"What are you staring at?" she asked.

"Shiver my sides, but I can't fathom you at all," I replied.

"No," said she, "and what good would it do you if you could?"

Nine

WHEN I HAD finished relating to Eliza and Dunn the history of my short life thus far, Dunn went over to one of the seaman's chests standing here and there about the house serving as tables or chairs according to need. He came back with a bottle of brandy.

"Straight from France," said he, as he set down the bottle and three glasses.

"Ain't we at war?" I asked.

"Which we?" replied Dunn. "I've not put my name to any declaration o' war. Sure, an' I'd rather have meself a glass o' wine or a Cognac from time to time. An' I'm not alone in that, neither in Ireland nor in England."

"An' mebbe enough like-minded folk for you to make a living?" I hinted.

"Mebbe so. The English call Kinsale an' Cork a nest of rogues. But they don't know what to do about it. It wouldn't surprise me at all if one day they forbid us to fish or to own boats. I tell'ee, John, in the eyes of the English, Ireland is no better than one of their Colonies in Africa or India. Me grandfather was at the Battle of Kinsale in 1601. Six t'ousand five hundred Irishmen under O'Neill an' a t'ousand Spaniards in Kinsale itself, against four t'ousand Englishmen who'd been besiegin' the Spaniards for t'ree mont's. The assault was launched on the night o' Christmas Eve, in t'understorms an' pourin' rain. In t'ree hours we'd lost everyt'in': our honour, belief in ourselves, our old traditions, our way o' life. If O'Neill had beaten Mountjoy, it all might be so different now."

"My father was Irish," said I.

"I know," replied Dunn, smiling at my disconcerted countenance. "Don't take me amiss, I've not been out pryin'. But when you told us your name, an' said the money in your belt was smugglin' inheritance, a light dawned. There was a Silver in Cóbh who used to sail to France, an adventurous younker, greatly admired. Me own father sailed with him for a few years, ere I was old enough to remember. But I do recall that my father used to say that a better man than Silver would be difficult to find."

Dunn and Eliza looked at me as if they were pleased for my sake that I had had a father to respect. And to think that I had always looked down on him, both literally and in other ways!

"He's dead," was all I said. "Drank himself to death. In a manner o' speaking."

"That's sad," said Eliza.

I said nothing.

"But now the question is, what shall we do about John Silver?" said Dunn, changing the subject, out of consideration, I assume. "Ye'd better keep out o' sight until Wilkinson has gone from Kinsale."

I looked at Eliza. Dunn followed my glance and shook his head.

"I suppose we'll have to be doin' what Eliza wants," said he, "as usual, though 'tis not the most sensible t'ing we could do. It wouldn't surprise me if Wilkinson has men out searchin' for your corpse so that he can be certain no one survived. Because if any o' the crew managed to reach land I wouldn't want to be in Wilkinson's shoes, to be sure."

Dunn stopped himself. It must have occurred to him and to all three of us simultaneously that I was actually a survivor, and had the right to avenge myself, before God and all other judges on this earth.

"Let him live," said I. "One day he'll find out that John Silver survived. That'll be punishment enough, because he'll be afraid ever afterwards that the truth will come out."

I saw relief in both their faces.

"That's good," said Dunn. "'Tis more than sufficient that me daughter has taken a likin' to a mutineer."

"I can go on my way," said I. "John Silver ain't a man to sail as ballast, you may lay to it."

"Very comical that sounds comin' from your big mouth," said Eliza.

"We'll say no more about it," said Dunn. "I have a boat, an' trade a little on the side, so to speak. A Kinsale hooker named *Dana*, a forty-foot cutter, seaworthy an' swifter than most, ideal for any number o' trips to Morlaix, Brest or St Malo. You ought to see her sharp prow slicin' t'rough the Atlantic waves like butter an' how she careens an' gathers speed as she gets her side into the water. Diff'rent from the hookers in Galway that bob about like corks on the choppy seas up there. No, the Kinsale hooker is made for the open sea, an' the more cargo you take on, the better she likes it. 'Tis a sweet delight to sail her, that 'tis. What d'ye say, Silver?"

I did not understand what he was angling after. I had never heard anyone speak of a ship with affection before. On the *Lady Mary*, before the mast at least, the talk was mostly of coffins, blood-buckets, wood-piles, deathships, floating Hells, leaking sieves, slaughterhouses, unruly whores, lopsided hulks, snail shells or worse.

"'Tis offerin' you a place on board I am," said Dunn, a trifle impatiently.

"I'm not forcin' you," he added. "You can choose for yourself whether you want to sail for a share o' the profits or sign on for a wage."

"For shares?" I queried. "As pirates?"

"Mebbe. Or just the way t'ings used to be. In the past no one took a wage on board. Everyone had shares, greater or smaller, from the ship's boy up to the captain. Profits an' losses were sometimes divided equally, more often on a scale o' shares. There were no crimps or runners. No one was pressed. T'ings move on in this world of ours, Silver. But if you put forty pounds into *Dana* you'll be good for ten per cent. Plus," he added after a short pause, "a five per cent bonus for Eliza's sake."

Once again my jaw dropped. Here was the father more or less offering to pay me to take advantage of his hospitality and his daughter, in so far as it was not the other way about, which it partly was, that I was to be reimbursed for making myself available to Eliza.

"Don't just sit there like a blockhead!" said she.

"Agreed for forty pounds," said I. "If I have it."

Eliza was beaming all over her face.

"Why have you gone red?" she asked.

"I ain't gone red," I replied.

"Let's drink to our partnership," said Dunn. "You won't regret it."

No, why should I regret it? There's no going back, that's my motto.

"There's just one more t'ing," said Dunn. "We have to bury John Silver."

"Won't crucifixion be enough?" said I. "If I'm to be certain o' rising from the dead."

"You'll need a new name in any case," said Dunn.

"What about Jesus?" suggested Eliza. "In Portugal I met a sailor who'd been born in Brazil. He was called Jesus, but looked like the Devil, with manners to match."

"What would you say to John Long?" asked Dunn. "There are Johns a-plenty, so there's not'ing in that. And Long has no particular signifi-cance."

Eliza clapped her hands.

"We'll take that," said she on my behalf. "John Long is fine, to be sure, because I can go on calling you John. And Long isn't so bad either, though you're not unduly long, except where it matters."

So that was the tack life took. In Eliza's hands I was no more than a lump of dough that could be kneaded and formed at will. When I took refuge in her soft warm body it felt as if I became another person, John Long, newly arisen, not much to do with John Silver the sailor, the man who had looked his own death in the face.

So much for that. And then there was Eliza herself, who had the quickest, most shameless and impudent tongue I have ever heard speak. With just a few words she could purge anyone of pride and vanity and they would end up with knees a-knocking, and feeling as if they had to learn to walk all over again. A spectacle easy to imagine. With her, I thought, I could talk sense. Not because she took me at my word, but because I could not lead her by the nose, even if I had wanted to.

Ay, all in all I fancied she suited me as well as the oiled leather gloves I now thought I might no longer need for their purpose of marking me for life and not for death. I seemed indeed to have acquired a new life, in every possible way. I was John Long, seaman, partner of Dunn, betrothed to his daughter Eliza, and newly arrived from the Colonies, that was how I was introduced and known in Lazy Cove. So I did not need my gloves any more. But I kept them on when I helped Dunn with his boat, *Dana*. For Eliza's sake! How foolish can you get?

I kept away from Captain Wilkinson, who rumour had it was in no hurry to take the next ship back to Glasgow. He must have been hoping that someone might have survived the catastrophe, someone who on his trustworthy word and testimony could be tried and hanged for mutiny. Only then could he feel safe in returning, head held high, and get a new command and escape the life on land he hated so much.

So I was a prisoner in Lazy Cove. Only a mile to the north my way was barred by Fort Charles, with its garrison of more than five hundred disorderly and unruly English recruits and suspicious arrogant officers who regarded every Irishman as a treacherous enemy, which indeed was true. Since the battle in 1601, Kinsale had been crawling with English soldiers; it was the best deep-water harbour for any Spanish or French vessels wishing to attack England from the rear.

Ay, my wings were clipped and I was mewed up, like an injured bird. I began to yearn to go to sea with Dunn, to feel the wind in my feathers. But as the weeks went by in delightful amity I was not so sure that I wanted Eliza with me. I thought about her all the time, in fact there was little else in my brain. I was considerate to her and respected her wishes and desires, not to say desire. Her goodness and thoughtfulness went to my head and made me giddy and unlike my usual self. It sometimes felt as if she was binding me hand and foot, as if her fondness for me was a noose around my neck.

Not that it made a great deal of difference to start with, because we wanted the same things, and probably did what we both wanted most. But gradually I began to reproach her for being in my thoughts so much. Not that I bore her a grudge for it or held her in less esteem. She was the way she was, but there were times when I felt I hardly existed in my own right. It was not in nature, it seemed to me, that she should take possession of me as she did. In my mind's eye I could see a whole lifetime of this, a whole life without being true to myself.

A few expeditions with Dunn on my own, I felt, could well provide a cure for all of this. But when I talked of sailing I got the firm response from Eliza that she would come with us. Partly, she said, to keep a watch on me so that I did not suddenly evaporate into thin air. For that was the sort of man I was, said she, one who could well disappear if she let him out of her sight! And partly to keep an eye on her father. She was afraid that he could not look after himself. He was made the way he was, and that was why she loved him above all else, but he trusted a handshake and took folk too much at face value.

"Although he knows better," said she. "He's not stupid, as you'll have observed, if you've a head on your shoulders. It's lucky I haven't inherited his good heart, because it makes life so difficult."

In one respect she was right, that it is not easy to live in this world with a heart as good and kind as Dunn's, if you want to be a human being, that is. Otherwise 'tis all one.

I learned to sail the *Dana*, really sailing in fact, since this was nothing like life as a seaman on the *Lady Mary*. Now I had to get a feel for the helm, turn my cheek or my face into the wind to judge the strength of a squall, estimate the speed before tacking, wait for the right wave so as not to let the sails slack and lie to directly into the wind, look at the wake to determine our drift – in a word, I had to think for myself. It soon made me the irrepressible spreader of joy I could be on a ship. Out of the corner of my eye I could see Eliza and Dunn exchanging glances that I would like to think betokened happiness – though not of the same kind of course – in having me at hand.

One day Dunn told me to head further on a southerly course, past Eastern Point and beyond the reef called The Bulman.

"You need to feel the pulse o' the sea in a little boat," said he. "'Tis not at all the same as in a lumberin' merchantman. An' then I'll show you somet'in' you might find interestin'."

We sailed first into The Pitt, the entrance to Sandy Cove, lay at anchor and had our repast while Dunn explained about the weather, winds and currents on that side of Old Head of Kinsale. He indicated landmarks ashore and explained how to come in after dark or in the teeth of a gale. Then we slid out along past Old Head in a light breeze and clear skies.

"I t'ink you should get the bearin's of your environs," said Dunn. "If the likes of us are to make our way in life we have to be smarter than the Excise. Knowledge an' cunnin', that's our insurance."

"So 'tis hardly for you at all," Eliza broke in.

"D'ye spy that little cove to port?" asked Dunn. "That's Cuis an Duine Bhaite, Drowning Man's Cove. Folk who live nearby say they can still hear screams an' cries for help when there's a storm."

I felt apprehensive. Dunn meant no harm, but he could have used his wits. It was no comfort for a soul such as myself to have it spelled out in black and white how easily a man's story can come to an end. Once was more than enough if you wanted to live as much as I did.

"The big cove is called Bullen's Bay," Dunn went on unperturbed without observing my mood. "You can lie at anchor there in westerly an' sou'westerly winds. But you have to watch out for sunken rocks at the southern end. You can avoid 'em if you take a line on Bottom Point over there, d'ye see it, the rounded headland?"

"'Tis so called," added Eliza, "because 'tis like an upturned backside. 'Tis treacherous, so I always think of it as a British soldier with his breeches down. It helps keep your eyes open when you're tiring on the way home."

We sailed close by an islet and slipped into the next bay.

"This is Holeopen Bay East, the best anchorage of all from sou'west to nor'west. You can leave a teacup on the table even if 'tis blowin' a gale round the other side o' the point. There's just a slight roll, because some o' the swell comes in. I'll show you what I'm talkin' about."

Dunn steered our course closer to the cliffs with an easy touch and I could see what he meant. In the cliff, in truth right through the cliff, I could descry the lower half of the sun that was setting in the sea on the other side.

"The sea has bored right t'rough the point," said Dunn. "At high tide you can even row t'rough in a dinghy unscathed. You can see where the bay got its name from."

I made no reply. My head was spinning and my breast was bursting. I had seen myself die once and thought that would suffice for the rest of my life, but now I understood that you could never stare your own death in the face enough and that I really had not gone to my grave. It was Eliza who had made me forget that you only had one skin to save, for as long as you were still alive.

"'Tis not impossible that a man could save himself that way instead o' bein' smashed against the cliffs on the other side," Dunn went on. "I've t'ought about that a lot, John, an' I reck'n that's what must have happened. You can t'ank the powers that be that you survived."

"And who should we thank for the ones who didn't survive?" I retorted.

"That wasn't what I was t'inking about," said Dunn calmly. "But you must learn to live with the fact that you were the only one to survive, without reproachin' yourself."

"Ay," said I, "I s'pose I must. Me an' Cap'n Wilkinson."

I was gloomy on the way back, and not even Eliza could cheer me, but I told both her and Dunn not to concern themselves about me, that it was just good that I had had a chance to see my own premature death again, and that I would soon forget I had ever thought it was all over with me for ever and ever. Amen. What I did not comprehend was that it was like talking to a brick wall. They must have reckoned they could teach me to live again. They did not understand that it was lesson enough to have almost died, and that I did not need anyone on this earth to tell me that I was alive.

After we had returned to Lazy Cove I told them I wanted to be on my own, and walked up towards the fort. Reaching the high, sloping walls I caught sight of some scarlet-clad soldiers on the parapet against the sky. I took it into my head to wave to them, but received no greeting in reply. I assumed it must be forbidden. The Governor of the fort, Warrender, was in Dunn's words a marvel of decrees and ordinances and had only the one religion and rule in life: discipline and more discipline.

"You're here to learn to obey without thinking," were always his first words to new recruits who came for training before being despatched, competent and obedient as few others, to the Colonies or as marines in the navy, the only men on board who made it a point of honour to obey orders.

I walked round the fort to the west side and sat down on a rock with my back to the wall. The sun had sunk behind Compass Hill, but it was still light and as mild as early summer days can be in Ireland. The for me prohibited town of Kinsale lay straight ahead, to port I had a view of the Atlantic, which was glowing deep ruby-red in the last rays of the sun, and to starboard the houses of Summer Cove were hidden behind the lush bright green hills that made you inwardly long to have been born a cow or a sheep. It was beautiful, the sort of scene poets would write about when they became tired of people – which can easily happen, if you ask me – and maybe it provided some relief even for the likes of me.

Anyhow, I dozed off into a dull stupor, for what else is it when we no longer think? But it was a state of mind not to be granted to me, for I was jolted into wakefulness by a musket shot. I pricked up my ears and at first could hear nothing, then a barked order or two, then silence. That in turn was broken by a woman's long-drawn-out scream, unlike anything I had ever heard, that almost made the hair on my head stand on end.

Shortly afterwards a new sound made me turn my head and look up at the top of the wall above me. And what did I see but, of all things, a bride, in a white dress and diadem, about to cast herself off the top! Whether she hesitated in the last moment of folly, or whether her mind was disturbed, I do not know, but it was certainly not a skilfully executed leap. She tottered and stumbled over the parapet, with a scream that pierced bone and marrow, and fell headlong down the thirty-foot steeply sloping wall.

I leapt up and sprang out of the way an instant before she landed with a dull crack of breaking bones and spurting of blood. Heads appeared over the top of the wall shrieking and swearing, moaning and cursing, weeping and wailing. I went over to the lady in white, knelt down and felt for her pulse. She was as dead as the rocks on which she lay shattered.

I was unsure what to do: take to my heels or stay put. But before I had time to decide I heard footsteps hurriedly approaching, and a redcoat appeared beside me, an officer to judge from the epaulettes and other frills.

"How is she faring?" he asked in a sharp voice.

"I can't say. But she's stone dead, no doubt about it."

The officer drew a deep breath.

"What a calamity!" he exclaimed. "This won't please the Governor!"

"Why not?" I asked.

"It's his daughter."

Two soldiers arrived, out of breath, and saluted without a glance at the dead woman. Presumably they did not dare to without an express order.

"Please inform Major Smith," said the officer, "that Miss Warrender is dead. Ask him to send down two men with a bier. Go to it!"

The two panting soldiers saluted again, turned on their heels and set off at full speed.

"I wouldn't like to be in the Governor's shoes when he hears this," said the officer, looking down at the woman.

"What happened?" I asked.

"It's hard to believe it's happened at all," he replied, somewhat bemused and perplexed.

Had we not had the tragedy at our feet, the officer would never have been likely to confide in a stranger and ruffian such as myself. But he obviously needed to unburthen his heart.

"Today is Miss Warrender's wedding day," said he. "She married Sir Trevor Ashurst this morning, a captain in the infantry. After lunch they were apparently walking along the wall by Devil's Bastion, which in truth has earned its name from this. Miss Warrender, or rather Lady Ashurst as she now is – or was, I mean – saw some flowers in the meadow at the foot of the wall. Ashurst, being the gentleman he is, offered to pick some for her. He told her to wait for him in the Governor's house. Then he asked one of the soldiers on watch in the Bastion to run down and gather a large bouquet, and took over the watch in the tower himself. Tired as he was from all the bustle of the wedding, he sat down on a stool and fell asleep at his post, the worst crime a soldier can commit. And what should happen then but the Governor himself came by on his daily inspection, wedding or no, discovered Sir Trevor fast asleep and shot him, his daughter's new husband, on the spot."

I could not believe my ears.

"But how in the name of Hell . . .?" I began.

"The Governor has always been implacable on matters of discipline. No one in the whole British Army can measure up to him in that respect. It's no coincidence that fresh recruits are sent here before they're trusted for service abroad or in the navy."

"Dooty is dooty," I put in, feeling mirth welling up in me. "But on his own daughter's wedding day?"

"Yes," said the officer, looking down at the newly wed corpse, "but he's had to pay a high price. His daughter loved her husband more than her father."

"I'm not surprised," said I. "Why didn't she shoot her father instead? I'm sure that's what I'd have done in her place."

The officer gave me a searching look, and was on the point of opening his mouth when we heard the second shot of the day from the fort, followed by silence, and then more tumult, cries, shouting and confused orders. A face appeared over the top of the parapet.

"The Governor is dead!" the voice shouted down to us. "He's blown his brains out."

"No! Oh no!" gasped the officer.

But I could feel my portholes bursting open. In this world, I thought to myself, we are supposed to behave according to the rules, as a sailor, as a soldier, as a citizen, and obey orders. For what?

I started to laugh. I could not help it. It felt as though the laughter was washing away all the mustiness that had accumulated in my keel since I went aboard the *Lady Mary* ten years before.

Of course I did not observe the officer's complete change of countenance, nor did it occur to me that he would have to give vent to his feelings of impotence sooner or later.

"Who the Devil are you anyway?" he demanded savagely as I tried to stem the flow of my mirth, at least outwardly.

And I, fool that I am – and yet when all's said and done am not – I of course said, "John Silver, known as Long, master mariner and more besides, at your service, sir," whereupon I turned and strode off, with my own peals of laughter ringing like wedding bells inside my head.

Ten

I WAS STILL chuckling to myself when I came back to Lazy
Cove and was confronted with Dunn and Eliza. They were
sitting close to the open fire, and however things were between
Eliza and me, I could not help a feeling of distaste at the concern and
anxiety that showed in their eyes when they saw me. They had saved
my life, was that not enough? Did I have to be diminished further? Was
I not a man who could laugh death in the face? I could do without their
troubled countenances.

Eliza brightened up when she saw there was nothing amiss with me.
But the very next moment her face clouded again in consternation. She
was staring at my legs as if she had never seen them before.

"What's the matter?" I asked.

"You've blood upon your breeches," said she in a quiet voice.

I looked down and saw that Miss Warrender's final act had been to
spoil the only trousers I had that were fit for land, a gift from Dunn.

"Well, have you ever seen the like?"

A smile came back to their gloomy faces. I kept them on tenterhooks
for a while longer before telling them word for word how close I had
come to an untimely end, and the events that had befallen me. But if I
thought my story would ease their minds, I was mistaken.

"You shouldn't laugh at a woman who was desperate enough to take
her own life," said Eliza.

"Why not?" said I. "What is more laughable than that?"

I looked from one to the other, but got no response.

"Imagine if it had been me," said Eliza.

"You?" I replied. "Why should I imagine that? For one thing I'd like
to see Dunn shoot his son-in-law for sleeping at his post. And secondly,
you wouldn't jump off a wall for my sake."

"What would you know about that?" asked Eliza.

"Yes," said Dunn, "who knows what I would do if my son-in-law brought misfortune on my daughter an' all?"

"Don't look at me!" I exclaimed, but that was just what he was doing.

"If I understood aright," said Dunn, "you t'rew your real name in the officer's face like a gauntlet."

"Ay, I did. An' shiver my timbers, I'd do it again if I had cause."

"That's what I'm afeared of," said Dunn.

"Don't distress yourself on my account," said I merrily.

"Sure an' I'm hardly likely to," responded Dunn. "I'm t'inkin' about Eliza."

I had to smile at that.

"If there's anyone who can look after herself in life, 'tis her," said I.

That was my honest opinion, and rare praise to issue from lips such as mine, a show of esteem; but I got naught in return.

"John," said Dunn, "I've taken a likin' to you. Eliza obviously has too. That has not'in' to do with the fact that I saved your life. I would have done that for absolutely anybody."

"Even Governor Warrender?" I put in.

"Even Captain Wilkinson," said Dunn.

I could hardly believe my ears.

"Yes, for sure I would, but you don't need to understand why, or to agree with me. We're talkin' about somet'in' else now. We gave you shelter an' looked after you. It's hard not to t'ink highly of you, John, whatever you may feel about it, yes, whatever we may feel about it. You chose to become my partner an' then Devil take me if my daughter isn't on the point of choosin' you as my son-in-law. That's no secret. An' now you go an' put everyt'in' in jeopardy by shoutin' out that you're John Silver, without t'inkin' that there's not'in' Cap'n Wilkinson would rather hear. For sure an' I t'ought you had more sense."

"I just said what came into my mind."

"Indeed," said Dunn, "that was exactly what you did. An' what d'ye t'ink will happen if it comes out that Eliza an' I have been harbourin' a mutineer like you?"

I made no reply. I had nothing to say, neither in my defence nor the opposite. I had shouted out my name to get a bit of air under my wings and to be myself, that was all.

"We would be hanged," continued Dunn. "Exactly like you."

"Well," said I, "we're in the same boat, then. For better or for worse."

"For worse, most likely," said Eliza.

Later, in bed, she took me, without a by your leave, as if our last hour was at hand. In the end I had to beg her for mercy.

"Mercy?" said she. "Do you have to beg for mercy, a big, strong man like you who can take on the whole world? Do you even know what the word means?"

"Ay," said I, "that I can't take any more."

Eliza laughed joylessly, as I had never heard her laugh before.

"You can't take any more!" she said scornfully and sorrowfully at the same time. "One day, John Silver, I hope you'll be down on your bare knees pleading for mercy. Like a human being."

"And what am I now?"

She did not reply. I did not understand. Why did she not say what she meant, as she usually did, straight to the point? And to make things worse, she began to weep.

"What's the matter?" I asked. "Mebbe I didn't think before I spoke, like enough. But I was true to myself. Ain't that why you've taken a fancy to me? Because I am the way I am? If you want me to go and leave you and Dunn in peace, just say so instead of blubbering like a baby."

A lot of help those words were – she wept even more.

"Can't you just tell me what the problem is?" I ventured.

"Yes," said she at last, "I can. The problem is that you don't understand."

The next day we put to sea in the *Dana* and set course for France. Both Dunn and Eliza seemed relieved to be at sea, with nothing but perhaps a covert glance as a reminder of the previous day. The wind was with us and *Dana* was sailing beautifully. Rainbows sparkled through the flying spray. The sun was reflected in the drops of water on the red cotton sails. The air cleansed all three of us, thought I at least, of all bad feeling and discord.

We hove to out of sight of Ouessant until smugglers' darkness fell, and then slipped in through Le Goulet, past Brest and into the River Aulne, where we anchored as close to Châteaulin as we durst in view of the tide. As soon as the sun rose we hoisted the French colours at our stern.

"Isn't it odd," said Dunn, "that so many folk are tricked by somet'in' so simple? But most o' them, especially officials, hold their flag so dear that it doesn't occur to them that the likes of us change flags just as we please."

We took the jolly-boat in to Châteaulin, on the flood tide so that we did not have to row, as if we were on a Sunday excursion. We went into a tavern called Le Coq, and Eliza ordered red wine for the five of us, for we were in company with two of Dunn's regular men, Edward England, an Irishman from birth despite his perverse and ill-fitting name, and a half-Frenchman, a result, I learned later, of an encounter between a French prostitute – no offence to that honourable profession – and a whoremonger of surprising origins. This progeny went by the name of Deval. Little did I suspect then what significance these two men were to have in my eventful life.

We were a happy group, at any rate. Dunn and Eliza had acquaintances from earlier trips: sinewy, red-faced, high-spirited Bretons not lacking in humour. Business was concluded with a handshake, without fuss, to the sound of corks popping out of bottles and the slurp of oysters slipping down throats. There were jokes and banter about the decision-makers of the world, with debate as fierce as among sailors, though more good-natured. Stories were told of excise cutters lured aground by skilful and risky manoeuvres. What fascinating adventures I heard of, and what scorn of danger and death, as far as I could grasp it anyway, since I was dependent upon Eliza's, Dunn's or even Deval's explanations in a language the likes of myself could understand!

We loaded up with Cognac before sneaking out on the ebb tide past the arsenals of Brest, through the Chenal du Four, and into l'Aber-Wrac'h as dawn broke and revealed to our vision the waters Dunn had steered us through. They were nothing but cliffs, islands, exposed or submerged rocks, and reefs mostly concealed at high tide.

To my weary and heavy-lidded eyes it was a pure miracle that we were still alive, but Dunn demonstrated night after night that Providence was the last thing he relied upon. A little moonlight or even just the glitter of the stars, a lead-line, a compass and a log were all he needed.

"By thunder, how did you learn to navigate like that?" I asked him, full of admiration, on the fourth night as we made our way into the Trieux River through an evil witches' cauldron of breakers glinting treacherously whichever way I turned. "There must be easier ways to earn our bread."

"To be sure, there may well be," said Dunn, "if bread is enough to satisfy you. But not if you want a little amusement besides."

That was true, I discovered. This was a life worth living, and no mistake. There was excitement and adventure, cunning and deceit, jokes and laughter, with hardly a serious moment except for wind and weather, and no religion other than a belief in getting home in one piece and making a bit of money on the trip. It was the first time in my life that I felt I was really free and master of my own happiness. It was an opportunity I did not want to miss and I wrought like a fiend to make myself indispensable on board. To learn something about navigation I took double watches, standing by Dunn at the helm in the narrow passages and by England on the long crossings.

"You ought to get to your berth," said England. "You're drivin' us all mad with your energy. You're givin' me a bad conscience."

"There's time enough for that when we're old," I replied, the way you think and speak without knowing what you are really saying.

"You're young," said England, who was not that old himself. "Take some good advice an' rest while you have the chance. You never know when you'll get the next."

Edward England knew what he was talking about. He was born, he said, of parents who had taken part in every single uprising against the English, and as a consequence had lost everything they owned, including, he could say, their half-grown son, who had wearied of the life of a fugitive, never spending two nights in the same place, never a full stomach, never anyone of his own age to play with. The day his parents were taken prisoner in a cave in the Wicklow Mountains and he himself was to be sent to the poor-house, he fled to Cork. There he had wanted to try to set himself up as a farmer, to get some firm ground under his feet, as he said, instead of the quagmire he had lived in since the day he was born. But what happened? Although as a farmer he was certainly standing in one place, the longer it went on, the more he felt he was sinking into bog and dung. That was no life either. He feared, he said, that all the running around had got into his blood, and gave him itchy feet if he tried to sit still. So he set off for Kinsale to be a fisherman, for the free life of the sea, as it was called by those who knew no better. For what was it but constant toil on the same thwarts, in and out, back and forth, never any rest for the sake of a change but only because the weather made it impossible to work. And even then you had to guard the moorings or be anchor watch! So that too was no life at all. Only after shipping with Dunn had he come to feel there was any meaning in his wretched circumstances. On Dunn's boat there was no hurry, at least if you used your head so that you did not get into difficulties too often. Quite the opposite, in fact: it was important to have a good sleep and be rested so that you did not make stupid mistakes from tiredness when the topsail of an Excise cutter was sighted on the horizon.

"That's why, comrade," said England, "you ought to listen to what I say an' get to your berth."

"I know what I can take," I retorted.

And I think all of them were amazed at what I could take. No rest or relaxation, yet always cheerful, laughing and jesting, that was me, and it was to be my mark, that and instilling fear, throughout my life.

As we approached the entrance to St Malo, with Cap Fréhel to starboard and the shape of the land visible in the moonlight, I was the one steering, with Dunn on one side and Eliza on the other. Dunn had told me about the landmarks and course in advance, and I felt as if I was taking my apprenticeship test. And shiver my timbers if I did not bring us in without Dunn having to correct me a single time. My pride and self-esteem knew no bounds – until Eliza brought me back down to earth, where I belonged.

"'Tis strange that you're so stupid yet can learn so fast."

She said it with tenderness, but it grated on my proud ears. Why should she destroy my happiness when it was at its height? But perhaps she was just afraid of the likes of me going his own way and no one else's, that I would not make the slightest effort to accommodate myself to others, since I was, after all, capable of mutiny. But I have always been ready to accommodate myself in most ways, at least as long as it served a good cause: my own.

The only other note of discord on this trip came from Deval. When we hauled in the anchor rope he could not keep up, and had to settle for coiling it on deck as it flew through my hands. When we had to trim the sails he was so slow that he was mostly in the way; hoisting and reefing was one thing I had learned on the *Lady Mary*. Whenever we moored at a quay I would tie bowlines with one hand, while Deval could only tie one knot, and in one direction. When we raised the jolly-boat up into the davits, Deval would hardly have got the bow out of the water before I had the stern level with the rail. No, he was not good for much when it came to any comparison between us.

I asked England how on earth Dunn could have taken on such an incompetent creature.

"There are two ways of lookin' at everything," said he, showing the understanding he later became renowned for. "It makes a lot o' sense to have a Frenchman aboard."

"But there must be better ones he could get," I objected.

"Not in our circles," replied England. "Have you met many sailors who could pass muster in any tongue other than their own? And ashore?"

I had to answer no to that. On board the *Lady Mary* there was every language you could imagine, except for French and Spanish, because of the war, but we had our own sailors' lingo too, an unholy mix of every possible tongue. But who could use that on dry land and be understood? Like enough no one at all.

"Besides . . ." England hesitated, "besides, you don't choose those closest to you, however much you'd like to."

"Closest to you?" I repeated. "What d'you mean by that?"

"I dunno whether I ought to say this, but I've taken to you and hope

I can depend upon you to keep your mouth shut."

"Shiver my soul," said I. "You can always depend upon John Silver."

"Deval's mother is Eliza's mother too. Deval and Eliza are half-brother and sister. In his youth Dunn visited a bawdy-house in France, the way we all do. When he went back there the next year he found he was father to a child, if you can be certain o' that with a whore, but the fact is Eliza was her father's spitting image. Anyhow, Dunn didn't hesitate. The child was his. Believe it or not, he wanted to take her, he didn't want a child of his to grow up in a bawdy-house if he could prevent it. Well, he could – you know what he's like – but at what a price, say I. The whore agreed, for a sum of money, but on top of that insisted Dunn should take on another of her progeny: Deval."

Deval and Eliza half-brother and sister! None could be less alike than they were.

"By the powers!" was all I could say.

"Yes," said England. "Dunn is the most honourable man I know, but we all have our weak sides."

At that moment Dunn emerged on deck. He went over to the rail and stood staring out into the darkness. England gave me a warning look.

"'Tis all right, Edward," said Dunn without turning round. "I should have told him meself. I suppose I was ashamed."

"Ashamed?" said I. "Why should you be ashamed?"

"For sailin' with an inadequate man. Because that's what he is, without a doubt. But I've given me word, so there's not much I can do."

Take it back, thought I, that's all there is to it, but I held my tongue.

"On the other hand," Dunn went on, "I didn't give me word that Eliza should know where she comes from. She doesn't know, either, and nor does he, for the same reason. I ask you gentlemen to keep that in mind. I don't need to say that to you, Edward. We all have our weak sides, right enough. Mine is Eliza. So now you know, John."

"I'll do my best," I replied.

"I mean Eliza to be happy," said Dunn in a voice that was not far removed from Wilkinson's.

He turned abruptly and went back below to his berth, where he had every right to be, since he was off duty.

"I'll never understand folk," said England quietly a while later. "Parents especially. D'ye know why I was called England? So that I should never forget our country's oppressors. So that I would rise agin' the English an' fight 'em with me bare hands, if need be. Can you believe it?"

He fell silent and thoughtful for a few moments before continuing, "But one thing's for sure: however much I like Dunn, I'd hate to be his son-in-law."

And I for my part was beginning to think there might be something in what he said, however I might regard Eliza and the free life of a smuggler at sea, which in every other respect seemed an enjoyable and proper way of life for the likes of me.

"Why should it all be so damned complicated?" I asked irritably. "Here we are leading as good a life as you could wish for. Except for this Deval, who turns sulky just because I happen to be a better man than him. And then we can't do anything about it. Not even throw the bastard overboard."

"Don't bemoan that," said England cheerfully. "Things could be worse, to be sure."

"There's two sides to everything, you mean?"

"Yes, that's about it."

I had food for thought, that much was plain. But I did not let myself be disheartened and I had no intention of giving Eliza up, if she would just let me be myself. Only one thing troubled me: what was Dunn's gauge for measuring her happiness? What did it consist of? Her not crying more than once a month? Her looking happy most of the time? Her talking as much as she customarily did, usually at my expense in any case? Was it my fault, for instance, in Dunn's eyes, if Eliza was saddened because in her opinion I was too stupid to understand what it was I did not understand? Would Dunn blame me for that? And so on and so forth, until I gave up, tired of asking myself questions I could not answer, at least not in all honesty.

Meanwhile, Deval's angry eruptions did not trouble me. On the contrary, I put myself out to be particularly friendly to him, now that I knew he was staying on board, for worse rather than better. My friendliness produced results beyond my expectations. By the time we hove to beneath the granite walls of St Malo I had led him by the nose further than I had either hoped or wanted. He had become almost like a dog, and would have licked my backside if I had asked him – which I was careful not to. It was bad enough as it was.

Dunn had business with the prosperous shipowners of St Malo, who were fitting out ships for everything from cod-fishing or privateering to conquest expeditions or simple trading. He took Eliza with him to prevent himself being cheated, which could easily happen with crafty dealers of that sort. England proposed that we three crew should have a well-deserved evening off. Without women and captains, as he put it.

So three high-spirited seamen set out through the crowds on the rue de la Soif, Thirsty Street, where inns, taverns, ale-houses, saloons and wine-houses stood side by side. We went from bar to bar, trying every possible kind of drink in all the colours of the rainbow, and a few more besides, cursing and laughing, roaring and bellowing, singing lewd and wanton songs; we span yarns about all the weird characters we had met in port and on board ship, boasting of feats in the rigging, lashed by storms, or in brothels when our feelings were overflowing; we slapped barmaids on the buttocks and got resounding cuffs on the ear for our pains; we picked a fight with four red-headed Dutchmen, and generally lived life to the full to let ourselves know we were alive – until finally, exhausted, squint-eyed and battered in body and soul, but happy with our night's work, we found ourselves lolling over a piss-warm beer in a hole that went under the name of Liberty Bar. Our strength and stamina were at an end, and as so often happens with sailors at a late hour, we turned to sentimentality, homesickness, self-pity and to thinking about all our various disappointments.

Even England, who for a long time showed no leanings in that direction, started to delve in the most melancholy reaches of his otherwise so apparently simple soul.

"By the powers!" said he. "For sure an' I should never have gone to sea! 'Tis goin' to end badly, I can feel it in my bones. I should've stayed on dry land, so help me. With a patch o' ground."

"An' drowned in cow-shit an' muck instead?" I scoffed at him. "Would that've been any better?"

Deval began to lament his dear lost mother who, according to him, had died before he was born, and his own worthlessness, the fact that everyone ignored him though he had never done anything to deserve such treatment.

"You exist," I said to him. "That's the root of the problem."

"What d'you mean by that?" asked he in a slurred voice.

"When people look at you they see themselves as in a mirror. An' obviously they ain't best pleased at the sight."

"Is that so?" said Deval and seemed almost to brighten up, as if his wretchedness had been given new meaning in life.

"An' what about you?" he went on, "d'you see yourself in me too?"

"No, God forbid. I'd hang meself from the nearest tree."

At that Deval laid his greasy head on my shoulder and, man that he was, cried a few tears.

"John, I want to be your friend."

"Deval," I replied, "you can do whatever you like for all I care, as long as you don't involve me."

So we left Liberty Bar, shouting and stumbling over our words and feet, as the boon companions we took ourselves in our drunken delusion to be. But if there was one thing I knew when I woke up on the morrow with my deadlights falling out of their sockets, it was that it did not pay me to drink to forget, if that was what I wanted. Nothing of any value, as I have said, went in one ear and out the other. That is how it remained all through my life. Others drowned their sorrows while I remembered them – theirs, that is.

Dunn laughed knowingly at our grave-digger faces the next day. Eliza was not so amused. She said our fumes had filled the cabin and given her a headache, but we all stubbornly refused to admit it. With some difficulty we loaded the last of the cargo that was destined to quench thirsts on the other side of the Channel. Dunn and England talked a little about the war while we waited for the tide to get us afloat – it was thirty-six feet hereabouts – but I turned a deaf ear. The war was no business of mine.

As we approached Ireland, we lay beneath the horizon till daybreak, and then sailed in and mingled with the hookers fishing on the banks off Old Head. We laid our nets all day to show that we were honest and upright folk, in case anyone should wonder. Towards evening we set our sails for home along with the others, headed in to Kinsale and anchored off the fish quays, after setting Eliza down in Lazy Cove.

We unloaded under cover of darkness, and were met by Dunn's comrades who helped us roll everything in through Nicholas Gate. The watchmen waved us through, because they knew what reward awaited them for turning a blind eye. A posting to Nicholas Gate was so coveted that neither the Sovereign, the Governor of Kinsale nor the English had ever succeeded in turning any of the watch informer. I heard much later from a Kinsale fisherman who joined Edward England's company that Nicholas Gate was unceremoniously walled up, and since then, and probably still, goes under the name of Blind Gate.

I was hesitant, of course, about setting foot within the walls that contained Captain Wilkinson. But Dunn himself said the risk was too slight to worry about. I was among friends who were used to moving around the town without being seen or heard. So I went with them and was led through narrow alleys to Tap Tavern, which belonged to the blacksmith's wife and was frequented by honourable and resolute Irishmen like Dunn, who frightened off any English soldier who might think of putting his nose inside.

I have been in many taverns in my day – it went with the job, in a manner of speaking – most of them best forgotten; but Tap Tavern was not like the others. Mary and her son Brian, the open fire with its leaping flames, the black cats – of which one, in good Irish fashion, was christened Cromwell, just as England had been baptised England – the cup-sized whisky measures hanging from hooks in the ceiling, themselves the blacksmith's own apprenticeship work, small bottles vying for space with the barrels behind the bar, benches, shiny with use, along the walls, tankards with the names of regular customers engraved on the handles, gleaming brass pump-handles: all this made even me relax and feel myself as much at home as the likes of me could ever wish or hope to be.

Mary, it was not hard to see, knew everything about everybody in Kinsale, natives as well as strangers like myself. With inquisitive eyes and vivacious lips that flashed into an all-embracing smile or an unfriendly scowl depending on subject or person, she seemed to be equipped, in her place behind the bar, to contend with anything and anyone. I can see now that it was thanks to Tap Tavern and Mary that I was later to buy the Spy-glass in Bristol. Why should I have hobbled around on my single leg searching for that swine Billy Bones when, like Mary, I could get all the information I needed in one place?

So *Dana*'s little crew raised their tankards to celebrate our first successfully completed voyage as partners. We had been paid for our goods and my pocket was weighed down with fourteen sovereigns. It was very different from the miserable wages on the *Lady Mary*, when you got any at all, even if some of the fourteen had to be put aside for the next voyage. I bought a round and would duly have recovered my outlay handsomely, as is the rule in Ireland, had not the door opened to admit a man who glanced briefly round the room and then came straight over to us. He nodded at Dunn and turned to me.

"Would your name be John Silver?" asked he, as if nothing in the world could be worse.

"And what if it were?" I asked.

"If it were," said the man, "you'd do well to fly from here like the very Devil. The new Governor in the fort has sent out hordes of men to hunt for you."

"The Governor? What would he be wanting with such a poor swab as John Silver? Has he done aught wrong?"

The man turned to Dunn, whose countenance resembled a thunder-cloud. It was quite touching, I thought.

"The English say he's a dangerous spy for France, an' that he was skulking around by the fort a few days ago."

Dunn's face grew even blacker, if that were possible.

"It can't be true, of course," the man quickly added. "But the fact they want to hang John Silver is for sure. But as for why . . ."

He spread his arms wide.

"So, they do, do they?" I exclaimed indignantly, unable to restrain myself any longer. "Then I'll be damned if I won't get in first! They want to hang me so that no one'll know what goes on in their immaculate fort and in their well-disciplined heads. But they'll get no satisfaction from me, as sure as my name's John Silver!"

And so I set about telling the whole story once again, at the top of my voice, to everyone who would listen. Mary pricked up her ears – no one who had eyes to see could be in any doubt of that – and thus there was no doubt that my story would soon spread like wildfire. But that was scant revenge.

"And should the likes of me, an innocent seaman, hang from the gallows for that?" I asked. "Is that fair and just?"

I heard a murmur of accord from all sides.

"And wouldn't you think that would be enough? No, because now I've washed their dirty linen in public, they'll hang me as a spy anyhow, so that no one'll dare believe my story to be true. That's how things are done in this world, in the name of God and the King. You're hanged for telling the truth, and you're hanged for voicing your opinion. But go up to the fort and ask to speak to Governor Warrender or his wench of a daughter and see what answer you get. Or ask for Sir Trevor Ashurst. Ask 'em whether he's woke up yet, the sluggard!"

I felt an arm round my shoulder. It was England.

"Take it easy, John!" said he.

"Easy? Why in Hell's name should I take it easy? You tell me that!"

"For your own sake if not'in' else," said England.

This time at least England knew how to put his finger on a tender spot.

"The way you're rantin' an' goin' on," he continued, "it won't be long before the redcoats are stormin' in an' hangin' you from the nearest tree before you've had time for your last prayer. Besides . . ."

"Ay, I know," I broke in, "besides, it could've been much worse. I could've been dead, for instance. One thing is true, you may lay to it, and that is that I'll never understand the Irish. But you may be right. What do you suggest?"

It occurred to me as I spoke that I should have put that question to Dunn, not to England. But Dunn was regarding me with a look that gave me cold shivers and goose-flesh.

"The best thing we could do would be to sail you to France," said England, "and for you to stay there until the worst has blown over."

Calm and collected, England put his hand on Dunn's shoulder exactly as he had with me, as if nothing had happened. But he was not the one who was going to be hanged.

"What d'ye say, Dunn?" England asked him. "'Tis a bit soon, o' course: we don't want to drown the whole populace of Cork in brandy, but we could sail John over an' take the opportunity ourselves to ship a new cargo. We could probably manage it."

Dunn shook off England's hand.

"An' Eliza?" he spat out.

And to think I had believed he had been distraught with anxiety over me! How we deceive ourselves. I had a good mind to point out that a few corns on his delightful daughter's feet were not much in comparison with the harm that could come to the whole of me if I had a noose around my neck!

"Why concern yourself about her?" asked England, ever the man of sense. "You know as well as I do that she can take care of herself an' that she'll wait for us in Lazy Cove. Why should anythin' befall her tonight? We won't make it any better by standin' here an' losin' valuable time, anyhow," he concluded in an authoritative voice which I would not have thought him capable of.

Thereupon he took command and propelled us out of the tavern. As the door was closing I met Mary's eyes and could see that she understood me and would do her bit. Before the night was out the whole town would know about the Warrenders, father and daughter, Ashurst the son-in-law and the alleged spy John Silver's insignificant role in the comedy. Too late it suddenly occurred to me that at the same time it would reach Captain Wilkinson's ears. But what did that matter? Might as well be hanged for a sheep as for a lamb! It made no difference whether I was a spy or a mutineer. And there were many who were hanged for less. The punishment was the same for stealing a sack of half-rotten Irish potatoes as for cutting the throat of a ship's captain. Why should I bewail my fate? There would be a certain justice in my hanging in any case, even if it were all a fabrication from beginning to end.

England drove Dunn and me in front of him like two sheep through the same dark alleys and passageways we had come through before. Deval trooped along behind.

"This here's your chance, Deval," I said to him, "to be my friend, as you wanted to be, if I remember aright. Help me out o' this fix and you'll be one of us, the friends of John Silver, no more an' no less."

"John," said Deval in a voice thick with gratitude, "you can depend upon me."

I had the greatest difficulty, despite the circumstances, in containing my mirth, but for once I was sure no one would understand what was so comical.

We reached the fish quay unhindered. We took to the jolly-boat and only when we were out of earshot of land did England explain what he had in mind.

"You an' Dunn take the jolly-boat an' sail straight round to Lazy Cove. Deval an' I'll make the *Dana* ready to sail an' follow as soon as we can. We'll anchor off shore an' wait for John. Or for all three of you. We can just as easily make the voyage with a full crew. What d'ye say, Dunn?"

"Eliza an' I will stay here," said Dunn. "You must see that we can hardly disappear at the same time as John. If we're not already regarded as his accomplices, we'd be as good as if we sailed now. An' what d'ye reckon would happen to Eliza then?"

"You're right, Dunn," said I. "I'll get off alone. I don't want to sail as ballast, as I said when we first met. D'you remember? You may recall that I offered to go away, that John Silver weren't one to be a burthen on others."

Dunn made no answer. It was really as if I had ceased to exist, all the while he did not know whether anything had happened to Eliza. It was an eerie trip in the jolly-boat, in light mist and drizzle, with the two ominous forts on each side of us and Lazy Cove as a dark and forbidding gap somewhere ahead of us. The only partial reassurance was the muffled sound of a block groaning and a sail filling, the *Dana* gliding along in our wake.

When we arrived, Dunn leapt ashore and ran up towards the house along the winding path. I had the sense to draw up the boat on to dry land before following at top speed, but not so fast as to forget to check that I had the pistol that Dunn had given me, nor to stop and load it.

And it was well that I did, for when I entered the house Dunn was standing by the fireplace holding a torn piece of cloth, the same white cotton, it seemed to me, that had so beautifully revealed the form of Eliza's body as she slipped in and out of the sunlit doorway a few weeks earlier. But I could also see in the failing light of the fire that the white cloth was stained with red. I looked hurriedly around. Everything was in a complete state of disarray. Chests had been opened or smashed and their contents were strewn over the whole room.

As soon as Dunn caught sight of me, if it was me he saw at all, his face contorted into an ugly snarl.

He has gone mad, was all I could think, mad and insane with worry. But not for me, that was certain.

"You've murthered her!" he screamed. "Murthered Eliza!"

"Like Hell I have!" I retorted. "You know that as well as I do."

But of course that was what he did not know. I saw his hand disappear behind his back, and in the next instant he was holding his sharp-bladed gully and hurtling towards me like the madman he had become. At the very last moment I raised my pistol and shot him in the chest. He probably died on the spot, but it was not enough to halt his headlong rush towards me at that speed, dead or alive, and he slit my trouser leg and a bit of my thigh. Then he crashed to the hard-packed Irish earth at my feet, and when it was all completely quiet again I knew that the person I had actually shot was not Dunn, but Eliza, if she was still alive.

It was hardly a pleasing thought to ponder, you may lay to that. Eventually, however, it hit me that I could not simply stay where I was if I wanted to live the only life I had. What would I say to England and Deval? Not the truth, for sure. Deval's promise that he was my friend was meaningless. Anybody could buy him with an ounce of amity. England was a different matter. Nothing seemed really to affect him, so it was hard to know where you stood with him. Things could always be worse and there were two ways of looking at everything. How could you depend on such a man? So to be on the safe side, I would have to invent, say something that could have happened. What, I wondered? That the English had been lying in wait, that they had shot Dunn, but I had managed to flee? That seemed natural enough. But the English would not have fired just a single shot. So I loaded again and loosed off several shots into the darkness as I made my way down to the beach and the jolly-boat. Hurling myself into it, I rowed for all I was worth, with a brief pause for a last shot that I fired off at water level so that it might hit *Dana*'s hull if I was lucky, to add to the plausibility of my story. I was living, it seemed, on credit. From then on, and for ever, my peaceful and affectionate life ashore was at an end. Maybe it was just as well, since such perfection was not really suited to the likes of me.

I rowed till the sweat was pouring off me, my face was red and burning and my wound bleeding profusely. The shape of the *Dana* was soon discernible in the darkness, as unreal as the *Flying Dutchman*, with two human figures bending over the rail ready to pull me on board. I let the jolly-boat hit the *Dana*'s planking with a thud and grabbed the rail with a final effort. I just had time to hope I was not overplaying it before feeling England's powerful arms hoisting me on board like a case of brandy.

"Get goin'!" I gasped. "The English are a-comin'!"

"Make fast the jolly at the stern!" England ordered Deval, without questioning me further. "We'll hoist it up later."

With the foresight he always displayed at the right moment England had let *Dana* drift instead of anchoring her, and it was not long before I heard the life-saving ripple of water racing beneath her hull.

But not until I felt the slow pulse of the swell making us rhythmically rise and fall, and the hollowness in my stomach that followed, did I sit up with difficulty and tell my story. They were anything but gladdened by the news, Deval and England, but they believed me; and thus, I imagined, a chapter had ended and a new one would commence in the story of my own life which would be hard to believe if not personally seen or experienced. There were two ways of looking at it, as England would say, but at least it was not tedious to be in the midst of it. Of course, I could scarcely forget or gainsay that it was not exactly heartening to be Dunn, Eliza or Deval, but their misfortunes were their own. Why should I be burthened with their lives, I who looked after my own problems and let others do the same?

But what about Eliza, was the thought I could not repress as the last flickering light from the beacon on Old Head of Kinsale disappeared over the horizon while I stood staring astern. Perhaps after all Eliza had been trying to give me something I lacked, but something which for the life of me I could not comprehend. I could not be expected to take the blame for that as well. I told myself in all seriousness that there must be others like Eliza among the millions and millions of women who inhabit this earth. There may well be, but as for meeting any of them in my long life, I'm damned if I ever have.

Eleven

O LIVE. AT any price. That has been my object, I do not mind admitting. But who has had to pay, I wonder now deep in my heart; at whose and what cost have I lived? I have sucked at life like a leech, and though I boasted the opposite, I seem in truth to have bled everyone. I convinced myself at the time that they were temporary loans, investments in the promising business of John Silver, which would be repaid as soon as I was in funds. But no one will ever get anything back, and now I sit here like a rich man, with masses of lives that will remain lying unto eternity like buried treasure without a map.

So I shot Dunn, in the heat of the moment; I did it without forethought, with no thought at all. Dunn saved my life, but on the other hand it was not in essence mine he saved. He was prepared to save any life at all, mine or Captain Wilkinson's, it was all the same to him as long as it was a life. So what did I really owe him? Should I have just stood there and let him finish me, transfigured and demented as he was, with a thrust of his knife that would have made that new chapter in my life the final one? Surely not.

The truth is that I shot Dunn and erased Eliza from my life with one and the same shot. It was nothing to be proud of, but nothing to be ashamed of either. I could tamper with the truth, of course, tell myself that I had my back to the wall, but what good would it do me? There was not a shadow of a doubt that I was standing in the doorway, with my back free, and that is all there is to it.

Nor is that the worst. If it was bad to shoot Dunn, I have been guilty of worse and still slept soundly. No, what has disturbed me is to find, in black and white, that this John Silver, who to all appearances was true to himself, seemed to live his life from hand to mouth, just as it happened, according to whichever way the wind blew. He grasped at one straw here and another there, took what was offered and what was forbidden, but did he have any compass or destination? Did he ever think about whither he was going or what he wanted, always priding himself on being sure of his ground, always believing himself better because he knew he was alive while others went through life unaware of it?

Ay, I know what I reckoned, that this, writing my true story, would keep me sane for a while longer, that this was what was needed, and more in the same vein. Balderdash, I call it, no more and no less. It makes me know that I am alive, right enough, but by God, if He exists, it was not how I thought it would be. But perhaps I can hope that the memories will become easier to face up to, and can then be cast overboard like so much ballast when they have been named, put in order and wrung dry. For is that not how life is extinguished here on earth? Always provided you are not hanged, that is.

Twelve

A NEW CHAPTER, then, as we say without thinking about it. *Dana* headed again for France with its indefatigable crew giving themselves no repose. There were no laurels to rest on, either, not for any of us. There was no question of England and Deval going back to Ireland without playing constant hide-and-seek, and England at least had had enough of that. And for me to return would be, to use an approximate likeness, akin to sleeping on duty for the sake of a few flowers.

So, France it was, naturally. We thought it would give us some cards to play with. To compensate for his lack of other qualities, Deval could be our interpreter, if he ever managed to understand what it was England and I wanted to say. England had made a score of trips to various places in Brittany with Dunn. He knew the waters like the back of his hand and was obviously the captain. I for my part remained a simple seaman, though a master mariner, and was content with that. Sticking out my neck to make decisions, in good times and bad, was not my strong point. I wanted to steer my own course, not one for others. Nobody was going to depose John Silver, that was the first of my articles. But as a safeguard I proposed that we should set up a ship's council to determine all the most important issues on board, whatever they might be, other than when, where and how we should put our only lives at risk to earn ourselves a crust.

Deval stayed in his berth the whole of the first night. While England and I did what had to be done to save our skins, to sail the boat, change the flag and name, make an inventory of weapons and stores, Deval wept over the death of Dunn. If you could believe Deval himself, he was the only one – and on this matter it was hard to disagree – who had shown Deval the little friendship and consideration that most people – and whatever could have made him think that? – had a right to expect. Magnanimously I let Deval put his head on my shoulder and have a good cry; in view of the circumstances that was the least I could do. When he had finished I bade him sharply return to his berth. We needed him rested and clear-headed when we reached Brittany on the morrow. Indeed, we would not be able to manage without him. My well-chosen words acted as a spur, and he swiftly disappeared below deck.

So England and I stood there together with the night before us.

"Devil of a soup ye've landed us in, John!" said England, directing a great gob of spittle over the side into the sea.

Admittedly he was now captain, with the right to piss into the wind if he so desired, but it was still foolish to spit windward – because the gobbet flew in an arc and landed on his foot. He looked disbelievingly down and then at me.

"But . . ." he began, and I interrupted him, not surprisingly.

". . . It could've been worse," said I.

"Not much," he replied, dispiritedly. "What could be worse than this?"

"You could've got the spittle back in your mug."

"John," said he, without even a flicker of a smile, "I thought a lot o' Dunn."

"Who the Hell didn't?" said I with some vigour.

"He had his weak sides, o' course," added England predictably. "One of them was his daughter. D'ye know what became of her?"

I gave a start. Eliza, of course. I had forgotten to account for her in my story.

"Don't take it amiss," said England considerately. "Even I can under-stand that 'tis not easy."

"No," said I slowly, and probably meant it in my own way, "it ain't. I can only assume the English had most likely seized her before we turned up. But not without a struggle, you may lay to that. You know what she's like. Dunn found a torn scrap of her clothing. With blood on it."

"The swine!" he exclaimed. "If they so much as hurt one hair of her head, damn me if I won't . . ."

He broke off, and I waited expectantly for what he might propose. For what in the world would he be able to do against a whole nation?

" . . . declare war against the English wheresoever they might be on this earth," he concluded determinedly.

"Like your parents?" I asked.

"Yes, Devil take 'em! They're right. There's no other way. And you, John, what'll you do yourself?"

"About what?"

From England's countenance I could see that I would have to be more on my guard if I was to be believed.

"About Eliza, o' course," said he, as I had comprehended, though a fraction too late.

"What can I do?" said I. "It's not her they're after. The only thing I'm afraid of is what she'll do when she finds out her father is dead."

As soon as I had uttered these words, it occurred to me that I was on the right tack. If Eliza believed it to be the English who had shot Dunn, all was well and good. Not for some Englishman, of course, nor for herself. If she thought it was me . . . ? But, I tried to convince myself, why should she ever suspect me, a man of honour with soft hands who, after all, she had become rather fond of?

England took my silence as a sign of emotion.

"We won't speak of it any more now," said he, to my relief. "When things have calmed down, we'll send her a message to say we're alive, thrivin' and in good health, that we're lookin' after *Dana* like a child, an' that she can come an' collect her share of our earnings. That an' her betrothed. 'Tis only right an' proper."

Despite the fact, I thought, not to be forgotten in the midst of all this upheaval, that Dunn had actually intended to kill me and bring my existence on this earth to an irrevocable end.

"No," said I simply, "I suppose so. If we have anything to share out, that is."

"That's very true, John," said England. "How are we goin' to earn our daily bread? An' a drop o' wine an' rum to boot?" He shook his head. "As I said, John, it's a Hell of a soup you've landed us in. Don't misunderstand me, I'm not blamin' you, far from it. I just thought I'd found my rightful place, a bit o' fun an' adventure, but calm an' peaceful as well. I'd even found meself a plump little thing in Kinsale, daughter of the butcher. Can you imagine anythin' more fittin' for an easy life? An' now this!"

He threw out his hands in a gesture of despair.

"Now I'll have to start all over again," he continued. "An' all because o' you, John Silver. I likes you, you knows that, but you're a dangerous companion, it seems to me."

"We all have our weak sides," said I.

"At least you listen," said he, finally giving a faint smile. "But that's the way of it. We really do all have our weak sides."

"What are yours?" I asked.

"Well," said England, pausing to cast a glance at the sails, "I sometimes have trouble tellin' the difference betwixt right an' wrong, port an' starboard, up an' down, wise an' foolish, take whatever blessed pair you like an' I'll probably mix 'em up."

"What about life an' death?" I asked.

"I can usually tell the difference. For the most part."

"So we wouldn't prosper as pirates, then?"

England laughed out loud.

"In this? With a crew o' three? I can lower meself to many things, but makin' meself more stupid than I already am isn't one o' them. Can't you see the sailors on even the tiniest brig pointin' an' jeerin' at us when we threaten to board an' enter – three men, one o' them Deval? No, I propose we continue smugglin', but mebbe to Bristol. Or Glasgow."

"Glasgow wouldn't be my favourite choice," said I, "nor Bristol neither."

"No, o' course, I forgot that. So where the Hell shall we sail?"

I would rather not recollect the rest, but for the sake of truth it cannot be simply avoided in bashful silence. We must have been the most foolhardy smugglers ever to have plied their trade in the English Channel, making a mockery of the profession and bringing the old *Dana* into disrepute. England could navigate and became more skilful over the years, though not remarkably so, because it took an age before he could distinguish between port and starboard. It was good enough for long crossings, with the compass to steer by, but in narrow winding channels or for speedy tacking it all went to pieces. He became known, quite justifiably, as the skipper who would do whatever came into his head.

That could have its advantages sometimes, I freely admit. I don't know how many Excise cutters England managed to throw off without himself being aware of how he did it.

It goes without saying that Deval was good for nothing; he became almost permanently melancholy and tearful, especially when he had had a drop to drink. He wept profusely over Dunn's death and his daughter Eliza, who had both been so good to him. It began to irk me, and I tried to convince England that we should deliver the son of a whore back to his whore of a mother. As if I did not have enough trouble forgetting Eliza for ever without having to listen to Deval's whining and lamentation. But England refused point-blank on the matter. He insisted to the end that *Dana* had a fourth share that belonged to Eliza, and that she would never agree with our leaving Deval high and dry. I toyed with the idea of doing away with him myself, but I knew England would probably see through me, however much he believed others.

When all was said and done, *Dana* offered the best chance for some sort of life for the likes of me at that stage. But to keep Deval quiet I told him, behind England's back, more or less the truth of the situation: that he was the son of a whore who had sold him to Dunn in return for certain favours, the nature of which he could easily guess, and that Dunn was then too kind-hearted to get rid of him. Deval went as white as a sheet and would not believe me until I went into detail and embellished it with a few flourishes. From then on he kept his mouth shut about Eliza and Dunn, but as for forgiving me, that he never did.

The worst thing of all on the *Dana* was not Deval but the fact that none of us had a head for business. Either we missed a chance, right under our noses, in a manner of speaking, or we were led by the nose, time after time. Buying and selling, hawking and haggling, adding and subtracting, wheeling and dealing, no, none of that could we do. I'll take my affy-davy we were too honest for it. But did we perceive it in time?

Needless to say, I had wished to avoid sailing to England, but if we were to survive there was not much choice. We invested half of what we had in goods, a bit of everything that Edward England said smugglers usually traded: tea, sugar, tobacco and lace, not forgetting brandy of course. We set sail for Bideford in Cornwall. We anchored off Lundy and it was with some emotion that I set foot on the island, since it had been a haunt of my old father, the man who had drowned himself in the harbour. But if I had believed that he would have left any trace behind, I was disappointed. What could the likes of him have left behind in life, anyway, except for empty bottles and a reputation, good or bad, in folk's talk?

In the lee of the west wind behind Lundy Island we met other smugglers waiting for a better wind and worse weather before setting sail for France. From them we learned the names of dependable people ashore. But when we got hold of Mr Jameson, a jovial and corpulent businessman, and told him what we had on board, he could hardly contain his mirth.

"Gentlemen," he said when he had stopped slapping his thighs, "I don't want to be disobliging. I'll buy the brandy, and give you a good price so you can sail back without too great a loss."

"Loss?" I queried in amazement.

"But the tobacco, sugar an' lace, then?" asked England. "They're of the best quality."

"I know," said Jameson, "I'm very well aware of it."

"How can you be so sure?" I asked, my suspicions aroused.

"There's no mystery about that," said he, with a further display of mirth, "the tobacco is what I exported to France myself not long ago with agents like yourselves. And I'll lay I'd not be wrong if I guessed the sugar and tea to have reached France the same way."

We looked at one another in disbelief.

"Gentlemen," continued Jameson, "I can see you're new to the profession. These are goods that go from England to France, not the other way about. Sail back to St Malo quickly and sell them for the same price you paid, that's my advice."

"By the living thunder!" England cried out, banging his fist into his other palm.

When we counted up our funds on return, after the sale of our twice-smuggled wares, we had exacty the same capital at our disposal as before, no more, but also no less. That was hardly any good for us to live on. A few more trips like that and we would be done for.

Our next voyage was to Falmouth and the hold was full of brandy and wine. We slipped into the Helford River and delivered it to a merchant for a good price in gold coins. But before we had the money in our hands the merchant set the Excise on to us so that we had to beat a hasty retreat.

And so it went on. A free life it might have been, but profitable or improving it was not. After six crossings I'll be damned if we still had no more than when we started, less, that is, what we had spent to live. After the seventh we had only half of it left and it was then I called a halt. If we were going to live, I thought, we should at any rate have something for it other than ridicule and disappointment. There should be something to enjoy, that was the least we could expect.

So I called together the ship's council, which was easily done, and presented my thoughts. I said we should take for ourselves whatever was on offer instead of hawking and haggling with the results we already knew. I proposed that we should sail for prize-money, bold and resolute, and that soon none of us would have anything to lose: anything was better than this, which was getting us nowhere.

"And where would that get us?" asked Deval, and that was probably the only perceptive question he ever asked in his life.

I made no answer but turned to England.

"Then what's your view?" I asked. "That it could be worse?"

"Yes," he replied, "indeed it could."

I called them all the names under the sun, but it did no good.

"You could just go," said England.

He was right, of course. I could always go on my way.

But not for much longer, as it turned out. There were rumours of peace circulating round the coastal towns of Brittany, and precious little benefit would it bring to the likes of us. The price of smuggled wine and other goods would drop to rock bottom, sailors' wages the same, as they always did when the navy began to lay off and lay up, and

I would not be so safe from the long arm of the law.

When the peace finally came, with posters, trumpets and declarations in every little town along the coast, England began to talk of sailing *Dana* back to Ireland and Eliza. That sent shivers of the worst kind through my body. One thing I could be absolutely sure of was that meeting Eliza would be tantamount to digging my own grave, one way or another.

Cautiously, so as not to arouse England's, or even Deval's, suspicions, I tried to make them understand how ill-considered it would be, or quite simply perilous to my life and limb, for us to return. I entreated, pleaded and begged, but to no avail. My facility with words, of which I had such high hopes, was not enough to overcome a sense of honour such as England's. I got nowhere with Deval either. I had taken from him both honour and integrity, what little he had.

So I did not have much choice but to take matters into my own hands. I bore them no ill-will, for that was not the sort of man I was. I could hardly have a score to settle just because they happened to be of a different mind from me. If that were the measure of it, I would have had to hate half of humanity. My intention was just to steer the two of them on to another course for a few years, until everything was forgotten or changed.

At that time there was a vessel lying at St Malo preparing for the Colonies. Placards around the town carried tempting offers: a free voyage and help with starting up in a land with an incomparable climate and undreamed of opportunities, to earn money in exchange for three years' work on the plantations. Three years was certainly better than five, as in Britain, but I knew from my voyages on the *Lady Mary* how things were conducted. The voyage was simple, the work was slavery, and there were a thousand and one ways of prolonging contracts. A white contract worker was at least as valuable as a black slave, maybe more so because the white man had signed his slave contract himself. Because of that he was even less likely to escape or revolt.

But out in the town I discovered that the French contract workers really were set free at the end of their three years. There was in fact a need for more people to cultivate the land, marry, bear progeny, carry arms and do everything else that was necessary to keep the Colonies alive. They had even despatched whole shiploads of women to the islands to persuade the men to stay. Ogeron, the former Governor of Tortuga, had his moment of triumph when he held a lottery of his women, mostly whores and women of dubious character, but tough and quick-witted. And these marriages, it was said, embarked on with the help of Lady Luck instead of the Holy Spirit, held up for no less a time than all the others. That was a subject, it occurs to me now, that I should have spoken about with Defoe, the man who wrote a whole book of four hundred pages to prove the excellence of Christian marriage.

The fact that the French let their contract workers go free decided the matter. I sought out a crimp. I offered him fifty *livres* straight off if he could arrange for England and Deval to be on board the *Saint-Pierre* as contract workers the day she sailed.

How he went about it was no concern of mine, but sure enough the two of them were on board when the *Saint-Pierre* set sail one bright summer's day with an easterly wind. I saw them standing at the rail peering towards the *Dana* to get a glimpse of me, certainly not suspecting me of being anything other than the good shipmate I could also be when the spirit moved me. According to the crimp, when he got his fifty, England and Deval had not had the slightest inkling that I was the one behind their new and promising future in a land with an incomparable climate and undreamed of opportunities. They had innocently let themselves be tricked with not a little liqueur and brandy and a handshake from the crimp's assistant. As usual. Thus I rid myself of Deval and England, I thought, for a good long time or longer.

I sold the *Dana* a few days later and got back my hundred *livres*, my whole wealth, and then began to think seriously about my own life and adventures. I could not stay where I was with all the peacetime connections and exchanges between Ireland, England and France. I began to think, from all I heard in bars and taverns, that the West Indies would be a suitable place to make one's fortune, even for the likes of me. A few months later when a frigate flying the Danish flag appeared in port bound for the West Indies, I presented myself. The captain was English, as it happened, discharged from the navy but obviously still believing he was in the service of the fleet. The ship, which rejoiced in the name of *Carefree*, did indeed have the West Indies as its destination, but would first call at Guinea to buy slaves. Of that, though, I knew nothing when I stepped on board with my worldly chattels, good for a hundred *livres*, in the year of grace 1714, to start on a new life – my third, you could say – as a free man on the high seas.

Thirteen

THIS MORNING, WHEN the sun rose above the horizon, the sky was ruby-red, though it was scarcely anything to be pleased about. The red presages rain and the blue-black clouds lurking behind the hills in the west will soon transform the deep lustre of the sea into mountainous grey billows.

My first intention today was to resume where I left off, but then I began to reflect on whether it was not perhaps just lack of thought that had led me so far to recall my life in chronological order, indeed with the precision of a chronometer. Had I not imagined that the only true life that could be said to be my own was the one that was rolling around in my head according to the way the winds of memory blew? And had I not surmised that this life of mine would be a ferment of recollections, where one thing would lead to another, first my leg, then Deval, followed by Dunn and possibly Edward England, who in turn would recall Plantain, whose blessed memory would lead me on to Defoe, and so on *ad infinitum* until I was empty? But I happened to write that I was born, a superfluous observation, I reckon, and from then on events proceeded in quick succession. Lack of thought? Ay, maybe, but also curiosity, as if my life was a good tale to be told before the mast. How on earth had it turned out as it had, I wonder? I may be starting to understand that this other life, the uncontrollable flashes of memory swirling around as if in a storm, cannot be written down. It is no more true than the other one, the one that begins with birth or whatever, for after all, both lives exist in my own mind. And so in regard to the truth of these lives, I am in a state of total confusion.

Would Defoe have been able to help me in all this, having himself written in order to avoid living his own life? No, I am inclined to reply. He persuaded others to believe his words, but did he know himself who he was among the hundreds of assumed names he used in order to be free? It was indeed his profession to pull the wool over people's eyes! He was a secret agent and an independent journalist at one and the same time. Could anything be better? Could one wish more of life? Ah, we were an ill-matched pair, you and I, Mr Defoe, but there was, I think, nothing remarkable in our meeting one another in the Angel Tavern in London. You as an historian of piracy and I as a first-hand witness of a rare kind.

At that time I had been sailing the Caribbean and the Indian Ocean with England for a couple of years. In the *Fancy* we had taken more and richer prizes than most of our brethren, almost always without a fight, since we were usually an hundred and fifty strong, and what merchantman, with at most thirty seamen aboard, would want to fight to the last against such superior strength to defend the shipowners' profits and their own miserable wages? But there were some captains foolhardy enough to order resistance for the sake of their honour. They had to pay double, firstly with the vessel and its cargo and secondly with blood and death. To what avail? And of course there were captains who just fought for their lives, tyrants who knew they could expect no mercy when the flag was struck and accounts were settled. Edward England had his weak side, and if he had been able to rule in sole command there would have been many captains, supercargoes and clerics whose skins would have been saved, albeit in destitution, on the ships we boarded and entered so mercilessly. But England was outvoted by the fo'c's'le council – if he even spoke up at all in the end – and execution was the usual result after consultation with the crew on how they had been treated. It really was as England had expressed it himself one day, that the only difference he could distinguish was between life and death.

And so things took their course. England was deposed, but escaped to Madagascar, against all wagers, except for mine, having wagered contra-riwise and won. He found a safe haven with Plantain and managed as best he could until it was time to strike his flag.

After his removal I stayed on Taylor's ship for a while with my newly acquired parrot, but with neither pleasure nor desire. The *Cassandra's* rich booty and the vast ransom for the Viceroy of Goa were like poison for most of the men. Every one of them suddenly had the wealth they had always dreamed and raved about and had believed would be the culmination of their lives. But what happened? Most of them behaved like madmen, throwing money around as if it were burning fuses and drinking as if their last hour were at hand. Pieces of eight and jewels, prizes and booty were the only things in their heads as we sailed out, and when they finally had enough to keep them quiet, they had no idea what to do with themselves. It was pitiful and shameful to see and to suffer.

I took my share to a safe place and set off for Ranter Bay as soon as I heard that England was still alive, if only just. I was with him until he died and made sure he had a decent burial, or as decent as it could be with all the reproaches he made of himself and his conscience before he hauled down the flag for good. His remorse became irksome, I have to say, and I was not myself for some time afterwards. I began to wonder what meaningful choice we had. What was it worth to be Long John Silver this side of the grave? What did the likes of myself count for in the chaos of life? Would it make any difference at all if I lived and died the same way as everyone else? Whither ultimately would the primrose path lead that I now seemed destined to tread? Was there no longer any sanctuary at all in life for the likes of me?

Questions such as these whirled around in my head and made me dejected and out of sorts.

What put me on the right tack again was Matthews' punitive expedition, set up with special orders to take prisoner and bring back to England and the gallows one single wretched life, Plantain's, a small-scale buccaneer who had retired with an assemblage of whores of varying ranks and complexion. Why? I asked myself as I loosed off shots and wielded my cutlass as never before to defend the lives of both of us. Why should marines be sent half way round the world to risk their lives and die simply for the mob to be able to see Plantain hanged? There must have been enough riff-raff to hang closer to home.

It began to occur to me that I needed to see and understand more of the world if I were to make the most of my life before I died. I was an outlaw with a price on my head, but who and what was I fighting against and watching out for? I needed to be present at a hanging in London, hear the cries of the mob, see the face of the hangman, the eyes of the guards, actually experience the sounds and smells of an execution through my own senses, on the very skin that I was so afeared for. I had always avoided the sight of the gallows like the plague, but were they not the measure of a life like mine and Plantain's? I thought I was courageous when I was the first to board an enemy ship and swing my cutlass on its deck. But courage meant always having the gallows in view, knowing that the death sentence was the only true gauge of a life such as mine. With that judgement hanging over your head and a rope around your neck you never need have recourse to doubt or despair. You knew what you were worth. Or so I believed.

I thus decided to make my way to London at the earliest opportunity, to see and to learn. In Diego Suarez I enlisted as a novice seaman on a brig taking raw sugar to London. If I remember rightly I called myself Zeewijk and made myself out to be Flemish. I think I never suffered so much. Not a sound that resembled language could pass my lips. I groaned and grunted like an animal or laughed like a madman, and that was the whole of my stock. That taught me one thing: in Hell, if it existed, everybody would talk their own individual language. But so well did I hide my inclination and desire to open my lively mouth, that no one had the least suspicion of my predicament – that I was bursting with thousands of words inside my body aching to see the light of day. I was aware that I aroused the admiration of the officers for my seamanship, for my willingness and sobriety, while bad blood emanated a-plenty from the crew for the same reasons. It made no difference to me. And why should it have? The men did not know who I was or what I was up to.

So we made landfall and docked in London without Mr John Silver having uttered a single honest word in two whole months, the closest he ever came to madness.

I took my miserable pay, signed off and let myself be swallowed up by London's seething, stinking hotchpotch of life. We had anchored in the Pool of London, one broad-beamed brigantine among a thousand other vessels carrying riches to fill England's already bulging coffers. Was this not a sight for the gods, I thought, if they had eyes to see? Several thousand masts, like an autumn forest denuded of leaves, rose from the mass of hulls. Hoys, prams, lighters, barges and suchlike plied to and fro. Sailors, dockers and water-carriers were coming and going, loading and unloading, shouting and swearing, laughing – though not so often, because their work was not that diverting – and chattering like crows, carrying and lifting, falling down and picking themselves up again – or sometimes not – fitting out or laying up.

There were hundreds of coal-barges at anchor in Billingsgate Dock. There were also dry-docks and shipyards with timber skeletons protruding above half-finished planking, and everything resounded to the noise of hammers and saws. Vapour rose from the steam-boxes where the wood was being softened and bent. The smell of burning tar was an irritation to eyes, nose and throat. Ship chandlers, sail-makers, riggers and rope-makers lined the quay, all the businesses necessary to the building and equipping of ships.

Never had I seen such a collection of vessels. The supply of prizes to plunder seemed inexhaustible. And it was not just London. I had seen Bristol and Glasgow with my own eyes, and then there were Portsmouth, Southampton and all the other harbours in England alone. How many ships could there have been on this side of the Atlantic? Thirty thousand? And how many were gentlemen of fortune? I counted up those I had heard of during my years with England. Twenty perhaps, at any one time. Fly-shit and gnats, that's what we were.

How was it possible that we had more or less put a stop to the West Indies trade? Well, it was not because the shipowners had been ruined, I could see that now. There were always enough ships getting back with their cargoes to produce a profit. No, it must have been fear. It was our reputation, that was it. Just think, that we had once been able to bring trade to a standstill simply on the basis of what was said about us, from uncorroborated assertions and wild fantasies. What encouragement for the likes of me! All those tens of thousands of ships, and the truth, that we others were no more than a score of gnats, was at total odds with people's imagined fear and horror.

I wandered this way and that through the turmoil of London for several days taking stock of it. I saw the bloated, well-endowed institutions that supplied capital for the shipowners and their vessels. I stood in astonishment outside the companies that provided insurance – for everything except the crew, that is – Royal Exchange and London. I marvelled open-mouthed at the shipping companies, East India, South Sea and Royal African, with all their pomp and ceremony. I was on my guard outside the Excise Office with its thousands of employees who would have wished for nothing better than to lay hands on the likes of me.

Ay, if I learned anything, it was how little the likes of me knew about the ways of the world. We had had no idea of the vast sums that were invested, risked, won and lost. How could we have survived and been invincible, as some imagined – Roberts, Davis and the others who challenged the whole world with their proclamations? No, seeking happiness on your own account must be the first priority. The chance of being trampled to death was too great if you were a gnat or a shipworm.

So in the end I also went in to the Admiralty, resurrected anew as Mr Power, Customs Prosecutor, and made enquiries about that worthless pirate John Silver.

"Do we have anything on him?" I asked.

"We have his name here," said a scribe whose pasty skin was in a state of putrefaction and in urgent need of fresh air.

"Mutineer on the *Lady Mary* that went down off Old Head of Kinsale. Reported by Captain Wilkinson. That's all. No one knows for certain where he went."

"I know," said I, cunningly and authoritatively, though within myself rather reluctantly. "John Silver is dead. He lost his head, luckily and quite literally, when Matthews made his assault on the pirates' hideout on Sainte-Marie not so long ago. You can strike the man off your lists. With a clear conscience."

The pallid man did as I instructed, and with that I departed this world. It was with an easier heart that I left that house of evil. After all, it was rather like stuffing your head into a lion's den. But I, John Silver, did it anyhow, a fact which created no little respect for my person when I returned to the West Indies and soon afterwards took ship with Flint.

Truth to tell, all this acting and pretence passed off comfortably and sweetly, since it was already in my blood. But if I had not known before, then I came to understand conclusively in London that the only thing that counted this side of the grave was the belief others had in your position. With such belief you could take liberties and perform miracles. But I learned too, there in London, among so-called respectable folk, that you had to look over your shoulder constantly to avoid being led by the nose. It was not enough to have the gift of the gab. You also had to have eyes in the back of your head.

Fourteen

T HE ANGEL TAVERN – that was the best place of all, so I had heard, to witness hangings. It was well known that Judge Jeffreys used to sit there to wash down the results of his death sentences with a tankard or two of ale. Without having to mingle with the common herd on Execution Dock itself, where the gallows stood lined up like scarecrows to instil fear into the likes of me.

When I arrived there, three condemned men were swinging from their ropes on three gallows. They were sticking out their purple tongues at me – or rather what was left of their tongues after the crows, jackdaws and gulls had helped themselves – and staring at me from their empty eye-sockets. Swarms of bluebottles buzzed around them eagerly, and there were even ants crawling over them. Their flesh was swollen and pecked to shreds by sharp, greedy beaks.

This was death, and no mistake, thought I. The men – our own and the others – who lost their lives in the raids and skirmishes on the *Walrus* were still warm and human when we threw them overboard or buried them in the sand. Some of the bodies, the ones who had been knifed in the back, could equally well have been alive as dead. But here, by God, so to speak, there was no question of whether there was time for extreme unction, even if it were wanted. Here it was far too late.

I tugged at the leg of one of the corpses as I walked past. The air was filled with insects and maggots, and the body swung to and fro like a pendulum in a *perpetuum mobile*. A yellowish, stinking sludge began to drip to the ground and was obviously a particular delicacy for the flies clustering round the droplets where they fell. I trampled a few hundred to death for amusement and drove away the birds. Even I was no more than human, though many would maintain otherwise.

"God bless you!" said a hoarse voice from behind me.

I turned round and saw a shrivelled old hag, hardly even still alive if you ask me.

"Why on earth should God do that?" said I.

"For chasin' off the birds an' the flies," answered she.

"That ain't enough to bring me a blessing," said I, making an effort to sound friendly, which was no small accomplishment. "If you'd had my luck in life you'd know that 'tis God's unfathomable will to feed birds and insects on sinful hanging corpses. So I'm afeared I've violated God's will."

"My son didn't sin nohow!" said the old woman.

I followed her gaze and looked more closely at one of the corpses, but could not distinguish any obvious likeness.

"What did he do wrong, then, to end up here?" I asked.

"He shot rabbits on the Duke's land. We 'ad naught to eat, I swear to you, sir."

"By the powers!" I exclaimed. "Can you be hanged for the slightest thing in this country?"

You certainly could; I had heard that before. How many men had become gentlemen of fortune because they would have been hanged in any case for this or that, mostly trivial things? Had I not seen, on my wanderings through London, proclamations about the new Shoplifters' Act nailed up all over the place? From now on, it said in black and white, thefts of a value greater than five shillings would be punishable by death. At least you knew what a human life was worth. Five shillings! But for shooting rabbits, that were breeding faster than you could kill them anyhow!

I stood for a while in front of the three bodies to imprint the sight on my memory for ever. After all, that was what I had wanted to see, with no frills or fancy descriptions. What still remained was to see an actual hanging in real life, to observe and learn from the very moment of death, the part I feared most of all. Not death itself, for that was nothingness, but the certain knowledge that the likes of me, who wanted to live at any price, would soon be no more than a rotting corpse sticking out its purple tongue at the whole world, of no benefit whatsoever to either side.

I nodded to the old woman, who was sitting praying with clasped hands, rather too late, I would have thought, and wended my way to the Angel. Someone had painted an angel on the door that received a punch on the nose every time a thirsty devil like myself opened it and entered. Otherwise the premises themselves were not very memorable, with the possible exception of the man behind the bar, who somewhat resembled the archangel in his own high or low person. I ordered a tankard of ale from this creature before taking a look round. It was the usual motley assortment of wizened drinkers of every shade and hue. Just one distinguished himself from the many: a man in a wig, though rather tufty and frayed, powdered, unevenly applied, with sheaves of paper in front of him and quick, lively, inquisitive eyes peering at me attentively from his window table with its unequalled view of the gallows on Execution Dock. The table was a large one, so I went over and enquired, courteously I think, whether he would have any objection to my sitting there, for the sake of the view, as I explained. With an affirmative gesture he continued to observe me openly as I drank and accustomed myself to the sight of corpses at a distance.

"I see that you are interested in hangings," said he, following my gaze. I nodded guardedly.

"You're not alone in that," he went on. "You should observe the scene here on the day of execution itself. There are as many people then as there are flies round the corpses after a few days. But why? Have you given that any consideration? What is it that entices so much that everyone sallies forth to witness the misfortunes of others? Is it to catch a glimpse of their souls on the way to Heaven or Hell? – one hopes the latter, for how would it look if those we punished here on earth ended their days in Paradise? It is none of this, I would say. It is a great deal simpler. People want to see how the living react to their own deaths, to be able to despise the weak who beg for mercy and to admire the strong who go to meet it uncowed, with head held high. Or, which is even more laudable, who go to meet it with laughter. That, sir, laughing death in the face, is the most coveted attraction of all. 'Tis always the ones who laugh and smile who provoke cries of encourage-ment, even applause. People wish so much to believe that death is not something to be taken seriously, that it is not something that needs to be taken into account. It is unbearable to live otherwise. The promises of Paradise and the Kingdom of Heaven that are handed out so liberally by the priests make little impression in this world, believe me. The authorities imagine that people throng round the gallows to mock and jeer at criminals, out of respect for the law. Or even that criminals come here to affright themselves away from committing crimes. If anything, the reverse is true. It is widely known, indeed, that the place is infested with pickpockets when the people foregather at the gallows. But of course that is no more than could be expected. An understanding of the common man, I venture to suggest, as one who possesses no slight familiarity with such matters, has never been one of the strong points of our judicature. Would criminals willingly lay themselves open to such an uncomfortable experience as witnessing their own possible end? What do you yourself think, for instance? What could be the rational purpose of such a venture?"

"Witnessing a few hangings can certainly make you think," said I. "'Tis by no means easy to live in the shadow of the gallows, if you want to go on living at all."

"Do you think so?" said he, with a smile, by no means unfriendly, and giving me a pleased and perhaps knowing look. "A very interesting thought. I'll commit it to memory, if you do not object."

"Why should I object?"

"Well, it was your thought, after all. And I have the unfortunate habit of turning the ideas of others into my own. I have observed that some people find that vexing. But if you will permit . . ."

"By all means. Take what you want!"

Nevertheless I was rather surprised when he picked up his pen and actually wrote my opinion down, in black and white.

"I am just making a note," said he when he had finished. "I am no longer so young, as you can see for yourself. I dare not depend on my memory any more. There is such an endless number of things that have to be remembered."

He seemed to ponder that for a moment, before turning his attention back to me.

"And what about you?" he asked. "What is it that you find so fascinating about a hanging?"

He put the question with the most innocent countenance, yet I was immediately convinced he was leading me by the nose, albeit in an amicable manner. For now I could not express my true opinion without myself becoming one of those living in the shadow of the gallows and treading the primrose path, for whom I had just made myself spokesman. Or perhaps he had seen through me from the beginning, something in my bearing or mode of dress, and tricked me into giving myself away. Who could he actually be and what was he after? He had rendered me speechless anyway, if only briefly, a feat achieved by few.

"I hope I have not offended you," said he, as if he had read my thoughts. "I did not mean to be intrusive. I just happened to perceive that you were showing an unusual amount of interest in the three poor devils out there, and was curious. That's another of my bad habits."

"Then we have something in common," said I, relieved at being able to turn the conversation to my own advantage, as I supposed. "I would quite like to know how you come to be sitting here, a gentleman as far as I can judge, with such piles of paper in front of you, in the Angel in Wapping, a seamen's district, spying on ordinary folk like me."

"Spying!" said he with a chuckle. "You've spoken a truer word than you might have guessed. Spying, yes, that's what I do and have been doing for as long as I can remember. But not only on ordinary people – which, by the way, I am rather sure you are not – no, I spy, indeed, but on all and sundry, without distinction, high and low, law-abiding and lawless, good and evil. I have become the archivist of our times."

I motioned to show that I wished to speak, but he misunderstood me.

"You don't believe me? Look at this!"

He put a paper under my nose.

"This has taken months to do. Can you conceive of it? Months of my life have been spent in simply counting what there is."

He said it as if it were a complaint, but in fact he was brimming over with what could only be described as self-satisfaction.

"Is it not strange to think that no one but I actually knows what there is in this ant-heap called London? I have enquired of King and

Parliament, of mayors and magistrates, but nobody, can you believe it, nobody has a sight of the whole. So I had to count up, from meat markets, of which there are fourteen, as you can see here, to prisons, all twenty-seven of them, as many, I should think, as there are in all the principal cities on the Continent of Europe together. That is the price, I'm sure you'll understand, that we have to pay for living in the country that prides itself on having the most freedom of all. I have reckoned up the dead and buried as well as the living and baptised, the sick and the cured in the hospitals, vagrants and beggars taken into custody, the condemned and the freed, I have counted them all. Churches too. Look at this! There are three hundred and seven churches in London, including fifty newly projected, and that is without taking the meeting houses of the dissenters into consideration, since according to the letter of the law they do not exist. You may wonder whether God really needs so many churches, three times as many as there are schools, and fifteen times as many as there are hospitals. To that, sir, there is no answer, as far as I can see. Yet you might also think the number of churches is far from adequate when you regard the prodigious number of gaols, primarily the general ones but also the debtors' prisons, where people with money allow themselves to be confined voluntarily until their debts are paid or the case expires, so that they avoid the shame of the ordinary gaol. Yes, that's how it is, and it is easy to discover by just taking the trouble to look round, like a spy if you will, and counting – being life's book-keeper, in a word. Does that not surprise you? Can you imagine, and you certainly cannot have known, that there are ten such private institutions – for whose services, by the way, payment is required – where people voluntarily allow themselves to be incarcerated? Just to avoid the shame."

"No," I exclaimed hastily, without thinking, "I'm damned if I can."

But as soon as I had said it I could see that I had laid myself open again. The old man had not answered my question about who he was and what he did, but instead had prattled on, eagerly and with evident relish, about his computations, only then without warning to ask a question that applied just to me. All I could do was bow and scrape and yield. It was naught but a game, that was what it was, as far as I could see.

"I suspected as much," said he with a smile.

"Suspected what?" I asked cautiously.

"That you were not the sort of man who would pay to be put behind lock and key to avoid shame."

I was about to object, but the old man forestalled me.

"Please don't be offended – I do apologise, that must be the second time I've said that to you, but I have my bad habits, as you will have perceived. I have made a study of human beings all my life, and cannot prevent myself putting my knowledge and experience to the test to check their validity. I have discovered that there are people, indeed such as yourself, sir, who seem to create a space around themselves. There is something, if you will permit me to say, as I am certain you will, in their posture and mien that recalls a pirate or freebooter, by which of course I do not mean the common sailor, a man who became a gentleman of fortune to escape from whips and blows, or because he was forced to make the choice between that and death when a ship was seized. No, I'm thinking of the names of renown: Davis, Roberts and Morgan, men who knew what they wanted, who had drunk deep of the chalice of liberty and then could not give it up. Am I right?"

The old man looked at me expectantly, and I must have squirmed under his gaze. I was careful not to answer too readily – I was not that foolish – but laughed instead, though it did not sound genuine.

"You presumably do not imagine," said I, "that I would tell you, who could just as easily be a magistrate or Excise officer as anything else, that I was a pirate, even in the unlikely event of that being the case."

"You misunderstand me, I think," he replied, with the same good-natured but sly smile as before, "quite apart from the fact that I am indeed not the extended arm of the law. I did not intend to accuse you of piracy in any way, and certainly not in front of the terrible view we have here. I simply wondered, out of sheer curiosity, whether you were not in some respect rather like them."

"How would I know?"

"You would perhaps prefer," went on the old man indefatigably, "to think yourself not like any other person at all, but unique. There are unfortunately also, I have discovered, many people like that, among the nobility in particular, but it is my honest opinion and experience that it is fundamentally pride and vanity. For the aristocracy, to be like others is a worse sin than all the rest put together, I can tell you. The First Commandment has been completely misunderstood. God, as you know, has no equal and will admit no equal. But is the First Commandment not one of vanity and pride? God Himself did not provide a good example. Humility is not, jesting aside, God's earmark, and that is why, sir, we all endeavour to elevate ourselves, above our ability, above our station, above everyone else. We are like rebellious children. We always want to show ourselves in an advantageous light and never be like others, for then we are nothing."

"God has never been my favourite dish," said I sharply.

The old man smiled.

"That I can well imagine, with no difficulty. And I willingly admit that you are not like others, not even pirates."

"Now I believe it is you who misunderstand me. I have not said that my like cannot be found."

"No, perhaps not. But the fact is that your words surprise me, and I have heard much in my time, I assure you. Nothing gives me greater pleasure nowadays than being surprised. May I therefore, with every good intention and without obligation of any kind, other than continuing this for me so agreeable conversation, offer you a tankard of ale?"

I was not a little surprised myself. I could not make out this courteous and sharp-witted man, whose like I for my part had never met and who so plainly manifested his interest in me, but about whom I knew nothing, while he with all his questions seemed already to have found out various things concerning me. I was afeared he would inveigle me into saying more than I meant to if things continued as they had begun. But I had no cause for quarrel with the old man yet, nor did I wish to have; if only I knew who it was I was talking to.

"It seems to me," I thus said in a more serious tone, "as if you, sir, have questioned me on various matters, with no ulterior motive, I'm sure, but as if my humble person had some special interest for you or somebody else. So if we are to continue this conversation, it would make sense for us to introduce ourselves."

"By all means," he replied. "Johnson is my name. And yours?"

"Long," I answered. "And perhaps we should give our profession too, in this spirit of openness."

"Book-keeper," said he.

"Trader," said I.

But in the same second our innocent and honest eyes met and we burst into resounding laughter, and the old man's wig fell askew.

"I think it would be just as well if we began again at the beginning," said he. "With all possible discretion, of course. On both sides."

He proffered his hand.

"My name is Defoe," said he, "perchance not entirely unknown, not even to you, but incommodious to bear at times, particularly now, nigh buried in debt as I am. Profession: writer. And you?"

"John Silver, not so renowned a name as yours, but perhaps more comfortable to bear, at least in certain circles. Profession . . ."

"Quartermaster with Edward England," interjected Defoe, but in a low voice so that it would not be heard out in the room. "Probably at the present time out of employment, since England was deposed off Madagascar. I am pleased to have met you, more than you could ever imagine."

He made a dismissive gesture with his hand.

"Do not look so surprised. The fact is that I am writing a book on pirates, the first complete description of their crimes and malefactions. Well, I've dabbled a little in something of that nature already. I wrote a play for the theatre about Captain Avery, without great success, I regret to say. Then I published the story of the life of Captain Singleton. That fared better, and several editions have been printed. You may perhaps have read it?"

"No," said I, "I've not had that good fortune. But *Crusoe*, naturally. Who hasn't read *Crusoe*?"

"Well, I have to say, a well-read gentleman of fortune, at that. Yes, I know they exist. Roberts was one. A wonderfully skilful writer in his proclamations. Irony was second nature to him, I opine."

Defoe pulled a book out of the bag standing next to him.

"Here's *Captain Singleton*," said he. "May I venture to commend it to you? I would much value your opinion on its credibility and veracity. People here in England are so credulous and easily deceived, indeed they seem to suffer from a feverish need to believe. They are firmly convinced that Captain Singleton existed; it has even been said in the newspapers that it was he who discovered the sources of the Nile. As you might suppose, I have been laughing up my sleeve. It was all invention from beginning to end. No, ordinary people and even the educated have such a desire to believe that everything that is written is true. They are no help to me as a gauge. But a man like you, you would be able to judge whether I have conjectured right about the essence and nature of pirates. Would you undertake to perform this task for me?"

"Certainly," was my ready rejoinder.

"And dare I also ask whether you would perhaps assist me with my book on pirates? My appetite was whetted, so to speak, with Avery. You must have been sent by God to have turned up so opportunely."

"By the Devil himself, more like," said I. "According to all the edicts of the Church that rule our world."

"Whichever, my good man, whichever. We have a lot to talk about, and it concerns me little who sent you. So if you will do me the honour. But first of all something to quench our thirst. If you would be kind enough to call for some ale or rum for us both, to go on my account, whatever you want, nothing would please me more than to treat such a widely travelled person as yourself."

I rose, crossed to the bar and bade the monstrous being behind it bring two tankards of ale and two glasses of rum, of the best sort, to be put on Mr Johnson's account.

"You can pay up for it yourself, then," grunted the man. "There ain't no drinking here on credit. People drink theirselves to death afore they manages to settle their dooes."

I turned round, and shiver my timbers if that same Defoe was not giving me his best smile. He had led me by the nose again. A game or no, I could not allow him to remain entirely uncompensated, and so changed my order.

"Two tankards of ale and two rumfustians, then," said I, and the creature from the depths brightened up with a smile of recognition as he mixed the beer, gin and sherry.

"Put a pinch of this in as well!" I told him, placing a little bag of gunpowder on the bar.

He nodded enthusiastically and his smile grew broader. His response was irrefutable proof that he had had experience of classic pirate drinks.

"So," said I when he had finished dropping a pinch of powder into each of the tankards and stirring it well, "what ship an' what cap'n?"

"*Queen Anne's Revenge*," he replied, "an' Teach was cap'n."

"I might have known," said I, taking out a gold coin. "Blackbeard was an ugly devil too."

The man took it as a compliment. I pointed at the coin.

"This is my and my friend Johnson's credit," said I. "An' what's your name?"

"Hands, sir. Israel Hands."

"Good, Hands. I can see you're a man as can be depended upon. Mr Johnson and I wants to be left in peace an' not disturbed by the curious and inquis'tive."

He gave me what he thought to be a cunning look and opened his mouth.

"Ay, I knows what you're a-thinking of," I forestalled him. "I weren't born yest'day. You'll be paid for services rendered. But remember, my friend, what it costs if you ain't reli'ble."

Hands nodded and I took the drinks over to Defoe.

"The gentleman, if I can call him that, behind the bar has given us credit, and at my request will see to it that we're left in peace."

Defoe's eyes lit up.

"Is he also . . . ?"

" . . . a first-class eyewitness," I interposed. "Ay, he is that, but you would have to pay for every single word of his that you made your own, and on top of that I doubt whether you would get anything but grunts as an answer, however much you paid."

"And you yourself, sir?" said Defoe in a troubled voice, as if he were a child who thought he saw a bag of sweetmeats within reach but was not sure whether they would end up in his mouth. "Are you expensive too?"

"Me," said I, laughing at his countenance, "I cannot be bought for all the gold in the world."

"There's a great deal that I would wish to know," said Defoe.

"Let's drink to that!" I exclaimed heartily, and Defoe in his elation took a great gulp of rumfustian, spiced with gunpowder, usually only done with pure rum.

I have seldom seen a face go through such a transformation, in colour or in shape. Tears streamed from his eyes and carved channels through his powder, leaving him streaked red and white where his burning cheeks showed through. It was my revenge for having so nearly had the wool pulled over my eyes. When he had finished coughing and had regained his usual colour, I explained in my most amiable fashion that I had simply taken it upon myself to share my knowledge with him, and that what was called rumfustian was what pirates drank to show they were worse than everybody else.

"Wash it down with ale," I added. "That's what I usually do. Rumbo tastes like the very Devil, you may lay to that."

"Never a truer word!" Defoe managed to exclaim, and started making notes as soon as he could hold the pen without trembling so much that he risked splashing ink on his cuffs, which were frayed, as was his wig.

"So you will permit me to ask you questions about various things?" he asked, as if he still did not dare believe that I was his lucky angel – understandably enough, when all's said and done.

"I have to say," he continued, "that it is not easy for the likes of me to talk with the likes of you. Before we know where we are, you may be swinging from the gallows over there, silenced both for me and posterity, or disguising yourselves behind assumed names and borrowed clothes. And no one can maintain that gentlemen of fortune are particularly concerned about their posthumous reputations. After us the flood, that seems to be their motto. Besides – but you can hardly be expected to be aware of this – I have my reputation to think of . . . No, don't misunderstand me again. It is not a matter of defending my good name, since I no longer have one. Sometimes I call myself Johnson or Drury, sometimes Captain Singleton or Colonel Jack. Believe it or not, I recently wrote the memoirs of Mesnager, the French Quaker – and the man exists and is living in the best of health in France! I would like to see his countenance if he ever got hold of the book. Wouldn't you? No, sir, my own name has been put in pawn, not simply because of my debts, but rather because of views and opinions that I thought I was investing for the benefit of mankind, without getting a shilling in return. On the contrary, as you may know, I have been sent to gaol and to the stocks for as much. I slink around like a criminal, condemned for my opinions. Defoe is no more than a shadow, a word on everybody's lips except my own, a supposition, a murmur in society, nothing but a memory in the bosom of my own family where I dare not show myself for fear of creditors. Yes, that is the way of it; but why should I sit here complaining to you? That was not my purpose. Yet I want you to understand that even the likes of myself can feel the noose around my neck, not to hang me, but just so that the rope can be tightened enough to prevent the air getting to my brain. Please do not think that I want to ensnare you with evil intent. But I beg you, not on bended knees, because I have hardly any left, having worn them out raking together sufficient means to buy my bread and butter, I beg you to remember that far too many people would like nothing better than to be able to declare me a friend to pirates and fellow-criminals, so that I could be cast into prison and silenced for good. Imagine the cries of malicious pleasure were I to place a small advertisement in one of our newspapers: Daniel Defoe wishes to meet pirate for exchange of information and opinions, to mutual benefit."

Defoe gave a cynical smile and drew his finger across his throat to indicate how it would end.

"So I am bound hand and foot, and too old to go on board ship and seek out pirates in their everyday lives. Yet I am not entirely without resources. I sit here in the Angel not only because none of my creditors would dare venture hither, but also to attend hangings and to listen to the language of sailors. That is part of it. And I have attended all the trials of pirates that have taken place in London; I have perused the proceedings of those that have been held in outposts of the Colonies; I have read log-books and journals. That is not discreditable, but is it adequate? No, far from it. Pirates are not concerned about writing and recounting their affairs, with few exceptions – Dampier, Exquemelin and Wafer, for instance. But can they be depended upon? John Locke and the others in the Investigating Commission of the South Sea Company thought so, and what did they achieve? Failed expeditions and unsound trade. No, Silver . . . Long, I mean – I won't repeat that error – quite different sources are needed to come at the truth. You can never depend upon what is said to be true in order to turn the course of the world in one direction or another, and I, of all people, should be aware of that. But to return to our own business, it would please me to offer you a princely recompense if you really are prepared to put yourself at my disposal, but I . . ."

He cast a meaningful glance at the bar.

". . . you must have already comprehended, but been too delicate to mention, that my funds are extremely limited . . ."

He threw up his hands and took a sup of his rumbo, this time without a grimace.

". . . not to say non-existent."

I put twenty sovereigns in gold on the table and pushed them over to Defoe.

"Take this!" said I. "You needn't concern yourself about repaying it in any way. On the contrary, I'll gladly pay to hear your accounts of this and that. I'm here in the city of London to look and learn. They say I'm an educated sort, because I'm one of the ones on board who's read something other than the contract of hire and the ship's articles. But that, I've come to understand, means little. Gentlemen of fortune such as I know very little of the workings of the world. We live on rumours, we're like headless chickens, and not much smarter neither, you may lay to that. Yet we think we'll stay alive all the same! No, I for my part believe I've learned enough to know that you can't watch your back unless you have an idea of how the world is ordered and how it functions. So I can talk about the tribulations of the piratical life if you in return can tell me how things stand in England. You have spied and computed, and can doubtless provide me with what I need. That will be adequate payment. There's only one other thing I would ask."

"And what might that be?" enquired Defoe as my twenty sovereigns disappeared into his inner pocket as naturally as could be. "Consider it already granted."

"You're writing a book about the misdeeds of pirates, and perhaps – why not? – the good deeds they've been guilty of, inadvertently one may well suppose. You're reckoning on this book being published and read?"

"Indeed. Otherwise it would be totally without point."

"My wish then is that I myself, John Silver, shall not be named in this book."

"Mr Long," said Defoe, "you never cease to amaze me."

I picked up my leather gloves.

"I've had leather gloves like these on my hands at sea," I explained, "ever since I was fifteen or thereabouts. They've protected my hands from wounds and scars: in other words, from the brands of the sailor. Surely you would not wish that to have been in vain, to furnish me with another stamp that will lead me straight to the gallows?"

"Your request is of no small moment. To ask that I should change facts, deviate from history itself."

"There's no need for big words. All you have to do is pretend that I didn't exist, exactly as you've pretended that others existed who didn't – Singleton and Crusoe, for instance. Am I not right? Is the one any better than the other?"

"I do not know," replied Defoe in a dispirited voice, as if I had trodden on a corn. "You may be right, that the death of one can be life for another in the world of words. It is possible. Stealing the life of somebody, like poor old Selkirk, who is forgotten for ever, and giving it to another man, Crusoe, who will live for ever if all goes well, at the cost of the first. Is that right? Did you know that some while ago a woman came to tell me that she had been shipwrecked on Crusoe's island, that she had gone with Crusoe when they had been rescued by a Dutch ship, and even that she had lived with Friday in London, and that I had stolen her story to write my own? And that I had also killed her off, silenced her for good, by not naming her in my story. What is right and what is wrong? Can you answer me that?"

"No," said I. "'Tis a puzzle. But just don't involve me in your book on pirates, that's all I ask."

"You have my word," said he, but regretfully, if I interpreted his tone aright.

So that was how easy it was to remove Long John Silver from the story, I thought. He had been struck out of the Admiralty archives and rolls and written out of the history books, as if he had never existed.

I leaned back and put my hand on the old man's shoulder.

"Don't take it so hard!" said I. "If that's the only thing you have on your conscience, you should see mine."

Whether those words helped, I don't know, but he became more cheerful, and when we left one another on that first day he seemed to be in the best of good humours. I for my part felt exhilarated and gave a sovereign to the wretched woman who was keeping a vigil and praying for her corpse of a son.

"God bless you!" said she, like a parrot who only knew a single verse.

"Devil take Him!" I replied, as a little variation.

Fifteen

I T GOES WITHOUT saying that I regaled Mr Defoe with the story of Edward England. Whether it was true is not so easy to know. At that time I was not so inclined to such a notion as truth. But it is as certain as an amen in church that I did not tell him everything of how and why England, through my good offices, became a gentleman of fortune, because I did not entirely trust Defoe's probity. All he had actually promised was that I would not appear in his history. If there was one thing I did not want, it was to end my own days as a Selkirk, or even worse, as a Crusoe.

But if there were a Heaven, if you, Mr Defoe, after all your lies and deceits, were to have gained entrance to it, and if up there you could hear what we other poor sinners are thinking down below on earth, I would like to tell you what truly happened to England and me. Then, when you and I were sitting in the Angel, it would have taken a day or two of your valuable time. But I presume, and hope for your own sake, that you are not in such a hurry where you are now, that you are not writing so frantically as before and in such a frenzy as to dig your own grave. And how would it look, anyhow, in Heaven? And why should you write books for the improvement of folk in Paradise?

So you ought to have the time and patience to listen to me now. I regret to admit that I have started to feel a sense of emptiness some-times, or even meaninglessness, in telling stories, including my own, into a void. I will confess to you that from time to time I wish there were someone listening to what I have to say, that this writing were not so damned lonely. But how could I have had any idea that that was how it would be when I started? You certainly did not inform me of the fact.

So in St Malo I went on board the good ship *Carefree*, as you will have heard if everything is going as it should up there, under its English captain, Butterworth, who was one of the naval captains who had to seek a new command when the war came to an end. Not that you could have told as far as he was concerned. He did all he could to make the *Carefree* resemble a naval ship. It was no wonder that the greater part of the Danish crew had signed on elsewhere when they got to London and had been replaced by a British crew. As soon as we had left Ouessant behind us, Butterworth began to drill us for battle.

"Men," he declared, "the war is over, the Lord be praised. There is peace in the world among nations. But you know as well as I that pirates and other marauders do not refrain from attacking and plundering just because there is peace. They obey no laws and continue to slay and pillage. So we have to be able to defend ourselves and be prepared to sacrifice lives for our freedom. We have twenty-four cannon on board. When I've finished with you we'll be able to engage in battle with anyone."

There was a muttering and groaning at Butterworth's speech and no mistaking the discontent. Butterworth should have remembered that he did not have marines at his disposal on the *Carefree* to force obedience on the crew; half of them probably wished for nothing better than to be captured in order to become pirates and as free as they were ever likely to be, for as long as it lasted.

I listened to Butterworth with half an ear. I would not let him anger me. I had signed on for a one-way voyage to the West Indies and I had no intention of jeopardising my assured passage by setting myself up against him. I had tried too many things lately, it seemed to me, all fresh in my memory. No, the likes of Butterworth were not going to provoke me to acts of folly.

But I had closed the account on Butterworth and myself too soon.

One morning when I came up on deck, a beautiful clear morning, since we had just caught the Portuguese northerlies, Butterworth had had a white line painted right across the deck by the mast. I was about to step over it when I was stopped by the first mate, who explained that the line was not to be crossed by us sailors except with special permission from the captain or himself. I turned on my heel with a ringing in my ears as if someone had hit me with a marlin-spike. I found out from a master mariner by the name of Murrin, who had served in the navy, that lines like this were common practice on naval vessels and that traversing the line without express orders cost fifty strokes of the cat.

This line on the *Carefree* made me forget all my good intentions. Showing me a white line that separated me from them was the same as laying a juicy bone in front of the nose of a starving mongrel and flogging it nigh to death if it so much as moved a muscle.

It will come as no surprise that in the end I stepped over the line. Foolish and ill-considered though it was, I was compelled to gnaw the bone. Almost as if I would otherwise have starved to death. Can you understand that, Mr Defoe? You who made a constant study of mankind, with your spying and your counting. I was the first one ever known to have crossed the line without a thought of mutiny, just head-long and headstrong as was my nature in such matters.

Not that it helped, of course.

"What have you to say in your defence?" screamed Butterworth, his face as crimson as a distress flare, when the first mate pushed me into his cabin.

"Defence?" I asked in genuine amazement. "For what, sir?"

"You know very well."

"No, sir. Beggin' your pardon, sir."

"Are you trying to make sport of me as well? You've refused to obey my standing orders, that's what you've done. That's mutiny, I'll have you know!"

"Mut'ny, sir? Never in my life! I signed on to get meself to the West Indies. That were all."

Butterworth's face twisted into a mocking sneer.

"That was all! You expect me to believe that? I've met your sort before. It's the likes of you that become highwaymen ashore and pirates at sea. You can't make a dupe of me."

"Sir, I wouldn't even try."

Butterworth turned to the first mate.

"You can see for yourself the kind of man we're dealing with. An impertinent devil who needs to be taught a lesson. Make ready for keelhauling!"

"But, sir . . . " the first mate began.

"No buts. I could have the swab shot. But he shall have a chance to improve himself."

Keelhauling! It was only when I came out into the bright light of the sun that it fully sank in how thunderously stupid I had been.

"I didn't think about the line," I entreated the first mate. "I didn't see it."

"That won't do, Silver, and you know it as well as I do. You've had your eyes on naught else but that line. Everyone knows it."

"I couldn't help it, sir. It were a mistake."

"You should've thought o' that a bit earlier."

"But I don't want to die, sir. Can't you talk to the cap'n? It won't happen again, sir. You has my word."

I begged and pleaded and demeaned myself to the utmost. I had no pride where my skin was at stake. There was little use for that when you were dead.

"All right, Silver, you've done good service up to now," said he. "I'll tell the men not to haul on the ropes too tight. I can't do more'n that."

That was something, at least, and enabled me to calm down so that I could think. Everything depended now on how the *Carefree* looked on her bottom. In my mind's eye I saw it covered in razor-sharp barnacles that would slice my back to ribbons as easily as a knife through butter.

It did not take long for the men to get the ropes ready, four of them, two on each side of the ship. I was stood at the bow, and tied at the wrists and ankles. I looked around me. In some faces I could see concern and anger – those, I assume, who had the brains to imagine themselves in my place. In others I could see for the most part happy expectation, and they were no doubt making bets on whether or not I would survive. For them a keelhauling was a spectacle, a welcome interlude in the voyage, as amusing as a hanging on land. I observed that the two who were to pull on the ropes on the starboard side were grinning and nudging one another. Anyone could see they would not concern themselves overmuch with the first mate's instruction to slack off the ropes.

At that moment Butterworth came out on to the poop deck. I could not see him, because I was standing with my back to the stern, ready to be dropped overboard and dragged feet first along the keel from bow to stern, the whole length of the *Carefree*, ninety-six feet, no more and no less. Because I was to be keelhauled the length of the ship, not athwartships, which was the milder punishment.

"Here is a man," Butterworth roared out, "who refused to obey my orders. You know as well as I do that it would have been my right, perhaps even my duty, to have him shot as a mutineer. Yet I'm not without mercy. The man shall have a chance to repent and improve himself. But let it be a reminder to you all. Next time I shall show no clemency."

Disgruntled murmurings could be heard from several quarters. Mutiny material, I just had time to think, before Butterworth shouted out an order and I was lowered down the prow towards the surging waves.

I fought against the terror that was rushing in and trying to seize me by the throat. I had survived death once, I reassured myself, at Old Head of Kinsale. It must not have been in vain. Live! Like a silent roar inside me. By all the powers I was going to live!

I did what the old Indian in Chesapeake had taught me about diving under water for lengthy periods: I took several deep breaths to cleanse my lungs before closing my mouth. My last thought was that I must not cry out. A single scream of pain and I would have spoken my final word this side of the grave.

The green waters enveloped me, the ropes stretched upwards and my back scraped against the keel. I had not gone many feet before I felt my skin being torn open and the pain rending deep gashes in my will to live. One thing I knew already: ninety feet of that would turn my precious body into a lump of meat and put an end to the story of Long John Silver. I was kicking on the ends of the rope like a fly in a cobweb. To what effect? I was bound hand and foot.

Hand! The sudden thought was spurred by a splinter of wood that stabbed my buttock and made me draw in my arms to my sides. I immediately felt the slack in the port-side ropes, one fathom, two fathoms, right, steady at that! The men on that side had heeded the first mate's instruction not to tighten the rope. Like that! More slack!

Now the two grinning rope-holders on the starboard side who gave not a damn for John Silver would find out what was what. I took their hawsers in both hands, braced myself against the keel and heaved on the ropes for king and country with a rush of strength I have never been capable of before nor since. My chest was pounding fit to burst and I thought I would split asunder, there was a shrieking in my ears like a hurricane, but before I blacked out I felt the starboard ropes slack off completely. I was free.

When I opened my eyes again gasping for breath I was already being hoisted up on to the deck by the port-side ropes. So I was alive, and as willing hands pulled me in over the rail, I bellowed out my joy so that no one could doubt that it was life coming aboard, even if almost out of its senses. I beat off helpful hands that were trying to hold me up, and slumped to the deck in a formless heap. I was cursing and swearing, spitting and sputtering, but managed to get myself upright by clinging on to the mainmast. The mainmast! I looked down at my feet. There it was, that damned white line, and upon my soul I was on the wrong side of it again, without express order. What incentive to live for the likes of me! A bright red stream of blood was pouring down my back, down my legs, out on to the deck and right over the white line, which it cut in two. I stared up and tried to catch Butterworth's eye. Before I collapsed again I wanted him at least to look me in the eye, if he durst.

He was standing as stiff as a handspike on the poop deck and could not take his gaze off me. I raised one hand and gave a trembling salute.

"John Silver, sir, reportin' for dooty," I gasped out, exposing my teeth in something meant to resemble a grin.

Only then did I become aware of the silence that reigned on deck. The men were gawping as never before, with admiration, fear and respect all mixed together. I looked again at Butterworth, who finally averted his gaze.

"That's enough!" said he in a strained voice, turned on his heel and disappeared down to his cabin.

That, without a shadow of a doubt, is what's called bliss! That was my final thought before my strength ebbed away and all went dark.

Sixteen

I T WAS TWO weeks before I was in good fettle again and could
make myself useful on board – in my own way, that is. Everyone will readily comprehend – will they not, Mr Defoe? – that
after such a resurrection John Silver could not simply carry on as if
nothing had happened. And in addition, I had heard a number of
things while I was lying on my stomach with my back covered in
scabs. Butterworth had forbidden the men to talk to me, as if I was
contagious, but one after another they sneaked down to the sick bay to
testify to their respect for me. And again and again I had to listen to the
wondrous tale of my rescue, because what I had not known was that
with my Herculean tug I had dragged down one of the starboard men
into the sea and that he had been instantaneously ripped to pieces by
sharks attracted by my blood. I for my part had been immediately
hauled up by the port-side men, who did not wait for Butterworth's
orders. He was mad with rage, of course, but durst not interfere. Even
a numskull such as he could see that mutiny would not be far off if
he let me be consumed by the sharks, which would not have been
the punishment imposed.

I had no doubt that many of the crew were on my side. In the stench
of my suppurating wounds murky plans were aired. If I would take
the lead more than half the crew were willing to mutiny, I heard. In
order not to be regarded as insane I had boasted that I had gone over
the line just to oppose Butterworth, and was believed, though the truth
was otherwise, needless to say. But on the question of mutiny I held
my tongue. I had done my bit, and I also had my assured passage to
the West Indies to keep in mind. There had been enough foolishness on
my part already.

But one day Lacy appeared and said that Butterworth had had my blood painted over as soon as it had dried. And then came Scudamore, the surgeon, with even worse news. I found out from him that the *Carefree* was not sailing direct to the West Indies after all.

"Haven't you heard the carpenters hammering and banging on deck?"

"No," said I, quite truthfully.

It had been all I could do simply to survive.

"Well, they are," Scudamore continued. "They're building palisades and huts for the crew on deck. We're going to take on a cargo of black ivory. We'll make the coast of Africa in a week."

Slaves! Of course. How could I have been so stupid as to ask only where we were bound and not the route before I signed on? I thought of Captain Barlow, who had warned me about exactly that. And to think I had bragged of my aptitude for learning and asserted that nothing went in one ear and out of the other. If you wanted to die, Barlow had said, the slave trade was the surest place to start. Slaves died like flies, of course, but so did the crew. Throw the captain overboard, mutiny, do anything to get out of it, Barlow had said.

So I began paying heed to what was being whispered and hinted in my ears. Many of the men wanted to mutiny immediately before the slaves came on board with their fevers and their sores. I was of the contrary opinion.

"For a start," I said to Mundon, Tompkins and Lacy, who were crouched around the head of my bed, "there can't be any mut'ny till I'm healed an' ready to get things going. Secondly, there ain't enough on us. I've a mind to let the negroes do the rough work. You has to look a'ter your own skin."

"How can you say that?" whispered Tompkins, who had a head on his shoulders, which was more than the other two did, who hardly knew they had one. "Why in Hell's name did you go over the line, then?"

"No one," I snapped at him, "remember that, Tompkins, no one tells John Silver what to do an' what not to do."

"I meant no harm," said Tompkins quickly.

"No, I'm sure you didn't."

I made my voice sound friendly and ingratiating.

"D'you think you'd have been down on your knees in front o' me discussing mut'ny if I hadn't a-gone over the line? D'you think I'm mad enough to cross a line like that for nothing?"

"Hell's bells!" said Lacy with a low whistle.

"But I made a mistake," I went on. "I thought there was men aboard who had courage. But they're naught but cowards. Not one swab lifted a finger when I defied Butterworth. An' now you comes along an' says we should mut'ny. Certainly, says I. But this time I'll be the one who decides. Is that plain? First of all go an' speak to the ones we can depend on. Ask 'em whether they believes in God. Without saying anything about mut'ny, o' course. That comes a'terwards."

"There ain't no sailors that believes in God, anyhow!" Tompkins exclaimed contemptuously.

"Ask 'em to swear to it," said I. "Ask 'em to swear on the Bible that they don't believe in God, then you'll see a goodly few on 'em dancing to a different toon when it comes to the point. I've known old sea-dogs who would be ready to smite any clergyman they saw with the Bible drop to their knees an' pray for their lives when things got really hot."

The three of them looked uncertainly at one another and obviously wondered whether they themselves would dare to swear on the Bible that they did not believe in God.

"What we'll do is this," I went on, "you gather as many as you can to our cause an' hold yourselves in readiness. Each on 'em must swear an oath on the Bible an' add his name to a round robin."

"What's that?" asked Lacy in all innocence.

"Well, shiver my timbers, I'm damned if I can believe you're a sea-faring man!" I exclaimed. "An' to think I have to get involved with swabs like you that are still wet behind the ears."

"Easy all, John!" said Tompkins. "We may not know as much as you, but we're not to be played around with when the trouble starts."

"That's good, Tompkins. That was what I wanted to hear."

I saw his eyes light up with pride.

"A round robin," I explained affably, "is just a precaution. On the one hand, everyone who wants to be in on it signs a declaration, so they can't withdraw when things start warming up. On the other hand the same piece of paper leads straight to the gallows if it falls into the wrong hands. But since it's always those as signs first as are viewed as the ringleaders you has to sign in a circle so nobody knows who started."

"By the Devil, that's a good 'un!" said Lacy.

"Ay, it is. You get things going! I'll be on my feet again in a few days' time an' then I won't be the on'y one who knows he's alive."

So much for that, I thought when I was alone again. Instead of a safe and peaceful crossing to a new life in the West Indies, I had to bear the burthen of another mutiny on my shoulders. This time at least I knew what I was doing. I would not show myself on deck, for example, before the round robin was ready and signed by the others. There was no point in sticking my neck out unnecessarily and risking the fresh skin I had got on my back, not before I had seen which way the wind was blowing.

When I was given a clean bill of health by Scudamore a few days later, and tottered up on deck with weak legs and my eyes squinting in the bright sun, I was barely able to recognise the ship. The white line had been completely replaced by two strong palisades right across the deck. Both projected over the side by a fathom so that none of the negroes could squeeze past that way. The palisade nearer the stern had two cannon set in it, and on the poop deck were three more smaller ones for grapeshot and case-shot, aimed at the rest area for the male slaves between the two palisades.

To my surprise I could see some of the crew rigging up fine netting along the sides of the ship; as a rule it was just used on naval ships in battle, filled with blankets and other soft materials to catch flying splinters of wood. What did we want them for? Was it another of Butterworth's military notions?

"Are we going into battle?" I asked Scudamore, who was standing leaning over the rail.

"Well, if it isn't Silver!" he cried delightedly. "Good to see you on your feet again."

"Why?" I asked.

He winked knowingly with a significant glance at the first mate who was standing within earshot.

"Because it's my job," he replied, "to patch up people like you. That's what I'm paid for. We'll need every man we have when the blacks come aboard."

Was Scudamore one of the mutineers? It gave me an idea.

"That'll be something for you to get your teeth into as surgeon, a couple of hundred negroes to look after."

"You can be damned sure it will," said he with a grimace. "They're not easy to handle."

"Do you need some help?" I asked.

"What do you mean?"

"Listen to me, Doctor. I've just shed my skin like a snake, and I'm tender over my whole body. I don't think I'll be able to climb the rigging like a monkey. Not yet. Can't you put in a good word for me with Butterworth so as I can be your assistant?"

There was no mistaking Scudamore's surprise.

"You? Assistant? Do you know what you're talking about? It's so cramped down there that you have to crawl on all fours to get the shit barrels out, mop up vomit and hand out food. That's what we use the ship's boy for."

"I know what I'm a-doin'. I'm good at getting on with folk. It would be best for all of us."

A glimmer of comprehension flashed across Scudamore's face. He was with us, no doubt about that.

"All right, Silver. I'll see what I can do."

"Thanks, Scudamore. I knew I could count on you. But what about the bird netting, what's that for?"

"It's to stop the negroes jumping overboard."

"Are they mad? They'd be turning themselves into shark fodder and striking flag."

"Yet that's what they would do, Silver. They're ungrateful savages. Many of them would rather die than live."

"The fools!" I gasped.

"Ay, they have a steadfast belief that they're reunited with their kinsfolk when they pass over. But while they can still smell land, most of them try to stay alive. On the other hand, that's when you have to watch out for insurrection. They get desperate, Silver, if they can smell that the ship is leaving land. That's why all captains of slave ships have orders to weigh anchor in the middle of the night so the negroes don't know what's happened until it's too late."

"Is that so?" I said, reflecting on what I had heard. "And how long d'you reckon it will be? Ere we weigh anchor, I mean."

"It depends entirely on how many slaves there are in camp at the trading posts. Sometimes you can get a full load right away. But you can also wait for months, and that's no joke. Then all you get is sickness."

"We can't wait that long."

"Wait for what?"

"To die of ague and fever."

I turned to go.

"One more thing that might be of use," Scudamore added. "Some of the blacks are magnificent fighters. They have amulets that they think make them invincible. With one of those round their necks they're formidable antagonists. That's why the amulets are always cut off and thrown into the sea in front of them. It makes them submissive with a flick of the wrist. But at the same time it's rather a shame to see them wither like autumn leaves, if you see what I'm getting at."

Scudamore winked meaningfully again. He must have assumed that he and I were more than in collusion, that we were bosom friends or something like it.

"Scudamore," said I, slapping him on the shoulder, "you're worth your weight in gold!"

"Ay, am I not?" the rogue replied.

He did as I asked, at any rate, and put in a word for me with Butterworth, who granted my request without hesitation. Butterworth was no doubt hoping that I would catch some convenient disease, the deadlier the better, and released me from my duties as a master mariner. At the same time he saw to it that my wage was reduced to that of ship's boy, but what else was to be expected?

Ten days elapsed before we came in sight of Accra and the Danish white fortress, Christiansborg. During that time I was a helpful little devil in my new-found freedom as ship's boy. I was everywhere, talking to all and sundry as I pried into every corner, noting where the powder store and weapons were, which bulkheads would have to be torn down to let the slaves up to the poop deck, borrowing the key of the slaves' shackles from Scudamore's bag to make a copy. Nobody else was taking care of these rudimentary preparations.

From Scudamore I learned what little there was to know about the art of healing, and it was, if I may say so, no great skill, at least as far as the inner man was concerned. The likes of Scudamore were good with wounds and they could amputate an arm or a leg blindfold. They were as dexterous with needle, bone-saw and branding-iron as we others were with lashing, ropes and marlin-spikes. But as for the rest . . . Leeches, blood-letting, hot and cold compresses, drops of camphor in brandy or just neat brandy, medicine to make them shit, medicine to stop them shitting, there was no more to it than that. But did it do any good?

"No bloody good at all," said Scudamore, spitting over the rail. "I've never noticed any difference. On one of my voyages I did nothing, apart from feeding them and making sure they got fresh air. And do you know what? – the number of negroes for auction when we arrived was neither more nor less than usual, if anything slightly more. I received the same pay and the same dividend, without working myself to death. I know what you're going to say, of course, that it could have been a coincidence; and I had to falsify the journals, for who would sign on a surgeon like me, educated in Edinburgh and so on, to twiddle his thumbs? No, Silver, most of what we do is as useless as the natives' own witchcraft. And what there is some point in, wounds and amputations, a sailmaker or a carpenter could do just as well. You'll see for yourself soon enough, now that you've been such a blessed fool as to ask to be my assistant."

"It won't be very long now," said I.

"Not if everything goes as it should and as you want. But does it always?"

Scudamore was looking me straight in the eye.

"What the Hell d'you mean?" I asked in a low voice. "Has someone been blabbing?"

"Not that I'm aware of," said Scudamore with a smile. "But I've seen the paper. Though there was at least one name missing, so far as I could see, as if there were someone who durst not stick his neck out. You yourself, for instance."

I did my best to present a surprised countenance, as if I did not know what he was talking about.

"Never fear!" said he, slapping me on the back. "I'm not stupid enough to stick my neck out unnecessarily, either. You can depend on me. I know how to trim my sails to the wind and cut my coat according to my cloth. I'm an educated man, after all. Like you."

When we arrived off Accra there was tremendous commotion on board. We anchored in the roads and fired our salute, nine shots with our four-pounders, and the fortress responded in the same coin. Boats plied to and fro between the fortress and the ship. We unloaded, first the post, despatches, and money under guard, and then goods. Butterworth went ashore, of course, dressed out like a peacock. His cabin-boy, I had heard, had been ordered to polish his brass buttons for two days.

While Butterworth was ashore negotiating the cargo, and the officers were busy with the unloading, I set about the bulkhead between the hold and the after-deck. The carpenter, Soakes, was a swab who obeyed orders and therefore not to be depended on, so I had to content myself with the tools in the surgeon's chest. It took some time. I went to work with the trepanning drill and then sawed two shoulder-width holes with the bone-saw, feeling in a mood to whistle quietly to myself as I toiled. This, I thought to myself, constructing secret passages, was a noble pastime for the likes of me.

That evening I got together the sworn mutineers for a game of dice. Some of them were already as drunk as lords. Their eyes were glistening with Dutch courage and pugnacity. Rum and brandy were their amulets and fetishes. Our sailors with hair on their chests and scars on their hands were not a jot superior to the negroes in that respect.

"I can un'erstand you needs some grog," I said gently to the assembled company. "If I'd a-been in your shoes, if you had any, I'd have drunk myself to death long afore now."

"Been in your shoes?" screeched Roger Ball, who was later, in characteristic manner, to try to blow himself up when under Roberts' command, rather than be captured. "What the Hell is so special about you? You're no grander than the rest of us, Silver. Just because you happened to survive a keelhaulin'!"

"You're quite right, Ball," I admitted. "The fact that I happened to survive a keelhauling means nothing. I'm sure you would've done too, thick-skinned as you are. There ain't much that could get the better of an ox like you. Ain't that so, messmates? Roger Ball is a devil of a fellow."

A few of them nodded ardently. They wanted to keep in with Ball, who was quick to anger and really was as strong as an ox. And they thought from my innocent tone that I meant every word I said. It was only Tompkins, I observed, who perceived that I had not yet spoken my final word.

"That's right," agreed Ball approvingly with a self-satisfied laugh which I would dearly have loved to ram back down his throat. "That's right," he repeated. "No one can tell me what to do, neither Silver here nor anyone else."

He looked round self-confidently. That is how it was on every ship. There were always a few like Ball, so full of arrogance and brute strength that there was no room for anything else inside their thick skulls. And what became of them? Cannon-fodder, and shark-food, or the gallows.

"Right again!" said I calmly. "You've quite a headpiece, Ball. You should just make use of it a little more often."

"What the Hell d'you mean by that?" he shouted threateningly.

"On'y this, shipmates," said I in a voice that came to me at such moments as a gift from Heaven, "that if this strong, smart, courageous fellow is to make claims, then he should've been the one to cross the line. Then it would have been him as dared to challenge Butterworth and stir up mut'ny. Not me. But did Roger Ball do anythin' o' that nature?"

There was silence.

"A big mouth you might have, Ball, but as far as my deadlights can see, you obeys orders without so much as a blink."

Ball clenched his fists and was choking with rage, but even he could see that I had all the support and he had none. I picked up the dice and cast them on the table.

"I hazarded my precious and on'y life when I stepped over the line," I said when the dice had come to rest. "That gives me precedence over the likes o' you. If anyone has any objections, let's hear 'em now."

The silence spoke for itself.

"Tompkins, have you got the round robin?"

Tompkins drew out a creased sheet of paper and threw it down on the table as if it burned his fingers. I looked at it, folded it up and stuffed it into my pocket.

"You've all signed and are sworn in. You know what that means. If this bit o' paper falls into the wrong hands you've condemned your-selves to the gallows or twenty years in Newgate. So none of you can pull out and let the others risk their necks."

"Why ain't you signed, John?" asked Tompkins, cautiously.

I fixed my eyes on him.

"I suspected someone would ask that. I thought you would be sharp enough to work out why, Tompkins. I'm afeared for my skin, for one thing. If you were all as partic'lar as me, I'd've signed with the greatest pleasure. We wouldn't even've needed a round robin. I would've taken on the whole affair and written my name, John Silver, in big fat letters right at the top. But look around you! Half o' these bold mutineers have a'ready started drinking to give 'emselves some courage. Is that the way to protect their skin and mine? No, muddle-headed and unpredictable is how you gets from drinking brandy. Why d'you think the likes of you have failed so often in your high-flown plans? Because there's always been someone who's taken victory for granted, got himself blind drunk and shouted his mouth off or lost his head. That's what happens. That's why I ain't signed and why I've taken charge of the paper. And now I'll say this. From now on until this ship has got an elected cap'n and free an' honest men on board, there'll be no more drinking. Not a drop, d'you hear? If I sees anybody running around drunk with a bottle in his hand, it'll be meself as presents this paper to Butterworth."

[155]

There was muttering and grumbling here and there, but nothing serious. No one was prepared to knock me down and get hold of the paper just just for the sake of a drink.

"When this is all over," said I, encouragingly, "I promise you you'll be able to drink as much as you can take, ay, drink yourselves into Davy Jones's locker if that's your dearest wish."

"Ease up, John!" said Tompkins. "We don't need any more sermons. What say you, men?"

Tompkins was impertinently frank, but acceptably so. At least there was one of them who understood what was at stake. The others acquiesced, even Ball, though he still had a dangerous glint in his eyes.

"What's the plan?" asked Lacy, even he with a new firmness in his tone.

"We'll take the negroes on board. I'll let 'em loose and give 'em what they needs to take control o' the ship. We won't need to lift a finger ourselves, let alone risk our val'able skins. When the negroes have swabbed the poop deck, we'll come out and help them get ashore. That's all they want, nothing more. What d'you say to that, gen'lemen? We can mut'ny without lifting a finger. We get a fine ship given us and can't even be hanged for it."

I picked up the dice again and rolled them across the table. Two sixes.

"Can anyone beat that?" I asked, with my best laugh.

Seventeen

ELL, MR DEFOE, you can easily see from these events in my life how hard it must have been for the likes of me to live among men who were no different from the way most folk are. The whole of my life, it sometimes seems to me, has been taken up with wrangling to make people see reason. But has it achieved anything at all? Has it ever made any difference to anything in the long run? Confound it, they can blame themselves for not listening. Is it my fault I am the only one left? Is it my fault I am sitting here on my cliff as the last of an extinct race?

I am out of sorts, I will admit. It is not very cheering to acknowledge that there were failures and calamities in a life such as mine. And then Jack comes in with one of the slaves I freed and his woman. All three of them looked at me with an air of subservience that did not improve my humour.

"What the Hell do you want?" I asked, straight to the point.

They both turned to Jack.

"We need to talk to you," said he, with some reluctance if I judged aright.

"Don't you think I can see that for myself? Out with it! I've got other things to do."

But they just shuffled their wretched feet and stared down at the ground.

"What the Devil's the matter with you?" I asked.

"The fact is this," Jack began, "these two want to go back to their tribe. Their parents are old, they don't want to let them die alone and they're the eldest in the family."

"What's that to do with me?"

"They would like your permission."

"And why not my blessing as well while you're at it?" said I in a sweet voice.

"It's not an easy decision for Andriaaniaka to leave you after such a long time," replied Jack. "A word or two to help them on their journey would make it easier."

"A word or two for their journey! D'you think I'm a man of the damned cloth? They can have a drink for their journey, that's all. Give 'em a keg o' rum so they can get drunk at their parents' wake."

"But . . ." said Jack.

"No buts," I replied, weary of the subject. "How many times do I have to explain that you're free men, free as the birds, free as the wind. Is that so difficult to grasp? I bought your freedom because I needed your help. I've had it, and I thank you for it. But I'm blest if I wanted to be burthened with a crowd of servile slaves who come and ask for my permission and blessing."

"John!" said Jack in the indulgent tone that he had the gall to use when he thought I was talking rubbish. "We are Sakalava. We've killed many who thought they could subdue us and we'll kill many more if they try again. We've stayed with you because you gave us back our freedom and took us back to our own country. We're ready to defend your life with our own."

"But . . . ?"

Jack gave a rather mournful smile.

"But it's not how it was any more. You're getting old, you just sit here writing and you'll probably die a peaceful death. You don't need all of us any more."

I thought of disputing the point, but did not know what to say.

"You won't be left on your own," Jack went on. "There will always be some of us here."

I was struck dumb with rage. By what right did the likes of him dare to show sympathy for the likes of me?

"You have my blessing," was all I said. "An' the Devil take you!" Jack brightened up. He must have thought I had chosen my words as I used to do.

"Thank you!" said he. "If you hadn't given your permission, they would have stayed."

Did I tear my hair? Ay, that I did, for what could I do about such stupidity? No one had ever subdued the proud warriors of the Sakalava tribe, that was true. Except me.

I watched them go. The sun was on its way down between the peaks of the mountains in the west. Blinded by the red orb, I managed to avoid seeing their waves of farewell from the ground below. They were loyal and true, Jack had said. And what if they were? What did it have to do with me?

I tarried there till dusk, looking not after them but out to sea and the unbroken horizon. Despite everything, I longed to return to that life without restrictions, as I had lived it, to a life that had a morrow, to a life that seemed to have no end, no full stop, only at the very most a comma here and there, a little breathing space, and for the rest naught but action and excitement.

Eighteen

HEN BUTTERWORTH CAME back the next morning the crew were toiling at the capstan hauling up the anchor rope. The sea-bed at Accra was so rocky that we had to inspect the anchor line daily for fear it would be frayed. But despite the fact that we were all so busy the first mate was reprimanded in front of the crew for not having given the order to pipe the captain aboard. It was obvious to everyone that it was unjust; the *Carefree* was not, however much Butterworth may have wished it otherwise, a man o' war. She was a simple slave ship, no more and no less, despite her cheerful name.

That is how it was. Slave-trade vessels had grand names and highly placed patrons, everything from earls and cardinals to the Virgin Mary herself. And the truth was that they sailed with the blessing of God and the Pope. I have seen log-books from slave ships we plundered, where thanks were expressed to God for various things, for favourable winds, a safe crossing, mutinies quashed, good auction prices and so on, in endless lists. On a certain voyage it had been noted that one slave a day had died, but that God's grace was so benevolent that He had requited the loss by securing high prices at the ensuing auction.

After the reprimand Butterworth summoned all hands on deck. He informed us of the happy news that we were the first in Accra this year, that the camp at the fortress was already at bursting-point, and that we would thus be able to take on our full load within a week and then set course for St Thomas.

"God be praised!" he concluded, as might have been predicted.

"What bloody luck!" exclaimed Murrin, who happened to be hard by me. "Three months a-waitin' for cargo in this shit-hole an' he'd 've had a mut'ny on his hands. Believe me, I seen it afore."

Murrin was right. It was very obvious that Butterworth's news had altered the mood on board. There was naught but grinning faces and spirited cries. Even Roger Ball looked as if he had forgotten all about any imminent mutiny. In his mind's eye he was probably seeing plump whores and cheap rum in the West Indies, enough for the likes of him to drown himself in joy. Only Scudamore seemed as unmoved as usual. I felt in my pocket where the paper containing the sworn oaths was safely hidden. They had forgotten that, of course, in their short-sighted exuberation. But they were going to be saddled with a mutiny as sure as an amen in church. I was not intending to risk my newly healed skin to carry a few wretched blacks afflicted with every kind of illness across to the other side of the ocean.

The male slaves started being loaded aboard the next morning. The poor devils looked totally dejected as their fuzzy heads appeared over the rail. There is nothing that can be said about it. They were chained together in pairs with foot-shackles, naked from top to toe and branded like cattle.

Scudamore and I received them and gave them a good going over to see whether they had pox or clap, for the one they died of like flies and the other made them valueless. Something I can vouch for is that none of them had an erection before Scudamore started to squeeze their members. But Scudamore was a real craftsmaster. He pressed his slender fingers beneath their scrotums and their pricks soon leapt up so that we could judge and reject.

To make the slaves stand still we had two burly seamen with cutlasses and muskets to aid us. But sometimes even that was not enough. A shackled pair contrived to jump over the rail through the hole in the netting where they had been hoisted up. After just a scream or two they had been ripped to shreds by the sharks that always kept close to any slave ship worthy of its name. And to think that only a few days hence I, John Silver, would give them every chance in the world to fight for their lives, and mine as well – more than enough for anyone.

But if I was distressed, it was nothing compared to their owner, Feltman the priest, a black-coat travelling as a passenger. He had a dozen heathens with him for his own use that he had branded with a cross so they would not get mixed up with the rest of the cargo.

Feltman was beside himself and utterly inconsolable when he heard that it was two of his crucifix-branded possessions that God's unfathomable will had chosen as shark-fodder. He said no prayers in their blessed memory, but yelled, swore and cursed for all he was worth. He would have done well for himself before the mast, such was his command of the language. He immediately promised the two sailors who should have been keeping watch that they would burn in Hell, whereupon he gathered up his flapping robes and rushed off to Butterworth to see whether he could have his promise fulfilled then and there.

Butterworth heard him out, but no more than that. He had no great love for priests; there were not many captains who had, because God represented a challenge to the supremacy of captains. In fact most captains banned black-coats from their ships. The captain and no one else was there by the grace of God. For that very reason, however, Butterworth felt constrained to discipline the two sailors. Next time it might be the ship's own slaves who jumped overboard, and it was on them that Butterworth got his fee.

"Every slave who jumps overboard and dies will be deducted from your pay," he told the two sailors curtly.

No more needed to be said. The value of two adult male slaves was considerably more than an experienced seaman could earn in a whole year.

Day after day, in the boiling, unhealthy heat, Scudamore and I stood on the baking deck with its swelling joints that were sticky underfoot. I had asked for two jobs which I carried out with zeal and efficiency, examining the natives' eyes for blindness and ulceration, and cutting off the amulets that made them invulnerable or protected them against every kind of sickness and ill-fortune, against everything except the white man's folly.

I began by taking off them this only item of apparel, apart from their brand markings, and saw so much hatred and fear when I stared into their eyes at a proximity of a foot or so that a lesser man than myself would have recoiled. But they were transformed when I secretly thrust their gewgaws back into their hands. They fixed their gaze on me as if I were a lifeboat on a sinking ship. Not all of them, obviously. Many had nothing left that I could take from them, not even pride or dignity. And some were in a state of such inner spiritual degeneration that they could not give a damn about anything.

When Scudamore and I had finished our part, others took over and drove them below deck. The first mate was there overseeing the loading. To make rebellion more difficult he consulted his papers and made sure that slaves of the same tribe and tongue were segregated. The need for that had been learned from bitter experience. If it had not been necessary to feed them to ensure their very survival, I am sure their mouths would have been sewn up too.

Last in this progression of male slaves came three tall and majestic men without shackles. They looked around, pushed away my and Scudamore's prying hands, headed straight for the first mate and presented themselves for duty.

"Slave-masters!" exclaimed Scudamore.

"They don't look like slaves," said I.

"But they are, just the same. You see, Silver, white men are not as stupid as they often appear to be. You take a few sons of kings, or similar ranks, ones that already feel themselves to be superior to the others, teach them a few words of English, enough to be able to understand the captain's orders, give them a whip and let them move around freely on deck and – hey presto! – they keep their own people in order. And I can assure you they don't do it just to protect their miserable privileges. No, Silver, the blacks are like us, neither better nor worse."

After the male slaves it was time for the women and their born or unborn children. They were naked and branded like the others, but with no shackles on their ankles.

"Are the women allowed to go around just like that?" I asked Scudamore.

"Ay, certainly. Why shouldn't they?"

"Ain't it a risk to leave them unfettered?"

"Silver," said Scudamore in a surprisingly friendly tone, "you have a lot to learn still, as experienced as you are."

He looked down covetously towards the first boatload of a dozen or so black female bodies gleaming in the strong sunlight.

"Have you tried mounting a woman who's shackled to another one?" asked he with a laugh. "Not that it would be absolutely impossible, but it's confoundedly difficult."

"I thought 'twas forbidden."

"Ay, there's said to be something to that effect in the shipowners' instructions to captains. But for one thing, the officers are just as much whoremongers as the men. And who do you think would report such excesses? The women slaves themselves? Would their word count for more than that of any white sailor's, even if it were the ship's boy? No, Silver, the field is free, and you and I have first choice before all the others."

Scudamore had not exaggerated about the ship's whoremongers, for when the women appeared on deck the men emerged like mushrooms out of the earth. Their grins and back-slapping, their brazen and lustful gaze at everything but the women's faces, and their hardened cocks that they were rubbing unawares – it all made them look like the most distasteful voluptuaries I had ever seen.

And what about me, was I not the same as them? Devil knows! Firm and supple female flesh certainly put me in a good humour, too, there's no gainsaying. But so what? What was the point of all the excitement afterwards, when your prick had had its fill? No, I was not like the others, because they did not know what they were doing when their sap was flowing. To be sure, I lost my senses with Eliza, and what were the consequences? That even I was not myself.

Butterworth was bellowing and cursing to get them to go back to their posts. But he too found it difficult to take his eyes off the visionary creatures that Scudamore and I were assembling on the port side.

"Now, Silver, it's my turn," said Scudamore, calling over a slave-master.

"Tell the women we're going to check them for disease, and then get below deck," he ordered.

"That usually pacifies them so that we can carry on for a bit," Scudamore explained when the slave-master was out of sight.

"Carry on with what?"

He laughed.

"I'll carry on down here," he replied, "and you look in their eyes as before. Then we'll see which ones are any good, and those we'll keep for ourselves."

Kneeling down like a priest he began touching the women in various places, calmly and methodically – ay, that's the sort of man he was – even gently, if you ask me. He let his slim, smooth fingers glide up and down their thighs, pressed them against their pudenda and finally inserted his eager middle finger into their cunts and made his thumb vibrate like the string of a lute on their clitoris. And what was I doing while Scudamore was so rapturously endeavouring to awaken the women's lusts?

I stood there staring straight into their eyes to look for a contagious disease that would make them blind. But I think I saw everything that eyes could possibly express on this earth and beyond while Scudamore was rooting around their genitalia like a miner hunting for a seam of gold.

"Tell me if there are any who look as if they want more!" said he from time to time. "If so, they're mine!"

But I kept my mouth shut, until suddenly I was looking into a pair of eyes that seemed to see right into my own soul instead of the other way about. Scudamore was busy with the one next to her and did not observe me.

"If anyone's going to be mine," I said to her, "'tis you."

She met my gaze without flinching like the others. I was utterly convinced that she knew what sort of man I was, even that she under-stood what I said. A moment later Scudamore came crawling over with his sticky fingers and put them on the woman's thigh. I stood there impassively letting it happen until I saw the hatred welling up in her eyes.

"Keep your shitty fingers off this one! She's mine!"

Scudamore visibly shrank, and to my amazement I perceived that he was afraid.

"Of course, Silver," he replied with a fawning grin, "of course she's yours. I've got a sackful already. As they say. More than I can manage."

Even so he could not help inspecting the woman from top to toe, or rather, from the neck downwards.

"By all the fiends in Hell!" he exclaimed, "I didn't know you were such an authority on women. And a mulatto too! There you stood, giving nothing away, and you were just biding your time."

"Shut your mouth!" I yelled at him, and he snapped it shut like a codfish.

But I looked at the woman's body too, and shiver my timbers if he wasn't right. She was sculpted like a figurehead of a mermaid on an admiral's flagship. And she was not shy, either. No, I thought to myself, this one was not like the others.

How could I, as ship's boy, the least significant of all on board, lay hands on her for myself? But I was racking my brain unnecessarily. Down from the poop deck came Butterworth and took the woman by the arm.

"I need someone to clean my cabin," said he. "My cabin-boy died the day before yesterday, as you know."

Indeed he had, a few days after having polished Butterworth's brass buttons, as the last good deed the whipper-snapper managed to do in his short life. Butterworth's lustful eyes were glued to the woman's golden brown body as if she was covered in sticky tar.

And I, what did I do but tell the bastard he could forget that bloody idea. He gave a start, and even in him I thought I could discern a hint of fear, before he remembered who he was and who I was.

"So, that's what you say, is it, Silver? I can't really believe that John Silver is questioning my orders yet again. After four weeks in African waters I would imagine the hull of the *Carefree* looks like a coral reef."

"Nay, sir," I managed to splutter, controlling myself with some difficulty, "I was just anxious about your health, sir. I think she's got the pox."

"Well answered, Silver! Unfortunately you're a man with a brain, though you make deplorable use of it. Frankly, I've never seen a health-ier woman in my life, healthy and as firm-fleshed as a new-slaughtered calf. Believe me, I've sailed this route before, and can judge a case of disease as well as a couple of bunglers like you. I won't be risking anything. On the contrary, this one is going to do me naught but good."

He looked round arrogantly before taking the woman off with him. I followed her with my eyes and could almost imagine that her glance tarried on me. And then I saw her smile, but a smile that might make anyone shake at the knees – in fear and trembling. It was not a pretty sight. Yet Butterworth was too busy with his thoughts of coming bliss to see anything at all. I felt Scudamore's hand take hold of my arm in a firm grasp.

"Don't do anything foolish again!" said he, sounding almost as if he meant it for my sake. "A woman isn't a white line on deck, she's just a slit. And there are plenty enough of them."

"What the deuce do you know about it?" said I, pulling my arm free. "If you think I'm stupid enough to have myself keelhauled a second time for the sake of a woman, you're wrong!"

"That's what I wanted to hear," said he, sounding relieved. "I don't want anything to happen to you. If the ship falls into the right hands, at least you know I was a dependable man. Now perhaps we should go down to our charges in the underworld and see how they're faring. Prepare yourself for the worst."

Nineteen

T O THINK, DOLORES, that it was nineteen years we were together, without ever talking about it. And now it is too late. You took your secret to the grave with you. Last night, after writing about how you and I met, I asked one of the women to sleep with me. She arrived with a smile on her face, as if she were pleased I had asked her. She undressed in front of me, displaying her black body, and lay down on my bed with open, inviting thighs. I also stripped naked, in my wrinkled, decrepit, dried-up and reddish whiteness, and lay down beside her. I asked her to lie on her side with her back towards me, and then I pressed the whole of my body against her, minus one leg, and held her tight all night long without moving. I could feel her warmth flowing into my numb and frozen corpse as I thought of you, Dolores, until I fell asleep at daybreak.

When I awoke again, the woman had risen and was putting on the few clothes she had. On one shoulder and one thigh I could see the impression of my vice-like grip. She gave me a questioning and, I think, sympathetic look, though it made no difference to me.

"Thank you!" I said to her in her own tongue, and her face lit up in delight.

It occurred to me that that was probably the first time she had heard the words from my lips.

You must excuse this outburst of emotion, Mr Defoe, but I am like an old compass in need of resetting. I can cope with the deviation and allow for it, but it changes with the course, the cargo and all the other unstable ballast on board. I was going to write about Edward England, that was it, all that I did not say when we talked in the Angel. But my memory has no deviation table. I set a course, but do not know how to compensate, and it is not long before I lose my bearings. Dead reckoning, it is called, Mr Defoe, navigating just by log and compass. Did you know that? That's the way it is, anyhow, the story of my life is no more than dead reckoning. You know where you are, but the further you get from the starting-point, the more uncertain your position becomes. The circle within which you should be sailing gradually gets bigger and bigger. So what do you do? You set up double watches in the crow's nest in the hope of sighting land before it is too late. You go back over the log-book weighing up one thing against another, the inevitable errors, drift from wind and current, helmsmen who bear up or make leeway in squalls, helmsmen who sail too slow or too fast in the dark. But can you ever be sure? No – on the contrary. The wise navigator is one who makes his circle wider and wider, who knows that uncertainty is the only certainty there is.

I went back over the log-book to see where I was, but it turns out that I have just been measuring my circle. Yet I have not set up any watch in the crow's nest, because I have understood enough to know that it was only imagination, vanity or wishful thinking to believe I had navigated through life in sight of land and with reliable bearings. No, dead reckoning has been my life; but perhaps – who knows? –I might manage to fix my position before I eventually sink.

Twenty

S O I FOLLOWED Scudamore down below deck with my mind in a state of turmoil. Thoughts of the woman and of the mutiny were raging in my head like a tornado. At that moment I was full of appetite for life.

But I cannot deny that it abated somewhat when I entered the cargo deck, heard the moaning and groaning of hundreds of voices and smelt the acrid, pungent stench of sweat, piss and shit. I stood next to Scudamore in the tiny space available by the ladder. Before me, in the faint light from the deck hatches wedged ajar, lay rows of naked bodies, eyes staring impassively. The moans and groans had died away as the faces had turned towards us, first the nearest ones and then on through the rows up to the last against the bulkhead at the stern. An oppressive silence followed. It was as if they were waiting for something.

"Well, you can see for yourself," said Scudamore in a low voice, in case any of the slaves could understand English, "three hundred and twelve negroes in all, top-class slaves, not counting the women and children. It's a prodigious amount of humanity for an area of seventy by twenty feet. It's lucky for us we didn't load chock-full; Butterworth is one of the worst tight-packers. He's one of those who lay the slaves on their sides to get in as many as possible. The more you squeeze in from the start, the more are left by the time we arrive, that's how the tight-packers reason. But the figures don't tally. I've sailed with both tight-packers and loose-packers, and the one earns no more than the other. The only difference is that the likes of us go through Hell on earth with the tight-packers. More die, needless to say, and you can hardly get in without shifting corpses out of the way, at least until the grim reaper has started to thin out the rows properly. And then there are the ones on the shelves."

I had not even observed it, but along both sides the slaves were lying double-banked.

"How the Hell do they think we can work when it's like this? Try reaching those ones there and you'll know what's what. There's scarce three foot above and below the shelves, so they can't sit up even if they want to. You also have to walk barefoot to avoid trampling the poor bastards to death. But do you think they appreciate such care? No, they're ingrates, the lot of 'em. The only thing that helps is to rub your feet in their excrement. That at least stops them biting you."

He laughed.

"That's my own little trick," said he. "It's not very pleasant, but it's effective. Do you see those half-barrels? That's where they relieve themselves. The women relieve themselves on deck, but it would be too much of a risk to let the men up every time they want to shit or piss. It's your job to carry the barrels up on deck and empty them."

He gave me an enquiring glance.

"I warned you," said he. "But you wouldn't listen to me. Now it's too late to change your mind."

"D'you think I'm stupid?" I asked. "It'll be over in a few days and we'll be free men."

"No, Silver, I don't think you're stupid at all, far from it. But do you always know what you're letting yourself in for? This is as close to Hell as you can get. A couple of days can break anyone. You ought to see what it looks like after a storm. Most of these blacks have never set foot on a ship before. They get seasick and spew all over the place. The barrels tip over and they have to piss and crap where they are. What do you think it's like then? And under the shelves? The ones above drop their own shit on the ones lying below. And the stench, Silver, imagine it! With the hatches battened down not a breath of fresh air gets in. It's so fetid down here that the lamps often go out. And the screams, the wailing and whimpering! Hell can't be worse than this, Silver. What you've taken on, my friend, is keeping Hell clean."

"Tell me one thing," I asked, "if this is as vile as you say, how come you've got involved with it, even though you don't actually have to clean up the shit?"

"What else can an educated man without connections do in life?" he asked, throwing up his hands, "apart from endeavouring to keep people alive?"

He looked at the negroes, who were still lying there in silence.

"And earn a crust from the misery and misfortune of others," he added. "Just like everyone else."

He took hold of the ladder.

"Now you'll have to manage as well as you can on your own. I do my rounds twice a day, and you can help me administer medicine and so on then. You'll get help yourself in handing out the gob gravy, as they call it, but you can reckon on a lot of them refusing to eat. We have special instruments for them. And the ones that are going up on deck for some fresh air will be fetched by guards. You just have to organise the sequence. Otherwise you're on your own."

Before disappearing up the ladder he turned and said, "By the way, take a piece of advice: forget all about that woman if you don't want to be keelhauled again. I can promise you that the ones I selected for myself are at least as good, and that there are enough and to spare for both of us."

A moment later the hatch was closed and I was on my own, confronted by three hundred and twelve pairs of eyes.

"All right!" I yelled. "Now there'll soon be an end to this Hell. Is there anyone here who can understand what I say? Anyone who knows anything other than a native tongue?"

The silence persisted, but then I heard a voice out of the darkness.

"Yes, sir," came a response from somewhere.

I made my way over and between all the bodies that, to my surprise, did what they could to let me through. There was a clanking of iron as they moved their shackles. Here and there I could see friendly smiles and hands stretched out to touch me. All that, I thought, because I had given them back a few miserable amulets and stared into their eyes.

"And who may you be?" I asked when I had found my way to one of the last pairs on the port side.

"Andrianamboaniarivo, sir."

"Are you making fun o' me?"

The negro looked at me questioningly. No, he obviously was not.

"D'you mind if I call you Jack?" I asked.

"No, sir," said he with a grin.

So he was not entirely wet behind the ears.

"And don't call me sir," I added. "I'm ship's boy on this vessel, nothing more, and my job is to clear up your crap an' keep this Hell-hole clean."

"Thank you, thank you," said Jack.

"For what?" I laughed. "For clearing up shit? I don't do that for your sakes, if that's what you thought."

"No, not that, not the shit. For giving us back . . ."

He did not know the word, but pointed at his neck where a crocodile tooth or something like it was hanging.

"Same applies, my friend. It ain't knick-knacks like that that'll save your skins. No, when it comes to life or death you'd do better to turn to the likes o' me, John Silver by name. I'm worth more'n a hundred o' your crocodile teeth and lumps o' coral, believe you me."

Jack stared at me uncomprehendingly.

"You want to get out o' here?" I asked. "Home?"

He understood that anyway, for there was no mistaking the hatred that glinted in his eyes.

"Now hearken carefully to what I have to say. If you don't understand, speak up. 'Tis important, can you grasp that?"

Jack made no response.

"You must be able to nod your head, even though you're black," said I, and nodded my own. "That means yes, in case you weren't aware of it."

After all it was not certain they had the same book of signals as we did. But Jack nodded and gave a smile. So he was not as stupid as all that. Things were coming along.

"In a day or two this ship will be ready to sail you all to Hell. Do you know what Hell is?"

Jack nodded several times and glanced about him expressively.

"Good," said I with a laugh, "then we're agreed on that, leastways. Now the fact is that slaves like you are not God's chosen children in the cap'n's eyes. The cap'n, he's the one who's king here, and it's against such people that you can rebel. And if you're so inclined you can kill 'em and eat 'cm."

Jack shook his head.

"All right, not that. No, like enough you wouldn't want to sink your teeth into a martinet like Butterworth, even if you were a cannibal. Anyway, Butterworth, the cap'n, thinks that you lot down here wouldn't come over to the other side o' the ocean with us if you had a free choice. So he means to set sail from Accra here in the middle o' the night while you're sound asleep. When you wake up the next day the smell o' land will be gone and then there's naught else but the great ocean till you gets across to the other side. But then, my friend, it'll be too late, because there in the West Indies we'll be met by soldiers with muskets who'll make sure that such valuable treasures as you gets safely ashore. Have you understood that? If we don't do somethin' now, it'll be too late, and then there'll only be an even worse Hell or shark-fodder to look for'ard to for the likes o' you."

"I understand Hell," said Jack very seriously. "How kill Captain?" he asked, looking down at his fetters and at his partner chained to him who was following our plans with the greatest interest.

Only then did I observe that it was still silent around us. So I lowered my voice and explained all about my preparations, about the stock of weapons, about the sworn mutineers who would be holding themselves in readiness before the mast, about the cannons on deck, about the hole in the bulkhead, and finally I gave him the key to freedom.

I'll warrant he opened his deadlights as wide as portholes.

"Why?" he asked.

"Why what?"

"You white man. Not black, not slave."

"What do that matter? As long as you gets free."

He nodded, but was still suspicious. There was nothing wrong with that.

"What about this for a reason?" said I, without expecting any answer. "When I sees the likes o' you I always thinks it'll be my turn next."

Jack looked me in the eye as if he had actually understood.

"You and me brothers," said he. "My people, Sakalava, submit to no one."

"No?" said I. "Then what the Hell are you doing here?"

That shut his mouth.

"That gave you something to think about, didn't it?" I added, sounding as cheerful as I felt.

"We brothers," said Jack obstinately.

"As you wish," I agreed magnanimously. "So long as you does what I've told you. And one more thing afore I forgets: make sure the slave-masters are in front when you storms the poop deck."

Jack raised his eyebrows, just as we do.

"Exactly," said I, "as shields. 'Tis no more'n right."

Jack brightened up, and I could not help thinking that we had understood each other rather well, better than I ever could have hoped or desired.

"Can you explain to the rest? D'you understand one another's lingo?"

"Some," said Jack. "But not hard to explain."

He made a gesture with his finger that anyone would have understood to mean that some might have to have their throats cut. I turned round and grabbed hold of the first latrine barrel that came to hand. As I shifted it towards the stern I could hear the expectant, even excited, murmuring and chatter that was spreading my message like wildfire, language or no language.

I need not have worried about whether the message would get round. Every time I came down from the deck to fetch another barrel I could see their countenances changing. And wheresoever I turned I met with friendliness, gratitude, respect and determination. When I thought of the churlish and petty mutineers that I had allied myself with, I almost regretted that I had not asked the negroes to cast the whole white race overboard, excepting myself, of course.

When I had thrown the last of the sweet-smelling muck in the sea I stayed up in the hot, shimmering but pure air for a rest. But you would think the likes of Butterworth had eyes in the back of their heads, for whose sarcastic face appeared by my side if not his?

"Are you off duty, Silver?" was his first remark.

I did not answer.

"Get back below deck where you belong, then," he shouted.

"Anyhow," he went on, hardly moderating the power of his voice, "it's about time I inspected the cargo. We set sail tonight. You go first, Silver."

Tonight! I clambered down and waited until Butterworth was beside me. The muttering subsided as soon as the slaves caught sight of us. Butterworth brought forth a handkerchief and held it to his nose and mouth. He durst not walk far into the mass of black limbs. When I stepped forward out of the darkness the chatter started up again, and you would have had to be particularly obtuse not to notice the vivacity in it. I raised my voice.

"This is Cap'n Butterworth, king on this ship. It's him and God we have to thank when we get to land."

The murmuring increased and I knew that Jack had translated and passed the words on. Useful, I thought, since now they all knew what the devil himself looked like.

"What the blazes are you telling 'em that for?" Butterworth asked. "Do you think they can understand a civilised language?"

"It ain't that, sir. 'Tis the tone that counts. 'Tis just like dogs, sir. Ain't you never talked to a dog? You has to admit they looks quite happy and content."

"Maybe," he muttered. "It certainly looks all right here. And it's lucky for you that it does. I'm watching you, Silver."

"Ay, ay, sir. But I knows how to handle folk, sir."

"Always excepting of yourself, obviously," he snapped, turning briskly and hastening back up.

As soon as he had gone I started to move fast. I told Jack it had to happen that very night, but that they should leave their shackles until Scudamore had done his round and they had been given their evening rations. I sent word to the others with Tompkins. The moment the rebellion started they were to withdraw for'ard of the mast and not lift a finger until I said so. That was the only way the negroes could know what was permissible quarry and what was not.

When Scudamore arrived to do his round I told him what was afoot and advised him to keep himself hidden before the mast if he wanted to see the sun rise on the morrow. He thanked me for the information, but showed no eagerness or enthusiasm. Nor had I expected any.

At eight bells that evening the slaves began unlocking their shackles. Their countenances when they sat up and rubbed their ankles were a sight for the gods – ay, even for me.

Four bells later, standing at the hatch, I heard the first mate ordering the men in a low voice to go aloft. I hurriedly climbed down again and was met by Jack ready at the base of the ladder. The three slave-masters were standing by the aft bulkhead waiting fearfully for whatever might befall. They were not so cocky now, which was no more than right.

I nodded to Jack and within an instant the whole black sea of humanity was on the move. There was little more for me to do, other than wait. I lay down on one of the bunks and closed my eyes. I heard the first shots and screams of pain, and was momentarily delighted, before suddenly my lights went out and I lost consciousness.

When I came round again it was still dark, and even before I opened my eyes I knew that something was not as it should be. Not just because my head was pounding and felt as if it would burst, not just because I could smell the odour of warm bodies, of excrement and other things hard to determine, nor just because of the strange feeling of not being alone even though I could hear no other human sound except a faint groaning – but rather because we were sailing, as sure as my name was John Silver. The *Carefree* was rolling gently, propelled by full sails, in a falling or rising swell, with the wind on the stern quarter. It was indisputable. And we would not be in that position if the mutiny had prevailed.

What had happened and where was I? I tried to get up, but one leg was held fast as if in a vice, and before I was even sitting up my head hit a beam and the pain doubled. Warm, repulsive blood, my own without a doubt, ran down my forehead, past my nose and on to my chin. I was suddenly aware of what the smell was that I had not recognised. It was blood, that was it. I pulled sharply on the leg that was stuck fast and something gave. But then I heard an unfathomable despondent voice at my side.

"Lie down, sir! It's all over now."

I felt with my hands alongside me and there lay a naked body. With the worst forebodings I felt around down at my feet and found a shackle on my ankle, chained to the body next to me.

"What in Hell's name is this!" I cried out.

"Everyone can be slaves," I heard the same voice declare, as if it came from the underworld. "Sakalava, white men."

I sank back on the bare wooden bench with no mattress other than the small amount of fat a man has on his own body. Only then did I become aware that I too was naked. I was a slave, God help me and be damned, I had been turned into a slave, me, John Silver, who wanted to be freer than anyone I had ever known.

I went into some kind of frenzy and screamed to high Heaven. Then I felt a hand take hold of me and shake me.

"No more. You not alone," said the same voice as before, quite resolutely.

And then I heard a mirthless laugh.

"Now we brothers you and me. You too."

The words were like the crack of a whip.

"What did you say?" I demanded vehemently.

"You slave, me slave, we slaves. No difference." It was Jack; it was he who was lying beside me.

"I'm no slave, by God I'm not, remember that!"

"Wait and see!" replied Jack.

What did he mean? I tried to think. At least I was alive. That was always the most important thing, staying alive. The mutiny had been quelled, there could hardly be any doubt about that. The how and why would have to wait. I must have been hit on the head with a heavy object and tied up here for the time being for lack of anywhere better. Of course I was suspected since I had been the only one below deck when the insurrection broke out. It was only natural that I would be held captive, I said to myself, and thought myself fortunate that I had not signed the round robin. As things stood there was no proof that I had been behind it all. I would be able to defend my reputation with my big mouth if I just used my wits and avoided getting over-excited. But why was I stripped bare?

"Jack?" said I. "What happened?"

"Happened?" he repeated, in a flat voice.

"Ay, just that, happened! Why are we lying here? Why didn't things go as they should have?"

I had to coax him and urge him to get him to say anything, so downcast was he. Someone must have betrayed us. Everything was ready to receive the rebels. The three slave-masters and two others had been permitted to seize control of the cannon and then give the signal to the others to rush out behind the palisades. When a hundred or so were in position, packed like sardines, the five at the cannon were simply dealt with – those were the shots and the screams I had heard before I lost my senses – and that made it plain to the others what would happen to them if they so much as moved a muscle. At the same time, more of the crew had attended to the ones who were clambering through the hole I had sawn with my own hands, easily effected because they emerged in such small numbers, two by two. Finally a group of seamen armed with muskets had got down to the cargo deck through a hatch at the bow and surprised the rest from behind. It was one of them, Jack thought, who had clubbed me where I lay. It was Jack himself who had made sure in the confusion that he got chained together with me.

"But how could it've been over so quickly?" I asked in astonishment. "It still ain't light, everyone's back, and we're under sail."

"Second night," said Jack.

That was it. I had been out for twenty-four hours.

"And now," Jack went on, "there's only Hell. As you said."

He could have looked happier, you may lay to that.

"They ain't seen the last o' me yet, as sure as my name's John Silver," I answered, and sank back down on to the bench.

I needed to gather every reserve of strength for what was to come, I thought. And by thunder I was quite right, though not in the way I had reckoned.

Twenty-one

THE FIRST THING I saw on the morrow was Scudamore's impassive countenance regarding me without a trace of human emotion.

"You might easily have been dead by now," declared he.

"It wouldn't have been the first time," I countered defiantly. "But I'm alive, as usual. Get this damned shackle off my foot and give me a few rags to cover my body. I can't lie here like this."

"I'm sorry to have to say it, but that's the only thing you can do."

"What the Devil do you mean by that?"

I fixed him straight in the eye, but there was no sign of fear in him.

"Captain Butterworth's orders," said he, and I thought I could discern the trace of a smirk on his face.

"To Hell with Cap'n Butterworth!" I roared. "He ain't got no right to use me like a dog. I'm a master mariner and can expect proper treatment."

"Butterworth seems to be of a contrary opinion," said Scudamore, grinning broadly now.

The grin put me on my guard.

"And what does he base that opinion on?" I enquired in a calmer tone.

"Well," he replied, "on one thing and another. They discovered the round robin in one of your pockets."

"They were led by the nose, then," I broke in. "I'd like to see Butterworth's ugly mug when I tell him I'd intended handing the paper over to him to prevent an almighty mutiny."

"I don't think that would be wise," said Scudamore.

"No? Why not?"

"For the simple reason that your name is on it."

"Like Hell it is," I screamed at the top of my voice. "Butterworth is lying to incriminate me."

"No," said Scudamore slowly, "in this case he isn't. He showed us the paper. Your name is there above all the others, John Silver, in big, clear letters. That was stupid of you."

"What?" was all I could utter in my dismay. "I didn't sign any paper."

"Well, as I say, there are different opinions about that."

"But you know," said I, recovering my power of speech, "that I wouldn't be stupid enough to sign my own death warrant."

"How should I know that?" he asked innocently.

"'Tis a forgery," said I, "and I'll be able to prove it if I can only come up and talk to the swab myself in his own esteemed person. He's the one who wrote my name, him or someone else who's out to entrap me."

Suddenly a thought struck me.

"It must be Roger Ball," I cried. "He must have done it. He hates me worse than the plague."

"It's quite possible. He's not the only one at present. Unfortunately, John Silver is not held in high regard on board this vessel."

"But I'm telling you I can prove I wasn't the one who wrote my name. Get me a pen and paper and I'll show you!"

"And send eight others to the gallows? Is that what you want? Butterworth needs all the crew he can get, and as things stand at the moment he's willing to content himself with you and pretend to over-look what the others did. And even you he's not intending to kill – on my advice, by the way. No, you needn't thank me. I didn't do it for your sake. It's never a good notion to put white sailors to death when you've got negroes on board. Sooner or later they find out about it and start to believe that it's not so hard to cut the throat of a white man after all – a simple surgeon, for instance, who happens to come within reach to administer medicine and help them keep body and soul together. So I proposed a less dramatic solution to Butterworth, which was also much more effective for all parties and gave you, my friend, a chance to survive. My suggestion was quite simply that you be placed here among the others for the duration of the voyage and then be put on trial when we arrived."

I did the only thing I could: launched a well-aimed gob of spit that hit Scudamore right on the forehead. He flinched, but regained his composure and wiped himself with a handkerchief.

"I can understand that you're angry," said he, unruffled but with some distrust in his eyes. "But I would advise you to keep on good terms with me. For your own sake."

"For my own sake," I hissed as derisively as I could.

"Indeed. If you're to prove to the court that you were not behind the mutiny, you need some creditable person to speak up for you. There are eight men up on deck with Roger Ball at the head of them who would swear on the Bible and their mothers' blessed memory that it was you and no one else who led the mutiny, quite apart from the fact that it's by and large the truth. They'll want to see you hanged to avoid being hanged themselves. I'm the only one who could say anything different and be believed."

"Why?" I asked, still raging, but minded to reflect upon it. "Why should a serpent like you be particularly believed?"

"Because I was the one who disclosed the mutiny plan to Butterworth. My star has never been so high as it is now."

"You?" was all I could say, too taken aback to shout, spit or choke.

I was speechless, it was as simple as that.

"You don't think," Scudamore went on, "that I'm foolish enough to wager everything on one horse. Whatever the outcome of the mutiny, I would be all right. You have to get by as best you can in this life, Silver, that's something you still have to learn. Instead of running about like a demented hen jumping over white lines that you could just as easily go round when necessary. You've got a backbone, Silver, I'm more than willing to admit. But a backbone can be broken. I'm just cartilage and muscles that bend and stretch and yet still hang together."

"You're a cowardly, deceitful swine," said I.

"That may well be so, but what use is it to you to be anything else? Answer me that!"

This time he sounded both pugnacious and dangerous. He was already sly.

"Well," he continued, "you've got time to think things over before you come up with some new stupidity. Life is a game, Silver. I played wisely and sensibly, and won. You staked everything on one card, and lost. That's the way it is. We need your eight brothers-in-arms to sail this tub across to the other side and to keep the blacks alive and under control, so that I get my usual fee. And if you rant on about forged signatures, I'll talk, here and in court, about who stole my instruments to saw a hole in the bulkhead, and who took the key to make a double. That should be enough to make sure you swing from the gallows several times over. I hope this is language you understand."

"Ay," said I, emphatically and humbly, because Scudamore was obviously right in what he said.

He turned and left. A leaden weight descended on me body and soul, and it felt in all seriousness as if I already had a noose around my neck. My fine new skin on my back, I thought in desperation as I felt the unplaned boards marking my naked body. But then there was the touch of a hand on my shoulder.

"Brothers?" asked Jack with a note of supplication in his voice.

I turned towards him.

"Slaves, at any rate," I replied. "That's a start."

And shiver my timbers if his face didn't brighten up, as if something like that actually mattered in the predicament we were in.

Twenty-two

CAN YOU IMAGINE anything more derisible, ridiculous and hopeless? There I lay, I, Long John Silver, nicknamed Barbecue, later to be so respected and feared, condemned to be a slave and bound hand and foot by my own stupidity and others' vengefulness. I never sank lower than that in the whole of my life.

For the first few days, I readily admit, I had no desire to do anything. I refused to eat, not because I wanted to die or show my defiance, but because I had lost my appetite. I refused to go up on deck to get fresh air, not because I wanted to rot away in the mustiness below deck, but because I did not see the point. I was no longer a human being, if I had ever been one.

That I stood up again at all was due to Jack. For while I declined to set foot on deck, Scudamore would not let Jack up on his own. To make Jack suffer because of me was Scudamore's own idea. He probably hoped that the blacks would turn against me and make my life Hell.

After a few days Jack quite justifiably started berating me, in order to get himself a breath of fresh air. He screamed at me and hit me hard about the head, which was no more than right. The pain eventually sank through to my benumbed brain. Then came a fear of dying while yet alive, slave or no; followed by the sight of Captain Wilkinson on the *Lady Mary* giving Bowles the preacher of doom the blow with the axe that knocked him overboard. Was I no better than Bowles? I asked myself. Had I no more shame than that in my body?

"You win," said I to Jack at last.

He put his hand on my shoulder, and I let him keep it there.

"That's good," said he. "My people never submit. No white flag like you. You are like us."

"How the Devil do you know how I'm made?" I objected.

"Why you lie here? With us?"

It suddenly dawned on me that the negro by my side had hit the nail on the head. Had anyone ever heard of a white man clapped in irons together with slaves? Even the criminals that the British sent to the Colonies were kept separate from the slaves if they happened to be transported on the same ship. The thought was comforting for a soul like mine and helped me back on to an even keel again.

The next day I opened my mouth and told Scudamore I would not mind an airing with the others.

"If that's all right," said I, as amiably as I knew how.

"Well, look at that," said Scudamore, "the corpse is stirring itself again."

"It's my mate who's got the itch," I replied.

"Your mate?" echoed Scudamore. "It's like that now, is it?"

"You have to take what's on offer."

Straight after dinner we slithered down from the shelf as best we could. I set off myself without thinking, and the next moment hit the deck with a thud. Jack had come to a full stop by banging his head against a beam.

"You and me brothers," said he. "Brothers do everything together."

"You're right," I replied. "I forgot. We're brothers, till Hell us do part."

And he was indeed right, though it was damnably hard to learn. The slightest movement, turning round, having a shit or a piss or clambering up on deck, had to be carried out with all due consideration of the other person. In everything you did, except breathing and thinking, there were suddenly two of you. It was a complete marvel to me that more of the negro pairs did not go mad and beat one another to a bloody pulp.

Just getting up the ladder was a spectacle. Not separating us for the trips up on deck was Butterworth's order. The mutiny had given him cold feet. It took us three attempts to climb up, and even then we had help from a slave-master who came along with kicks and lashes of the whip. There was such confusion trying to climb the ladder that we emerged on deck grinning from ear to ear.

"What a clumsy bastard you are," said I.

Only then did I observe the silence around us. There were no cries to be heard, no shouting, oaths or conversation, just the roar of the sea and the whining creak of rigging and hull. And what was the reason, but my stark-naked ghostly white appearance on deck! The whole crew had gathered round to stare themselves silly at my pathetic figure. Heads protruded over the palisade walls wherever I looked. Not even Butterworth could restrain his curiosity, but stood stiffly on the poop deck with an approving smile on his face. And both cannon were manned, in my honour.

"What the Devil are you staring at?" I yelled. "Ain't you never seen a slave afore?"

Then I directed my gaze at each and every one of them, one after another, and saw some of them shrink back or look away. I was really beginning to feel human again.

But when I turned round I saw Jack staring up at the sky. There beneath the yard-arm hung three negro bodies with their hands and feet chopped off and their pricks still glowing as red as tomatoes after being rubbed with salt, pepper and ashes, the usual custom.

"Now you ain't such a big-mouth, you bloody slave!" cried a shrill voice.

It was Roger Ball.

Soon more voices could be heard, mocking, jeering and swearing. They all called me the same, "slave", and that is how it remained. "Slave" became my name, as if there were no others on board, and I even think the negroes received better than usual treatment because of it, except for Jack, so that I would get what a real slave rightfully deserved.

While the taunts were raining down I looked at the three hanged men, but it took a while before I saw whose faces were on the bodies: it was the three slave-masters. That, I thought, was true gallows humour, and I started laughing at the top of my voice. When I stopped I discovered that my laughter had silenced all the jeering. Mad laughter like that could obviously scare people out of their wits, for I saw consternation in the countenances that none was able to avert from me.

But when Jack and I had been stuffed back in like sardines on our accursed shelf, doubts began to assail me. I may have silenced the crew and the captain, created a little confusion and uncertainty in their minds, maybe even a slight fear. But that was all – and was it a good thing? No, for often it was people like that who stopped thinking and just hit out all around them to appease their questionable consciences. There was a limit, a sort of line, in a manner of speaking, which I ought not to transgress if I wanted to keep my precious skin on my body. I could of course turn myself into a madman, completely unpredictable; that would save me from floggings, since there was no insolence to knock out of lunatics. On the other hand, they not infrequently ended on the gallows, to get rid of them. So even that was no way to extricate myself from my dire straits.

So I was despondent, and things got worse when two days later we sailed into rough weather. It was not a fully-fledged storm, just a steady gale that made the *Carefree* roll like a pendulum while pitching in the counter-swell from another storm far away. But it was enough for the hatches to be battened down and for the Hell to break out that Scudamore had warned of.

There was a wailing and a howling from the blacks, who, as wretched landlubbers, were convinced they were going to die. It was hard to understand, but there were many of them who would rather die than live, and some who had voluntarily given up eating to help death on its way; yet those same people, while the storm raged, vied with the others to scream the loudest. And they were all seasick and spewed, pissed and shat where they lay. I think Jack and I were the only ones who tried to make use of the barrel, not because Jack was really so inclined, but because I told him I would push his own shit down his throat if he didn't do as I said. Not that it made much difference in the long run, because we were wedged in like the joins between the planks, like pins hammered in between the boards of the deck, among others who were beyond caring whether they lay in their own excrement or not.

At last, in that vale of sorrow, I lost my temper and roared in my strongest voice that by all accounts could pierce marrow and bone and certainly penetrate every corner of a sixty-foot-long cargo deck, "Stop your bloody wailing, damn you! You ain't a-goin' to strike flag just because of a little bit of a breeze!"

And to Jack I shouted, "Can't you explain to those accursed blockheads that we ain't a-goin' to sink to the bottom?"

"They won't listen," said Jack encouragingly. "They think death is nigh."

"Shiver my timbers!" I screeched. "If you think I'm going to go along with just anything, you're wrong! Now do as I say. Tell 'em this is a good ship, that storms like this are nothing to be afeared of. Say I've been out in weather like this hundreds o' times and I'm still alive, as they can see, even if not in the best o' health. And make 'em understand that there's nothing unusual in feeling like shit at first when the ship starts pitching and tossing. It'll pass. And they won't die of it neither, whether they wants to or not."

Jack had little sympathy for my views, but in the end I managed to persuade him that what I was saying was the truth, and I could hear him muttering to the nearest sorry wretches on both sides of us. But it sounded feeble.

"To think you're supposed to be a Sakalava!" said I in scorn.

In a flash I felt a pair of weak hands fumbling at my throat.

"So," said I jocularly, "you're going to throttle your own brother?"

The hands fell away and the next instant I heard a faint chuckle in the darkness. I'm damned if he wasn't laughing, and I felt a touch of pride in what I could achieve in my better moments. Making people want to live has always been one of my strong points. But I didn't make life easy for anyone either. You can't have the one without the other, that's what I've always said, if anyone would ever give me an ear.

When Jack spoke up again he did at least try to make himself heard. It took a while, but gradually the din lessened enough to become bearable.

My good humour started to revive and I slapped Jack on what I thought to be his back but turned out to be his solar plexus, and so winded him.

"I'm sorry, shipmate," said I magnanimously. "Now I think we can start to do business with this crew."

"Business?" said Jack wonderingly.

"The first thing is to make sure this mob understands what we say. If we're going to keep our noses above water, we have to get our mouths to do more than eating. Silence is the same as death, that I can tell you. If we can just understand one another I reck'n we can give this ship Hell, and have our revenge. That'd be no more'n right."

Jack was eventually carried along by my ardour and started doling out questions and advice to port and starboard.

It took two whole days to get order into the chaos. It was no easy task, you may lay to it, to keep account of near enough three hundred slaves with nothing to write with. We had to position those who had knowledge of languages so that messages would spread as quickly as possible. Some knew a little English and over a hundred knew at least two languages. Many had been taken in battle and served as slaves to other tribes, perhaps even for several years, until one of their kings had finally hit upon the idea of earning some blunt by selling them to the whites. No, the blacks were no better than us in that respect.

I asked Jack whether there were any more of his indomitable tribal brethren aboard, and he named a dozen. None of the names was pronounceable without twisting your tongue. But they were Sakalavas, and when I found out that Jack was a descendant of one of their kings I understood at once that they would look up to him and do his bidding, as is the way with most folk. So it was with these Sakalavas that I began to organise my grand reshuffle, to make life difficult for Scudamore for a start.

It was a sight without compare. Negroes crawled and clambered around one another, over and under one another, caught against one another, knocked into one another, pushed and pulled, the whole time two by two, in helplessly indivisible pairs. It went well enough when both were willing and made their way together. But some had to drag along cumbersome burthens, either because their partners were so infirm that they could no longer move unaided, or because they had given up and lost all hope, which was also a sort of infirmity, though of the mind. Or because they were stone dead and no one had yet cast them overboard.

The groans and lamentations could not be eliminated in every corner, but at least I had managed to make it plain to them that some of us would end our days like the three slave-masters if it were discovered what we were plotting.

By daybreak most of us, myself included, were so exhausted that half the cargo hold was snoring. I summoned my last ounce of strength to watch Scudamore's face when he came down to do his morning round. I shall not forget the sight for a long time to come. He must have perceived that something was different as soon as he arrived, because he halted at the bottom of the ladder.

"They're asleep!" he exclaimed to Tim Allison, the youngest on board, who had taken over my hardly enviable task of keeping Hell clean.

"What else should they be doin'?" he asked, reasonably enough.

"They're like cats, Tim. They sleep with their eyes open and their ears pricked. And they're wide awake as soon as they hear our footsteps. They're afraid we'll murder them while they sleep. Yet now they're sleeping like logs. Something's happened here in the night. But what? Be on your guard, Tim. You can never be too careful."

"No, sir."

Scudamore took a few tentative steps forward and bent down to inspect his first invalid. I could imagine his crafty eyes opening wide.

"What in Hell's name is this?" said he.

Tim hurried over to him.

"What is it, sir?"

"What is it?" Scudamore repeated to himself disbelievingly. "Yesterday this man was on the point of dying of fever. I'd more or less written him off. And now he's lying here fast asleep and as healthy as you or me as far as I can see."

"That's good, sir," said Tim. "You've cured 'im."

"Maybe," said Scudamore thoughtfully, "maybe."

He was no less perplexed in his evil soul when he examined the others on his list of the sick. It seemed as if every one of them had recovered overnight. Tim spoke of miracles, but Scudamore was not that stupid. He began running around all over the place and very soon found some nigh on lifeless ones lying elsewhere. He muttered and cursed because he had to start again from the beginning and examine each and every one anew. It took nearly the whole day, and when he had finished he was so angry, confused and exhausted that I burst out laughing at him. My mirth knew no bounds, and he was soon standing over me with a countenance that boded no good.

"What the Devil do you look like?" said I. "You must have got out of bed the wrong side this morning."

"Silver," he snarled, "I don't know what you think is so funny, but you'd better watch yourself. Don't forget that you're living on grace, on my grace."

"I haven't forgotten, Scudamore. I'm eternally indebted to you, you know that."

"Don't try it on, Silver. You can't deceive me!"

"No, Scudamore, don't fret yourself, I'm smart enough to see that you're invincible in that respect."

"Have you had a finger in this game?"

"What game?" I asked innocently.

"Playing hide-and-seek with the blacks."

"You'll have to pardon me, Scudamore, but I don't know what you're talking about."

"No?"

"On my honour, Scudamore . . ."

"Your honour," said he with a coarse laugh. "I wouldn't give a lot for that."

"It ain't for sale, neither," I replied. "If you don't believe me, that's your business. I don't have to answer for your foolishness, on top of everything else I've been punished for."

He gave me an unforgiving look, turned abruptly and left. My first good deed would be to send Scudamore mad and out of his wits if I possibly could. I had some success in my endeavour, for in the two months the voyage lasted, we shifted some of the sick around every single night, until finally he could stand no more and asked the Captain if, in addition to our fetters, we could be chained down in the ship, as far as he was concerned for ever and a day. But the first mate, who had taken over from Butterworth, rejected his request. The death tally among the slaves was lower than the average, and so he did not want to make any significant changes. And it was true that fewer than was customary had been struck down, but no thanks to Scudamore. In all modesty, I'll warrant that it could be ascribed in part to your humble servant, who coaxed a not inconsiderable number of the negroes into wanting to live for a little while longer.

Butterworth, on the other hand, did not survive the voyage, and no one can say that his demise was any great loss, if indeed it is in the case of anyone; with the exception of my good self, needless to say. He only had himself to blame: his lust was his undoing, and he had plenty of time for remorse before he died. We were two weeks out from Accra when to my inordinate joy I heard the whole story from Tim, who without too much trouble I had been able to draw into my confidence. He felt sorry for me, and I let him think there was every reason to be, as indeed there was. The fact that I was in good spirits was not as it was intended to be.

Tim came running across, as well as he could in the jumble of arms and legs, and blurted out that Butterworth was within an ace of dying.

"Don't look so afeared, lad!" said I, since he had an air of great affliction. "I'd gladly exchange places with Butterworth rather than lie rotting here. If you on'y knew how often I'd wanted to fall asleep for good."

But Tim was so overwhelmed that he hardly heard what I said.

"Mr Silver," he croaked, "'tis a dreadful thing!"

And I'm damned if I didn't see moisture clouding his eyes.

"Calm yourself down!" said I sharply. "One cap'n more nor less ain't naught to grieve over. There's enough on 'em as it is."

"It ain't that, Mr Silver. Cap'n Butterworth's 'ad 'is prick bitten off!"

"What?" I exclaimed, overcome by astonishment and delight.

"I saw it meself," Tim went on with sobs in his throat. "The cap'n 'ad given me orders to stand guard at 'is door an' not let anyone in, whoever it might be. Then I 'eard a terrible scream from inside, but I didn't rightly know what to do. I durst not open the door without an order. But then it suddenly opened an' one o' the negro women rushed past afore I could stop 'er. I looked in the cabin because I could 'ear moanin'. An' then I saw 'im, Mr Silver. 'E was a-sittin' on a chair with 'is legs all bare, pale as a corpse 'e was, like as if 'e was dead a'ready, an' 'oldin' the stump of 'is prick. Blood was pourin' out, Mr Silver, it was 'orrible. It was comin' in spurts, like a bilge pump. Oh, 'twas fearful to be'old!"

His legs would no longer support him and he collapsed at my feet. I heaved myself and Jack up to a half-sitting position and patted Tim on the head in a fatherly fashion.

"Don't take it so hard!" said I. "Life's like that sometimes. But you gets used to it. Think of all the men in the navy who're a-muck with blood in every attack. How would it be if they was to burst into tears at ev'ry scratch?"

"But it were 'is prick," said Tim, his voice cracking, "it were . . ."

The poor lad could get no more words past his trembling lips.

"Pull yourself together, now!" said I. "Butterworth won't have any need for his member up in Heaven as far as I'm aware. That kind o' thing's taboo up there."

Tim gazed up at me with a pleading look in his eyes.

"Snap out of it, lad!" I insisted. "The negroes will think you're cryin' over Cap'n Butterworth. Us down here and him up there wasn't exactly the best o' shipmates."

"No, no," said Tim, shaking his head. "I don't like 'im neither, but . . ."

". . . but you've a good imagination. You must've thought about what it would feel like if it was you that had been docked. But it ain't. Yours is still there where it's always been. No one, mark my words, lad, feels any better for putting himself in the shoes of others. You might as well jump overboard without further ado. No, be o' good cheer, an' do your friend John Silver a service. Go up on deck an' find out what's happened, whether that fiend of a cap'n will live or not. An' the woman, d'you know who it were?"

"No," said he, a faint rosiness returning to his ashen cheeks. "I 'ardly saw 'er, an' they all looks the same, the whole lot on 'em."

"Not if you got any eyes in your head, Tim."

"I 'ad to fetch Scudamore," he said by way of explanation and apology.

"You done right!" said I emphatically.

Nothing could set a low-spirited and despondent younker like Tim on his feet again so well as a little praise. And indeed he rose and went on his way, though with faltering steps, as it looked to me.

I lay back down and related to Jack what had happened. He grinned and thumped me in the stomach, as I had done to him by mistake and that he now imitated, before sending round a few carefully chosen words to the others. In a few moments there was no doubt of the sounds of joy I could hear. The blacks who shared my fate sometimes hoisted flags that were not to be found in my list of signals, but they were not that damn difficult to understand if you just listened. And for once the heathens' gods and witchcraft had surpassed the Almighty and brought Him to His knees.

Later that same evening Tim was back again.

"The cap'n's gone," he declared, without seeming too upset about it.

He had already managed to forget what it was that had been so dreadful.

"What d'you mean?" I asked. "Shiver my sides! Couldn't our skilful surgeon handle a trifle like that, ampytating a prick an' staunching the blood with a branding-iron?"

"He weren't even allowed to try. The cap'n refused to let Scudamore touch 'im. An' when 'e fin'lly lost 'is senses, it were too late to do anythin'."

"By the powers, Tim, I thinks I understands the cap'n."

Tim gave me an enquiring look.

"Ay," I explained, "who wouldn't rather strike his flag than let Scudamore play about with his holy of holies? 'Cause I can tell you one thing, he's a real sodomite and a real heathen. Nothing is holy to him. You be on your guard agin' him!"

Tim nodded and understood the serious tone of what I said.

"An' the woman?" I asked in passing.

"God knows!" Tim burst out. "It were o'ny me as saw 'er, an' yet I didn't see 'er. The 'ole thing is my fault."

"Your fault? How so?"

"The fact that we can't punish 'er for doin' it!"

"Punish?" said I. "She ought to get a reward, if you asks me! Do anyone think they knows who it might've been?"

"No. Butterworth 'ad so many, it might be any one on 'em. An' 'e kept it secret. He fetched 'em hisself an' thought no one saw him. Because it ain't allowed."

"Then he's on'y got hisself to blame, that's what I thinks. So nobody'll be punished?"

"Ay, a dozen are goin' to get a taste o' the whip. But no more'n will heal by the time we reach port."

So no one was going to be hanged, not even the woman who had bitten so well, like a real man if you ask me: the woman I'd picked out for myself. For I was sure of it – it must be the very same woman that Butterworth had stolen right in front of my eyes who had brought his life to an end. And that, I thought with a sense of satisfaction that flooded through me like a river, surging over the banks and smashing all dams, that was a woman to my taste and after my nature, no more and no less, as sure as my name's John Silver.

What I did not know was that Butterworth's shameful end frightened the crew out of their wits, or, at any rate, out of their lusts. In no time at all the *Carefree* became the most celibate vessel ever to ply the seas on the triangular route. And best of all, even Scudamore was scared into curbing his filthy lechery. It was not long before the whole crew looked like a bunch of grave-diggers, because women were their only joy, except for rum, and that was rationed. Ay, as time went on I think I probably preferred lying where I was, despite the stench, the shackles, the chafing, the moans and wheezing of the sick, the fatalists who did not want to live at all, the mess of grain that was our only provender till we neared land, the excrement that seemed to get everywhere whenever there was the slightest breeze and the hatches were battened down, the jeers that rained down on me whenever I showed myself on deck – ay, any of this was preferable for the likes of me. I was the one accomplishing something of value, after all, not the men on deck. But I will gladly admit I envied the woman who had so simply and painlessly, in a manner of speaking, known how to put the whole crew of the *Carefree* in their place.

I did what I could myself to dispel the state of miserable dejection that prevailed below deck. I provided encouragement and used my head and my words to help them, hard enough as it was to think of anything at the beginning. But as Jack and I came to know each other better, a plan started to form in my mind. I was damned if I would not make sure that the slave-dealers who bought slaves from this cargo would get more than they bargained for.

So I started telling all those who would listen what I knew of the worse Hell that was awaiting them on the other side of the ocean. I did what I could to explain, for instance, that the idea with the likes of them was that they should be profitable, and that white men did not take slaves in order to punish them, only to fill their coffers.

But as far as the negroes were concerned it went in one ear and straight out of the other without leaving a trace. They were even more sceptical when I told them they would have to toil on the sugar plantations, dig, sow, harvest and till the earth. Ay, some of them even began to laugh, thinking not even white men were stupid enough to have men doing the work of women. Their custom was for the women to till the soil while they themselves went hunting or to war. Anything else was beneath their dignity. I told them I didn't give a fig, their dignity was of no interest to me, but that they would soon find out that the plantation owner cared even less than I what they felt about the matter.

They only began to believe me when I started listing what would happen if they did not work until they dropped, or if they took it into their heads to escape into the mountains, going maroon as it was called. On St Thomas they did not content themselves with an honest four-strand rope whip and an equally decent hanging. No, they had additional punishments: the amputation of a leg or a hand, branding on the forehead, clamping in red-hot irons, breaking limbs on the wheel, severing ears and other small but vital parts.

Finally, I said, since I was beginning to understand something of the negroes' way of thinking, there was no point in their letting themselves die after their hundred and fifty lashes or worse. They would never get back to their homeland and kinsfolk, leastways not in one piece, because if anyone suffocated himself, or just let himself die, the body would be chopped up into portions to be hung in a tree, so that all could see that the dead man was still among them, whether he wanted to be or no.

Words like these made an impression, but obviously they did not exactly raise spirits on board. There was woe and lamentation everywhere. Even Jack grumbled that I was completely taking away their will to live, that they could not live without something to hope for.

"Well I'll lay to it there's masses of folk who lives without hope or anything. But at least they don't take their own lives like some o' these fatalists that we have to put up with on board. No, first of all you have to know you're alive, and then perhaps you can do something about it."

But without Jack it would not have been possible to get the negroes to see reason. He was not only the grandson of a king: he was also a person the natives regarded as having soul. It was not easy to comprehend what that meant, but for his fellow-tribesmen Jack's word was law, and they obeyed him blindly. Ay, in that respect he outshone by far a captain appointed by the grace of God, who needed the cat, keel-hauling, his fists, marlin-spikes and much else besides to keep his men subservient. And Jack had also observed enough of white men to know they held nothing sacred, but only perceived in things whatever might be to their advantage. And he could handle a flintlock and had seen what devastation a twelve-pounder loaded with grapeshot and case-shot could wreak on a crowd of natives.

But even Jack could not open the eyes of the ones I called fatalists. A score or so, like enough, came into that category. Scudamore called it chronic melancholy in his jargon, and the result was almost always deadly, and no wonder, since they just lay down to die. And as if that were not bad enough, I had one of them right by my side.

He was as silent as the grave, and I would hardly have noticed him had not Scudamore begun attending to him. When I inspected him closely I too could see that he was not much more than skin and bone and a pair of feverish, watery eyes.

"The bastard hasn't eaten or drunk anything for a week," said Scudamore.

"What's wrong with him?" I asked.

"His head. He's made up his mind to leave this world for good."

"What do you mean to do about it? You ain't going to let him get away with it?"

"Are you mad? He's perfectly healthy otherwise."

Scudamore pulled out of his pocket an instrument that reminded me of a cross between a pair of compasses and a corkscrew, what was called a *speculum oris*, a mouth-opener. He parted the negro's thick lips with one hand and tried to push the two ends in between his teeth. But the negro bit hard and I could see his jaw muscles tensing. Scudamore was not to be deterred so easily; he just pushed harder until two teeth fell out and let the points through.

"The teeth aren't so firmly fixed after a while," he calmly explained. "The difficult thing is not to press so hard that it goes right through into the neck."

"Ain't none o' them worked out the trick?"

"What trick?"

"Holding tight and then suddenly opening their jaws when you're least expecting it. That way they'd die as fast as they liked."

Scudamore looked at me in admiration.

"No," said he, as if he'd had a revelation. "They haven't. Strange, now you come to mention it."

He screwed the wheel so that the two arms moved apart and forced the negro's mouth open. Then he started pouring the gob-gravy, as the mess of food was called by the blacks, down his throat. And the negro swallowed, that he did, when he could equally well have let himself choke. I have come to understand as the years have passed that the business of suicide and how to go about it is not that simple, because some methods seem to be regarded as worse than death. But the negro was leading both Scudamore and me by the nose in any case, because as soon as Scudamore had turned his back he spewed all over me. I gave him a resounding thwack on the head. Wasn't it enough that I had to lie there watching him die by his own choice? Did he think that on top of that he could do just what he damned well liked? He could at least show a bit of common decency.

The same spectacle was repeated the next day, the only difference being that he spewed in the opposite direction. Scudamore was getting nowhere and I was getting more and more nettled.

"Ask him," I said to Jack, "why he's so bloody keen to die!"

Jack had to ask over and over again before he got anything resembling an answer out of him. But making him say something was enough to bring him back to life a little. It was not much of an answer, 'tis true, no more than expected. He was unhappy and he wanted to go home. He felt like the very Devil, of course.

But what was it, I got Jack to ask him, that was so special about him and his situation? Why didn't we all just take our own lives if he was right that it was so terrible lying there as we were? Didn't he understand that his depression was a slap in the face for the likes of us who were doing what we could to keep up our spirits in this vale of tears?

And so it went on day after day. I left him no peace. But did it help? Did he listen? Ay, he must have heard some of what I said. One day I explained the trick with the mouth-opener to him and said he could at least take his own life speedily so that I didn't have to have such a shameful wretch beside me. And shiver my timbers if he didn't see the point, in a manner of speaking, because the next time Scudamore started pushing, the negro opened his mouth so suddenly that the implement shot through his teeth and pierced his throat. Scudamore swore with rage when he pulled out the opener and saw blood gushing from his mouth and neck. He did not even attempt to stem the flow. In an instant the *Carefree* was one negro the poorer and Scudamore had lost a dividend.

He glowered at me, as if it was my fault.

"By all the fiends in Hell, I'm glad he's gone!" said I, and meant it. "He put me out of humour."

"It was you who told him what to do!" Scudamore spat out. "It was you who killed him!"

"No, Scudamore, now you're going too far. How would I be able to explain anything at all to the likes of a negro from Angola? I may be able to speak Latin, but d'you think a negro would understand it? And who was holding the mouth-opener, may I ask? Was it me? No, sling the bastard in the sea. That's what he most wanted, after all. Don't look so gloomy, Scudamore. One negro slave more or less makes no difference at all in the long run. Not even to your purse."

Scudamore went off muttering, and no wonder, because it was far from easy for him. Things got so bad in the end that he hardly durst show himself on the slave deck, purely and simply for fear of being beaten or bitten to death. That was something to be pleased about, and I was, because it irked me to know that I could not get the fatalists to see reason. That's how it was then and that's the way it has always been. With the likes of them it makes no difference what words you use, that's my experience. They don't listen. All they hear is an echo of themselves in their empty heads. They're not bothered whether I exist or not, that's all there is to it, and nothing to be done.

As the voyage neared its end the crew and the new captain livened up. We were taken up on deck again and again to wash and rub one another with oil. For the first time our food was as it should have been according to regulations, including rum, since now it was known that the stores would last out. We had managed well. Sixty-five slaves and eight seamen had perished. The cargo hold was sluiced down with saltpetre and fumigated with juniper twigs. The hatches were opened wide and let in warm but fresh equatorial air. Even the sores from the unplaned boards began to heal, and the new captain reduced sail so that we would all look as fresh and healthy as possible by the time we reached harbour.

And I continued my stories and explanations throughout. I don't think I've talked so much in the whole of my life. When I had finished, everyone who had paid heed knew how to load a musket, how to spike a cannon, how to stick a knife in from below and upwards into the ribs for the best effect – all the useful little things that I had picked up in ports and on board ship in my ten years with Wilkinson. So one thing I was sure of was that the slaves on the *Carefree* would create sheer Hell for their owners and make them a loss like no other they had ever sustained. For if they did not rebel sooner or later, they would escape and join the maroon negroes in the mountains. That was as certain as an amen in church, and vengeance as good as any. And if there is aught in my life that I am proud of, it is that I put the blacks on their feet again, against all the odds and despite the fact that they had nothing to risk or lose.

I had no time even to ponder much on my own situation, as I became aware when the first mate arrived of a sudden on the slave deck a few days ere we were due to make landfall.

"Silver," said he, "in my opinion you've been sufficiently punished."

"Sir," I replied in a respectful voice, "my signature on the round robin was counterfeit."

"I've heard rumours of that nature. 'Twill be for the court to determine. If 'tis as you say, you'll be freed, like enough. But I want to set you free now. It don't look good to put a white man ashore with all the blacks."

"Sir," I entreated, with all my powers of persuasion, "I've got too many en'mies on board. If it comes to court, 'twill be my word against others. It won't work out, sir. I'll be hanged. Ain't it enough that I've been keel-hauled and a'ready spent two months in this Hell?"

The first mate was silent for a few moments.

"What's your plan?" he asked eventually.

"Sell me to the highest bidder at the auction as a contract worker, along with the others."

He looked at me in amazement.

"I can't do that," said he. "You're white and a Christian."

"Contract workers go under the hammer, no matter how white they are."

"Ay, but not alongside the blacks."

"But don't you understand, sir? 'Tis my only chance to pacify them as are agin' me. Naught would please 'em more than to see me sold as a slave. In their eyes there could be no better punishment for the likes o' me. They'd be very content for me to be humiliated and crawl in the shit, you may take your affy-davy on it."

The first mate looked at me long and hard.

"You're the on'y one worth anything on this hulk," I added. "You must see how 'tis."

"Have it your own way, Silver," he exclaimed, "but I'm damned if I understand you."

"You don't need to, sir. Thank'ee kindly, sir. I never forgets a favour. You can depend on John Silver."

"No," he replied, "the risk of you forgetting is pretty small after a few years on the plantations. Well, you've only yourself to blame."

"Ay, ay, sir, 'twould never occur to me to think otherwise."

The voyage had lasted two months, which was as ordinary and as fortunate as could be expected by any standards. A fifth of the cargo was lost to the pox, chronic melancholy and other sickness. For a tight-packer like Butterworth it was nothing, and his family, if he had any, must have thanked God for the fine profit, and not just because it was in the captains' instructions that God should be thanked in a special service for a successfully completed slave voyage.

Almost a third of the crew died as well: that was nothing to grieve over, either. They had never had the means to invest in the game of life, and it was quite fitting that they should lose the only thing they owned, their lives, the only thing they had to hazard. That too was something to thank God for if you were a shipowner or a captain, though silently of course. The homeward trip did not require as many crew as the slave route, and by this means the number was reduced in the most natural way conceivable. But astonishingly, none of the mutineers was among those who died. They had to wait until they came under Roberts' command and were hanged, together with forty-six others, among them Scudamore, by the Fort of Cape Corso, below the high-water mark as was the custom, in the year of grace 1722.

So this crossing counted as a success, for those who knew no better, but this opinion was doubtless not shared by the likes of the first mate, who had taken over command from Butterworth, and Scudamore, who heaved sighs of relief when the soldiers came streaming on board and delivered them from further obligation for the welfare of the negroes. For the inhabitants of St Thomas had probably never before set eyes on slaves of the kind that came ashore from the good ship *Carefree*.

They were looking around them, chattering away in their own tongues, and behaving almost like ordinary people. They knew what awaited them. They no longer believed they would be slaughtered like kine, but understood, on the contrary, that there was an interest in keeping them alive for as long as they might live, and that they had nothing to lose other than their lives, as long as they lived.

And that, I thought with no little pride as I walked among them, as stark naked as the rest, as oiled in the same glistening grease as they were, to pull the wool over the eyes of the plantation owners at the auction, that was my work! I, John Silver, a naked, lily-white master mariner in their midst, had employed my quick tongue to give them something to live for in Hell, the knowledge of what it was like and the price to be paid for passively accepting it. Not even Butterworth had been able to prevent it while he lived. He had turned me into a slave and had only himself to blame. Now there was a trouble-maker being offered for sale, no more and no less.

Behind us trudged the *Carefree*'s own crew, gaunt, disheartened, sickly and in desperate need of drinking themselves into oblivion to forget their misery. They looked the way crews usually look when they have survived the slave run. There was nothing remarkable in that. For them there was no hope. They did not know what life was worth, other than that it was something to be drowned in brandy. That was also a kind of vengeance, although I could not take the credit for that myself.

Twenty-three

SO I WAS taken up to the fort on St Thomas along with all the rest on the day after the *Carefree* had anchored in the roads. We were herded into a warehouse and given hand-some quantities of food, porridge with thick layers of sugar, fresh meat with rind and fat on, vegetables and poor-quality rum, what the blacks called killdevil. That was what they used the rum for, after all, to kill the Devil in their Hell of a life.

Scudamore went round to see if he could remedy any of the most obvious ailments at the last minute to wring out every shilling of his coveted fee. He cured three men suffering from diarrhoea by pushing a plug of rope into their arseholes, one of the usual old stratagems.

For four days we were fattened up, washed and oiled, while messages were sent out to the island's plantation owners to tell them that a new cargo of slaves had landed and would be sent to auction the following Sunday, after Mass.

The day before the festival Scudamore took me to one side.

"Silver," said he, "it hurts me to see you here amongst the others, even if you are a contract worker and have a few rags on your body. Your white skin offends the eyes. The negroes might get the idea that there's no difference between them and us."

"That's hardly my fault," I replied.

"There's still time to repent," said he.

"And be taken to court and hanged! No, thank you. If the mutineers are happy with me being sold as a contract worker, that's preferable to a trial that can have only one outcome."

"You're forgetting my testimony."

"Not in the least," I replied. "I know how well you wish me. Butterworth is dead, however, and he was the only one who could vouch for your words. You'd be one single surgeon against six experienced seamen. It ain't a risk I'd care, or dare, to take."

I did not say what I was really thinking, of course, that the greatest risk of all was that Scudamore would entice me into court and then bear witness that would ensure I would leave this world for good. After all, he was afraid of the likes of me staying alive, even as a slave, because I think he understood by the end that I was not to be trifled with. Life was not the game Scudamore reckoned, because a game has rules. But on matters of life and death there are no rules on this earth. So it does not pay in the long run to cheat, the way Scudamore and so many other educated folk did.

On the day of the auction we were let out into a fenced enclosure. Clusters of expectant people were hanging over the fence or standing around in excited groups. The air was full of yelling and laughter, whispering and murmuring, fingers were pointed, and there were cries of delight and insolent jeers. The last, to be honest, were mostly directed at me. For there was no doubt that I was a special attraction at this meat market.

I looked around for the woman I had found so much to my taste. She was standing by herself, off to one side, with a haughty air as if she were not interested in the rest of us in the slightest. I made my way through the crowd and stood before her. I saw what I had wanted to see, that she was not the sort to submit to anyone, not even to me. But she responded to my gaze and gave a hint of a smile.

That was all, because suddenly there was the sound of drums and a man in a frilled shirt came forward and announced that the auction was about to commence. I kept close to the woman, because I knew what to expect. It had been explained to us that this auction was to be a scramble, as was customary when it was a seller's market and the plantation owners had to take what they could get. The company set a fixed price per slave and let the plantation owners into the enclosure. They then bought for the stipulated price the slaves they managed to lay hands on.

The signal was given. I took the woman by the hand, and she gave no sign of objecting. My idea was that we should be taken and bought together, just as other women were pressing their children close to them so that they would not be separated. Not that it did any good for the most part. It was even known for a woman and the child in her womb to be separated, though not at a scramble, obviously.

The plantation folk threw themselves upon us. They grasped and pulled at arms or whatever they could get hold of, amidst all the noise, shouting and laughter. Children screamed when they were torn away from their mothers. Oaths rained down when people crashed into each other in the confusion and started fighting over the same slave. Some had the sense to examine the slaves as they grabbed them, and let go a few, while others with flushed cheeks raked in their purchases indiscriminately. It was one of them who with a lecherous grin tugged at the woman by my side. I let myself be dragged along too, but was stopped by a blow on the chest.

"Go to Hell!" said the man to me in my own tongue. "I don't want any bloody traitor!"

"I'm a slave," said I politely. "I can pull my weight."

"Go shit yourself!" was the curt response.

Plainly the rumour had travelled. And sure enough, I then caught sight of Roger Ball's pig-like snout in the crowd outside the fence. He was pointing at me and saying something to those around him, and guffawing in his loud, taunting, self-satisfied and mirthless way. I was not far from losing my head and rushing over and breaking his neck. But I had at last begun to learn the price that could often be paid for losing your head, and calmed myself.

Gradually the worst of the hubbub and turmoil abated. Sweaty and breathless plantation owners stood around here and there with groups of slaves they had selected. I saw Jack in one group with the woman and three men from his own tribe, the Sakalava. That was as much as he could have hoped for. I also observed that the three whose arses Scudamore had plugged with wads of rope had been sold. I myself, the arch-slave, and two others who had the clap were the only ones that nobody wanted.

The man in the frilled shirt made sweeping gestures and said a whole lot of words in Danish. He was evidently trying to drum up enthusiasm for the three of us who were left. After a while a well-dressed man went up to the official and they could be seen arguing back and forth before shaking hands, whereupon the well-dressed man walked over to the two infected slaves and took them away with him. It was no doubt the local surgeon who, because of the scramble, had missed out on his usual consignment of the sick to cure and sell on.

The only one left at the end was me, Long John Silver. The auctioneer was waving his arms with even more vigour and stressing the usefulness of a strong and intelligent man like me, correctly handled. But the crowd remained silent, except for Roger Ball, of course, who could not resist bellowing out, "You're gettin' what you deserve, Silver. No one's a-goin' to touch you with a barge-pole!"

This brought a few scattered chuckles from the crowd. The auctioneer looked round almost in desperation and shouted something to the gathering, perhaps, I thought, that he was now open to any bid whatsoever. It was not long before the crowd parted to let through a man with white hair. But only when he came fully into view did I apprehend what he was, a black-coat, a man of the cloth. He crossed over to me at a slow and stately pace. What the Devil was the meaning of it? Was I to receive absolution for my sins before being hanged after all? Had they all been leading me by the nose?

"Come with me, my son!" said he in a paternal tone, in broken English.

"Why?" I asked.

"Why?" he repeated. "To go into service on the mission's plantation, of course."

Well, of course, what else? That was where Father Feltman's slaves branded with a cross must have been intended for, because on reflection it occurred to me that they had not been there at the scramble. And what about me? Was it pure greed that had made the priest take pity on me? He would not be able to convert me, leastways, since as a white man I was already of the right faith, whatever I might think of it.

"Father!" said I. "Have pity on a poor sinner!"

"I shall indeed!" said he without turning round.

Suddenly I could restrain myself no longer, and burst out laughing at the top of my voice. They must all have thought the priest should not have bought a madcap like me. I thought so myself. For me to be a slave of the God-fearing must have been a manifestation of the unfathomable will of God Himself. I asked the priest and discovered it was as I thought, that he had got me for nothing and taken me out of charity. The contract would run for three years, and after that I would be free to take employment wherever I wanted.

I must admit my thoughts turned momentarily to England and Deval, not to regret their fate but to curse my own. In my mind I went through my life so far and could not see much to be proud of, even though I say it myself. Well, I was going to be punished for it anyhow.

I was put in with the plantation negroes. To be a house slave you had to be trusted, which I was not, with some justification. I found myself among a score of blacks whose eyes widened when I walked into their hut. I had learned from Jack a few words of greeting and pleasantries in African tongues, and I made use of them now, but it turned out that these negroes spoke Danish. As luck would have it, two of them had been bought from Englishmen on Jamaica after the great uprising and were able to be spokesmen for me.

I let the negroes stare at my appearance as much as they liked. It was a baleful gaze, partly because I was white, and partly because I was a *bussal*, an ass, which was what they called all newly arrived slaves. Ay, even among these serfs there was a ranking, and I was on the lowest level. I nipped it in the bud, however, by asking respectfully who was their leader, having him pointed out to me, a man with the most self-righteous countenance of them all, and going up to him and seizing him by the throat. I pressed harder and harder, calmly asking my spokesmen at the same time to explain to the others that I, John Silver, might be a slave and a *bussal*, but that I was untouchable, invulnerable, taboo, and had a soul, together with much more in the same vein. When all of them, including their elected oppressor, seemed to have understood, I let go and lay down on a bed of straw that was like pure goose-down after the unplaned boards on the *Carefree*. Before I fell asleep I remember thinking that the time had come to be done with half-measures, and I think it was from that instant that I always had the red flag ready to hoist. The black one, the Jolly

Roger, I had, in a manner of speaking, hoisted long before.

On the morrow I was awakened at daybreak by a well-placed kick from a foot protruding from a priest's cloak.

"Up with you!" said the priest's voice.

Even he knew a few words of English. They were educated, at any rate.

"What in God's name are you kicking *me* for?" said I. "I'll do whatever's expected of me." I struggled up under the priest's watchful eye, and out we went into the fields. The priest was behind us with a whip in one hand and a wooden club in the other. He cracked the whip in the air from time to time as if we were a team of oxen. The priests obviously depended more on themselves and their God than other plantation owners, because they made no use of any slave-masters.

As soon as we could see our hands in front of our faces we were hacking the hard clay soil with our picks. We dug holes, nothing else, holes in straight lines, one after another, without repose, from dawn to dusk, in the baking sun that burned the white skin of my back. By midday I had large suppurating blisters on my hands. It could only end in one way. Shortly before we were to get our third ration of sugar water and rum, the fuel we were stoked with, I started lagging behind. By that stage I could hardly hold the pick. Before I knew where I was, I heard a whishing sound and felt the sting of the whip cutting into my flesh. I had to summon all my restraint to stop myself killing the swine of a priest on the spot, but I was not that stupid, because I would not have got far, half naked and with gashes on my back and scars on my hands. So instead I turned to him.

"For the love of God, Father, show some mercy!"

"The likes of you should beware of taking the name of the Lord in your dirty mouths. Here it's you who work for us so that we can work for God."

"But I'm a Christian, Father. Baptised in holy water an' all. I didn't think Christians had to taste the whip."

"Well, you thought wrong. The only thing that's not allowed by our regulations is for a negro to lay hands on a white man. Everything else is permitted. And we keep to the regulations, my man."

This priest was not to be moved. I learned later that Holt, for such was his name, was the cruellest of them all, and it has to be said that none of them were God's favourite children in that respect. A couple of weeks earlier Holt had beaten a two-year-old boy to death with his bare hands. And he used the plaited silk whip on the children constantly, though it was intended for adults. He was unrivalled in his domain, was Holt, notorious over the whole island.

So I bit my lip even though I was roaring and screaming within as my lacerated hands strove to hold the pick. What saved me from more lashes of the whip was the others, I have to say in their favour. When they saw how things were going they slacked their pace imperceptibly, just as much as they could risk without Holt observing. That evening one of the women mixed an unguent which she put on my back and my hands. She repeated the same treatment three days in a row and my hands healed without mark or scar. It goes without saying that I counted myself lucky with my hands that I had tended so carefully ever since my conversation with Captain Barlow.

One night I crept over to the woman to show my gratitude. But just as we lay there with our juices mingling I was pulled away from her, given a few kicks and thrown out of the hut.

The next morning we were all lined up in front of the chapel. The woman had to be punished in the name of God for her immorality with a hundred and fifty lashes of the plaited whip.

Nowhere else on the island were the women punished for their lust. But the priests of course had their own wives sent over from Copenhagen, unsighted, selected by lot from the congregation's meagre stock of uneven quality. Thus it was that the head, Martin, had a sixty-five-year-old hag round his neck whom he could not bear to look upon, not even in the name of God. No, it did not surprise me in the least that the priests flogged young, firm, gleaming black, delicious female bodies as soon as they got hold of them. They could not touch them, for then they would be banished and have to suffer the torments of Hell for the rest of their lives.

In accordance with custom it was us slaves who had to carry out the punishment. When the whites had brandished the whip or the red-hot irons the negroes had gone completely wild instead of being frightened into submission. But now they more often than not kept in their place. Can people be so stupid?

We stepped forward one by one to administer our lashes, and had to listen to the woman's screams until she finally fell senseless. When I let the whip whistle through the air for the fifth time her back was one almighty bleeding wound. I hoped by God, if He existed, that one of the others would be able to brew up her healing salve afterwards.

It goes without saying that I was not happy where I had ended up. I started trying to become familiar with the high priest, who was more of an understanding person, at least in comparison with the others. He quickly saw for instance that I had certain linguistic gifts and that I could turn out a legible hand. I never became a house-boy, but he would borrow me sometimes from the cane fields to copy something or produce a final fair version. I still remember a letter to the mission from a newly baptised slave. He expressed his thanks in the letter for his salvation, while at the same time asking pardon for not being able to write the letter himself, hardly to be wondered at since he had neither hands nor feet. He had had them chopped off after running away as a maroon.

To think that people can be so utterly stupid.

My first thought was a simple one, to get away with a weapon in my hand, steal a boat and escape. I made myself useful in every way I could, but it was always some negro who was given the job and the affidavit that allowed him to be on the road when provisions had to be fetched. It has to be said in the priests' favour that they were not as easily fooled as might have been expected when it came to being on their guard with the likes of me.

There was nothing to be done but to trust in Providence – in myself, in other words. Once more I fanned the glow of the natives' simmering hatred, stirred them up with my poker, and soon enough they were aflame, in a manner of speaking. I promised them green forests and gold, as you have to in such circumstances, and in two weeks it was just a matter of adding one little spark to ignite them, which is literally what I did, because I set fire to the priests' house.

While the black-coats were running round like crazed chickens, forgetful of all prayers, I sequestered their weapons in the chapel. I took three pistols for my own use and distributed the rest to the negroes. It was not of much benefit to us, because most of them did not know how to reload. To help things along I brought down one of the priests with a well-aimed shot. I don't know which one it was, nor does it really matter *sub specie aeternitatis*. But it had its effect, for the other priests abandoned their attempts to quench the fire and rushed over to the chapel as if the flames were at their heels.

We could hear the heart-rending laments when they discovered their arsenal was empty, and then the silence that followed as they began to speculate how God might save them from their plight. The dwelling-house was soon completely engulfed in flames, the shadows of which were playing on the chapel. I told my men to shoot the moment they saw a glimpse of a black-coat, while I went round to the rear to see what I could do. If anything went wrong, I added, they should run off into the hills, because after this, they would be hanged. But, I selflessly proposed, as an alternative they could try to convince the priests that the whole affair was my fault. They would not hear of such a thing; they would rather take their chance as maroons, they said.

I said my farewells, a little ceremoniously, which is always an advantage in the event of meeting again, and crept off towards the chapel. When I peered in through a window at the back I saw one of the priests on his knees praying, to be on the safe side, while the others were conferring. It seemed to be Holt who was chosen to go in search of help, because he went to the church door and opened it cautiously, only to be greeted by a volley of three shots that thudded into the wall. He closed the door again with a resounding bang, and it was obvious that he was frightened out of his wits. Now that he no longer had the whip and God on his side he was not quite so courageous.

"We're lost!" he shrieked. "We'll never be able to get out of here and fetch help."

No, it was true, I thought, they were trapped like rats, because the chapel had only one exit.

"Halloo in there!" I shouted, making them all, even the priest at prayer, jump out of their skins.

"'Tis me, John Silver."

That certainly did not make Holt any calmer.

"I got away from those damned niggers," said I. "They mean to shoot holes in every white person they set eyes on. I can go and fetch help."

"Can you?" asked Martin.

"Ay. The coast is clear. The negroes are lying in wait around the door of the chapel. They're as stupid as sheep: they can't see that they could shoot you all through these window apertures. They're just a-waitin' for you to come out. I'll have no trouble getting past them, believe you me. Give me an affy-davy so I'll be believed, and I'll run as fast as my legs will carry me, as sure as my name's John Silver."

Martin and his brothers were hesitant, that was plain, especially when Holt muttered something that was certainly not to my advantage.

"Hurry!" I urged them. "You ain't got all night if you wants to see the light o' day again!"

Only afterwards did it strike me that it was perhaps not the best way of convincing the likes of them who had a secure future assured in Heaven. But Martin scribbled down the requisite words on a piece of paper.

"If you help us, Silver, we'll be eternally grateful to you. We'll all pray for you."

"Please do!" I replied happily, and snatched the paper. "Put in a good word for me in Heaven. It can't do any harm. I'm off. You're in safe hands, brothers!"

I stepped back, although I wasn't quite finished with them. I waited a few minutes and then sneaked back to the window aperture. I could see them all on their knees praying for their lives. I took aim, shot Holt through the head, and left to the sound of screams of fear and more shots fired at random by the negroes.

At last, I thought, as the noises died away behind me, I could feel pleased with myself. Not because I had freed the world from Holt – I was not that foolish, for there were always others to continue in his wake, just as one dead captain by God's infernal grace was always replaced by another before you knew where you were. Nor because I had meted out to Holt his rightful punishment for all the lashes. Who knows, perhaps he had already been received into Heaven, and what was the value of my punishment then? Nor because I had given the priests a sleepless night or made them believe the negroes were not as stupid as sheep after all. No, if I was pleased it was because I had led them all by the nose, negroes and priests alike, to my own advantage, and was at liberty again, for the first time in nearly a year.

With my safe-conduct in my pocket I made haste slowly towards Charlotte Amalia in the mild and starry night, surrounded by the blessedly peaceful chirping of the cicadas and the confoundedly irritating buzz of gnats and mosquitoes. It was still as black as pitch when I arrived and slipped past the sentries on the fort with no trouble. There was a spritsail tied up at the quay, belonging to one of the traders that was anchored off shore. Appropriating it, and using the ship's anchor lights as markers, I was able to steer out of the bay and set my course to the east.

Let no one think it was easy sailing, four hundred sea miles single-handed in an open boat, but I made good use of all that Dunn had taught me. Knowing how to meet a wave was vital, because it was the time of year when the trade winds were blowing at their strongest. No sooner had I left the lee of the islands than I encountered heavy, powerful, foam-crested waves thundering down on me in an endless succession. I had to steer with one hand and bail out with the other for more than a day and a night until I managed to make my way into a sheltered cove where I could put down anchor and have a good sleep.

It was even worse a week later when I reached eastern Hispaniola, one of the Spaniards' most fortified strongholds. I had to lie hidden in mangrove swamps by day and make my way forward as best I could by night in the light of the moon. In these accursed and appalling conditions I was not much more than skin and bone when I finally felt I had left the Pope's followers behind. My tangled hair was as stiff as a brush with all the salt. My lips were tight and split and I could hardly utter a word. My skin was as dry as tinder and I was sweating as if from a forest fire. I could hardly sit because both my buttocks had the worst sores imaginable, from chafing. And although I had slept in the bottom of the boat, I had sometimes had to anchor so close to land that I had been eaten alive by a host of bloodthirsty flying insects. Ay, John Silver was no sight for the gods, or maybe that is exactly what he was, when he was finally found and picked up, with not many more days to live, by some buccaneers of the old school who decided to make him their own.

Twenty-four

FREE AND WRETCHED as they were, those last surviving bastard crosses between hunters and pirates, for them time seemed to have stood still. They were sentimental old devils, still dreaming of the great expeditions to Panama and Cartagena, unable to understand that their time was past. They talked about the good old days with Morgan the Traitor, L'Olonnais the Bloody, Monbars the Exterminator, Grammont the Atheist, Le Roc the Brazilian, and Van Horn, who had no nickname but was known for running around the deck in battle and shooting anyone who displayed the slightest hint of hesitation or cowardice. They stuck rigidly to all their old customs and rituals, and most of them were fitting enough. They had councils and voted. They shared everything alike and owned everything in common. They had no surnames but called themselves by forename and nickname, so that who they were and where they came from counted neither to their benefit nor to their disadvantage.

As hunters they had no equal, and they were experts with food and cooking. They could make chocolate, a jealously guarded secret of the Spaniards, and knew that wild boar that had lived on apricots were tastier than others. They made monkey meat appetising with coarse salt, and were able to shoot the scoundrels without getting covered in shit. Believe it or not, I have myself seen monkeys doing it into their hands and then flinging their excrement on to the hunters for all they were worth. It was no easy matter to shoot them down from the trees either, because every shot had to kill them outright; if it did not they would hang on by one leg or one arm until the others came to the rescue and carried off their wounded comrade with fearful shrieks and jabberings that would distress the most callous.

There had to be meals upon the table, and the old buccaneers knew how to do it. And how to cook so that you salivated like dogs at the aroma – they knew that too. I learned a lot about cooking from them and picked up a skill that stood me in good stead later in life, both in the good old Spy-glass tavern in Bristol and on board the fateful *Hispaniola* that so nearly brought disaster upon me.

There were other things that were harder to put up with. They were God-fearing, those devils, saying grace at table and reading the Bible. I kept my counsel because I needed their good will to get on my feet again after my flight. But I cannot say I liked it. I had to hear over and over again, until I was sick of it, the eternal story of the buccaneer called Daniel, who took a man of the cloth on board at an anchorage and asked him to hold a service. They had not had God for a long time, he said. A temporary altar was set up on deck and the priest began to go through his usual patter, though in such fear that he was shaking. They had no bell to ring for prayers or hymns, but Daniel made up for it by firing off a cannon instead. All went well until the Communion, when one of the crew poured a whole bottle of the blood of Christ down his throat and started swearing and cursing extravagantly. Daniel rebuked him, but when the exhilarated man refused to show the proper respect, Daniel drew his pistol and shot him in the head.

"Don't concern yourself about that!" said he to the terrified priest. "He was a ne'er-do-well who didn't understand what we owe to God, and now I've punished him to set him on the straight and narrow. You carry on!"

My buccaneers used to tell that story over and over again, to great roars of laughter. It did not amuse me too much, because you can guess whose side I was on: that of the sailor three sheets to the wind on the blood of Christ!

But somehow they came to accept me, and even take a liking to me. Stranger things have happened in this world.

One day when I had been with them a few months and fed myself back to health, their chosen leader came and took me to one side. He was a big man, with the beard and hair of a goat, who had probably been elected on the basis of his brute strength rather than for his headpiece, as far as I could judge. He looked at me familiarly and put an arm round my shoulder, as if we were friends.

"You've been with us for three months now," he began solemnly. "You've learned to shoot like a real man, cut up an animal an' cook on a barbecue an' a boucan. You've your own oddities an' do foolish things, but you've been a good messmate an' one of us. You knows we favours justice, that we shares what we has an' makes sure nobody's set above anybody else. Brothers o' the coast is what we calls ourselves, an' it ain't just an empty phrase. We're brothers, we're like one big family. What d'you say, John? Will you jine us? 'Tis a hard life, but healthy an' free, though you won't die a wealthy man. But how many o' the likes of us would? I don't think you'll regret it."

He stopped speaking and gave me time to think. There was not much to think about, as I saw it at that moment. Their talk of brotherhood had little effect on me; I had heard enough of that among the blacks on the *Carefree* to last me a lifetime. They too had wanted to make me one of them, as if they could have changed even my skin for me. And now these brothers of the coast wanted to take me into their community, make me swear an oath of loyalty and such like, promise to behave as I should. Well, gladly, if that was the way they wanted it. Oaths and promises were only words, after all.

Besides, at that time I had no clear notion where I was going in life or in the world. I was already an outlaw in numerous places, and could not make my way without taking care where I set foot. I possessed nothing to speak of. Butterworth and his successor had laid hands on my money for their own account. My gun and my clothes were not my own, they belonged to everyone for the common weal, according to the buccaneers' rules. I might just as well stay where I was as anywhere else, until an opportunity presented itself for something more enriching, in every sense.

"Fine!" said I to Pierre le Bon, as he was known. "I'll join you. On one condition."

"What might that be?" he asked with some curiosity.

"That I be excused prayers at meal-times."

Pierre le Bon was not God-fearing enough to refrain from laughing so much that his beard twitched violently.

"I don't think anyone'll deny you that."

Nor did they. On the contrary, when we came back to camp and Pierre announced the news as if they had all got a first-born son, there were congratulations and back-slapping all round, and naught but happy faces. Had I not lately been so engrossed in regaining my health and strength, I might perhaps have had my eyes open and suspected that all was not above-board. Experience has taught me that it often is not, with people who in order to live together have to promise one another fidelity until death do them part or as if they will never die at all.

So a great feast was to be made ready to celebrate my initiation into the brotherhood. The whole camp – a score of buccaneers, their black or chocolate-coloured women, and an equal number of ordinary slaves – set to work to prepare the victuals and drink. The fatted boar was to be slaughtered in my honour. The feast would commence in the afternoon, and everyone would be blind drunk by sunset, for that was when the mosquitoes came and made life Hell.

There was a fixed boucan in the camp, a smoke-house, its sides covered in leaves, eight feet high, with a grill of cross-bars across the top, on which was placed meat that had been rubbed in coarse salt the night before. Inside the boucan a fire was lit of dried boar skins and bones. It was better than wood, because the salts in the skin and bones of the boar suited the meat better and gave it flavour, whereas the fumes from wood did not seem to be absorbed so well. And it was true, since the meat was so tender and juicy that you could eat it without any further seasoning. It could also be kept for months, and was thus the favoured provender of all gentlemen of fortune. The only thing you needed to do was to dip it in pimentade, a sauce of melted boar fat, the juice of two lemons and some spices.

When the meat was ready and drinks had been served from the common stock, the buccaneers said their confounded meal-time grace and thanked God for all the food they themselves had sweated to procure. After the repast, out came the pipes, and some had even adopted Spanish customs and rolled tobacco into so-called cigarillos. When they had all been lighted, Pierre le Bon stood up again and made a speech in which he welcomed me as one of the fraternal band. He had much to say about loyalty and comradeship, about unity and helping hands, about sharing what there was, about staying together and remaining amicable, not just when things were going well but even in adversity, for better or for worse, as he said. It would not have surprised me if he had been a priest earlier in life.

After these formal words I was sitting sucking on my pipe, suspecting nothing, when Pierre le Bon, with a beatific smile on his face, brought over a stooped little devil of a buccaneer. He looked as dry and hard as stone, the sort you could not joke with about anything, and certainly not about life and death and prayers. His scraggy mug tried in vain to crease itself into a smile that might indicate friendliness.

"This," said Pierre, "is Tom, called Crackshot. He's one o' the best marksmen we have. Ask the others. They get tired of hitting oranges and the like, because Tom will shoot off the stalk without even grazing the orange."

At this Tom looked mighty pleased with himself.

"Tom's mate was taken by the Spaniards a month ago when we was pursuing a herd o' wild boar into their territory. We was confronted of a sudden by a whole troop o' matadors an' monteros. They hunts on horseback with long spears, so we seldom has reason to fear them, with our guns. But we'd fanned out an' the villains managed to spear Yann afore the rest of us could get there. But Tom had his revenge. He shot eight Spaniards afore nightfall, despite their horses an' dogs."

"I should've shot more," said Tom, with loathing in his voice. "Yann was worth more'n a score o' them tyrants. He were the best man I ever been paired with."

"Paired with?" I asked.

"Ay," said Pierre le Bon, "that's one of our customs."

"What kind of custom?" I asked.

"Pairing ourselves in twos, being inseparable and sharing everything."

"Everything?"

"Ay, everything," replied Pierre. "We calls it *matelotage*, an' that's the way we've lived ever since we've been in existence. 'Tis like being wed, no more'n that."

"No more'n that?" I echoed. "Are you sodomites, the whole lot of you?"

That made them both roar with laughter.

"No, God preserve us," said Pierre. "What joy would we have in that? No, you see, John, we even shares our women, then we avoids any bickering an' squabbling. Let's say you an' Tom was to come across a beautiful woman, at sea or on land. What we does is toss a coin to see which of you'll wed her. But then you takes turns in bedding her, because you shares everything, right?"

"I see," said I, feeling rhyme and reason deserting me, "but why should either of us need to marry her if it's all the same anyhow?"

"So that nobody else can make any claims on her."

What do you say to that, Mr Defoe? You've studied humankind, and deviants in particular, but have you ever heard of anything as ingenious as that? But that is how it was, I was to be paired off in *matelotage* with this wizened character called Tom, known as Crackshot, whose only virtue seemed to be that he could shoot the stalk off an orange at thirty paces.

With that I knew that my time with these buccaneers was at an end even before it had begun.

But that was a day of surprises. Tom took me by his sweaty hand and led me to his hut. That was where we were to live until death did us part, said Crackshot Tom, and then inherit each other's guns, slaves and hut, the only things that were ours, for the common good.

"But the hut hardly counts," he explained. "With a negro you can knock up a new one in two days. Clearin' land usually takes a few weeks."

What did all this matter to me? I thought as I listened with only half an ear to his ingratiating chatter, stuffed so full of consideration that by all the rules I should have had a lump in my throat.

He dragged me over to the slaves' camp a little way off to show me his dearest possessions, of which he had three. The first was a woman who according to Tom was good both in bed and at cooking. The second was a man, who, also according to Tom, was strong and capable. He had once carried home six hundredweight of meat, unaided, in a day.

"The third, on the other hand," Tom went on, pointing at a shrunken figure in the far corner of the big hut, "ain't up to much. He only un'erstan's the whip, an' hardly even that. But that's the way it is with a lot o' the white contract workers as comes here. They've been promised green forests an' gold by some fool on the other side o' the Atlantic, when in fact they're signin' up to work their guts out just to earn their daily bread afore they'll be free again a'ter three years. Some of 'em seems to think we're running a charity when we takes 'em on, an' we ain't got enough ourselves even to put anything in the church collection."

Tom spat accurately between the legs of the poor wretch, who did not even look up.

"No," said Tom, "that's the last time I lays out any money on a white contract worker. Even if they costs nothin' to buy, they're dearer in the long run. It's better if you're under the English 'ministration, 'cause you can extend the contract without anybody botherin'. I heard o' one man who managed to extend a contract for twenty-one years. He slung his hook afore it ran out. The French Governor's a really finical devil, because he needs everyone who can walk or stand, even if the contract workers ain't much good by then. Look at this one here! I've had him a year, but what use has he been to anybody? Not to me, at any rate!"

I stepped forward so that my shadow was on the ground immediately in front of the poor wreck. Perhaps it was the shadow that made him look up, but imagine my surprise and repugnance when the creature began to undergo a transformation at the sight of me. His eyes started rolling in their sockets and the whole of his emaciated body began to shake.

"John Silver!" he cried, trembling with emotion and throwing himself at my feet, clawing at my legs to raise himself.

"John Silver," he croaked, breaking into copious tears.

"What the Devil . . . ?" I managed to gasp.

I took hold of the man by his matted hair and twisted his face upwards, drenched as it was in tears that seemed to be pouring out of every orifice.

I was rooted to the spot.

"Deval!" I exclaimed at last. "How in Hell's name did you end up here?"

Twenty-five

ESTERDAY AFTERNOON I thought I glimpsed a sail on the horizon, but by the time I picked up the telescope it was as if it had been blown away. Had I been mistaken? Maybe. But nevertheless it filled me with a yearning to go to sea again. I have sat here poring over my life and a mass of worthless characters who keep looming up in my memory with the speed of a hawser running out through the anchor hole. I have hardly been beyond my door for several days.

But the mirage of a sail had me upon my foot and out of the house. Everything was quiet outside. I called, but not a soul appeared, nor answered.

Well, I thought, it was naught to do with me where they were. If they had had the sense they would have gone for good long ago, just like the couple who had asked for my permission and blessing.

I hobbled down the steep path on my stiff leg. What had happened to the agility I once possessed? I had to support myself and hold on at almost every turn of the rocky path. Down below on the flat ground I had to stop and get my breath. What was to be done with a leaky hull like mine? It was more trouble than it was worth. Would I even be able to climb back up to my clifftop?

I made my way slowly down to the beach. There was no better sand anywhere on this earth, as white as chalk and as fine as powder. I threw off my clothes, removed my shoe and sat down heavily with my foot in the water. The sea was warm, and scarcely even cooled me. It was pale turquoise, a shimmering green beryl and aquamarine. It was strange, but true all the same, that every ocean had its own colour, various individual shades of blue, green and grey mixed by currents, winds, sandstorms, angles of the sun, cloud and temperature into the special blend of each particular sea. That was also something I had discovered and experienced in my life. It is so easy to forget such things in a life like mine. Who would have believed that there was room for beauty in the midst of all the hullabaloo? Yet I have had my precious stones, my jewels, and all the hours I have spent leaning over the rail just looking at the ocean. I have watched the sun go down in a flaming sea of fire, and seen it rise again as burnished copper. I have seen the moon reflected in the slow surge of the swell, making the veils of the night sky glow like phosphorus. I have seen the water so smooth and the air so clear that the firmament of stars has been mirrored below so that you no longer knew what was up and what was down and thought you were sailing inside a glittering globe. I have seen skies and clouds that it would take an artist a whole lifetime to try to imitate. Ay, there have been such things in my life too, and well worth living for, though they do not stick in the memory like so much else.

It was over now. All I had left was this corner of the Indian Ocean that was Ranter Bay. And I could not even see that clearly any more. Everything in the distance was blurred and indistinct. And to think I had always seen the horizon as sharp as a knife blade! No, Long John Silver was not up to much nowadays, by most standards. His story would soon be at an end. Good to be rid of him, the old wreck.

Thus I sat thinking at the water's edge, until it occurred to me that I was thinking of myself as if it were a different person, John Silver, who did not have much to do with me and who seemed to take what he wanted from life with a good appetite, but at my expense. That is how far things had come. The life I was writing about with such zeal was no longer my own.

I could not help thinking of you, Mr Defoe, whom I admit I have neglected of late. You gave life to Crusoe at Selkirk's expense, immortalised the one and consigned the other to obscurity, as if he had never existed.

But in that case am I not doing the same, I asked myself, with all those poor wretches like Deval who seem to have encumbered my life without my wishing it? Am I not giving them life undeservedly? I remember, Mr Defoe, that you wrote about rogues of all kinds so that they would serve as warning examples; again and again you felt yourself called upon to place extra emphasis on just how ungodly, sinful and unhappy they were until they mended their ways. But could you really be sure that no one would imitate them? Moll the whore, Singleton the pirate and Colonel Jack found happiness in the end, after all.

Although on the other hand, no one would be mad enough to want lives like those of Scudamore, Deval, Wilkinson or Governor Warrender's daughter. I may have given them life, but no harm is done as far as I can tell. And what does it matter? I am writing for your eyes only, Mr Defoe, because I have nobody to talk with in my own way, and you are not in a position to have to express an opinion. Where you sit now, you are home and dry, we can assume.

It was heavy going to make my way back up to my fortified abode. Heavy-headed, heavy to drag my leaky hull, heavy-hearted at leaving the water's edge, to come up to what? – to the echo of words in my mind, to silence and emptiness. There was still no answer to my calls, and I was horrified to discover that I missed life and movement around me, the sound of people, whoever they might be, carrying on their futile activities. For the first time in ages I picked up a bottle and drank till I dropped. It may have helped, for when I awoke there were negro faces gazing at me anxiously, Jack most of all. So not everyone had left me yet. There was still time to bring things to a close, before it was too late.

"What are you staring at?" I asked. "Ain't you never seen a drunken sailor afore? Yo-ho-ho, and a bottle of rum!"

Twenty-six

SO THERE I stood with Deval, who by that stage I had blissfully forgotten, and had him clinging round my neck. If I had been a God-fearing man, I would have thought both then and later when he took my leg that Deval was the punishment for all my sins. He was not, of course. He might have been the punishment for my stupidity in letting him hang round me in the belief that vermin like him could not do any harm. I deceived myself as I had deceived him. Unfortunate, self-loathing, wretched, bitter and pitiful creatures like him should not be played with. In order to stand on their own two feet they have a constant need of someone to hate and calumniate. And, mark you, sooner or later, if you remain in their proximity, they will knife you in the back when you least expect it.

"Take me away from here, John!" he pleaded. "I can't endure it any longer."

"What became of England?" I asked.

"I don't know," he replied. "We were sold to different people."

"Sold?" said I.

Deval looked ashamed.

"A crimp got 'is claws into us, drank us under the table an' tricked us into signin' a contract for three years in the Colonies. We let you down, did Edward an' I."

"So it seems. But it has happened to me too."

"You let someone down? You?"

"That wasn't what I meant. I was tricked aboard my first ship by a crimp."

"Take me away from 'ere, John!"

"I'll see what I can do," I promised, to shut him up.

Tom Crackshot was open-mouthed, of course, but I gave him an expressive wink and told him the truth, that Deval was an old acquaintance that I had been burthened with by chance and not for my sins, as you might think.

"No," said Tom as we walked off, "who would want a fawnin' rat like Deval as a friend? He ain't got no pride. Demeans himself in ev'ry way. Except by workin'. But mebbe you can talk him into improvement."

"Mebbe."

The next day I asked Tom to show me their little brig, but the buccaneers' vessel was nothing to be proud of. She was watertight at the bottom, Tom asserted, but leaked like a sieve if she had to work on the open sea. The sails were half rotten and might just about withstand a fresh breeze. All the spars were cracked by the sun and the rigging had not seen a trace of tar in many years. And this horror of the seas went under the name of *Tonton Louis*.

"It's been a while since we've taken her out," said Tom.

"She looks as if she needs a bit o' maint'nance too," I opined.

"May well do," said Tom, who was quite obviously not very conversant with the sea, however many orange stalks he could shoot off.

"Lend me Deval for a few days," said I. "He's not doing any good where he is. Then I'll have this old hulk in trim in no time."

"We need you on the hunt, Silver."

"You know you'll manage as well without me, with your shooting skill. Come and let's talk to Pierre!"

Pierre was all ears. He understood perfectly well the advantage of having a seaworthy vessel at the ready. Not only, as he explained to the others he had gathered together to express their views, so that they might be able to capture a Spaniard with useful cargo on board, but more in order to be able to flee if the Spaniards suddenly took it into their heads to send matadors and monteros to throw them into the sea. Pierre's words impressed them favourably, and it was agreed unanimously that I, John by name, had permission, can you believe, to make the *Tonton Louis* ready for the open sea, for the common weal.

I fetched Deval, who was overjoyed when I informed him of the news that he was to work under me. He had misgivings, however, when during the course of the work I started to explain my plan, which was that we should take some trustworthy negroes on board and try our luck at sea. He said he could not understand my purpose.

"No," said I, "thinking was never one o' your strong points. Perhaps you'd rather rot here, hardly better treated than an or'nary slave, even worse in fact, because they wants to suck everything out o' you in three years instead o' spreading it out over a whole lifetime. Leastways with slaves they earn more by keepin' 'em goin' as long as possible."

Deval shook his head.

"You've made it impossible for yourself on the French islands, if you flees," I went on. "I myself dare not set foot on the Danish. And neither of us can risk being recognised on the English islands, not to speak o' showing ourselves on the Spanish. The sea, Deval, is the only place left for the likes of us. With a pile o' pieces of eight we might've bought ourselves freedom and respectability, but we're scraped bare."

"What did you do with the *Dana* an' our joint funds?" Deval asked.

"I sold the *Dana* and followed you to try and find you and free you from your contracts. But I lost the money, robbed of everything we possessed and owned."

Deval's mouth dropped open.

"Did you sail to the West Indies to 'elp us?"

"Ay," said I, "I swear by all you hold sacred."

Deval took me at my word, of course, because he could scarcely afford to be fastidious.

"John," said he, "I'll follow you to the ends of the earth if need be."

"I truly hope not," I replied.

For some time afterwards Deval was the most tractable and compliant tool imaginable. Tom was astounded when he saw how Deval was working and that he never left my side, other than when I told him to go to Hell.

With Deval's energy and ardour the work made rapid progress. We careened the ship and scraped the bottom. We caulked her and replaced some of the deck planks. We cleaned the water barrels and made them tight. We stocked her with provisions, for as I said to Pierre, there was no sense in having a boat without food and water if she were to serve as a Noah's Ark for a group of landless buccaneers. In the end the whole of the little community joined in the preparations eagerly. Those who were old enough to have sailed with the filibusters in former times began to talk of going to sea again. They had called themselves adventurers, with every reason, in the good old days, and their eyes sparkled as they recounted their memories of the great expeditions to Panama and Cartagena. Pierre had difficulty convincing them of the advantages of the peaceful life they were leading now. Had it not been for their confounded *matelotage* and God-fearing ways, I might have felt inclined to agree. Or at least have been tempted to take on board a whole crew of their best marksmen.

Instead, I had to make do with Deval and a negro when we cast off one moonless night. I would love to have seen the buccaneers' faces when they discovered the boat was gone the next day, and with her all the hopes they had lately cherished. But you cannot have everything in life, not even I, and certainly not credulous buccaneers. And I am sure too that Pierre and some of the others may have spared me a thought or two of gratitude for disappearing and taking with me their dreams of another life. And, if you ask me, those buccaneers must have lived happily for the rest of their days, till death did them part, each from the other.

We had not been sailing many hours, first south and then east so as not to be caught by the sunrise while still within sight of land, when Deval raised his bright little voice.

"An' what shall we do now?"

"We'll capture the first ship that comes our way," I replied.

"We ain't pirates, are we?" he objected.

"Ay, Deval, that's exactly what we are from now on. If you don't want to be, I'll gladly set you off on the nearest spit o' land. No one shall ever say that John Silver were the sort to make others dance to his toon."

"I won't desert you," said Deval. "You know that. But must we . . . ?"

"You don't have to do anything in this life," I interrupted him, "that's my motto. But my mind's made up, anyhow. I've lived as I could, without ill intentions as far as I'm aware, and what's it led to? I'm outside the law 'most everywhere, I risks the gallows in at least two places, I've been flogged and thrown in chains for naught. One thing I've come to understand is that there's always a cost for the likes of us in keeping to the straight and narrow. It's always the ones who're rolling in duff and gold who has the right o' way and takes the windward position in any battle. No, guineas, pieces of eight, louis d'ors, moidores – they're the only things to have if you wants to lead a respectable life while it lasts, says I. Ah, that's the only way to be counted, Deval, in this world. The more doubloons you has, the more you counts, you may take your davy! Who bothers about a destitute wretch like you, for instance? You don't count, you may lay to it."

"Not even for you?"

"No."

"John," said Deval slowly, "it ain't always easy to be your friend."

"No," I replied cheerfully, "and why should it be?"

Some time later we sighted a small brig, not unlike ourselves. We lay to windward, and I slacked the sheets at once.

"What are you thinkin' o' doin'?" Deval asked uneasily.

"Boarding her, o' course."

"You're crazy," he exclaimed.

I was not stupid enough to think I could just jump aboard and shoot wildly around me, naturally. No, cunning was my way, the only thing you could depend on in the long run.

We were hailed, as was customary, and I responded that we had come out of Charleston, Virginia, and were making for St Thomas.

"Then you've come a Hell of a long way off course," was the short answer from the brig.

"I know," I shouted back. "Can I come over and compare positions?"

No one suspected anything was amiss. I was welcomed aboard by a ruddy and genial captain who slapped me on the back, invited me into his cabin and opened a bottle. He even warned me about all the pirates that had begun to turn up in the West Indies after the Peace of Utrecht that had put thousands of sailors out of a job. I thanked him for the warning and laughed, then drew my pistols and held them to his head.

"You should look out for yourself," said I, and bade him call in his mate.

When he came I made the captain bind him to a chair, and then we repeated the same with one seaman after another until there were no more chairs left and only the helmsman on deck to hold the course. I made the swabs a short speech and spoke in a persuasive manner of service with me on the *Tonton Louis*. There were plenty of victuals and drink on board, the finest barbecued meat and rum, and the more there were of us the less each one needed to do. With cunning like mine, it was not hard to take prizes like this one, as they had seen for themselves, without risking life and limb. If they sailed with me, I said, they would have a better time than in Paradise. It would be wisest, I added, to take the opportunity while they could, because they would not get such an offer twice.

Things went as they usually did in those days: four of the five joined me and helped me to transfer everything of value. They gaped in amazement when they discovered that I was alone on board, in a manner of speaking, and their respect for me rose several notches. A few bottles of rum when the work was over and done helped convince them that they had actually landed in Heaven. Was that not just what they wanted for themselves in Paradise?

They called me Captain and bowed and scraped, not having understood a thing. Paradise, I yelled at them, was not having to bow and scrape, not having to ask for permission, not having to fit into the ranks and line up for inspection every five minutes. It was about electing your own captain, and deposing him when you felt like it, and so on and so forth.

"Now," said I to them all, "I proposes Deval here as cap'n. He's a capable man, if I ain't mistook, and he's sailed as a smuggler 'twixt Ireland and France."

The suggestion met with jubilant approbation. The fact that in Paradise they should think for themselves never occurred to them, needless to say, not before it was too late. Deval stood in silent astonishment to start with, but then a grin spread over his face, pleased and eager for revenge as he no doubt was.

"Steer west-nor'west," said he authoritatively to the negro at the helm.

"What d'you have in mind?" I asked him.

"You'll find out, 'long o' the others, when the time comes," was the curt answer.

I was not surprised. It would have been either that, or he would have shrivelled up, wept and wailed at the thought of having to steer a course and act as captain. But Deval was one of those – and they are legion – who kick away the stool that helped them up. But also one of those who forget to look around to make sure they have not stuck their neck in a noose hanging from the ceiling.

We took another brig or two, which strengthened the pride and confidence of the crew. If I had suggested it, I am sure they would have rechristened the *Tonton Louis* the *Seventh Heaven*. We had a prodigious quantity of rum on board, eight men now with the latest recruits from our newest prize, and most of them were as drunk as lords nearly all the time. It was just right. We had also acquired a musician, who led the deuce of a good life, I can warrant.

It has always surprised me that pirates should set such store by their musicians. They were tempted on board with all sorts of promises of extra shares in the profits, free Sundays and more besides. They were let off the dirty jobs, changing sails and even boarding in battle, as long as they played a ditty as soon as they were bade.

I recollect one time with Flint, towards the end, when his cruelty knew no bounds. We had captured a Dutch snow, with proud snub-nosed Flemings aboard. They were foolish enough to put up resistance, so we hoisted the red flag and boarded them. It did not take long to force them into submission, but Flint was in a raging temper afterwards.

"Bloody Papist!" he screamed at the captain as he severed his head from his body, with some difficulty in his agitation. "Why couldn't you strike your flag from the start? Risking the lives of innocent seamen for naught! Blackguard!"

That's how he went on.

"And the rest o' you?" he bellowed, fixing his eyes on the crew, who were standing in a terror-stricken huddle before the mast. "You let him do it! Mutiny, I say! Why didn't you mutiny? Ain't you got no shame in you, not a damned bit of sense?"

He took aim and kicked the bleeding head right among the men.

"Why ain't you saying anything?"

"Let's make 'em sweat!" cried Black Dog with an evil grin. "Make 'em sweat!"

"Do whatever you want," said Flint magnanimously. "Make 'em see what it costs to hazard sailors' lives for naught."

Flint had a good eye for dead sailors, as I have said. The living, on the other hand, he was not much interested in, hard to comprehend as it may be. But I knew how it would be. He would go back to his cabin, pour a whole bottle of rum down his throat and grieve for the captain he had just put an end to.

Black Dog for his part was a-fired with excitement, in a manner of speaking, because that is what sweating was. With help from the others he set up a circle of candles and torches on the middle deck. The man to be sweated was driven into the centre of the ring of fire. Our men stood all round, armed with knives, sail needles, forks – I even saw a pair of compasses from the navigation table in someone's hand.

"Music!" shrieked Black Dog to the clamorous approval of the others. "We must have music!"

Somebody fetched our two artists, who played a lively dance while the men lunged out with their own instruments, stabbing wheresoever they could reach. There were howls of mirth and exhilaration, sweat was dripping from the faces of the elated pirates, and the musicians increased the tempo until the air was filled with glinting lights, reflected from the stabs and blows lashing hither and thither to the sound of screaming from the ones who were being sweated. It was a noise unlike anything else, and not improved by the music.

But that is how it was. Every time we boarded and entered, as far as I remember, in the midst of all the powder-smoke, musket-fire, boom of cannon, crashing of splintered wood, screeches of the slain and the slayers, in the midst of all that our musicians would be standing blowing for all they were worth, enough to drive you insane. But was

that not the object of their handiwork, when all's said and done –
to whip us into a frenzy so that we acted like madmen and forgot
who we were? It was like rum, and they worshipped it in the same
way, to imbibe the courage to live. And to think that musicians were
given pardons and safe-conducts everywhere they went! They were
the only ones of Roberts' men who were freed when forty-six others
were hanged or condemned to seven years' hard labour. As if the
musicians had not played their part in the mischief. You may lay
to that!

Our own musician on the *Tonton Louis* was certainly a gift from
Heaven. Yet the sound was abominable whenever he struck up a tune
in response to demand, whether at good or bad moments. I made no
objection while it lasted. The men were happy, pleased with their lot,
and left me in peace. That was how I liked it, if I were to get anywhere
in this world.

But after a month or so of this unfounded feeling of contentment
we sighted a ship in the shimmering midday heat in the lee of one of
the islands. A real old hulk she was, riding almost still on the silky-
smooth water. There could be no doubt that she was a lumbering
merchantman.

"Make the ship ready an' out with the oars!" Deval ordered, to
everyone's delight.

But as we drew nearer the valour of some began to ebb away. She was
a large vessel that might have twice the number of men on board that
we had. She was flying the English flag, and we hoisted the same, one
we had taken from our first prize. Only when we came within firing
range did we change it for the black one. There was a ghostly silence
on board, despite the fact that we could discern the outline of a helmsman. It was quiet on our ship too, I can warrant, so quiet that I could
hear Deval biting his nails. The others did not have much to say for
themselves either. The halcyon days were over, and now it was up to
every man to show what he was made of.

"What are we waitin' for?" I roared.

"That ship has sickness aboard her," said Greenwill, a timid older seaman, full of superstitions and visions.

"Like Hell she has!" said I. "How come she has a helmsman at the wheel, then?"

"She's prob'ly full o' soldiers," suggested O'Brian. "They're just a-waitin' for us to come in range."

"We a'ready are, you blockhead!" said I.

Deval said nothing. He was standing as if benumbed on the poop deck staring straight ahead.

"Helmsman," said I to my trusty negro, who seemed to be the only one apart from myself who still had his wits about him, "hold course to their stern!"

"Ay, ay, sir," came the prompt response.

Only then did Deval come to life and start raging to the skies that he was the captain and not me. But it was to me the men turned.

"Let's take a closer look at her, anyhow," said I. "It might be an abandoned mut'ny or a plundered prize. We could do with a bigger vessel than the *Tonton Louis*."

"She's sick," insisted Greenwill.

"We've a'ready heard that, you confounded ass!"

"Can't you smell the stench?" said he.

No sooner had he uttered the words than it came to me what it was: a slave ship. Since we had approached from windward we had not been aware of the smell before. We began to hear cries of anguish, a great moaning that seemed to rise and fall in time with the swell.

"But where in Hell's name is her crew?" exclaimed Johnston, who was standing ready with a grappling iron at the prow. "I can't see a soul apart from the helmsman."

"It could be a mut'ny," said I. "The negroes have thrown the others overboard and kept the helmsman to steer the ship to shore. If so, we could be rich men in a trice. We could help 'em make land, get 'em to the nearest port, and sell the whole lot."

"They'll murther us if we go aboard," said Deval.

"You, mebbe," said I, "the way you look. But don't fret, I'll go aboard myself. I knows how to deal with slaves. I've been one myself."

The men looked at me in astonishment.

"That I have," I added. "Sold at a scramble, an' all. I won't be risking anything."

But I could already see that something was wrong. If the negroes had mutinied, the deck would have been crawling with blacks. But you could hear from their wailing that they were still chained below. An abandoned pirates' prize, then, was my best guess.

We went alongside without having been hailed. Johnston threw over the grappling iron and I climbed up.

I have had a lot to forget in my life, but the question remains whether the sight that greeted me on the *Rôdeur* was not the worst. There were a few wretched sailors sitting or lying here and there on the deck, and there was a nauseating odour of death and putrefaction rising from the open hatches. It did not need a great deal of imagination to comprehend that there would not be much life left in the hold. What was this? It was as if no one saw me, even though their strangely empty stares appeared to go beyond me. The whole lot of them looked like death masks or grave-diggers, except for the helmsman. I took a few steps in his direction before he caught sight of me. He sank to his knees and clasped his hands together.

"Thanks be to God! Praised be the Lord!" said he, in a voice that bore the mark of madness.

"Why?" I asked, naturally enough.

"He's answered my prayers and sent you, sir, to save us from destruction."

"I wouldn't take your affy-davy on that," said I.

"What d'you mean, sir?" he asked.

"I don't mean nothing," said I. "But shiver my soul, I'd dearly love to know what adversity has befallen this ship, that I would."

"Help us, for God's sake!"

"Can't you belay your bleating about God and tell me what's happened?"

"Sir, no such calamity has ever afflicted a ship! 'Tis God's punishment for our sins."

I did not say what I thought, but it is not hard to guess.

"We got sickness aboard in Africa," the helmsman went on. "It spread like wildfire, sir. We threw thirty-nine slaves overboard to put a stop to it. But nothin' helped. Nothin', sir. Now everyone's infected, blacks an' whites alike, sir, everyone save me. Half o' the negroes are dead an' I'm the on'y one who can steer."

"The on'y one? What's wrong with those seamen there, might I ask?"

Some of them heard my voice at that very moment and rose with difficulty and began groping their way around the deck like sleep-walkers. They stumbled and banged into each other, one fell over and opened up a bloody gash on his forehead, and all of them were entreating me and God for mercy. I could feel fear knotting my stomach, I will readily admit.

"They're blind, sir, the whole lot of 'em. Every man aboard, except for myself by the grace of God, has lost his sight."

I started to back away, beyond the reach of all the outstretched arms.

"Help us, for the love o' God!" came the wail from the blind sailors.

More and more voices joined in and their cries of woe spread like their sickness. The noise of pain and misery from the hold grew in strength until finally it was as if the whole ship were one all-pervading dirge of death. I continued backing away towards our grappling iron, being careful to stay out of reach of all the groping hands that were trying to grab me and drag me down into the depths. The helmsman's resentful gaze followed me.

"You can't just leave us, sir," he appealed, so loud that you could hear it above all the grief and lamentation. "We're white like you! Don't think about the blacks, sir. They can't be sold in any case. You can't leave us. We're Christians like you."

"What the Hell d'you know about that?" I screeched back. "I ain't stoopid enough to stay on board a ship that's accursed. But keep on a course of a hundred degrees and you'll strike land in a day or two. If God stands by you. As He obviously has till now."

Then I seized the rope, flung myself over the rail and started climbing down. I must have lowered myself a fathom before I discovered there was no *Tonton Louis* waiting beneath my dangling feet. The cowardly swabs had pulled away and were already a cable length off.

I called down every conceivable imprecation on their heads until they turned and came back to pick me up where I was hanging. I think the whole lot of them were deadly pale. I gave them a good bawling out, and soon assured myself that it was Deval who had decided on retreat.

"I never thought you'd come back alive," said he, wriggling like a worm to avoid my eyes.

I made no answer, and it was a long time before I spoke to him again. In all honesty I did not have much to say to him, either. He was and remained nothing but a spineless weakling.

The encounter with the blind *Rôdeur* left its mark on the *Tonton Louis*, and even on me. I awoke in the middle of the night sweating, with the screams of the slaves resounding in my ears. I could hear them, but not see them in front of me, which made my terror no less. For what remains of a life if you have no eyes? Just rumour and empty talk. If anyone should know, I should. And how would you be able to see over your shoulder? How could you watch your back?

The good mood on our own ship was as if swept away. The men were bad-tempered and obstinate. Deval was unbearable. The rum ran out ten days later without anyone being in a better humour for all they had drunk, and the days that followed were a total disaster. The meeting with the *Rôdeur* had been a bad omen, the others said, and sulked even more. There were not many sailors who trusted in God, but they were superstitious. They imagined first one thing and then another, without improving the situation. And to think that I had put up with them and tried to do them a service! I probably should have had Deval deposed and myself elected captain. But I had my principles, and not becoming captain was one of them, in memory of Captain Barlow. I was always on the side of the crew, whoever they were, and spoke up for them. Not because I was one of them, but to be able to be myself.

For months we sailed back and forth the length of the islands with the wind, and not so much as a glimpse of another sail. We took one single wretched prize, the French ship *L'Espérance* from Dieppe, which did not exactly leaven the mood. The contents of her hold were enough to drive anyone mad. Twelve sacks of pepper and six hundred tons of cotton were all right, although we had no use for either. But what were we to do with three hundred and sixty parrots and fifty-four monkeys, in need of food and drink as we were? I was against it, but our crew took a number of parrots and monkeys for amusement. And amusing it was, though not for the monkeys, who ended up in our pots, salted in the buccaneers' fashion; nor yet for us, who did not have a quiet moment until the parrots died miserably of hunger.

In the end everything was running out, not just the rum and good humour but our fine barbecued meat and the water. The crew was up early in the mornings sucking on the ropes to catch the dew that had fallen during the night. We slaughtered rats to have a bit of fresh meat to survive on. Someone even suggested that we should do the same with cockroaches. If the French could eat ants, we could surely manage that.

There was a constant bickering about what we should do. Some of them had begun to lose their heads and were all for sailing in to the nearest inhabited island to seek our fortune ashore. Others suggested a raid on the nearest town to get women and rum. Several were raving deliriously about sailing home to England – dross about girls they had left, parents they had not seen for decades, the smell of horse dung and heather, rainy, freezing cold winter days out on the heath and copious streams of ale in the taverns.

I had to explain to them over and over again that they had put themselves beyond the law and were thus lawful booty for anyone, including the prizes we had taken, and that now there was no way back, whatever they might think or want. I harangued them from morning till night, and eventually I managed to improve their humour. We made a few trips ashore, went hunting, gathered fruit and found water. It did no harm that we had to make do without grog. On the contrary, it would make the men all the more courageous when we went into battle.

Not that it made any difference when it came to the point, for one morning in the half-light of dawn we found ourselves a couple of cable lengths from a schooner, staring straight into the mouths of twelve open cannon-ports.

"All hands on deck!" shouted the helmsman. "Make the ship ready!"

I was the first to rush up, and it did not take long to work out that defence was out of the question. At the very moment I cut the rope and struck the flag came the explosion of their broadside. They had aimed high and when the smoke of the powder cleared, our rigging was in tatters and the mainmast was hanging from its shrouds over the rail. But we had struck our flag, though not to a Spaniard but to a gentleman of fortune, for at their stern flew the Jolly Roger. There were cheers and jubilation on board our ship, because the crew had thought they were about to reach the end of their short lives.

It was not long before our little deck was crawling with drunken, grinning pirates. One of them, Pew by name, as thin as a withy, slippery as an eel and with eyes transparently falser than most, ordered Deval as captain and me as quartermaster on board their ship.

"The cap'n wants to talk to you," said he, with such a coarse and cruel guffaw that Deval started to tremble violently.

Deval was probably thinking of the stories of men like L'Olonnais the Bloody, who had cut out the heart of one prisoner and started chewing it to make the others reveal where they had hidden their silver and pieces of eight. But we need not have concerned ourselves. It was just Pew's little eccentricity that he liked to instil fear into everyone who came in contact with him. That was the sort of man he was. And the ones who showed fear he despised. But to those who told him to go to Hell where he belonged he went down on all fours. In my opinion you cannot but be astounded by the variety of humankind. If we are God's work, we cannot accuse Him of lacking inventiveness.

On the other hand, there was perhaps nothing unfathomable in the fact that the captain who stood before us on the poop deck of the good ship *Fancy*, the captain who had nearly sent us to the bottom of the sea, was in his very own two-sided, confused, honourable and good-natured person, none other than Edward England.

Twenty-seven

S O YOU SEE, Mr Defoe, that I have returned to our business and come to the point at last – I am not a man who forgets his promises, leastways if they were given to someone who was not concerned about them. Because I have observed that between folk who are dependable no promises are expected. I shall stay well out of the matter, for who would take me at my word, save Long John Silver himself?

But with you it was in fact more open to question. I once asked you straight out whether you intended to take me at my word about Edward England and the others, whether you intended to stick to the truth in your book on pirates.

"Stick to the truth!" you exclaimed, leaning across the table. "Certainly the book will be truthful, with all the documents and information I have collected. But it actually matters little what it be if it be not believed. That is why we write all those prefaces where we say how true everything is. Crusoe needs no preface. He stands on his own two feet and is believed as he is. But look at what I have compiled on Roberts, Davis and Low! What is it? Nothing but fragments of the wreckage of their evil and shameful lives. No – Roberts, Davis and Low cannot stand on their own two feet. But you shall see in due course!"

"See what?"

You laughed fit to make your wig twitch. Like a little boy about to play a prank, that is what you were!

"Do you know what I have done?" said you in a low voice, as if it were another of your secrets. "I have written a long chapter about the life of Captain Misson!"

"Who the Devil is Misson?" I asked.

I had never heard of him, which was very odd, because I had been part of it for so long that I was aware of most of them.

"No," said you with your most self-satisfied smile. "How could you have heard of Misson? He does not exist."

"Doesn't exist?"

"No, I have invented him, from start to finish."

"Invented him? Ain't there enough pirate cap'ns as it is?"

"Indeed there are. I have thirty-four captains on my list and am reckoning on about six hundred pages. But do you not understand? You shall see that Captain Misson is one of those who will go down in history! He will be just like Crusoe! It will be Misson who will inspire writers and be cited in serious books! What say you to that?"

Without waiting for my answer you continued, "I have observed that you gentlemen of fortune have many excellent points. I do not expect you thought you would hear that from the likes of me, but so it is, none-the-less. You do not submit to authority, you drain your cup of liberty to the full, you are offended by any injustice to the weak; with you right comes before mercy, you vote on everything and let everyone have his say. You make no distinction between those on board, neither of race nor religion. Yes, there is much that is good in this that our leaders could learn from if they durst, because power is what makes your blood boil most of all, and that is what the high and mighty are not so inclined to hear."

You made a gesture as if to apologise.

"Pray do not take this amiss, but every single living pirate captain and his crew ruin all their good intentions with their cruelty, avarice and shameful way of life."

"That's what they live for," I interjected.

"I am well aware of that," you replied impatiently. "But the problem is that I cannot praise the good sides without seeming to excuse the bad. But evil, Mr Long, if you will permit me to say so, can never be counterbalanced. That is why I have created Captain Misson, a pirate who has all the good qualities without being burthened with cruelty and infamy. That is what I have done."

"Shiver my timbers, what a man you are!" said I in genuine admiration.

"Indeed," you replied.

[242]

"But I can understand why you ended up in the stocks."

"It is worth it," said you decisively. "If the gallows be the measure of your lives, then the stocks are the same for the writer. If he be worthy, that is."

And in that you were probably right. But you never understood what it was that drove all those gentlemen of fortune to live in the shadow of the gallows, despite your eternal questioning.

"Mr Silver," you once said to me when we were stretching our legs out of hearing of others and passing the corpses that had been hanged on Execution Dock, "have you observed their countenances?"

"No," answered I, "as far as I can see they ain't got much countenance left."

"There you are wrong," you replied with your usual fervour, "you simply have not regarded them properly. I admit that these particular corpses are not the best examples of what I have in mind. Bodies are like nobody, if you will forgive the pun, when they are hanged in chains from the gibbet for public inspection, after first being suspended below the high water mark to be cleansed – yes, that is what it is called – in the stinking waters of the Thames. It is indeed fortunate for the authorities that we are not afflicted with sharks in our waters. That would be something, would it not, if there were only a trunk hanging on the rope when the water receded on the ebb tide?"

And then you laughed so heartily that I began to wonder whether you yourself might not have made an excellent pirate when all's said and done. You had a gallows humour, I can vouch for that.

"You have to be up betimes," you continued, "if you want to see with your own eyes how it is when their last moment is nigh. Some, my friend, look as if they have atoned for all their crimes. Their faces are serene and peaceful, with no fear, no dread of the unknown that awaits them. Others are distorted into frightful grimaces, terror-stricken and out of their minds at the prospect of what is to come. They fear punishment for their sins. Can you explain it? How can it be that there are some who can go to meet death with defiance, without a murmur, and calm in spirit? If you will allow, I would like to confide to you something I have not revealed to anyone else, perhaps hardly even to myself.

[243]

I am afeared of dying. The mere thought that I am going to die frights me out of my wits. You who have seen so many die, or strike the flag as you would probably say, do you think there is a cure? Not for death, because that we know is irrevocable, but for the confounded fear. All those pirates, yes, I have counted all of them too, you see . . ."

You took a crumpled piece of paper out of your pocket and showed it to me, with the same proud, childlike smile you always had when you thought you had acquired some information about the world you believed was yours alone.

"I have counted the number of vessels and taken the mean number of men on board, which was eighty. I have deducted some who served several masters, added in the ships whose crews we do not know and assumed the usual manning, and behold!"

You pointed at several numbers, underlined twice.

"Five thousand pirates, give or take a couple of hundred! Yes, I can see you are amazed. You did not believe there were so many of you. It is also only a half-truth, for many sign off and new ones join. But let us say fifteen hundred at any given time. A fifth of our own Royal Navy. A formidable force if assembled under one command and a single will. But to return to our own business, which was death, if you have no objection . . . ?"

Not that you waited for my response. For the most part in our conversations I was unable to get a word in edgeways. You were so talkative, despite the fact that you did nothing but write down words all your life. I would have thought you would have had enough of it all. But words, I have found, are for some, like you – and me, in my own way – a kind of illness and a poison, as God is for priests, and rum for gentlemen of fortune.

"Fifteen hundred pirates, then, playing with life and death as if it made no difference to them. By my computing, sir, with Roberts now as the latest inclusion, about four hundred have been hanged and already atoned for their crimes. And how many have struck their flags in battle and sickness? A third can have their death ascribed to syphilis. Yet it does not seem to distress any of you unduly. Some repent, as a matter of course, when the rope is round their necks, but seldom ere that. I believe in God, Mr Silver, in a life after this, in the forgiveness of sins. Why can I not be as free from care as you gentlemen of fortune? Why can I not look death in the face with confidence while I live? Can you answer me that?"

I could not, but I do not think you expected me to. Now I would say that you feared death because your belief in a life after this was just deceit, trickery and secretiveness, like everything else you undertook. Why on earth should you otherwise have suffered from such a burning desire to write down everything you had on your mind? Could it not equally well have waited for Paradise? Your complexion was sallow and you had cramp and pain in your writing hand. To what avail, if you were immortal? No, sir, if you feared death, it was because you knew in your heart of hearts, just like me and the other gentlemen of fortune, that there was only one chance to live and it was then that everything had to be done.

One day I invited Israel Hands to our table so that you could see for yourself. You would at last be able to meet a real pirate, one who was like the others, one of the sort you called free from care, one who hardly cared whether he lived or died. I would have a good laugh, you may lay to that. There was no question of the two of you understanding each other.

Israel Hands took up my invitation and joined us. He looked calculatingly at me, knowing what I was good for, and greedily at you, because you had promised him a guinea for his trouble – at my expense, plainly.

"Hands," you began, "I understand from my friend here that you have some experience of the pirate life. May I ask why you became a pirate, or gentleman of fortune as it is called?"

"I was a-sailin' to Bermuda, from Bristol, with a Cap'n Thurbar. We was taken by Teach – Blackbeard – the ugly bastard, and had to choose. We could go with Blackbeard or be set ashore."

"And you chose Blackbeard?"

"Ay, so help me! A nasty devil he was, shot me in the leg just for the fun on it. He were a swine!"

"He shot you in the leg? What was the reason for that?"

Hands spat fulsomely on the floor.

"Blackbeard were a devil," he repeated, "an arsehole, a son of a whore. I were his helmsman, and he shoots me in the leg. To amuse hisself, the swab. We was a-sittin' in his cabin, a-drinkin' of a bottle. We was drunk and worse 'cause we'd taken some good prizes. My share were a hundred sovereigns by then. That's real money, that is. With five hundred you can make a life for yourself, buy papers and live like a gen'leman for the rest o' your days. But Blackbeard wouldn't hear of aught like that. Being a gen'leman o' fortune, he sneered, was a calling, like being a priest. He didn't want no fops aboard. They poisoned the air with their stinking perfume and showy manners. Gen'lemen and lords was vermin, dung, cow-shit, bastards, arseholes and the like. If there was any o' his crew who wanted to throw in their lot with them they could do it in Hell and good riddance. And while he was yelling and raging he pulled out his pistols. Alow the table, the devil, without any on us seeing. And then he laughed, like a boy about to play a trick, and fired, haphazard I should think, and hit me in the leg. I still can't walk right. A curse on the evil bastard!"

He spat another hefty gobbet at the floor.

"And what did you do then?" you asked. "Was the wrong avenged?"

"What the Devil d'you think? No, the crew had voted for Teach and laughed along of him. They all reckoned it was bloody funny to see the likes o' me hit the deck. And Blackbeard bawled out that if he didn't shoot someone from time to time they'd all forget what rogues they were. No bugger would vote for me as cap'n, you may lay to that. I could steer a ship and plot a course, that I could. And fight. But with my leg in tatters I was worth nothing. I invoked our articles and demanded comp'nsation for the maiming. I wanted four hundred pieces of eight, but only got two hundred, since the swabs on the council insisted that the articles only referred to battle. An' damned if I weren't myself to blame for sitting in the way o' Blackbeard's bullets. All in all they reck-oned I come out of it lightly. I signed off, took the King's amnesty, came back to Lon'on, bought myself this here inn and that were that. I were bloody lucky, I can tell you, gen'lemen. Two months later Maynard caught Blackbeard in the James River, Virginia, and settled the hash of more or less all on 'em. They fought to the last man, they did, but now the whole lot on 'em's gone to Davy Jones's locker. A good crew it were, gave way to none. Boardin' an' enterin' with them were a delight. It were a bit diff'rent from standing here in this shitty hole pouring ale for nex' to nothin'!"

"Are you not grateful to be alive and to be able to lead an honest life?" asked you.

Hands looked at you as if you were a blockhead.

"What? Grateful? I ain't got no devil to thank for nothin', write that down in all your papers. Honest life! Give over! What d'you think an honest life is for the likes o' me? It's wearing yourself out for nothin'. Who d'you think 'tis who makes blunt from me being honest? 'Tain't me, I'll warrant you."

He banged his fist on the table so that our tankards jumped.

"This ain't no life," said he. "No, give me a good ship and a smart cap'n and I'd leave this stinking hole tomorrow. Shipmates, fights, gallons o' rum, whores a-linin' up for you when you comes ashore, basking on deck in the sun doin' nothin', that's an honest life, the Devil alone knows."

"Is it worth the gallows?" you asked delicately with an expressive glance towards Execution Dock.

Hands looked at you with an artful countenance.

"You're s'posed to be a clever fellow, or so I've heard," said he. "That's as may be. I don't give a damn. But I'll tell you one thing, if it wasn't for the gallows, there wouldn't be many who'd have been pirates. 'Tis like goin' to war. If you couldn't die from it, there wouldn't be no point in it."

I looked at Hands. He hardly knew what he was saying nor even what he was thinking, yet he was spouting some sense at any rate. Though it was not what you had expected or hoped for. You stubbornly refused to believe that there were people who put their lives at risk for naught. Gentlemen of fortune they called themselves, but they were bunglers as far as fortune was concerned. A short life and a happy one was their intention, and where are they now? Dead, the lot of them. Being flayed alive in Hell, if there be one. Just think, they were so punctilious, elected their captains so that they could be deposed, voted on everything and nothing with every man's voice counting equally, shared their booty fairly and so on and so forth. Punctilious, ay, but did they know what the actual point of it was?

No, they were hanged for their own folly, and rewarded with the short lives they had set themselves. They blamed everything and everyone, but whose fault was it that they died like flies, if not their own? You, Mr Defoe, asked questions about justice and injustice, about good and evil, about freedom and oppression. Well, they understood injustice and tyranny, as well as and better than most, but in every other respect they were as blind as bats. And in that they were not significantly different from ordinary folk.

Twenty-eight

S O WE WERE reunited, Edward the honourable, who said he could distinguish betwixt life and death, Deval the contemptible, who was ready to sell himself for a friendly slap on the back, and myself, Long John Silver, who was ready to sell anyone at all if necessity demanded it.

There was no doubting England's genuine joy in our reunion, however misplaced it might be. He had no eye for people, he saw only good in them. Ay, England was a puzzle: mainly to himself, but also to others, who could see him wavering backwards and forwards, from one side to the other, so that in the end you hardly knew where you were. Why was he elected captain? Because he was a good man who could be depended upon. If there was one thing the crew knew as certain as an amen in church – unlike England himself – it was that England would never adopt the manners of a captain by the grace of God. And that was worth even more than pure gold in their eyes.

You, Mr Defoe, never understood England. You wrote in your history that he possessed such intelligence that it should have made him a better person than he was. He had, according to you, a substantial ration of good nature, and was not lacking in courage. He was not greedy, and abhorred the mistreatment of prisoners. He would have contented himself with more modest plundering and less evil ventures, you argued, if only his companions could have been persuaded to see reason, but he was generally voted down, and as he was part of that detestable company he was forced to be a participant in their dirty handiwork. That is what you wrote.

Ay, you made it sound as if England's heart was as pure and good as an angel's. I must take some of the blame myself, since I spoke in his favour then and indeed do so still. But England was not so bad a case that he would run the risk of ending his days in Heaven, though he had bitter regrets when he knew he had one foot in the grave. But you see, Mr Defoe, what you did not take into consideration was that no one forced England to be captain. He could have avoided it, as I did.

When we were alone together, in England's allotted cabin, I related the same story I had told Deval, though I added a little and suppressed a little here and there to be on the safe side. England swallowed the whole lot, a tribute to me, for whatever was said about him, many-sided as he was, there were plenty more stupid than he.

His own story was that he had had enough after a month on a plantation, that even the cow-shit in Ireland would have been better than sugar cane, and that he had had an itch like raging ants all over his body from not being able to move from the one spot. I well understood that all the wandering had got into his blood. He had escaped, signed on as mate on a sloop, which in turn had been captured by a pirate named Winter, who had asked England to join them and take command of the sloop with the consent of the crew, whereupon Winter and their good selves had been separated by a storm, and here he was now, elected captain and freed from his itch.

"If you'd be willin' to be our quartermaster, Silver, no one would be happier than me," said he.

"You may lay to it. If the men'll have me, o' course."

"They will in time. I don't know anyone who can make himself as well liked an' respected as you. If you show your good side."

"And Deval?" I asked innocently. "After all, he was our cap'n on the *Tonton Louis.*"

"Are you jestin' with an old shipmate?" asked England.

"No," said I, "I proposed him myself. Thought it would do him good."

"An' what happened?"

"He got the idea into his head that he was the on'y one aboard who was worth anythin'."

"That doesn't surprise me," said England, but without a trace of ill-will. "He'll never make a sailor."

"Amen to that," said I in confirmation.

It went as England had foretold. I made myself liked and was soon
elected quartermaster. Even if I am the one to say so, I think it was
with England that I finally found myself and earned respect and more
besides. How else could I have been elected a few years later quartermaster on Flint's *Walrus*, with the worst crew ever to have tramped the
same deck?

A short while after we had been picked up it was decided by the
fo'c's'le council that the ship should set her course for the coast of
Africa. Some of the men had heard, and said they knew for sure, that
there was rich booty to be had there. From the north came the slave
traders with gold, silver, weapons and the knick-knacks they used as
payment to buy negroes. Not to mention the stores and necessaries for
the factories. From the south came the East Indiamen with cloth,
precious stones, spices and sometimes ready money being carried to
London for safe-keeping.

It sounded promising, and the council made their decision on the
basis of these rumours. There was seldom anything else to go on. Ay,
that is how it was, when I think about it, for the most part. We sailed
six thousand sea miles, right through the horse latitudes and their
accursed lack of wind, with the sun burning through our necks and
bodies, all because of a few overheard words. First it was said that an
English man o' war had set out from Antigua to hunt pirates. So we
sailed south towards Barbados with our tail between our legs. Next
someone maintained that the King was intending to declare another
amnesty, someone else that it was just a false story plucked out of the
air, and so the council voted for first one thing and then another, to
write a petition and then to stay as we were. A third person had definite
information about a Spanish silver galleon leaving Cartagena the
following month, and so we lay in wait off Hispaniola for five weeks,
without catching a glimpse of a sail. Then the boatswain had heard that
Roberts was gathering a large pirate fleet in a bay in southern Jamaica.
We shifted the helm and sailed there, but all we found were three
Indians in a canoe. The first mate swore by all he held holy, which was
very little, that there was fresh, clean, cool spring water to be had on

the island of Aves. When we arrived there we found a stinking mud-pool full of lizards and such-like vermin. And so on and so forth in a never-ending stream of uncertainty. We gentlemen of fortune wandered around in a constant haze of rumours and reports, of hear-say and fancies. So it was not just my miscalculations, ascribable to dead reckoning.

There was a wrangling and bickering on board about everything and nothing, almost beyond endurance, for nobody apart from me had the patience to live in this cloud of unknowing. There could be squabbling for days on end about what there might be hard by. Words, nothing but words, into the air, at random: I think, I believe, I've heard, I've read, anyone who can read, I know someone who said, I can promise, on my honour, everyone knows, I don't give a damn, you can stake your life on it. When I tired of it all I would step in and tell them what was what. That stowed their talk, because I had the gift of finding words that were worthy of their belief. It was hardly to be wondered at that they thought I preached and laid down the law. Quite so: I had as much right as the others.

We had been out for three weeks when we sailed into the Doldrums as if into a wall of glass. One moment all the sails had been drawing, singing and roaring, the way wind-filled sails do. The sea was ruffled and foamy white. And the next we were in smooth and eddying waters, the sails flapping, booms and gaffs creaking, halyards and sheets hanging loose, and the cheering rush of the bows fell silent as if for ever. Even our words ebbed away as we all turned our unhappy faces towards the sails and the still and sluggish water. Then everyone swung round to look longingly astern at the frothy foam and sparkling white horses that had so merrily and easily brought us this far.

"What in Hell's name are you all starin' at?" I screeched, breaking the deathly silence. "The world ain't comin' to an end just because of a little calm!"

"What d'you know about it?" I heard a defiant voice cry, someone who did not have the sense to understand that I was only trying to instil some good cheer.

Soon enough, in the next few days, the same big mouth was making surly noises about ships that had been becalmed and rotted away with their crew and all, about ships with half their crew dead of hunger or thirst, about men suffering heat-stroke, or going mad and running amuck with knives and pistols, about gigantic whirlpools in the midst of the calmest sea that had even sucked down ships of the line. Tall stories, of course, superstitious jetsam floating around in sailors' wild imaginations and doing no good. Fine tales in themselves, I'll warrant, but such dung-spreading should surely not be allowed.

I took up the matter with the swab in question, Bowman by name, but he turned a deaf ear.

"I've ev'ry bloody right to say what the Hell I like," was his answer, on behalf of the crew, to my request to keep his views on the right tack till we reached land. "Ain't there no freedom o' speech on this damned coffin?"

"It depends," I replied in a gentle voice, "on what you say."

"Oh, it do, do it? An' where in our articles is it written that I ain't got the right to speak my 'pinion as it stands? I'm just as bloody good as anyone else here."

"I ain't said otherwise, nohow. But you ain't exactly a harbinger o' joy."

"So that's what you're gripin' about. Do you have to be some kind o' performin' fool to open your bloody mouth on this ship? What sort o' bleedin' art'cles are they? Can't folk bear to hear the truth? Go to Hell!"

"And what might the truth be, pray?"

"That this accursed ship is doomed to founder. What the Hell did we want to go to Africa for in any case? Weren't everythin' shipshape in the West Indies? They knows how to brew up a decent rum there, anyhow, and the whores are white. Now we has to fuck blacks, heathens and poxy cunts – 'cause that's what they all are. If we ever gets there, that is. Afore we gets half way through these calms most of our best men will be in Davy Jones's locker, I'll warrant you, you damned half-nigger. D'you think I ain't heard? Sold at a scramble with a load o' slaves. Of your own free will! D'you think I don't know the sort you are? You're the sort that's on the side o' the blacks!"

And he aimed a juicy gobbet of spit just short of my feet. What was I to do with a thick-skulled dung-beetle who was destroying the mood on board? Speech was free, by God it was, but we had to survive too. A person like Bowman could easily ruin everything, spread poison and pestilence, till the others went as crazy as he was.

"You got a headpiece," said I. "You knows we can't turn round at this point. We can't sail agin' the current without there's a wind, an' even if there was a wind, we wouldn't be able to sail into it an' get back to the West Indies without coverin' twice the distance that's left to Africa. A smart lad like you must see that?"

"Flattery won't do, Silver. I've got somethin' between the ears, you're right there. But no bugger's goin' to come along an' tell me what it's to be used for or what I should un'erstand or not. You just mind that!"

"I'll mind it, Bowman, you can depend upon John Silver. I got a mem'ry like a horse."

I contented myself with that for the time being. There was no hope of persuading the likes of Bowman to see reason. Not even friendliness would get through to him. He was a grave-digger, and that was all there was to say about it.

I let him disseminate so much bad feeling that the men began to look about for a scapegoat. A lot of small quarrels had already flared up and sharp words flew through the air when a sheet or halyard had to be raised to take advantage of the occasional breaths of air that came and went when least expected. Even England had begun to see what was happening, but true to character he just went among the crew with a kind word for every man jack of them. Much good did it do. That's how it is with the kind-hearted: they have difficulty in opening their eyes to evil until it is too late.

"What's goin' on?" he asked me after being met everywhere with scorn and derision. "I thought we were agreed on Africa, but now they're all sayin' it's a hellish venture an' blamin' me for pushin' it through. That's unjust, John, don't you think? You remember that as cap'n I kept my mouth shut an' didn't cast a vote for either view. I thought they all seemed of one mind."

"They've forgotten that. We've got a grave-digger aboard spreading gall. He's made the others believe we'll perish in the calm. Now they need somebody to blame if it goes badly. Who else but the cap'n?"

"But I didn't vote! An' they elected me themselves!"

"Nat'rally, but on'y to have someone who could navigate an' someone to hang if it goes to the Devil. Depend upon John Silver. I'll square it all."

Several days passed in the oppressive, suffocating heat under a burning sun that made the pitch and tar in the joins melt so that our feet stuck fast to the deck. We swabbed the decks all day long so that the hull would not open like a sieve, but in the end there were only a dozen of us keeping the pumps and the buckets going. The others sat or lay about on deck, heads hung low, swearing and cursing, drinking of the rum that was left, and concerned even less than usual whether they lived or died. Only Bowman was still going strong. He was bounding around like a hare, with a contented grin on his face, doing what he could to dig a grave for us all.

One morning, before the rum had got a grip on most of them, I called all the men together for a council. It was my right as quartermaster. No one was missing, for they thought they would be able to vent their spleen, avenge themselves on whomsoever they could, on the whole world if necessary.

"Shipmates," said I, with an ominous ring to my voice that made many of them pay special heed, "you knows how things stands on board, 'tis a living Hell, no more an' no less. There ain't naught but moanin' an' complainin'. If it goes on like this, we'll be cuttin' one another's throats long afore we sees an end to this damned calm."

"That's right!" shouted Bowman, as expected. "That's what I've been a-sayin' the whole time. We should never 've set out on this 'ere crossin', that's my view."

"An' which of you voted agin it when we took the decision?" I roared. "Who? Do I hear a voice?"

But all was silent, until Bowman spoke up again.

"There ain't naught wrong with changin' your bloody mind, is there?" said he triumphantly, looking round for approval.

And there may have been a few who nodded agreement, but they did not want to hear it from a rat like Bowman. They cast menacing glances back and forth in search of someone they could hold responsible. Someone would have to be beaten half to death to get the men on to the right tack again, you may lay to it.

"No," said I, "we all makes mistakes, even the best of us, like you yourself, Bowman. Ain't that right, messmates, ain't Bowman the best of all on us? He knows what's what in life. Ask Bowman, an' I'm damned if he can't tell any of us what's what. Ain't I right?"

Bowman grinned and looked round again. He wanted only one thing in this life that he otherwise cared so little for: to be heard, whatever it might cost, even his own, or our, downfall.

"Ain't Bowman worth ten o' the rest of us?" I shouted. "He tells us the truth that none o' the rest of us can see. He tells us exactly what the situation is, that not a single devil of us is goin' to survive this voyage. All we can do is tug our forelocks an' say thank'ee, an' take what's a-comin' to us. If Bowman has signed our death warrants, there ain't much we can do about it."

The men cast malevolent glances at Bowman. Who the Hell did he think he was? No one had the right to tell them what they ought to think and feel, let alone sign their death warrant. Bowman's complacent grin had faded away.

"I proposes Bowman for quartermaster," I bellowed above the muttering that was getting louder. "If there's anybody who can plead our cause with God an' the Devil an' the wind an' the weather, it's him."

"Like Hell it is!" cried a voice from the crowd.

They were the words that opened the flood-gates. They unleashed a torrent of threats, fists and curses. The men nearest to Bowman lunged out at him with ferocious blows. A marlin-spike came flying through the air and hit him in the stomach and he fell. Before he could get up the others were upon him with knives, cudgels and whatever weapons they could lay their hands on in their haste.

"Belay there!" I yelled in my weakest voice, so that the only thing that could be heard was Bowman's wailing.

Bowman turned his terror-stricken gaze towards me.

"Save me, Silver!"

I let out a scornful laugh.

"Why should I?" I asked. "We're gonna die anyhow, the whole lot on us, includin' you, if we can trust your prophecies. To Hell sooner or later, what do it matter? Tie the devil to the mainmast!"

Bowman let out an horrific scream as he was dragged across the deck and lashed to the mast. The crew gave him an agonising and drawn-out death so that he certainly knew he was alive while it lasted. He could have had a quick and immediate death as far as I was concerned. But if the men had slain him on the spot, they would never have got the poison out of their blood. As it was, there was naught but happy and contented faces when the sharks had removed every trace of our evil spirit and of what only an hour before had been a fully living person, even if a deformed variety of the species. I received expressions of thanks from one and all. Quite justifiably, perhaps.

The only man not blinded by my skill was England. He gave me dark looks for weeks afterwards, while the others had soon forgotten there had ever been a human creature called Bowman. I did not bother trying to explain to England that a scapegoat had to be sacrificed if we ourselves wanted to live a while longer on this earth. The likes of England, who by their own claim can distinguish betwixt life and death, do not understand that sometimes we have to choose betwixt the one and the other.

A week or two later the water was ruffled by a steady, fresh west wind that took us to the coast of Africa. For once the rumours were true. We captured eleven prizes in a very short time, without losing a single man in battle. We set fire to some of the ships and scuttled others, two of them we crewed as gentlemen of fortune, because we had a super-abundance of men with all those who wanted to join us, and the remainder were permitted to sail off as best they could, though empty. Lane and Sample were elected captains on the two vessels that were to try their luck on their own, *Queen Anne's Revenge* and *Flying King*, as for some inscrutable reason they renamed their ships. Little luck it brought them, for what a ship was christened, so let her stay, says I, though I am not fond of such rituals in general. Lane and Sample crossed the Atlantic and lay in wait off the coast of Brazil. They managed to take a few prizes of modest value before they met a Portuguese man o' war that settled them for good and all. Twelve died in battle, thirty-eight were hanged on the spot, and the rest, negroes and Indians, were sold as slaves.

I heard the news of their wretched end many years later, to no avail, and as always too late to grieve or take revenge, even if I had wanted to do either. The way things were, the best course was always to forget your shipmates as soon as they were out of your sight. They vanished without trace for the most part in any case.

And so we met La Bouche and his parrot in a desolate bay, Whydah Road, on the coast of Africa. England became richer by a parrot, we had a merry feast and declared our brothership, and took solemn oaths to make common cause against the rest of the world and to meet again on the island of Johanna. But life took its usual course, and having sailed together for some weeks we encountered a storm, were separated, and never had sight nor sound of each other again. La Bouche sank off Mayotte, built himself a new boat and went off to Madagascar, and I have heard no more of him since.

Ah, such was the life of the pirate, then, I have to tell you, Mr Defoe, and all you others who made yourselves their chroniclers: a circle drawn round their ship, lacking in goals and human contact. We were not like other seamen. Our ships did not sail to get anywhere. We called ourselves brothers and shipmates, but family and friends were the last thing we were interested in. Christians called us enemies to mankind, and in a way they were right, because nobody could be our friend, not even ourselves. No, our memory was short, and had to be, as far as humanity was concerned, if we were to keep ourselves in good spirits. Who missed La Bouche when he disappeared? None of us, you may lay to it, with the possible exception of his parrot. We had seen too many swallowed by the sea of uncertainty, on which we drifted like holy spirits with neither wake nor bow wave.

All in all we took twenty-six ships under England, with ease and skill, except for the last: *Cassandra*; and the first off the coast of Africa: the *Eagle*, a pink captained by Rickets, Cork her home port – as if I had not had enough pother as far as Ireland was concerned. Not that Rickets was foolish enough to put up resistance with his six cannon and seventeen men against our two hundred. He struck his flag before we even had time to fire a warning shot.

England and Deval were naturally overjoyed when they saw we had laid hands on an Irishman. England invited Rickets in, a stocky figure, bony and bent, with a big scar at the side of his mouth that made him look as if he was sneering all the time. England took him off to his cabin, to the vexation of our men, who had wanted to amuse themselves a little at the captain's expense. But England stood his ground for once, and declared that not a hair of his countryman's head should be touched, and that those who wanted to join us should do so of their own free will or otherwise be given free passage.

"In compensation," said he, "I'll forego my two shares of the booty this time. You can split 'em squarely amongst yourselves. But no brutality, mind!"

England explained to Rickets that if he had been able to prevail, the *Eagle* would have been allowed to sail on her way with her cargo and all, but that he could not do just what he wanted on a ship that flew the Jolly Roger.

"But," said he, "I undertake that you shall leave here unharmed in life and limb. No one shall say of Edward England that he mistreated his fellow-countrymen."

"Edward England," said Rickets with a start. "Is that your name?"

"Indeed, an' it is so," said England. "Born in Wicklow of honest Irish parents, and lately fisherman an' sailor out o' Kinsale."

Rickets' eyes at once took on a frightened look, though it was hard to discern with his incessant mocking grin.

"What's amiss with that name?" I asked menacingly.

"Amiss?" stammered Rickets.

"Don't try to fool the likes of us," I persisted. "There ain't many who've done that and lived to tell the tale."

By this time Rickets was beside himself with fear.

"What's got into you, John?" asked England angrily. "Rickets is our guest."

"Let me take care o' this!" I replied.

"John," repeated Rickets, drawing a deep breath. "John Silver?"

"You see?" said I to England. "The swab ain't got a clear conscience."

I grabbed Rickets by the collar and jerked him up from the chair.

"May we hear," I roared, "what's wrong with bein' called Edward England and John Silver?"

I had to give him a good shaking before anything intelligible emerged from his crooked mouth.

Perhaps I should not have been so persistent, but how was I to know what he would spill out? What we heard was that I was wanted for murther, and that England and someone called Deval were wanted for aiding and abetting, and that all three of us were accused of theft and unlawful contact with the enemy during the last war.

"Murther of whom?" said England in astonished disbelief.

"Of a fisherman from Kinsale, Dunn by name," said Rickets.

"What did I say?" I interrupted quick as a flash. "The English want to hang us, me most of all, for telling the story of that damned governor and his daughter."

Rickets shook his head amiably, thinking to reassure me.

"No," said he, "it ain't the English. 'Tis the fisherman's daughter. She's the one behind it."

"It's a lie!" I screamed.

"Easy all!" said England. "There must be some misunderstanding. Eliza can't have accused you."

"Like Hell it's a misunderstanding," I retorted. "This blackguard's lying to save his skin."

Before England had time to think or Rickets time to expand his text I drove him out on to the deck. England undoubtedly thought he could distinguish between life and death, but what would he do if he found out that I had murthered Dunn and left Eliza high and dry? Not to mention Deval.

"Messmates!" I yelled. "Here's a man what's spreadin' lies about your cap'n and your quartermaster. What d'you say to that?"

My words were met by a bellow of anger from the men. England came rushing out of his cabin, but too late. Our reckless crew had already seized hold of Rickets, and it was not long before he was silenced for good and the world was one captain by the grace of God the poorer. While Rickets was being drained of life, I made cautious enquiries among his crew, but I was lucky, for they were a collection of dregs from all the corners of the earth, and the four Irishmen among them had never set foot in Kinsale, and certainly never heard of Edward England or John Silver. Not only that, but Rickets had been a slave-driver of a captain. Not the most extreme of tyrants like Captain Wilkinson, but rough, brutal and mad enough for the crew not to mind in the least seeing him run the gauntlet of knives and daggers and hearing him cry out to the heavens as he was sliced up.

Afterwards, England was in a fury.

"You don't kill people just because they're stupid enough to believe any lies an' lunacies that are going around."

"But don't you see?" I ventured, "Rickets would've told all an' sundry who we were and what we were a-doin' if we'd let him live. We'd have been doubly hunted and pursued."

"John Silver," said England, in a sorrowful tone amidst his anger, "I ain't a fool. We've took liberties in this world that'll lead sooner or later to the gallows, you may lay to that. But to start murtherin' folk for false accusations, that's somethin' else altogether."

"Not even for the sort you can be hanged for?" I asked. "So when should we murther anyone?"

"Never, John. D'you hear? Never!"

He took me by the collar of my coat and shook me as I had done with Rickets. He had strong hands, had Edward England, I can warrant. I did not attempt to defend myself. In my heart I knew, I think, that England could always distinguish between life and death, including mine. Was that not why he was holding me in his iron grip? He was one of the few who left everyone to lead their lives as they saw fit, no matter what.

It was about that time that England began to show signs of remorse when we set upon a ship, plundering it and humiliating its crew. It began with Rickets and became even worse with the *Cadogan* from Bristol, with Skinner as its captain.

This Skinner was unlucky in life. He was a captain by the grace of God, but he had no help from on high. Providence in this case was on our side. We had on board a dozen of Skinner's old crew, including our coxswain, Graves, who never forgot a wrong, though his memory in other respects was no more to boast about than anybody else's. The fact was that Captain Skinner had come to regard Graves and his cronies as lazy, unruly good-for-nothings and had therefore put them on a navy ship, where they had been straightway pressed into service. Skinner had also refused to pay out the wages they were due, because pay, in his opinion, was a reward for work, not for mischief and obstruction that put the vessel's safety at risk.

Graves and I were standing at the rail to receive the *Cadogan*'s crew as they were led on board the *Fancy*. England was still on the *Cadogan* with a score of men taking an inventory of the booty.

When Skinner's head appeared above the rail, Graves started jumping up and down in eagerness and clapping his hands like a child.

"Nay, but is that the Devil I see?" said he with a jovial laugh when he recognised Skinner's mug. "Ay, it is indeed. This man, John, is no better than Satan himself. Welcome aboard, Cap'n Skinner. A thousand welcomes. To what do we owe this honour?"

When Skinner recognised his old crewman his whole body began to shake, like Rickets and the others before him, and he would have lost his grip on the rope ladder had Graves not caught hold of him and hoisted him aboard.

"No, my good man," said he with a reproachful look, "it won't do to leave us so soon. I'm greatly indebted to you, as well you know, and would dearly love to repay you in the same coin."

Graves called to his mates, who were almost as delighted as Graves himself. They bound Skinner to the capstan and started bombarding him with bottles that slashed deep wounds. Then they chased him round the deck with whips till they could run no more, Skinner begging and pleading for his life the while.

"My good cap'n," said Graves finally, out of breath but in the same rapturous tone, "since you've been such an honest and just cap'n, you're goin' to have a painless death. No, don't thank us now, please, you can do that when we meets up again in Hell."

Upon which Graves drew his musket and shot him through the head.

When England heard the shot he hastened back as fast as the oars would carry him.

"What's goin' on here?" he asked of me, not as John Silver but as quartermaster of the *Fancy*.

I explained what had happened and why. England's face fell. He went over to the remains of Skinner, looked at him long and hard as if he were trying to restore him to life, and then turned to me.

"Silver," said he, "see that the man has a decent burial, an' clean up the deck. A slaughter-house, that's what we've become, no more nor less. An' then you can provision the *Cadogan*. I propose Davis as captain, an' let him take that devil Graves an' his mates with him. If they stay on board my ship, 'tis certain I'll finish them off at the first opportunity, an' what good would that do either them or me?"

"I understands how you feels," said I.

"Like Hell you do, Silver. You're no better than the rest o' them."

"There you're mistaken, Edward," said I. "I has my faults, like all on us, but I don't murther folk unnecessarily just for the fun of it."

"What about Rickets?" said England with a bitter look.

"That was necessary. One day you'll thank me for it."

"Never, John, d'you hear! An' don't tell me you did it for my sake. You did it behind my back an' without askin' my opinion."

"You can believe what you want, Edward. But I'm your friend, whether you likes it or no. You ain't got no other aboard this ship, nor hardly any elsewhere, with the life you've led. Remember that: the only one who would come to your defence is me."

He made no answer, but returned to his cabin with stooped shoulders. Before closing the door he called back to me.

"An' Silver, I don't want my shares from the *Cadogan*. 'Tis blood money, that's what it is. Dole the shit out amongst the crew!"

This was picked up by sharp ears. Of a sudden, amidst all the activity, Pew's croaky and malicious voice could be heard.

"An huzza for Cap'n England, lads!"

And so there was a cheer for Captain England, until I put a stop to the din with a roar that frightened most of them. For certain I was of one thing: mockery and humiliation were not Edward England's due.

Twenty-nine

CAPTAIN SKINNER WAS the beginning of the end for England. He mostly kept out of the way, brooding in his cabin and leaving me to sail the ship, apart from the navigation and during an attack, when he came up to prevent atrocities and misdeeds. It was as if he were endeavouring to buy his freedom for eternity and appease his conscience by sparing all the lives he could. I for my part occasionally tried to persuade him that by this time no one would thank him for it, not even God if there was one, but it was a waste of effort. England had got it into his head that he should poison the rest of his days in self-reproach and remorse.

After the *Cadogan* we lay up in a bay for careening. Not far from thence was a native village, and when the work on the ship was complete the crew went into a frenzy. They chased off the men and fucked their women for several days from morn to night. They wanted to make up for what they had not had since the West Indies, six months before, and take an advance on what they would not get for many months to come. Events went as might have been expected. After a few days the men of the village returned with reinforcements and attacked from all directions. We shot a couple of dozen, and lost a handful ourselves. But none on our side grieved about it. We came off lightly, they thought, for such an orgy.

England had remained in his cabin almost the whole time, as if he did not want to know what was going on, but he emerged once we had raised the anchor and sailed the ship out of the bay. It has to be said that he had become a remarkably good captain as time had passed. It was many a long year since he had confused port and starboard, calculated our drift in the wrong direction, or paid out instead of taking in the sheets. But there is not much to sailing a ship. It was with people that England had difficulties, save when they were dead.

We headed for Malabar, in India, and in less than a month we took seven rich prizes. In the end we were so low in the water that we had to close the cannon-ports in the slightest swell. So the fo'c's'le council decided to sail to Madagascar, where we stayed for a month. We replenished our stores of meat and sold some of our booty to local chieftains, who paid us in gold, silver and precious stones. The men fully understood that we could not sail around so heavily laden without endangering the ship. This time they kept themselves in check.

Then we set course for the island of Johanna, north-west of Madagascar, where we had agreed to meet La Bouche, who gave England the parrot that later came into my possession and was renamed Captain Flint. By then England was devoting himself as much to the parrot as to the ship and the rest of us, when there was nothing else afoot.

On the way to Johanna we met up with Taylor in the *Victory* and joined him. England would rather have avoided him, because Taylor was a brute who showed no mercy. The crew of the *Victory* liked and revered him, because his cruelty was excessive and notorious; in fact by the end only Low and Flint surpassed Taylor in that respect. But that is how it was with most crews: there was no one they looked up to as much as those who were worse than themselves. That was the only forgiveness of their sins they craved.

With Taylor in our wake we sailed straight for Johanna, and what did we meet there but two Englishmen, the *Cassandra* and the *Greenwich*, and a brig from Ostend with twenty-two guns. We had sixty-four at our disposal, thirty with Taylor and thirty-four of our own. Making the ship ready did not take long, whereupon we headed straight into the bay: against England's will, but he was outvoted.

The brig put her tail between her legs, made her way out through the shallows, and slipped off up the coast. But who would have believed that the captain of the *Greenwich* was such a coward that he would follow suit, thus leaving the *Cassandra* to look after herself? Nevertheless it was foolish and arrogant of us to sail headlong into the channel as we did. The *Fancy* with her deeper draught ran aground and stuck fast mid-channel. Not a single one of our guns could be brought to bear, whereas the *Cassandra*, which had anchored across the channel, raked us with one broadside after another. Taylor in the *Victory* behind us could not return fire without sinking us, and had to throw out an anchor and pull himself past.

It was a blood-bath. We lost thirty men in twenty minutes, with the same number wounded or maimed. Yet it was England who looked the most tormented of all. Being the man he was, he took the guilt for all the dead on himself. It was his fault, he thought, even though he had voted against it, that the *Fancy* was streaked red with the blood running out of the scuppers.

But England knew that the only way to put a stop to the massacre was to silence the *Cassandra*'s guns. He, with me alongside, as was my nature when life was at stake, raced round like Furies on deck among all the corpses, screams, cannon-balls and splintered wood, to exhort the living to fight for their lives and mine. England put himself at the head of a boarding party, fifty men who set off with terrifying battle cries just as Taylor was able at last to let his cannon sweep over the *Cassandra*'s deck. It gave me, and a few courageous men, time to move our biggest guns into position, the eighteen-pounders, more accurate than most in the right hands. And we had a gunner on the *Fancy* who was second to none. In everyday life an obtuse blockhead, but he had no equal in aiming a cannon, strange as it may seem. I told him – because somebody had to do his thinking for him – to shoot off the *Cassandra*'s anchor cable, and after three attempts we saw the *Cassandra*, to our delight, turning about and firing her broadsides, already more uneven, out into nothingness. It was high time, for they had already sunk one of our boats with a ball that transformed eight of our men on the starboard oars into shreds of meat.

The *Cassandra*'s guns fell silent, to our cheers and jeers. But do you think that made her strike her flag? No – her captain was one of those who would sacrifice a whole crew for the sake of his honour. The flag was still flying from the stern when Taylor put his boats in the water with one hundred and fifty men, to support the *Fancy*'s fifty with England at their head, ready to do battle. Why in Hell's name did not they strike their flag? I thought to myself. They surely had not put a fuse to the powder store? I yelled and screamed where I stood at our shattered prow, but was I heard? No, our men in the boats thought I was urging them on, and boarded with an infernal howl that soon turned into anger and disappointment.

There were only the dead and wounded on the *Cassandra*. The uninjured survivors, the officers among them, had fled under cover of their own powder-smoke. Taylor was raging at the miscalculation, despite not having lost so many men as we had, and wanted to put to death those of the *Cassandra*'s crew still remaining. No, that monster knew no restraint, despite the fact that he was scarce able to move his hands at all. He could just about hold a musket, but had to depend upon a few selected helpers, including his quartermaster and boatswain, to carry out his daily work for him.

But England stood up to Taylor and said there were sufficient dead as it was. Seventy of England's men had been lost and twenty more would die of their wounds.

"Ain't it enough?" bellowed England, just as I myself came climbing up on deck.

Taylor remained motionless, except for a wink and an imperceptible gesture of his crippled hand. It must have been a signal, because before England had a chance to see what was happening, Taylor's boatswain had pulled out his cutlass and finished off three of the *Cassandra*'s wounded crew. Everything went completely quiet and still on board, but only momentarily. Then England let out a roar that made even Taylor step back a pace, whereupon England drew his cutlass, and with a majestic blow that only he was capable of, as good as clove the boatswain in two equal parts, neither more alive than the other. Taylor gave a flicker of a smile, as the connoisseur he was, but everyone else was transfixed.

"Any man," said England, his chest heaving like the swell of the sea, "who assaults a wounded man or a prisoner will follow this devil to Davy Jones's locker. Is that plain enough? Is there anyone of a different mind?"

There was not.

"Cap'n England is right!" said I in a clear and distinct voice. "The *Cassandra*'s men didn't fight o' their own free will, you know that as well as I do. And now we've lost seventy men. We need every man who can walk or stand.

"Don't we, sir?" I added, then went up to Taylor, placed myself before him at a distance of less than a foot, and glared straight into his dead eyes. "Don't we?"

Taylor blinked and opened his mouth, but his deformed hands did not move.

"Don't we?" I repeated a third time, now in the voice that made most people's hair stand on end willy-nilly.

Taylor gave a slow nod, and his eyes, in that topsy-turvy world of his, came to life, for fear is also a kind of life.

He told his men and ours, in a hollow voice, that they should always give ear to the likes of me.

"Booty first," he went on, to give the impression of having thought for himself. "Securing the prize and our booty, including the *Cassandra*'s brave crew, that's the mainstay, so it is. Mr Silver is right, you may lay to it."

The men cast me admiring glances as I went by. England had lost his head and his temper, that was one thing, that could happen to anybody. But I had very deliberately stood up to Taylor when he had just suffered a defeat, in a manner of speaking. That deserved respect.

I went over to England, who was standing off to one side by himself, head hung low. I for my part was careful not to show that I felt some elation in being right and England wrong. For he himself had now struck down with his bare hands one of those whom the world could probably do without.

"You see, Edward," said I in a friendly tone, "you needs me if you wants to stay alive and in good health for a while longer. Taylor ain't to be trifled with, as you knows."

"John," he replied, and it was the first time he had called me by my forename since Skinner, "I don't give a fig for Taylor an' life an' health. I've killed a livin' bein'. D'you understand what that means?"

"You were fully within your rights, Edward. 'Twas for a good cause."

"No, John, there you're wrong. There's never a good cause, I can see that now, though 'tis too late. Not takin' life, John, that's the highest cause. An' takin' life is the greatest crime of all."

"Even if you saved the lives of half a dozen or more o' the *Cassandra*'s men that Taylor's bo's'n would've chopped the heads off, if he'd been allowed to do his worst?"

"Even then. I tell you, John, the bo's'n has his conscience to contend with an' I have mine. An' in any case, how can we be so sure that he would really have despatched the others? Did I ask that afore I lost my temper? Just think! If you hadn't turned up, Taylor would've set all his men on me an' on those who would've defended me. It could easily have been a worse blood-bath than the one I tried to stop. No, there's only one Commandment, thou shalt not kill, an' I've transgressed it. For sure, 'tis the end o' me, John, as a human bein'."

For once he looked as if he was absolutely certain in his mind. But his eyes were staring straight ahead, dead and empty of the life he held so sacred.

It took two weeks to clean up after the bungle with the *Cassandra*, burying the dead, getting the *Fancy* afloat, taking an inventory, apportioning the *Cassandra*'s rich cargo, and getting one of the vessels into good shape. The *Fancy* was so badly damaged that we let her lie where she was and devoted our energies to the *Cassandra*, which was to be our new ship.

No one would have said that our spirits were high. England made an effort to do what was incumbent upon him, but he was a sorry sight. Taylor stayed on board the *Victory* for the most part. But first there was a dispute about the medicaments on the *Cassandra*, because half of Taylor's crew were rotting away with syphilis or the clap. I put a stop to it by pointing out that Taylor's men needed all the help they could get with such a madman for a captain. With the *Cassandra*'s quicksilver, I said, they might have some relief from their Hell, and our men could think themselves lucky they had not as yet been condemned to death for fornication.

After that, whenever the wind blew from Taylor's direction we could hear his oaths and curses at the moral weakness and frailty of some folk, at those who should not be allowed a command under the Jolly Roger, at those who brought shame and dishonour on the proud band of gentlemen of fortune, and at those who undermined the evil reputation of pirates, so valuable for affrighting most people out of their wits.

It was not long ere there were murmurings among our own crew again. I defended England, naturally, and reminded them that under him we had become quite rich, and that there were not many who could lay claim to such success. Just look at Taylor, I said, who was swearing and carrying on. Envy, that's what it was. He wanted to get at our booty by being elected captain, for what had he managed to seize himself? – a handful of coasters as poor as church mice, naught else. That was language our men understood. They kept to themselves for a bit and answered back when Taylor's men mocked them for having chosen as captain a coward who could not even stand the sight of blood.

These would never have amounted to more than skirmishes, and we would have sailed off peacefully, if Captain Mackra, of the captured *Cassandra*, had not suddenly appeared in our midst with a request for free passage for himself and what was left of his crew. Demanding free passage and the return of his ship after having killed four score of our men! Had it not been for England, I would have raised no objection to Captain Mackra's slow death, in accordance with the wishes of the crew.

It was lucky for Mackra that it was England on the *Cassandra* that he appealed to first. Taylor had promised a reward of ten thousand silver dollars to the man, whether native or gentleman of fortune, who delivered Mackra on a plate, dead or alive. England received Mackra on board with some reluctance. It was obvious that the latter had not grasped a single thing about how gentlemen of fortune regulated their affairs to the advantage of all. Mackra imagined that England could decide everything as he thought best, that he was appointed by the grace of God, like Mackra himself.

"My good Cap'n Mackra," explained England, "unfortunately I don't think you've understood the sort o' people we're dealin' with. They hate cap'ns, all cap'ns, even their own, except for the very roughest, like

Taylor. They detest you very particularly, since they hold you accountable for eighty dead."

"I was only doing my duty," said Captain Mackra vehemently.

I was there as the representative of the crew, and had to burst out laughing.

"If you wants to get out of here alive," said I, "I'll give you some good advice. Never let the word dooty cross your lips again. It wouldn't be very sensible with an hundred an' twenty dead on both sides an' on your conscience."

"On my conscience!" exclaimed Mackra angrily. "Who was it that attacked? Didn't I have both the right and the duty to defend myself?"

"No," said England curtly.

"But we would have been slaughtered to the last man," objected Mackra.

"How can you be sure of that?" asked England, predictably. "I'll tell you this, Cap'n, the only duty you have is to save lives. For that reason and that reason alone I'll do what I can to let you sail away from here with your men. But don't expect any compassion or sympathy. You haven't deserved either, any more than we have."

Mackra looked at England uncomprehendingly.

"'Twill not be easy," England went on. "I'll do what I can, but you'll also have to mollify Taylor yourself if 'tis to work."

"And how do I do that?" asked Mackra.

England threw up his hands.

"The Devil alone knows," he said. "But ask Silver here! No one has the measure of ruthless ruffians better'n he has."

Mackra turned to me.

"The best thing," said I, after a moment's thought, "would be to throw yourself on Taylor's mercy an' be hanged or quartered. That might appease him enough to let your men go free. But that's no help for you, o' course. England here would stand up to him, but you don't look as if you've got that kind o' bravery in you. So I suggest you invite Taylor here, fill him with rum, express your respect and admiration for the devil of a cap'n he is, and hope for the best. More'n that you can't do."

*

Taylor came aboard later the same day. He was in an exceedingly violent temper, shouting and swearing as he was hoisted aboard. With his disabled hands he was unable to climb a rope ladder without aid. Neither England nor I was there to receive him, because it vexed and humiliated Taylor to show his infirmity before those who were not subject to his command and rage, before those he could not threaten with death when the mood took him.

"Where in Hell's name is that lily-livered swab Mackra?" he yelled as soon as he had both feet on deck. "I'll cut the ears off the bastard!"

But that was playing to the gallery. Not even Taylor could think that Mackra would be so obtuse as to come back completely empty-handed.

He kicked open the door of the cabin, bellowing for all to hear.

"Hell an' damnation, England, ain't you broken the arsehole's neck yet?"

But he closed the door after him, to find out what Mackra wanted before he took any further steps. I placed myself hard by a hatch to the poop deck so I could hear what went on.

Mackra was brave enough behind his guns, but now he was down on all fours pouring out words of praise in Taylor's honour. The latter said very little, just drinking one noggin of rum after another while he waited to hear what Mackra's business was. But it never came, and finally Taylor lost patience.

"Out with it!" he shouted. "What is it you're after?"

And Mackra, not having comprehended a thing, replied that he needed a ship of some kind to sail himself and his men home.

"I see," said Taylor, as sweet as syrup, "and what would we get in return? Can you compensate us in some way, Cap'n?"

"But you've already got my ship, the *Cassandra*, and her cargo. Ain't that compensation enough?"

"Got?" screeched Taylor, suddenly beside himself with fury and contempt. "Got! We took her, at the cost of eighty dead master mariners. We've paid a hundredfold for that damn hulk. And you think you can buy yourself free passage with somethin' already in our possession. Ain't there no sense or wit in that cap'n's head o' yours at all?"

Taylor stamped on the floor, as he always did when he was in a rage, since he could not make a fist and bang it on the table.

England sat in silence. Then I heard Taylor get up.

"If you imagine, Mackra," said he, walking over to the door, "that we owe you anythin', you're mistaken. My men detest you for the scum you are, and now you're going to pay in our coin."

He kicked open the door.

"Taylor," said England suddenly in an authoritative voice, "for once I'm with you. Cap'n Mackra does not deserve our sympathy. He has eighty dead on his conscience. But you an' I ain't much better in such matters. I've said it already, but you wouldn't listen. We've seen enough blood in this accursed bay. So I'm tellin' you now, Taylor, it'll be over my dead body if you so much as lay a finger on Mackra."

There was silence for a moment, and then I heard Taylor hiss, "All right, it'll be as you say, England. Over your dead body."

Then Taylor shouted, "Quartermaster, come here!"

He had forgotten in his wrath that he was not on board his own ship. And I strode into the cabin with an expression on my face that would have struck terror into the worst.

"Where's Cap'n Mackra, cap'n of the *Cassandra*?" I roared.

Taylor jumped at my words. Mackra cringed and England looked at me as if he had seen a ghost. I drew my cutlass and thrust it into the table with such force that the blade quivered. Fear glistened in Mackra's eyes, and not even Taylor was entirely at ease. He probably thought he knew how I would view things and may have felt a mixture of delight and apprehension when I came in.

I took a few steps towards Taylor, and he in turn could not help taking a step back. But then I poured out four big glasses of rum and raised one of them.

"A toast to a brave cap'n."

Taylor looked at me uncertainly. He must have known I could not mean him.

"A toast for a cap'n abandoned by his own men," I went on, "who yet defends himself against trebly superior forces. That's a bit different from shits like you who wouldn't attempt to hurt a fly unless you'd ten men to the enemy's one!"

I looked long and hard first at England and then at Taylor.

"So a toast for Cap'n Mackra!" I bawled, with my hand on my cutlass.

Taylor first, hurriedly, and then England, more slowly, with a scarcely perceptible smile on his lips, picked up their glasses for a toast.

"May he survive us all!" said I, draining my glass and banging it down with such force that it shattered.

"By all the fiends in Hell!" said Taylor, full of admiration.

He had an eye for performances like mine, no two ways about it.

Ah, that's the way they were, as often as not, these cruel pirate captains – like weather vanes. One minute they would be blustering that they were going to exterminate half the world, the next all their intentions, zeal and enthusiasm were as if swept away by the wind. They lost all interest, let captains and other riff-raff live that they had sworn would suffer hellish tortures and die. No, they were never good murtherers, whatever appearance they gave, and they would have been utterly useless as hangmen, because they would soon have tired of the monotony of such an occupation. But that is the way of things when you do not know what you want or what the point of it is. Taylor, Flint and Low make a poor showing when compared with such artists as Cromwell and Saint Dominic, if you ask me. That is something I have to say to you, Mr Defoe, who never made such comparisons, and to all those who cry out for vengeance on the likes of me.

Thus I saved the life of Edward England, and of Captain Mackra into the bargain, since from then on Taylor wanted to keep on good terms with me as the best in my field. Mackra was presented with the old *Fancy*, shot to pieces as she was, to do with what he would or could. He managed to set up temporary rigging, take on food and water, and make his way to Malabar. There he received all kinds of honours, was made Governor and then sent out at the head of a squadron to hunt and destroy pirates. But one thing is certain: had I ever met him again when I was on the *Walrus*, I would not have hesitated to put an end to his richly rewarded life. And by the powers, it would not have surprised me if even Edward England, in Hell or Heaven by then – if either existed – had given me a nod of gratitude despite everything.

He was not so bad a swab that he would not have done so.

But all this was not enough for him to carry on as captain. We sailed as far as Mauritius, in company with Taylor, without encountering a single prize. The men used that as an excuse, called a meeting of the fo'c's'le council and deposed England. It was inscribed in the log-book, for these things were recorded scrupulously, that England had shown too much humanity in the case of Mackra and was therefore no longer fitted to be their captain. In the struggle for life and death, one of them said, you could not have a captain with such a weakness for folks' well-being. That could be mortally dangerous, it was felt; and not without reason.

England was put in a small boat to make his way to Madagascar if he could, but without his parrot. I was burthened with that.

Taylor was elected captain of both the *Victory* and the *Cassandra*. I was elected his quartermaster and stood up to him every time the crew had a grievance. But I was also the one who dealt out punishments on his behalf, according to custom. And so it turned out here as everywhere, I became feared and respected by everyone. Incorruptible, that was my reputation, a man who could not be bought for money nor for aught else.

I sailed with Taylor for six months. We captured rich prizes and were as cruel as few others, now that England was gone. I and many with me became rich when we captured none less than the Viceroy of Goa and were able to demand a ransom. So I was half way to being a man of substance when we came to Madagascar, and with no great eagerness to continue this free but narrow existence.

Not that I had anything else to put in its place. I signed off on the island of Sainte Marie, with the permission of the ship's council, and thus was able to take my share of the booty with me, despite the fact that the company was not breaking up. This was against the rules, but I think that most of them were secretly pleased to be rid of me, the only sort of conscience they could boast. I went to Plantain on Ranter Bay where England had found a final refuge, and saw him die. If he was pleased at my being there, he did not show it. I must have been his evil genius from beginning to end, the one who had dragged him down to perdition.

Even so, he was the most upright of men. He would submit to no one, and he let every man live in the way each found good. But to his own detriment, you may lay to that, as sure as my name is John Silver. For if anyone died a tormented and unhappy death, of remorse and bad conscience, it was Edward England. And it brought neither benefit nor joy to anyone.

Thirty

SO, THERE YOU have it in the end, Mr Defoe, my account of Edward England, with flesh on the bones, not just the names of all the ships captured by him and Taylor, jointly or severally. For you must admit that your own history of Edward England was rather scant: little more than a lifeless skeleton that no one would have believed had it not been for your good name.

Yet a whole living life is something very special, as England thought in his own way. Do you not think so too, Mr Defoe? I have found myself wondering, after all, what the meaning was of a life like England's. Is there any point in having so kind a nature as his? Ah, you are no doubt rubbing your hands, Mr Defoe, and thinking that I am beginning to regret my criminal life, as England did, and that I will be lying awake at night, sleepless with remorse at my sinful and godless life. But there you are wrong. I was not so good as England, nor so evil as Taylor, and that was that. My own articles were to watch my back; that is one thing, and good and evil are another. I am sorry we cannot speak further about that, but you are as silent as the grave wherein you now repose.

Here, on my cliff, silence has enveloped me more and more, if it be not simply that I am going deaf. At any rate, there is not the same noise and bustle there once was. Most of the blacks have left me to my fate, which is only right and proper. I cannot even trouble myself now to get angry when they come to ask my permission and blessing before they take their leave. It saps your strength writing down a life like mine. Ay, I am probably hastening my own death by trying to shake some life into this corpse of memories. I must have become like you in this respect, Mr Defoe.

You always arrived at the Angel for our discussions panting for breath.

If it were not one thing, it would be another: a politician whose views you were raging against as if the world were about to be destroyed, a creditor dogging your heels, an opponent you wanted to quell for good, a printer you wished would burn in Hell because to save his own skin he had revealed you as the author of some controversial polemic, a critic you sought to crush because he had accused you of dissimulation or because he had not understood one of your writings. There was always something to make your blood boil and get you raging like a Fury at the folly of mankind.

One day when you arrived I was already settled at a table in the window, and had just seen a jackdaw pecking at the ear of one of the hanging corpses on Execution Dock, which pleased me immeasurably, at the jackdaw's expense.

You seated yourself heavily at the table. Your eyes were rheumy and red-rimmed, your skin pale to the point of transparency, as if the blood were drained from your body, and your right hand looked as if it was stiffened in cramp round an invisible pen. I called for two large glasses of honest cane-sugar rum and you quaffed yours in one, without blinking. It would not have surprised me if I had actually heard the liquid splashing down into your stomach, so emptied of everything did you seem.

"My good friend," said you, when the rum had infused a few drops of life into you, "being a writer is a painful business. I have been inscribing page after page throughout the night. Struggling against the plague, running around the whore-houses with Moll Flanders, teaching Colonel Jack how to steal, and, as if that were not enough, I have finally demonstrated, after four hundred pages, the principles of good Christian marriage. Two books last year. Almost four thousand pages and a couple of essays a week. Can you imagine that as a life anyone would willingly lead? You were at least able to wear gloves. But look at this hand of mine, fixed as it is in writer's cramp. Look at me, completely spent, empty as a barrel when the rum's been drunk, you could say."

"Why?" I asked. "You'll kill yourself if you go on like this!"

"I know it," you replied with a weary smile. "That is exactly what I am doing. All my life I have been waging war with my pen on one subject or another, both for and against, with all the tricks and stratagems at my command, permitted or proscribed. I was the extended arm of government, in good faith at first, but later not even that. My pen was my weapon, sharp and keen, but was I the one holding it?"

You suddenly gave a hollow laugh.

"Do you know, Long, for twenty years this right hand was not my own. I was paid by the government to write in Mist's rag – Mist, the arch-enemy of the government. I was paid from secret funds to moderate his criticism of the government. My life has been one extensive sequence of make-believe and deceit. In short, it has not been my own. So now I am writing about Crusoe, Moll Flanders, Singleton and the others to avoid being myself. Or perhaps for the first time in my life to be myself. Does that make sense to you?"

"No."

"Well, at all events, that is the way of it. When I write about Moll Flanders, I am alive as never before."

"In that case this new life must be a confoundedly tiring one," said I, "to judge from the look of you. Who is Moll Flanders, might I ask?"

"A whore," said you, in an apologetic tone.

It was my turn to laugh.

"Now I understand why you look so troubled. Couldn't you have picked an easier woman – no pun intended – since you had a free choice? A rich lady of the landed gentry and that happy Christian marriage you've written about?"

But no, obviously you could not. You only wanted to write about the doomed and the sinful, and for that you had to take the consequences. One thing is certain: I did not envy you the life you led. I asked you whether you were happy with it.

"Quite honestly," you replied, throwing up your hands, "I have never had the time to ponder the matter."

But one day, the final occasion we met, you came rushing in with eyes that for once were sparkling with excitement and anticipation.

"Today at last you will see one!" you shouted as soon as you came in the door.

"See what?"

"Why, a hanging. Three pirates from Taylor's band of robbers are going to be hanged today."

"You're pleased about that, I see," said I.

"More than that, my friend. I am overjoyed, both for your sake and for my own. You wanted to see a hanging, did you not?"

"I didn't say that. You did."

So you did, in black and white; but, sly fox that you were, you had worked out how things stood. To take delight in it the way Defoe did, however, that I could not. And they were from Taylor's crew, sailors I had known inside out after having been their quartermaster for half a year or more. But not even Defoe was aware of that. There were not many who did know that I had sailed with Taylor.

"Well, whichever, my good fellow," said Defoe. "But a hanging is always instructive and worth seeing, you will have to agree with me there, and I thought we were in accord before. Do not misunderstand me, I am not happy about the poor devils who must die. That is not my nature, I hope. But nevertheless, dying is in some way the acme of life, whether it is premature or at the right time, if there is such a thing. Not its acme measured in happiness, not at all, but the point when the whole of one's life stands out in the clearest light. That is when one has to decide irrevocably whether one's life was worth living. Do you not agree? Is death not the measure of life?"

"No," said I, "'tis the sentence of death that's the measure."

"What was that?" he said with a smile of pleasure, taking notes, rogue that he was. "It is the sentence of death, do you say? So how can we measure the lives of others, then, the majority, the ones that are never sentenced to death?"

I had no answer to that at the time, nor was it my concern.

Defoe hauled me off to Execution Dock, where an eager and expectant crowd had already gathered. He had the ill grace to use a pair of sharp elbows to carve himself a path through the torrents of abuse he received in return, until eventually we stood in the front row, only a few fathoms from the three gallows and the hangman who was engaged in checking the nooses to make sure they ran free and easy. I cast glances to both sides and was on my guard. I knew how it could be with crowds, they were not to be depended upon. With a few rhythmic refrains, an agitator's fervour, spurred on by fear or by rum, they could suddenly break away like a team of eight and run amuck. And there might be any number of peculiar characters hiding in their midst: informers, magistrates, Excisemen, the kind of people who would love to destroy the likes of me.

Soon there came the sound of drums. Constables shouted and bellowed to make the crowd divide and let through a tumbrel with the three condemned men on it, and a priest who was mumbling endless strings of prayers. Two of the three had their heads bowed, you could see that from afar. The third, on the other hand, stood straight-backed, shouting impudent remarks to all the young girls standing hard by. They blushed, completely forgetting that very soon the man would never be able to fulfil their secret desires. Some of the men applauded the bravado of the doomed man, in the belief that they themselves would have done the like, had they been in his shoes.

"Do you see the difference?" said Defoe. "How can it be possible?"

I made no answer and scarce heard what he said. I could not take my eyes off these men who would soon exist no more. I, who had seen other men turned into slivers of meat by cannon-balls and splintering wood without turning a hair! But this was something else altogether. Here there was no question of hope, nor of fighting for your life. Here there was no choice to make, other than demeanour, a straight or a bent back, a brave face, or despair: as if it made any difference. Defoe obviously thought their attitude was significant, that it said something about their life. Maybe, but I saw only sham and clowning in the defiance of the unbowed man. He should have held his tongue. Trifling with the gallows, scoring a cheap point when it was too late, that was shameless. No, these men should have harangued the crowd and called upon them to examine their own shabby lives. For if there was one thing I felt sure of, in the shadow of the gallows, it was that my own life was worth living, even if only to avoid dangling from the rope.

"Do you feel unwell?" Defoe suddenly asked me, giving me an abrupt dig with his elbow.

"There is naught wrong with me," I managed to utter. "Leastways, not compared to those poor devils."

"You are not being of much help to me," said he reproachfully. "I thought I would get rather more from an experienced man like you."

"Such as what?"

"That you would be able to see from them what sort of pirates they had been in life. That in them we would find confirmation of how to live in order to meet death with head held high. I had really hoped for a little more assistance."

Since I had no wish to disappoint him, I observed the three men closely. And sure enough, now they were much nearer, I recognised them. Ay, they were Taylor's men, three ordinary seamen who had probably never made much of a mark or displayed their qualities to any great extent. Like most, they had joined us at sea when we had captured a prize. They disliked their captain, were living on poor victuals, had to work themselves to the bone because of undermanning, had naught to hope for either then or in the future – the usual old story, in other words, and there was nothing more to it than that in their case, as far as I could tell. They had just wanted a little easing of the wretchedness of their lives. And for that they were to be hanged.

They were pushed up on to the platform and each placed before a scaffold beneath the noose. And now we could see that the bearing and impudence of the straight-backed man was simply outward show. At the sight of the rope he fell silent and was no more arrogant than the others. On the contrary, his legs began to shake so much that he could hardly stand upright.

"You see," said I to Defoe, giving him a prod in return, "the only difference was that he couldn't imagine how it was going to be. He had to see with his own eyes first. There are plenty of that sort among pirates: you can write that down in your little book, too."

At that moment the solemn reading of the judgement began.

"You, Thomas Roberts, John Cane and William Davison, have been severally sentenced in the name of our gracious Sovereign, George, King of Great Britain, and on his authority, as follows: Whereas, in open contempt of and transgressing the laws of your country to which you should have shown allegiance, you did conspire to unite with evil intent and to enter into an alliance through articles to harm and destroy His Majesty's trade routes at sea, and that in accordance with such malicious intent you were party to thirty-two attacks on vessels in the West Indies and along the coast of Africa; you are indicted in particular on the testimony of honourable and trustworthy citizens, as traitors, robbers, pirates and enemies to mankind."

None of the condemned men seemed to hear. They stood with heads bowed as the execution order was read out:

"You, Thomas Roberts, John Cane and William Davison have been severally sentenced to be taken back whence you came, and thence to a place of execution, which is Execution Dock, there between the high and low water marks to be hanged by the neck until you are dead. Thereafter you shall each be taken down and your bodies hanged in chains."

That was what I had come to see and hear. And what was it I had to listen to: that I was an enemy to the whole of accursed mankind, no more and no less! Was there anything to argue, for the likes of me? If those poor wretches, who had hardly hurt a fly, were condemned to death, what rejoicing would break out in the name of justice if they got hold of the likes of me? I was not in the Admiralty rolls, that was certain, and Defoe would not blab, but a single testimony from such a citizen as was called honourable and trustworthy would be enough to send me to the gallows. What use would my gloves and unblemished hands be against that?

"There is yet more to come," said Defoe of a sudden.

The official took out a new document.

"I shall now read out a declaration from the condemned men: We, Thomas Roberts, John Cane and William Davison, greatly bewail our prophenations of the Lord and our disobedience to our parents. And our cursing and swearing, and our blaspheming the name of the glorious God. Unto which we have added the sins of unchastity. And we have provoked the Holy One to leave us unto the crimes of piracy and robbery; wherein, at last, we have brought ourselves under the guilt of murther also. But one wickedness that has led us as much as any, to all the rest, has been our brutish drunkenness. By strong drink we have been heated and hardened into the crimes that are now more bitter than death unto us. We could wish that masters of vessels would not use their men with so much severity, as many of them do, which exposes us to great temptations. We hope we truly hate the sins whereof we have the burthen lying so heavy upon our consciences. We warn all people, and particularly young people, against such sins as these. We wish all may take warning by us. We beg for pardon, for the sake of Christ, our Saviour, and our hope is in Him alone. Oh that in His blood our scarlet and crimson guilt may be all washed away. We are sensible of an hard heart in us, full of wickedness. And we look upon God for His renewing grace upon us. We are humbly thankful to the Ministers of Christ for the great pains they have taken for our good. The Lord reward their kindness. We do not despair of mercy, but hope, through Christ, that when we die, we shall find mercy with God, and be received into His Kingdom. We wish others, and especially the seafaring, may get good by what they see this day befalling of us."

The voice of the official rang out across the silence of the grave. Some were manifestly affected by this gibberish. The men of the cloth were sitting there with contented grins on their faces. But their God lifted not a finger to help a sailor in need. He stood on the side of the captain when he let the cat lash the backs of the sailors, when he withheld their food rations, kept back their wages, forced them up into the rigging in storms, and let them die of sickness, if it saved money for the shipowners. And who was it that sent storms to wreck ships, who was it that whipped up a squall that made the frozen hands of the sailors lose their grip on the yards so that they fell overboard to their deaths?

The condemned men looked up, now that their confession of sins had been read. At the same moment the official pronounced further.

"Let this give cause for reflection!"

I could restrain myself no longer.

"Like Hell!" I roared in my quartermaster's voice. "God don't give a fig for sailors and or'nary folk!"

Not a sound was to be heard. But I, and all those around me, could see the three condemned men give a start and come to life again. My eyes met theirs where I stood in the front row. And then, without warning, Thomas Roberts, who had something in him after all, shouted out, "Silver, John Silver. Save us from the gallows!"

There was commotion and excitement without equal, that was plain to see; and lucky there was, for otherwise it would have been the end of me. I managed to slip away in the crowd. When I was further off, I let my voice be heard again.

"Flee for your lives!" I yelled. "Taylor's gang are here to loose the prisoners!"

There was even greater uproar, and it was an easy matter for me to follow the stream of people,make my way across the river, and into the Angel. And what did I see from there, with my tankard in my hand, but Mr Defoe, surrounded by constables as if he were Taylor himself; Defoe, I assumed, had simply not thought to make good his escape. Well, it was no more than right after all. He had not wished to be known, as he stood next to me when I began to bawl, and for that he had now got his just deserts. He would be able to feel for a while, as he sought to extricate himself, what it was like to be regarded as an enemy to mankind. And perhaps he came to understand in the end that the stocks were nothing to write about when measured against the gallows, you may lay to that.

The crowd had become less dense by now, and naturally none of Taylor's men were to be seen as far as the eye could scan. What I accomplished, however, was to let Thomas Roberts, John Cane and William Davison die in peace, honoured be their memory, for when the noose was finally pulled tight there was only Daniel Defoe looking on, head bent, fearful of death himself as he was.

"Hands," said I to the landlord, "this is no life. I'm a-goin' to take the first possible ship back to the West Indies an' seek my fortune under a good cap'n. D'you want to come?"

His face lit up like the sun – leastways, by his standards – and he gave me a noggin of his best rum, which tasted like gnat's piss.

So that, Mr Defoe, is how I came to leave you and London – a stinking hole if you ask me – in the company of Israel Hands, shot in the leg by

Blackbeard, and, at the last and unlamented, removed from this earth for ever by that young whipper-snapper Jim Hawkins.

I left you then, as I thought for good and all, though you managed to send me, by round-about ways, your book on pirates, signed and dedicated: "To Long John Silver, may his life be long." You kept your promise not to mention my name and I thank you for it. But I discovered of course to my delight that you could not resist putting me in a corner of the scene between England, Taylor and Mackra. "A fellow," you wrote, "with a terrible pair of whiskers, and a wooden leg, being stuck round with pistols, comes swearing and vapourising upon the quarter-deck and asks which was Captain Mackra . . ." This is what you wrote, and we will let it go at that, though you did not stick to the truth, since my crutch was the only wooden leg I had, and indeed I had not lost my leg by then. I say this just for the record, if the truth is to be told, which I thought was the intention.

I will leave you again here, Mr Defoe, and this time I think for ever. What is left of my life is not really for your ears. You found it hard to write about the cruelty of pirates, about blood and death. My time with Flint, as you have no doubt understood, had plenty of both, and the Devil knows whether even I can face telling it in detail, or whether I would be able to if I wished. Unlike you, I did not count how many we killed, how many ships we captured and sank, how much booty we laid our hands on, or how many sea miles we sailed and whither.

I do not suppose we shall meet in Heaven, you and I, even if it were to exist. But you kept me company at a time when I needed someone to talk to in my loneliness. I am grateful for that, although you had no choice. We all need someone to talk to.

Thirty-one

THE DAYS ARE merging together more and more, each one like the other. I wake up, rise, breakfast, write, remember and write, dine, sleep again and dream. I wake up, write, stretch my leg, say a few words if anyone happens to be at hand, which does not seem to be very often, write, and sup. The sun goes down, I stare out into the darkness, see nothing, hear noises, remember again, a face I did not know had been in my life, the tone of some-body's voice, I know not whose, a smell of nearby land at daybreak, but where? – a cutlass – is it mine? – opening a gash in a man's chest, and the scream that follows, a pirate with no name, his pockets stuffed with gold coins, not myself anyhow, choking on the vomit from his own rum; another, myself, flailing my limbs in the air as the noose is drawn tight around my neck. But no, that cannot be a memory, at most a fear, because I am still alive, though at times I doubt it. It is just a monstrosity in my imagination. I carry on staring out into the darkness, call to someone to chase away the silence and help me forget my fear and memories, but there is seldom anyone within earshot. I curse myself for setting them free, my natives, who are not mine. Even a slave would be able to fill the silence. Time passes nevertheless, I fall asleep, dream as if awake, a new day dawns, but how do I know it is not the one that dawned yesterday or the day before?

For the first time in ages, as I thought, Jack came in. He looked aston-ished at my joy. But I was really pleased to see him. I needed to know that there was someone other than myself alive, someone who was not just an echo within myself.

"Where've you been keeping yourself of late?" I asked.

He looked at me uncomprehendingly.

"Keeping yourself," I explained, "where have you been, in other words?"

"I understand what you said," he replied. "I've been here."

"Here?" I repeated uneasily.

"Ay, where else should I have been?"

"I've been calling . . ." I began, but stopped myself.

Had I just imagined that I had called Jack or anybody else? Dreamed it?

"I'm out sometimes," said Jack. "Fetching food and provisions."

Ah, quite so, I thought, we have to eat in order to live, whether there is point in it or not. Mayhap I had called just when he was out getting fresh produce or more stores. It also crossed my mind that he took care of the meals himself, not even asking me what we needed or how to pay for it. Was it right or fair that he should look after me for John Silver's sake?

"I hopes the others lends you a hand," said I. "I'd like to do my bit, but you know how it is. It ain't so easy for the likes o' me to run around in the undergrowth hunting little pigs."

That was a lie, of course. As far as I could remember, having only one leg had never prevented my doing what was needed. Yet it rang true.

"I know," said Jack.

"Know what?"

"You're getting old, like everybody else."

"Old an' infirm an' losing my mind, says you. Not much good for anything, eh?"

"No," Jack replied, honest soul that he was.

"Why d'you stay here, when all's said an' done?" I asked. "You're free to go wherever you want. Why don't you go back to your tribe like the others? You don't owe me nothin'. I didn't buy your freedom for you to look after me."

"I know it."

"Well, then."

"My tribe gets along without me."

"What in Hell's name d'you mean by that? Wouldn't I get along by myself? I ain't done naught but that all my life. I can still damn well hop around on my one leg."

"It ain't your leg," replied Jack. "It's your head."

He pointed to my papers.

"Is that any o' your damn' business?"

"I'm waiting."

"For what, may I ask?"

"For you to finish."

"Was that what you came here to say? That I'm crazy to sit here writing? That I should do somethin' else? Have I asked you for advice? If that was all you wanted, you can go to Hell, as sure as my name's Silver!"

"No," he replied calmly. "That wasn't what I came for. A ship's coming into the bay."

"A ship?" said I, bringing my mind to bear on it at once.

"Ay," said he. "Shall we teach 'em a lesson they won't forget? Ain't that how you usually like it? They're anchoring within firing range."

I grabbed the telescope and went out to the side overlooking the sea, but with some difficulty. No, I was not so nimble and light on my foot any more. My one leg had probably begun to tire from having done the whole job on its own, without the customary assistance, for all these years. I could hardly complain about that.

I put the telescope to my eye and the first thing to come into view was the British naval flag fluttering listlessly in the gentle breeze. But English merchant ships had also been granted the right to fly the navy ensign south of the equator. They reckoned that pirates and other riff-raff would be hoodwinked, we who knew better than any how to recognise and judge ships!

I counted twelve cannon-ports on the starboard side of the ship below me, all closed. I could see some ordinary seamen on deck, but not a sign of a redcoat. It was not a navy ship, not a punitive expedition, just an inconvenient interruption in the passage of time, quite serious, but no more than that. Suddenly I began to long for someone to talk to, for word from somewhere else, news even. Perhaps nobody, it occurred to me, nobody other than Jack and the people on the island, actually knew that I existed.

"It's only a merchantman," said I to Jack. "No cause for anxiety."

I trained the telescope on her again. They had put out the boats and begun to pull her into the anchorage, right beneath our guns, without knowing it. From the sea my fort looked like part of the cliff it was built upon. Jack was right. We could sink the ship at any time if we so wished. She settled at anchor and turned her stern towards us and I was able to read her name: *The Delight of Bristol*. How could anyone name a ship that? I wondered. Bristol was about as far from delightful as it was possible to be, as far as I could remember.

"We'll hold off with the cannon," said I. "She may have news."

"News?" said Jack.

"She's from Bristol. That's my home town, if I ever had one."

From Bristol, I thought to myself. The place where Trelawney, Livesey, Hawkins and Gunn were wallowing in Flint's treasure by this time, driving in a coach and four and powdering their wigs, probably the only concerns they had in life. This was an opportunity for me to find out where I stood in the world. Had Trelawney kept his promise not to bring me to court? Had he been able to keep his blabbing tongue under control? Probably not. And what was I in that case? Hated and feared, of course, as was only natural, but what else? Did people think I was alive? Were there men desirous of nothing more than sending out a punitive expedition in my honour? Or had they done what they could to make me forgotten, as if I had never existed? Ay, there was suddenly quite a lot I wanted to know.

"I have a mind to invite the cap'n to dine," said I. "Can you manage that?"

Jack nodded, though with no great enthusiasm.

"We might be able to buy some merchandise from them," I went on, perhaps feeling the need for an excuse.

As if I required merchandise, with the short time I had left this side of the grave! The way I looked now!

That made me think I had better get a mirror and see myself. To be able to say to myself, without any hesitation or doubts, that this was John Silver, this is what he looks like and what he has become, and to Hell with all the memories and reminiscences that tell another story!

When Jack returned I stood waiting for him in the doorway.

"The cap'n's comin'," he declared. "Gladly, he said. I called you Smith and said you were a trader."

Shiver my timbers, I had forgotten that! The corpse might still be alive, but had cast caution to the wind.

"Well done," said I, apprehending what might have happened if a captain from Bristol had found that John Silver dwelt in this place and had spread the intelligence to all quarters.

We would have had to scupper the ship and do away with the crew. To the last man. As in the good old days.

"What was the cap'n's name?" I asked.

"Snelgrave," said Jack.

"Snelgrave? Does he yet live?"

So he did. Good for him, and for the seamen who sailed with him. Snelgrave was one of the few captains who had slipped out of pirates' hands alive. His crew had put in a good word for him. They had sworn that he was never violent towards them, and that they had always received their agreed rations and the rum stipulated in their contracts. Davis, who sailed with England and me, and later as his own captain, was not usually in the habit of restraining himself in dealing out appropriate punishments. But he had treated Snelgrave like a respected guest, and offered him a ship and cargo, so that he could return home without loss. Snelgrave had politely refused. He had been afraid, with some justification, I'll warrant, that no one would believe him when he got back, but rather would assume he was in collusion with the pirates who had taken his ship. Davis was not too stupid to perceive what Snelgrave had so judiciously inferred, and continued to entertain him as a guest until he could be sent home on a Dutch brig that happened to venture into the estuary of the Sierra Leone River. Because of Snelgrave, and only for that reason, the crew and captain of the brig escaped with naught but a frightening experience.

And now here was Snelgrave in person, in a ship from Bristol. He of all people must have heard of John Silver. With a little shrewdness and cunning I could surely find out what an old man like me was worth nowadays, what price was on my head, how hated, loathed and despised I actually was, or whether I was just forgotten, and had lived to no avail.

Captain Snelgrave thanked Jack for his kindness when he invited him to step in. He came alone, which was good, without fear or foreboding. He came towards me without hesitation and proffered his hand.

"It's a pleasure to meet you!" said he warmly, and seemed to mean it.

"I've been out for almost a year and a half," he went on, "with the same officers and crew. It gets tedious eventually. We must have had every possible subject of conversation a hundred times and haven't got much more to say to one another. And we know the books in our library off by heart."

He laughed.

"You sometimes wonder what sort of people they are who choose books for our ship's library. We had a *History of Scotland* in four volumes, which was always something to pass the time with. But what say you to *A Treatise on the Mineral Waters of France*! As a diversion for deep-sea sailors! It's hardly to be wondered at if it gets wearisome on occasion. You can imagine how vexed they were at my good fortune when they heard about your invitation . . . Mr Smith, was that right?"

"Quite so! And I'm equally pleased to meet you, Cap'n Snelgrave. 'Tis an honour."

"Oh, it's not so remarkable to be a captain, when all's said and done."

I could not restrain a smile.

"I suspect you're more or less alone in that opinion," said I. "There are not many cap'ns who would agree with you. I've actually only ever heard of one who would go along wholeheartedly with that."

"Oh ay? And who might that be?"

"Your good self, sir."

Snelgrave roared with laughter before it struck him that my answer might be saying more than it appeared to.

"You know who I am, then?" he asked, plainly somewhat surprised.

"Ay, and I'm sure I'm not the only one."

"How do you mean?"

"If nothing else, then for your *Account of the Slave Trade*. An extraordinary book. Though I must admit I had difficulty in believing that you yourself were true, to begin with. There weren't such right-thinking cap'ns in this world, as far as I knew. But then I had it attested from irrefutable witnesses."

"May I ask who they were?"

"Certainly. One was Cap'n Johnson, the one who wrote that history of the pirates."

"Have you met him?" Snelgrave interrupted. "I don't know anyone else who has. I'd give a lot to meet him myself."

"Johnson's not his real name."

"I thought as much. And who was the other who presented me in such a favourable light? I had a great deal of opposition in London when my book was published, you know. Sea captains thought a hard regimen was the only way to drive a crew, and that I had slandered them and undermined their professional reputation. Shipowners thought I was lying about Howell Davis and his offer of a safe voyage home. They called it the product of a vivid imagination, and spread the rumour that I had really been in league with the famous pirate."

I laughed, naturally enough.

"There you are. The other reliable witness was in fact Howell Davis himself!"

Snelgrave clearly did not know what to believe.

"As a trader in Madagascar," I explained, "I couldn't help coming into contact with some questionable characters, gentlemen of fortune among them. Many of them settled here, as I'm sure you know."

Snelgrave's countenance did not change. A notable person, this Snelgrave, I thought to myself, who could hear the words gentlemen of fortune without spitting bile.

"I was wondering," said he, "how you ended up here in the middle of nowhere. There must be places more fitted to the conduct of trade than this."

"Indeed," I replied cheerfully. "On the other hand the competition was not as murtherous here as in other places. But now I've retired, to have some peace and quiet in the autumn of my days. As you can see I'm getting on in years, and upon my soul, I've worked hard enough in my time to scrape together the necessities of life and a little over."

"But it's miles from civilisation, is it not?" Snelgrave asked.

"It depends what you mean by civilisation."

"I was thinking of merchandise and stores, the necessities of life as you called them, and maybe that little bit more. There can't be many ships that put in to Ranter Bay nowadays."

"That's right, and indeed I do run out of this and that from time to time. But then a topsail appears on the horizon, an Arabian merchantman or an Englishman like you, who can provide me with a few requisites."

"I'll be pleased to be at your service," offered Snelgrave, "if we happen to have what you need."

"Let's talk about it over dinner. Which must now be ready, I think."

I showed him into the dining room. The table was laid magnificently, with all the available silver, porcelain and crystal, as was customary when we had guests. It was one way, as good as any, to ascertain a person's nature and likings.

"You're clearly not in want," said Snelgrave cordially. "My men should see me now. They'd be filled with envy."

"If you are willing," said I, "we could lay on a feast for the crew. A real barbecue with roasted pig and goat. I could provide the food and you the rum and beer."

"In exchange for what?" asked Snelgrave. "I'm accountable to the shipowner, you know."

"Oh, it wouldn't cost you anything. Let's say those books you know off by heart. I've read every word in my own library. And maybe you could spare me a mirror."

Snelgrave raised his bushy eyebrows.

"Ay," I went on, "would you believe that I no longer have a mirror, and hardly know what I look like? It must have been pure luck that my aspect today didn't scare you out of your wits."

"It's not that bad," said Snelgrave courteously.

I smiled to myself.

"No, but bad enough, I can tell. I'm fortunate you're used to having sailors around you. They don't usually look like God's favourite children, as far as I can remember."

"Maybe not," said Snelgrave with an expressive shrug of his shoulders.

"But I'd like to see God's favourite children reef a sail in a raging storm with the rain lashing down so hard that you have to keep your eyes closed if you're not to be blinded for the rest of your life."

"Ay, you're right there. With one hand for yourself and one on the Catechism there wouldn't be much reefing done. But what d'you say? Shall we put on a feast?"

"Agreed," said Snelgrave after a few moments' thought. "I can always placate the owners somehow. My difficulty is that I always give the crew the prescribed ration of food and rum. So I can't save anything on that score. And since for the same reason they don't die on me, I don't make anything there either. You know how it is, twenty per cent or so tend to perish on a voyage to the East Indies. That saves a corresponding amount on the victuals – that's how many of my colleagues see it. Isn't it strange, when you think about it? Captains of slave ships get a fee for every slave delivered alive to the other side. But you earn more on the crew if some of them die on the voyage."

"Ay, I know a bit about that," said I. "But don't concern yourself about the accounts. We'll simply do the whole thing at my expense. I've enough to see me out and to spare till I die."

I was exhilarated by the prospect of a real feast with piles of food, rum and healthy sailors who knew how to enjoy themselves without thinking of the consequences on the morrow. Snelgrave set to work with a good appetite on what I provided. Even the smallest variety of frogs' legs, what the natives called nymphs, he ate quite happily. The lobster, with crushed lemon and green peppercorns, made his mouth water at the very sight of it, and the fruit basket, filled with every kind of fruit in the world, except for cherries, which do not grow on Madagascar, almost made his head spin with delight.

"No," said he, "you're certainly not suffering any deprivation. I doubt whether anyone, even in London, even the King himself, eats so well."

"It has its advantages, living miles from civilisation," said I, handing him a pipe, which he lighted with enjoyment.

"Tell me," said I when he had lighted up, "how are things in Bristol these days?"

"Do you know Bristol?"

"I was born there, according to what I was told by my mother. Whether it was true I was in no position to know. I grew up there, leastways, before being sent to school in Scotland, and then went to sea."

"And have you never been back since?"

I hesitated. To say that a one-legged man like me had been the landlord of the Spy-glass would be tantamount to deliberately telling him who I was.

"Ay, I was there on business and stayed for a while. That must have been about ten years ago."

"And visited your parents, I presume?"

"Well, you could say that," I replied, for lack of anything better to say.

I had not considered that it would be natural for him to ask about my parents. I was not so quick-witted any longer. It must have been all that writing about how things were, all that truth, straight to the point, that made me forget how you have to behave in the world.

"My father struck his flag early," said I, which was true. "And my mother had gone to her grave by the time I came back."

"Smith?" said Snelgrave. "I don't think I know anyone of that name in Bristol. It's English, is it not?"

"Ay, but 'tis possible my father was living under borrowed plumes, in a manner of speaking. If I surmised aright, he was a smuggler in Bristol Bay."

"That hasn't changed, at least," laughed Snelgrave. "Smugglers thrive and flourish as never before. The last I heard they had fifteen per cent of the trade in the bay. You have to admire them."

"And shipping in general?"

"Is the way it always seems to have been. Bristol is second only to London in volume of trade and numbers of ships. Someone told me that you can usually see a thousand vessels in Bristol, up the river and in the harbour, and that of fifty thousand inhabitants, two thousand are seamen. That's no small number. The market in Tolsey is livelier than ever. You probably know that Bristol has also become the centre of England's slave trade."

"No, I didn't know that."

"Ay, so it has. A filthy trade, if you want my opinion, but profitable. Quite a number of the big landowners have diversified, as they say, to spread their risks. From cattle to slaves. Chalkley, Massie and Redwood are among those who have accumulated enormous fortunes in just a few years. And Trelawney, of course . . ."

"Trelawney!" I interjected, hardly able to control my voice.

"Ay," said Snelgrave, but if he was surprised at my outburst he did not show it. "Do you know him?"

"I had some business with him," said I cautiously. "And was cheated. Well, not by the man himself, he was too dull-witted for that, but he had an adviser who helped him to think and make decisions. He made himself out to be a doctor."

"Livesey," said Snelgrave, sucking on his pipe.

"That's it! Livesey. He had his head screwed on the right way, though I'm not so well endowed by nature myself that I can judge for sure. But who knows, if it hadn't been for Livesey I might have been sitting in Parliament by now."

"And what would you have done there?" asked Snelgrave, catching me unawares again, because what I might have wanted to achieve in Parliament was something I had never seriously considered. It was just something I used to say on the *Walrus* when the others got angry with me because I had not squandered my prize money the way they had.

"Ah, well," said I, "I could have started by making sure that the likes of Trelawney and Livesey were put under lock and key until they'd paid back what they owed me. Then I would have brought in laws to make the lives of sailors more bearable, the way you've done yourself, but everywhere, with severe punishments for cap'ns who wouldn't obey orders. What else? Abolish the slave trade, contract labour, press-gangs, the cat, hang all crimps, pardon all pirates. Put an end to trade monopolies at sea, including the Navigation Act, dissolve the big companies. A bit of everything, as you see. There's a whole lot for the likes of me to do if I just sit down and think about it."

"From what I can hear," said Snelgrave with a smile, "it's not in Parliament you should be sitting; it should be the Admiralty for a man like you."

"Ay, maybe. But it's too late for that now, and I'm content with my lot. I drew a few blanks to start with, but then things improved. Leastways, except for Trelawney and Livesey. But tell me, how would the likes of them have got the capital to equip themselves for the slave trade?"

"Haven't you heard?"

"No," said I. "What should I have heard?"

"That Trelawney sailed to the West Indies and found Flint's buried treasure, a fortune without parallel. It was said to be greater than that which Drake brought home in his *Golden Hind*, even though that's hard to conceive. Drake came back with six hundred thousand pounds, more than the whole of Great Britain's cash reserves for an entire year."

"Shiver my timbers!" said I, with a whistle. "You don't say so. Flint's treasure? And more than Drake's booty, Drake who was raised to the nobility, as well?"

"Ay, so it was. There was talk of nothing else for months afterwards. Trelawney and the others were lucky to escape with their lives from the expedition, you know. Some of Flint's old crew had come to hear of it, and managed to sign on with Trelawney's ship. Flint's former quarter-master, John Silver by name, had gained Trelawney's confidence, to the extent that he depended more on Silver than on his own captain."

"I'm not surprised," I interrupted, "when you think of what most cap'ns are like, if you'll permit me."

"Seems to have been an extraordinary person, this Silver," Snelgrave went on, "who could make the best and the worst of them dance to his tune. Trelawney had to pay dear for his credulity and greed. Most of those who sailed out never saw England again, some honest and inno-cent men among them, ay, maybe even in both camps."

"It sounds an unpleasant story," said I. "But if I know that Squire Trelawney, he probably thought he got off lightly for such a fortune. That's the sort he is."

"I'm afraid that's true. He doesn't suffer from scruples. But it's more difficult to believe that Livesey, a doctor after all, should involve himself in the slave trade."

"It doesn't surprise me. Should surgeons be any better people than others because they happen to save a life now and again, and just any life at that? Without surgeons the slave trade would go under, and return nothing but losses."

"The subject seems to be dear to your heart."

"I've been to sea too. And you know what sailors are like. They've never had any time for doctors. They were called cap'ns' weather vanes, if you'll pardon me for saying so."

"I know," said Snelgrave seriously. "That's why I make my surgeons berth before the mast. I don't want the reputation of surrounding myself with informers."

"But tell me, this John Silver, what became of him?"

I looked him straight in the face, but he did not avert his eyes, nor did he cast a glance at my amputated leg.

"The most fantastic rumours and yarns abound concerning him. That he lives on some island in the West Indies like a king with his negro woman and his parrot, Captain Flint. That he returned to Flint's island, together with a young lawyer, Jim Hawkins, who had been ship's boy on the earlier expedition, to fetch what still remained of the treasure. Someone I met myself, a drunken sailor by the name of Gunn, insisted that Silver was in Ireland living with a woman from his youth whom he'd never been able to forget. Another maintained that Silver had changed his name, exactly as Avery once did, got himself a wooden leg with a shoe and was living in disguise amongst the rest of us. Yet another . . . but I'll stop there. I could go on all night."

"That was a considerable amount already," said I, laughing to hide my agitation.

"Ay, and it's even been put into print."

"Print?"

"Ay, true enough," continued Snelgrave. "John Silver, and Flint too, for that matter, have become arch-pirates. They're on everyone's lips, as if there had never been any others. Captain Johnson would probably turn in his grave if he knew that the only pirates he didn't write about are the ones who live on."

"Ay," said I, laughing again, but in genuine amusement this time, "knowing him, he would indeed. But what about yourself, then? What do you think about this John Silver?"

Snelgrave had a look around the room.

"Well," said he, "if I had to believe anything at all, I'd like to think that he'd retired to a place like this."

I would have gone as far as staking my life that Snelgrave was not being devious. He may have had his suspicions, but in that case he was concealing them so well that they escaped the sharp nose I had for that sort of thing.

"But who knows," said he, obviously thinking aloud, "perhaps we're all wrong. A man like this John Silver doesn't seem to be subject to the same laws as the rest of us ordinary mortals. The way he managed to get away with his life and part of Flint's treasure in his hands is proof as good as any."

"What other articles might he be subject to, then?"

"Possibly the ones that apply to fiction," said he. "Some of the stories told about him are so unbelievable that they simply cannot be true."

At that I really had to laugh again. Snelgrave was putting me in a good humour, there was no doubt about it.

"You should probably go and ask the poor devils who crossed Silver's path whether he was a figure of fiction!"

"Ay, I probably should. And maybe I ought to know better anyway, having met pirates in flesh and blood and knowing the cruelty they're capable of. But the strange thing is that Silver doesn't exist, so to speak. Johnson had nothing on him in his book. The Admiralty have nothing either. I looked into the matter myself."

"You what?"

"Looked into it. Tried to solve the mystery of John Silver."

It was by no means easy for me to keep my presence of mind and not let my mask slip. What right did this man have to take such an interest in me, to look into the matter, as he damned well chose to call it, as if I was nothing more than a yard-arm?

"For what purpose?" I enquired. "To get him hanged?"

"Far from it," protested Snelgrave. "That's not my intention. No, I'm just fascinated by the fellow. It would please me to know what he was really like."

"Then we have something in common," I blurted out.

"You too?" said he.

Now, I thought, now it's coming. But nothing happened.

"Ay," said I, "from what you say he seems to be an odd sort. And I've always loved a good yarn. You get a taste for them before the mast."

"Then I've definitely got something on board that might interest you."

When he had gone, I still could not fathom him, but quite possibly he felt the same about me. I had steered the conversation very carefully away from the treacherous waters around John Silver. But I had found out enough to know that the gallows awaited me if I so much as set foot in Bristol. Not because of Trelawney. He had kept his word after all, as far as I could ascertain, and not taken me to court in my absence for mutiny and murther. But the story of the discovery of Flint's treasure and how it got into the wrong hands, that had been spread far and wide. And the fact that I was at liberty, most probably rich, perhaps even happy, that was clearly a thorn in the flesh of all right-thinking people. But even with the gallows looming over my head, there was no reason to despair. I might be a thorn, pricking at the flesh, but I was alive, that was irrefutable. I existed – in several incarnations in fact, and as far from forgotten as anyone in my profession could ever hope to be.

The next day I spoke with Jack about preparing the feast, and remarked that it would be like the good old days when the merry-making used to reveal folks' true nature. I told him to spare nothing, for the sake of Snelgrave and his men. We left our fort at midday loaded with food and drink for a whole crew. Jack stayed ashore to set up a big barbecue. He had been in the West Indies for years with pirates and buccaneers and needed no instruction on such matters. I myself rowed out in the jolly-boat to the *The Delight of Bristol*, hailed them and was hoisted aboard by block and tackle like a sack, as if I was too old to climb a rope ladder with my one leg.

Snelgrave received me with open arms, showed me round the ship, introduced me to the men, who responded with cheery greetings, and then took me into the aft cabin where dinner was laid. He asked me straight what it was we needed by way of stores, and I mentioned gunpowder, salt and lamp oil, as well as the other things we had spoken of, the mirror and the books. He motioned towards a package wrapped in sacking and said it was a personal gift from himself. Then he called and asked – ay, that *de facto* was what he did, not ordered – a ship's boy, who must have been his attendant, to load the package and the stores into the longboat. I laid a little purse of coins on the table.

"Despite having been a trader," said I, "I don't really keep up with prices and exchange rates any more. But here's twenty Spanish pistoles. Will it be enough?"

"More than enough. It's about as many pounds, at the current rate."

"Then you can keep the difference and share it out among the crew."

"That's very generous," said he. "And magnanimous."

"Magnanimous? I hardly think so. I simply do what I feel like when the mood is on me. No more than that."

"Just so," said Snelgrave.

Over dinner we talked about ships and sailing, the way sailors do when they are together, as if they had not had enough of it at sea. Snelgrave also told me, with some indignation, about the complicated fraud that had been exposed in the South Sea Company, where the servants of the company, both high and low, had embezzled thousands of pounds of the company's money.

"It was more than the losses the company had suffered from pirates over ten years," said Snelgrave.

"And how many of the cheats were hanged?" I asked.

"None," replied he. "They had their patrons. Some ended up in the Marshalsea for their sins, at most."

Afterwards we rowed ashore to the beach, men and all. Jack and some of Snelgrave's sailors had lighted a fire, and two whole pigs were being roasted slowly in the heat from burning dried shit and wood shavings, in the proper way. There was rum and ale, and Jack had even managed to get some women from the neighbourhood, despite it being white men who were to be honoured. And damn me if he and the ship's carpenters had not knocked together a long table and benches. There was a murmur of expectance from the crew. Snelgrave looked at me in admiration. When everyone had sat – or, in most cases, thrown themselves – down on the fine sun-baked sand in which they buried their calloused sailors' feet, made hard by all the barefoot tramping over the planks of the deck and coils of rope, I prepared myself for what I knew would be, with all the certainty I could wish for, my final appearance as the Long John Silver, called Barbecue, that I had once been and would remain, come what may, I thought, until I died.

"Men," I shouted, in the voice that only I had been capable of in my prime, "may I crave your attention for a friendly soul who wishes to say a few words?"

The murmur of conversation died away and silence reigned, but not like the grave, for this was a feast and I had voice enough for that.

"Not very far from here," I began, "measured by the size of oceans, that is, which you as deep-sea sailors are accustomed to, is the island of Sainte Marie, or Nosy Boraha as it's called in the native tongue. Ay, there is such a thing, in case you happened to think otherwise, an' I can vouch for the fac' that you can curse an' swear in it as well as in any other language, though 'tis devilish hard to pronounce. Jack here, the closest o' my men, is called Andrianamboaniarivo, an' I'll warrant you, if I'd had bones in my tongue they'd 've been broken into tiny pieces by now, so long have I lived on the island, an' you may lay to that."

There was a ripple of laughter from most.

"Anyhow," I went on, "Sainte Marie, as you may have heard, was the refuge an' hidin'-place of pirates: ay, their Paradise, no less. An' should we begrudge it to them, when all's said an' done? – for they were unlikely to see even a glimpse of a Paradise in Heaven, I shouldn't think. With some justification. I'd like to have seen Saint Peter's face when he opened the grille to cast his eye over Blackbeard, Roberts, Davis and Flint as they asked for admission into the Kingdom of Heaven. 'Tis a good thing for God that He's almighty, or He'd have had a touch of Hell to contend with, by gum, if I know those four men. No – pirates, gentlemen o' fortune an' all the other names they were called, both for 'em an' agin 'em, were not God's favourite children. But leastways they knowed one thing for certain, there were no point in grieving in advance: there'd be grief enow an' to spare when their time was up . . ."

There was a mumble of approval here and there, in fact more or less everywhere.

". . . an' a feast was a feast. Celebrating, drinking, singing, playing and dancing was at any rate somethin' they knew how to do, whatever might be said an' thought about 'em otherwise. Now we ain't pirates, not so far as I knows, at all events, but why should we be any diff'rent from pirates when it comes to a good feast? As you can see, there's all that's needed, victuals an' drink till you chokes an' drops. 'Tis no less deserved than ever 'twas by the pirates on Sainte Marie. If I'm to believe Snelgrave, your cap'n here hard by me, he ain't never sailed with a better crew. The Devil might believe it, I s'pose, but that's what he said . . ."

There was more laughter and the men looked at one another with what seemed to be a childlike pride – that was how little it took.

" . . . but one thing you can take your affy-davy on – an' I know what I'm a-talkin' about, having survived all that life has throwed at me – you've had some damn good luck to have Snelgrave here as your cap'n. If they'd all been like him – but they ain't, as you well know – no profession in the world would've been able to measure up to the deep-sea sailor. Ain't I right, me hearties?"

The men shouted and yelled.

"So I propose a toast to Cap'n Snelgrave!"

I raised my glass and there was a cheer of a sincerity that could almost have moved a heart like mine. Snelgrave himself looked self-conscious, if I was not mistaken, and he reddened.

"One more thing!" I cried, quelling the roar. "I've jawed about the gentlemen o' fortune on Sainte Marie, and intends to do so again. Not that you should follow their example. No, the pirates' time is past, and a good thing too, I'll warrant you. They may have thought they were riding in a hunt for happiness, but they most often fell off their nag an' broke their necks into the bargain. And it ain't much to follow, if you asks me. That's what I says. They may have been happy in a way, but to what avail is it now? That applies to all on 'em, without exception. They had a rule that no one was better'n anyone else, neither in life nor in death. An' that rule, me hearties, we have here too, just so's you don't make any mistakes. The blacks you see around you ain't slaves, an' the women ain't whores, they're free men an' women like yourselves, an' should be treated accordin'ly, neither better nor worse. Eat, drink an' be merry, as you deserves, for this is as near to Paradise on earth as the likes o' you an' me will come in a whole lifetime."

There was a moment's silence, because I'd slowed down the last bit in a serious tone, but then a voice was heard from the crowd that I'll never forget: "Long live John Silver! Long live Long John Silver!"

And before I had time to think or to grasp what was happening, the men, and Captain Snelgrave with them, began to cheer from the bottom of their hearts, for even I could hear that it came from the heart, that as far as they were concerned I should live as long as I desired. Taken aback as I was, it could nevertheless not be allowed to stand unrefuted.

"I thanks you for the acclaim and the toast," I spoke up again, "even if it weren't me who were the subject of the honour. My name is John Smith, and if there's anyone who wants to believe anythin' diff'rent, let him come forward so we can settle the matter now."

No one moved, because my voice had changed.

"That's right, men!" Captain Snelgrave intervened in his captain's voice – which he had after all. "This is John Smith, trader, you have my word on it. And what good would it do to wish someone a long life and cheer them so noisily that it would lead straight to the gallows? I propose a toast to John Smith, who has also bought merchandise from us so that every one of you will have a gratuity when we reach Bristol."

The cheers were resumed with a tremendous noise that only increased as the men tucked into the food and drink with yells and laughter.

I dropped on to the sand, tired and heavy as never before, but also, I have to admit, with a strange, unfamiliar, unbelievable warmth in my breast. To think that there were people, in full possession of their senses, leastways not frightened to death or blind drunk, who wished John Silver a long life, exactly what he had wished most for himself all the years he had lived! Maybe, I thought to myself, I should have sought out the sailor who had believed he knew who I was, and cut off his head to frighten the others into silence. But shame to say I could not bring myself to do it. My time was past, whether or not there were exhortations for a long life. Who would trouble to bring home a decrepit piece of wreckage like myself to the gallows? I was not capable now of harming a fly.

The feast continued at full tilt, I observed, but without me. I drank a bit, but without getting drunk. People came and spoke to me in a friendly fashion, one after another, thanking me for this and that, but I do not know what I answered. I saw a sailor dancing on the table, two others playing dice, Snelgrave deep in conversation with Jack, a sailor with a laughing native woman on his knee, another black and white pair disappearing, secretly as they thought, into the bushes, some poor sod spewing on to his feet, another throwing his clothes on to the sand and himself into the water. It was going as it should and the way it always had done. This, I thought, was at all events something to remember, in a life like mine.

I took my leave of Captain Snelgrave at sundown, with heartfelt delight at having met a man such as him, and with great sadness in knowing that I could never expect to meet him or his like again. I did not ask him the only question that had been on my lips all day – whether he knew who I was, whether the men, when they cheered and wished me a long life, did it in full knowledge that I was who I was. That was the difference, anyhow, when all was said and done, between me and a tyrant like Captain Wilkinson. For him the men's huzzas were jeers, a mockery, a punishment. For me the toast was the proof that I had lived, and not in vain. And to think that I had believed the gallows would be proof enough.

I limped up to my house and sat down for a while to watch the bonfire and the shadowy figures around it. I was tired, in body and soul, but contented too. Now there was not much more to live for, as far as I could see. I had taken my leave, and my reminiscences had begun to run dry; they no longer seemed inexhaustible. I could see the end steadily approaching, and I welcomed it. My only wish was to draw things to a close myself, in order to have lived, right up to the last, as I had preached.

Thirty-two

COUPLE OF days ago, in the half-light of dawn, *The Delight of Bristol* weighed anchor, set her sails and glided slowly out of Ranter Bay, heading back to civilisation. Through the telescope I could see hands in the rigging and on the deck, waving in my direction, without anyone having asked them to. I saw Captain Snelgrave on the poop deck, as soon as manoeuvres had been ordered and the course set, turn round and stare up towards me and my fort. It could equally well have been wishful thinking or pure imagination, but at that moment I'm damned if I didn't think that the whole world, if the need arose, could learn to like John Silver, look up to him and respect him as the good and open-hearted shipmate he could be in his best moments when the spirit moved him.

There sails a decent man, said I to myself as I watched the ship start to roll in the swell of the open sea. I stayed there until the sails had faded into the obscurity that was now my near horizon, without giving a thought to past, present or future, if I had any. I felt I knew deep down inside that this was the last I would see and experience of the wonders of civilisation. Captain Snelgrave and his crew had taken part in a celebration, without knowing it, for my final voyage. John Silver was going to be decommissioned and broken up, for now and all eternity, and that was that. I had led death by the nose many a time in my life, but there would come a day when not even my most varied talents would suffice.

Behind me is the mirror and the present I received from Snelgrave. I have not touched either yet. There will be time enough for that, as there always is at my venerable age. If anything is too late, you are not aware of it and do not miss it.

*

So here I sat, at peace with the world, having taken my leave, or so I thought, watching Snelgrave's ship and its first-class crew of capable deep-sea sailors disappear into my own myopic mist. That was that, I thought. A few more words about the history of John Silver and then full stop. What more could the likes of me reasonably expect?

How stupid can we be? Why should I have peace and quiet now when I have never had it before?

If I had been able to, I should probably have torn my hair and invoked my pact with the Devil, as Lewis did when he climbed up the mainmast, ripped out tufts of hair and threw them into the sea, in honour of Satan, to get some wind. Or like the old bard at Hangman's Point, who had forgotten his thousand-year-old stories and killed himself because of it.

But I cannot even tear my hair. I did not have much of it left, as I discovered when I first looked in the mirror. I saw my miserable mug, sunken, blear-eyed and tallowy pale. That was only as it should be, I thought. I had certainly not expected to see much more than a living corpse, and was not disappointed. Nothing to complain about there.

But then I opened Snelgrave's gift, which he had said I would find particularly interesting. Interesting! Enough to send me out of my senses and out of my mind, more like! What did my rheumy and short-sighted eyes see before them? A book from the hand of Jim Hawkins, printed, bound and plainly for sale, accessible to anyone, to do with what they would! There it was, in black and white on the title page, the name of Jim Hawkins, the one who hindered me from getting my rightful share of Flint's treasure, which had no more belonged to Flint than to anyone else. *Treasure Island* was the name he had given the book – as if there had ever been an island with a name like that!

I opened it with the deepest misgivings. And what did I find straight away but Flint's accursed map, that had come so near to being the death of me, and caused the death of so many others. And then? Next came Billy Bones, the swab. And next? Next came Long John Silver, nickname and all. Barbecue on every page. I read and read, as I had never read anything before, and was transfixed, in a manner of speaking, by the whole gamut of human emotions. Here was another John Silver, full of life. Yet another John Silver to detest or approve, according to your sensibilities. Yet another corpse to throw overboard.

I do not know how many times I read it. I was entrapped, bound hand and foot, and could no longer think straight. I forgot that it was me, that words had been taken out of my mouth, that someone had been playing with my life without consulting me. Ay, I have to admit that I was laughing and crying at the slightest thing as I gulped down the words to the last drop. He could write and tell a story, this lad, enough to make you forget who and where you were.

But then I awoke from the intoxication of words, forced to be myself and look into my own dried-up face. I had a strange taste in my mouth from the drink, and my head ached so much that I did not know whether I was coming or going. Ay, I had indeed been made aware that I was still alive and kicking.

What had that damned Hawkins gone and done? He had not only displayed me to general view, brought me into disrepute and made me an object of ridicule. He had not only put me in a cage to be spat at, the way the Danes did with the pirate on the quayside of Langelinie, to put fear into all the sailors who were bound for the slave routes. No – more than that, he had delivered in print a damning testimony that could send the likes of me straight to the gallows. Could Hawkins be nothing but a simple informer? And we made an agreement, he and I! It is there in his words, as true as it was spoken. "But, see here, Jim – tit for tat – you save Long John from swinging." And Jim answered that he would do what he could, it is written there for time everlasting.

I held to my part of the bargain, that I did, and saved his wretched carcass. But he did not keep to his. Is that the thanks I get? And these are called honourable folk!

But it is not as easy as that to get the better of John Silver, as sure as that is my name. I cannot sail to Bristol and take the life I saved, nor would it serve any purpose to silence him. The testimony is sworn, even minuted for future generations.

Yet the last word is never spoken, I can see that now, having thought I had brought everything to a conclusion. If there is anything you should never count on in advance, it is your own end, especially mine.

Jim Hawkins had his eyes open, I'll lay to that, but so by thunder did John Silver. He feared no one, and he was as brave as a lion. That is true, as Hawkins wrote. He was only afraid of the gallows, true enough, as written. He had a way of talking to each, and doing everybody some particular service – also true as stated. He was no common man, quite right too; he had been to school and could speak like a book when so minded. He was the best of shipmates, that is also irrefutable, quite the gentleman if he wished to be, and the only one of his kind; all of it quite right. A strange fellow he was in that world of his – nothing to object to there, either. All that was as it should be, and Hawkins has not perpetrated untruths.

But do not forget that it is also as true as an amen in church that John Silver's former shipmate who betrayed him did not do it in the same world as old John. And remember there was never a man looked me between the eyes and seen a good day afterwards. Would you expect anything else from me, Jim?

Thirty-three

DEAR JIM HAWKINS!

I don't know whether this letter will ever reach you. On the other hand I'm quite sure you needn't trouble to compose an answer, unless you're able to convey your letter straight to Hell, where I would be if there were such a place. At any rate, I shall be dead by the time you might be reading this and have managed to discover the whereabouts of the remote corner of the globe in which I spent my last happy days.

Though now I'm lying, of course, as was my wont when it suited me. My days have not been so happy of late, if I'm to be truthful. And 'tis your fault, Jim, I'll have you know. Not just yours, I'll admit. I also have things to answer for myself, as far as my peace of mind is concerned. But how could you hang me out on display in words as you did, may I ask? Didn't you understand that your story is a testimony that could lead straight to the gallows for the likes of me? I saved your life, in case you've forgotten, and you promised to do what you could to save mine. And now this! Could that have been your intention, not just to put me on show in the stocks, but actually to get me hanged?

No, I can't believe that. I believed it at first, I won't pretend I didn't, when your book came into my hands, but now I've pondered and thought about it. You were an honourable lad in many ways and came to my defence, and not only, I'll warrant, because I saved your life. No, Jim, you also liked me for the man I was. That shows through in your book, despite everything, doesn't it, even though you were in mortal fear of me at the same time? But who wasn't? You're in good company – as you heard for yourself. Even Flint hesitated to intervene when I laid my hands on somebody.

So you liked me, I'll wager my head on that, even though it's not as valuable as it once was, leastways not for me. How then, my friend, if I may call you that, could you so thoughtlessly write, for all the world to see, that I may be living in comfort with my old negress and my parrot, and that 'tis not at all certain that I'll receive my punishment here on this earth?

I don't ask you to understand what I myself have begun to comprehend, that nothing would be a greater sin than to let John Silver die on the gallows. Humaneness, Jim, is what John Silver needs, a man like no other. Without a price on my head no one would know what it is worth to be alive.

Ah, Jim lad, I've become so arrogant in my old age – though modesty was never my watchword – that I'm quite serious in my opinion that the world would suffer a perceptible loss if I were hanged like a simple bandit and then forgotten. For that's why 'tis done – the likes of me are not hanged as a punishment, or to fright off others, but to make everyone forget theirs was ever a life as worth living as any other. Ay, if the likes of us are regarded as enemies to mankind, sentenced to death and hanged, 'tis because the rest of you wouldn't know else what was good and what was evil here in this world.

You can see, Jim, that I've been doing a bit of thinking here at the end. There's not a lot else to do when you're standing with one foot in the grave, especially when like me, as you know, you've only got one leg and could fall the wrong way at any time.

But it would be asking a great deal to make you understand. You're still a young man, and naturally, and quite rightly, think you have the whole of life before you. Why should you measure your future life against such a singular fellow as me with a price on his head?

You maintain that it was Livesey and Trelawney who asked you to write your memoirs. Why? I ask. Because there were unflattering rumours going round about those who were led by the nose by the likes of me? Because Long John Silver stole the whole show in the popular imagination? Or was it just because Trelawney, as was his wont, was trying to make money out of something that didn't belong to him? Ask yourself those questions, Jim, go on!

One thing you ought to consider is that I could lay justified claim to

Flint's treasure, more so than any money-grub like Trelawney. You had your share of the treasure, of course, and must be a rich man by now. But I have to tell you, Jim, you are no better than any of Flint's old crew. You're living off their dead bodies, remember that when you're driving in your coach, powdering your wig, taking your snuff from its gold box or being courted by ladies as the excellent match you have doubtless become. How much are you worth? Ten thousand pounds, perhaps, enough for you not to have to lift a finger for the remainder of your days. I envy you there, as you might guess. I had to keep working constantly just to have a few years as an idler here at the end. I didn't have your good luck. Be careful with your money! Buy your freedom, Jim, that's the only point of money!

You'll observe that I'm not the same man as I was of old, when all was action and adventure, and I would hoist my topsail in anything but a full storm, make or break. I suffered many a shipwreck, but always saved myself. No one can say that I didn't do what I could, or that I didn't have a life worthy of me. The important thing is that on the whole I was not a dissimulator. I never pretended to be anything but what I was: whereas others pretended to be better, but were the same as me.

Why, though, you should have lied about dates here and there, to no purpose, I cannot understand. Every sailor in Bristol knew when the *Hispaniola* set sail and returned. The map is not the original either. Would Flint have given it to Bones in 1754, as it says? Would Flint have survived for thirty years in that case? No, you can try that on someone else. Flint was a real man, 'tis true, and hard as nails, but he only sailed for eight years, the last three with my good self. And 'tis fine as it was, don't you think?

On the other hand I have to admit that you caught me to the life sometimes, such as when I was following the others on the way up to the spot where Flint had buried his treasure, with you tethered to a rope. You had your eyes about you, I've always thought that. You saw that I had a foot in both camps till the last, and that my word of honour would not have been worth a jot if we had indeed found the treasure. What you did not understand – but you were only a boy, after all – was that I cared as little about the pirates as about the rest of you. You made me out to be a weather vane, Jim, but no one was as steadfast and principled as I was. The treasure and John Silver first, the gallows last, those were my articles, and I kept to them strictly, you may lay to that.

But I have no desire to be churlish, and can let all this pass. You shook some life into the old carcass, even though it was not the full truth. In any case – but how could you have suspected? – I've been writing my own life, just as it was, the truth, I can warrant, not figments of the imagination. I don't know why. I thought I was doing it to keep my mind active, until death did me part. That was foolish, because if there's anything you should stay away from for the sake of your mind and wits, 'tis writing.

Now, you might think I'm trying to make a speech in my defence, or to draw attention to the fact that you were not a reliable witness. What would I achieve by so doing? I'm not too stupid to recognise what passes for good and evil in this world, and on which side I myself belong. But good and evil are only man's invention, like right and wrong. Why should I concern myself with all that, when by those very same tokens I have forfeited my right to live?

Well, I'll lay I know what you're thinking. I could simply have carried on with my tavern, the Spy-glass in Bristol, and kept myself to myself, been an upright businessman, if there are any such. But I'll tell you, if I returned to Bristol, it was only to get hold of Billy Bones and Flint's map, and what I did, I did at the risk of my life.

Bones, the swab, decamped when Flint died. It was his revenge for the fact that we treated him as he deserved. Well, you know what he was like. Loud in the mouth, but mean, cowardly and petty. He must have reckoned that he could equip a vessel and lay hands on the treasure for his own account. As if he would have been capable of that! Rum was all he had in his head, and there was plenty of space for it. The little he had in his skull from birth, he'd killed off long before with the amounts of spirit he poured down his thirsty throat.

But 'tis an ill wind, as they say. Bones lost his mind, but got the map instead. For who was it who kept Flint company when he drank himself to death in Savannah, if not Billy Bones? If Flint had been in full possession of his faculties – if he ever was – he wouldn't have let the map go to a coward like Bones. Flint got his reward, because as soon as Bones had the map he left Flint to choke to death on the vomit of his own rum. It was Darby M'Graw who found him. M'Graw became anxious when Flint didn't bawl and scream for his ration as usual, a bottle for every broken glass.

I remember it as if it were yesterday. What a rumpus there was! Ay, you won't believe your ears, Jim lad, but there were men who wept copious tears, I'll warrant you. It probably wasn't grief in the usual meaning of the word. They just lost heart. All their lives they'd lived without seeing further than the horizon. Astern they'd forgotten most things, and didn't want to know about them anyhow. Ahead everything was as empty as the grave. Now, with Flint dead, they would suddenly have to think for themselves, make decisions and steer their own course through the confusion of life. It was as if they suddenly had a fear of heights and the wind against them, the whole lot of them.

Even I was affected. Without Flint, everything was finished. He was the last of the great pirates, and the only one who had escaped with his life until he himself put an end to his misery. Without him we were at everyone's mercy. Ah, he was feared and even hated on board, but he was without equal in his field. He had taken liberties at the expense of the men, had women on board for himself against all the articles, buried a large part of our common proceeds so that no one should go soft and pull out, had killed a dozen or more of our own hands for cowardice: but Flint was Flint, a magnificent captain in battle, careful of his own, mine and our skins, and a gifted sailor. No one – and we had many first-rate seamen on board – could outdo him in navigating and manoeuvring a ship when things were hot.

So a day or two had probably passed, with Flint on his *lit-de-parade* and rum-sodden men on vigil, before I was the first to think of Flint's map. I overhauled him from top to toe, with no success. We turned his cabin upside down, and indeed the whole of the *Walrus*, without finding the tiniest little drawing from Flint's fist. Only after that did someone – 'twas Israel Hands, I think – ask about Billy Bones, who had

[316]

drunk with Flint to the last. Then we discovered that Bones had taken to his heels and the gig was gone.

A roar of anger went up from the men. New oaths were taken that our company would not be broken up before Bones was dead, the map found and the treasure raised. I was elected a sort of captain for part of the crew, you know which. Flint was thrown overboard without ceremony, now that we again had the courage to live. Under my supervision as quartermaster our booty was split equally. We built four smaller boats out of the timber of the *Walrus* and then burned what was left of her. Finally we had a feast, the like of which had seldom been seen, finishing up all the drink and all the victuals that there wasn't room for on the smaller boats. We worked for a week, and I've seldom seen such a hideous and pitiful crowd of buccaneers as the pallid and poorly men who set off in their boats and steered their courses in different directions without so much as a glance behind them.

So there you have the tale, Jim my son. That's how it was when the last of the pirates, and the worst of them all, went to their graves, to the delight of all the wealthy trading-houses. What became of the other three boats of thirty men, I do not know. You can reckon that some were captured and hanged, others drank themselves to death or ended their days as poverty-stricken beggars – the usual, in other words. Not the ones under my command, you may lay to that. We picked up Bones' trail and found out that he had returned to England. There's your answer, Jim, as to why you met me in Bristol. I didn't go back to lead an honourable life, as 'tis called – how could I have, with a history like mine? – but simply for the sake of my blood money, that was all! I went back to Bristol in constant fear of my life and skin, the little I had left – remember that!

For that's another thing I must tell you before I forget it: that for the likes of us who are called enemies to mankind by King and Parliament, or *terrorista* by the Papists, for us there's no going back. There are only two paths from which to choose if you wish to live as a human being with some meaning until you die. One is to hold your course. The other is to let yourself be hanged. No other ways are open to you. If you don't want to sneak around for the rest of your days continuously in

[317]

fear of your life, and not daring to trust a single person. Amnesty, says
you. There are gentlemen of fortune who have taken advantage of
amnesties, but what became of their lives afterwards, I'd like to know?
His Majesty can grant amnesties and pardons, but do ordinary folk do
so? And the rich?

Thirty-four

AY, JIM LAD, so I'm writing my life, as it appeared to me – the truth, Jim, and nothing but the truth. Does that surprise you? Indeed it does, says you, for you know as well as anybody that I turned a blind eye to most things that had to do with the truth. Credibility was my business. That was what got me on in the world.

In other words, for this past year, more or less, because you don't keep such a careful watch on time at my age, I've sat on my backside scribbling black on white to try to put some sort of order into the life that seems to have been mine. As you can imagine, 'tis a hard day's work, and not something for indolent idlers. But you will be well aware of that, having compiled your own account of Treasure Island!

You may be wondering why I'm turning to you in this way. The fact is that it is lonely being a writer – lonelier, I've discovered, than living – and I know what I'm talking about. So I'm writing to you and you'll just have to accept it.

And you're not the first to be so honoured. Can you believe, Jim, that I've narrated half my life to Defoe, the author? You'll think I'm mad, dead and buried as he is, but I had to have someone. I should have thought of you. You're alive and well, I hope, and can read. So I've decided on this, to write to you until my sap dries up and my veins shrivel. It ought to be of interest to you in any case, because what remains to tell of my life is the time with Flint, apart from what you called Treasure Island, of course. You did me the service of sparing me having to recall and give an account of that wretched misadventure that came about because of my fondness for a stripling like you.

It must have been in the year of grace 1723 when I stepped ashore again in Port Royal, Jamaica, after my new experiences in London, where, with Defoe's help, I had endeavoured to find out where the likes of myself stood in this world. I was in the company of Israel Hands, who was not the easiest partner to dance with. He started drinking like a pig as soon as we left Gravesend behind us, and so he carried on until his death. He was an ugly villain, was Hands, and there were times when I could have wished Blackbeard had aimed a bit higher. No one should upbraid you, Jim, for having shot him in the end.

So now I hear you ask your old shipmate Silver why he ever dragged along such a swab as Hands. Well, I'll tell you.

By that time the days of the pirates were numbered. Most of them were stone dead, and there was bounty on the others. The Spaniards transported their riches in convoys of hundreds of ships. And gentlemen of fortune were not bent on self-destruction, after all, even if they were careless whether they lived or died.

In addition to this, the governors of the islands had been granted shares in honest trade. Before that they had handed out privateers' licences, taken a proportion of the profits of their raids, owned whorehouses and taverns, and argued the pirates' case against King and Parliament. But when profits fell it became more advantageous to invest in ordinary trade, and so the likes of us acquired enemies who were far worse than all the guns and men o' war. You may lay to that, Jim: a worse enemy than what they call inadequate profit and poor return is hard to find. Fighting against it is like pissing into the wind: you sully yourself, and you stink ever afterwards.

It had become plain to me that it would be no easy matter to get a crew together and find a captain who was willing to try his fortune, and take on the rest of the world, against all the odds. The likes of Hands, without fear or scruple, would be necessary if I were to be able to buy my freedom one day. I had put away nine hundred pounds after my time with England. That was not bad, and it was in a safe place, with a goldsmith in London, as was the custom, so I could present bills of exchange elsewhere in the world for ready cash. But it was not enough to retire in peace. Three hundred pound a year was the minimum needed to invest in bonds that would allow you to set up as a gentleman in earnest, and not have to lift a finger, if you could stand it. Let no one think Long John Silver sailed with Flint for his own amusement, or for lack of anything better, like most of the others.

Flint, however, was hard to run down. At that time he did not even have a name. News had reached me that a pirate was wreaking havoc among the islands of the Antilles, as in the good old days. But who he was and whence he came, nobody knew. Ay, to begin with, it was not even certain that it was a pirate. Ships simply disappeared into the void, as it seemed, yet with no reason to suspect wind or storm.

But then a crew from an American brig was found, that had been attacked by a real living pirate. None of the crew, however, had seen him or heard him called by name. As soon as they had struck their flag they had been lined up along the rail with their backs to the pirates. Many fell to their knees and prayed in the name of God for mercy. Some of them were thrown overboard, while others were bound, driven below deck and put ashore on an island with victuals, weapons and a few necessities for survival.

Two months later the same story was repeated, the only difference being that all the officers had been beheaded, for having, so it was said, ordered resistance and risked the lives of peaceful seamen. Then came information from the Spaniards that a new pirate had captured and set fire to three of their ships, sparing no lives other than the slaves on board.

So it was clear that there was at least one pirate in those waters, and that it was a clever and resourceful vessel, manned by people who were careful of their own skins, if not of others'. But for ordinary folk and the authorities, the unknown pirate was a phantom, terrifying but not completely real, like God and Satan or the Holy Spirit and the angels, though without priests to encourage stories and superstitions.

But how, I wondered, was I to make contact with a ghost and a shadow of himself like this pirate?

I bought an old hulk for more than it was worth. I made a special request that the purchase should be kept secret, since I was intending to carry valuable cargo and was afraid it would come to the knowledge of pirates. Naturally, the news spread like wildfire, which was exactly what I had counted on. It went so fast that Hands, to whom I had mentioned not a word about the matter, came to me the very next day and asked if it was true, as he had heard, that I had bought a ship.

"Who in Hell's name told you that?" I asked indignantly.

"Easy all, John," said he. "I'm the on'y one who knows about it. I was told it in conf'dence, an' swore to keep me mouth shut. Though I knew you'd tell me. You wouldn't let an ol' shipmate down, I thought to meself."

"Never in a thousand years," said I.

"When do we set sail?" he asked. "An' where to?"

"Tomorrow."

He looked at me in amazement with his rheumy, bloodshot eyes.

"What about a crew? Weapons? Cannon?"

"We're sailing without 'em."

Hands looked as if he did not understand anything: that is to say he looked very much like his usual self, give or take a grimace or two.

"We ain't sailing as pirates," said I. "We're sailing as a prize."

I could do no more. Sooner or later the feared, nameless and elusive pirate would get wind of me and reckon that no easier booty was to be had. But to be doubly sure, I also spread the word that I would be sailing to St Thomas, collecting merchandise and coming back.

St Thomas, says you, wasn't that rather foolish? Ay, but I reasoned that no one would recognise me in my finery after having seen me as a half-naked savage. It was only the black-coats who'd had the advantage of studying me more closely. And I had my reasons, that I breathed not a word of to anyone, least of all to Hands.

It took ten days from Port Royal to Charlotte Amalia, a quick crossing with only two men on board. But Hands was a capable seaman as soon as he had slept off his drunkenness. Without rum he was even a good shipmate, singing, trimming the sails, taking double watches, as happy as a child at being able to be himself again at sea.

We saw not a sign of a sail on the entire crossing, and came into Charlotte Amalie unmolested. We saluted the fort with our muskets for lack of cannon. It sounded ridiculous, but we received a prompt response of two shots fewer than our own, as was the custom. Anchoring in the roadstead, I took the jolly-boat in while Hands stayed aboard on watch. He was to show himself on deck at frequent intervals, in different accoutrement, so that people on shore would be tricked into thinking we had a full crew on board.

I reported my arrival to the duty officer in the fort, and was registered in the book under the name of Johnson, in honour of Defoe's memory. I asked for an audience with the Governor, was escorted in, wearing my best clothes, and made a formal request for permission to take on provisions and add to my crew. I had lost a number of slaves who had escaped, I said, and needed to replace them. Would that be possible?

"It depends," replied the Governor. "We have seven thousand blacks on the island at the moment, but that doesn't go far with the present demand for sugar. The plantation owners are buying every load that comes in, down to the last man and woman."

"But . . . ?" I interrupted.

"But there are always some that are not much good. Partly the sick, of course, and also the disobedient and defiant who can't be taught to behave. Strange to say, Captain, a few years ago we had a whole cargo of such rebellious souls. They had been stirred up by a white man who had been put in chains on the slave deck to await trial for attempted mutiny. We've never known the like. They were as meek as lambs to start with, and then suddenly the whole island erupted. First we had a revolt on the clergy's plantation, but that was crushed before it spread. A good sign, we thought, that the others kept themselves in check on that occasion. But the devils had thought further ahead than we had, and just when we believed the danger was past and reduced our guard, all Hell broke loose. They killed an hundred whites before we managed to suppress them. They hacked an hundred men, women and children to pieces and hung them up in trees all over the island."

"How many were killed on their side?" I asked in some dismay.

"None, Captain," said the Governor, throwing up his hands. "Not a single one!"

"What?" I exclaimed. "How was it possible?"

"None as far as we know," he corrected himself. "When we went out to quell the uprising, everything was as smooth as a mill-pond again. Some had run off as maroons into the mountains, and the others denounced them as the guilty ones. We took five of them, tortured them and killed them without getting a word out of them. We've never seen the like before."

"What does it have to do with that particular cargo of slaves?"

"All the whites who were killed had bought slaves from that ship-load."

"And now," said I acidly, "you want to foist on me the agitators and trouble-makers? Is that it?"

"Don't take it amiss, Captain! I just want to be honest with you. In principle there are no slaves for sale on St Thomas. But since the uprising we've constantly had some from that ship-load under lock and key. At the same time we have to compensate the plantation owners who have to do without them. 'Tis a costly business in the long term. It would be better if we could sell them on and disperse them. Now do you see? We don't know whether they're trouble-makers or not. We're simply taking precautionary measures. The worst of it is that the plantation owners need every one of them, and they're all strong and healthy. If the owners hadn't still been scared out of their wits, they would never have let them go. Would you like to take a look at them?"

The Governor's voice was almost pleading.

"It can't do any harm," said I, with a show of reluctance. "But I'd like to inspect them on my own. In my experience they often dissemble and behave differently in the presence of guards and people in authority."

"Certainly," said the Governor without the least trace of surprise.

"And the white man?" I asked, in a tone of general interest. "The one who stirred them up. Did you catch him?"

"John Silver!" the Governor spat out with sudden venom and disgust. "No, that devil fled after murdering two priests. He put two of the clergy to death, deliberately, despite the fact that they had taken him on as a contract worker. It was a real service, because otherwise he would have been hanged. And I'll tell you one thing, Captain, if I were ever to get hold of him, I'd slay him with my bare hands!"

I said nothing, deeming it safest. The Governor, having recovered his composure, took me to the cells, explained the situation to the two soldiers on guard, and gave me admittance.

It took a moment to acclimatise myself to the semi-darkness and the stench. When I was able to make out anything at all, I saw a dozen black bodies side by side against the long wall, as far away as they could get from an open barrel full of piss and shit across the room. No one moved a muscle when the door opened and I went in. They might have been dead, the whole lot of them: but then I perceived that several pairs of eyes were watching me in the gloom.

"All right," said I, in the same tone of voice I had once used on the *Carefree*. "Is there any devil here who can understand what I'm saying?"

That caused a stir. Up sprang Jack like a cat – it was him, no more and no less, staring me straight in the face.

"John," said he, but quietly, clever fellow that he was. "John Silver!"

"In person!"

"Prisoner?" he asked.

"No," I replied with a laugh, "on the contrary. I'm as free as a bird. And in funds. I've come to buy your freedom, if you want."

"If I want?" he repeated.

But in the very next instant I could sense his hesitation.

"The others are Sakalava. I can't leave them."

I thought for a moment. I had the money to buy them all, certainly, but what would I do with them, a whole body-guard? On the other hand, it also occurred to me, it was far from certain that I would have the opportunity to share my resources with the unknown pirate. It could equally well come about that I would end up sailing on my own account.

"Fine," said I, "I'll buy the whole damn flock, if you'll stand guarantee for 'em."

Jack's face lit up and he gave me his friendly punch in the stomach. He had still not learned that white men just slapped each other on the back on such occasions.

"D'you remember the woman?" I went on to ask. "The one who bit off Butterworth's prick?"

Jack's smile became even wider, if that were possible.

"She's here too," said he. "In the next cell. They're more afeared of her than they are of the rest of us."

"Is she your woman?" I asked, as the thought suddenly came to me.

"She's nobody's woman," said Jack proudly. "She's her own woman. She's half Akwambo. They're like the Sakalava, submit to nobody."

"Good," said I, "then I'll buy her freedom too."

He punched me in the stomach again with a broad grin.

"I'm going now," said I. "Today or tomorrow you'll be taken out under guard to my ship. Explain to the others that I'll personally chop their heads off if they show with the slightest look that they know who I am. And tell 'em, if they ain't already understood as much, that they're free men the moment they sets foot on my ship. I ain't a slave trader."

I knocked on the door, was let out, and asked to see the woman who was the only one of her kind. I did not sound so arrogant when the next iron door closed behind me, even less so when I saw that the woman I called Dolores, for lack of anything better, was alone. She was standing in the middle of the cell, with her back towards me, as if she had stood there nailed to the floor ever since being incarcerated. She did not turn, though she must have heard me enter, so I had to go round her. She looked as I remembered her, haughty, impassive and self-contained. But as we faced each other I felt sure her eyes flickered. I was certain she recognised and remembered me.

"Do you understand English?" I asked courteously.

She nodded, but said nothing.

"You know who I am," said I, "John Silver, the white slave on the *Carefree*. I've come to buy Jack's freedom, with his Sakalava. I'm prepared to buy your freedom too. I need a woman like you. But I don't intend to lay down any conditions. I'll tear up your certificate as soon as we're on board. If you want to be my woman, all well an' good. If you don't, 'tis all the same. I'll get by without you, and you will too, I should think. But if you want me to buy your freedom, you must say yes now. I must at least hear a yes."

She looked at me, indulgently, then I had a view of her teeth as her lips parted to let out a continuous ringing laugh, the like of which I had never heard, so strangely pure did it sound.

When it stopped, she said "Yes", loud and clear, and then nothing more.

I could not take my eyes from her full lips and white teeth. I imagined how it must have looked when she clamped them round Butterworth's erect and lustful member.

A woman to my taste, no doubt about it, I thought, and left her where she stood, with her back to the door, just as when I came in.

I returned to the Governor.

"Do you know," said I amicably, "I'm of a mind to buy the whole lot, if you give me a good price. Some of them will make quite decent seamen; my mate knows how to deal with unruly savages. The others I can sell. I'm doing you a favour, remember, so I hope you'll allow for that in the price. What do you say?"

The Governor stood up and looked as if a great weight had been lifted from his shoulders.

"Even the woman?" he asked.

"Ay," said I, "the woman too. For my own account, if you know what I mean."

"Of course, of course, I understand," he spluttered with all the good will in the world.

But what he was thinking was as plain as a pikestaff: that the woman was the last thing he could have conceived of himself wanting.

"And the price?" I asked in a businesslike manner.

"Seventy dollars," he replied. "That's reasonable. Then you can make a bit if you sell on."

"Done!" said I, without haggling.

"Captain!" said he, "let me offer you a glass. You've rendered me a great service: I'll not forget it. You'll always be welcome here on St Thomas if there's anything you need."

He raised his glass to me and promised that my slaves would be taken aboard before sundown. We could settle the payment the next day. The temptation to get them on board and sail off without paying out a single dollar was great, but then of course they would not have been bought free according to the rules of the game. So I insisted on having all the papers drawn up immediately, counted out the agreed sum, and received in my hand the certificates that gave me the clear proof I wanted that I was the owner of thirteen slaves, twelve of them male, and a female of uncommon kind.

I did not go directly back to the ship. I sat in a tavern first and ordered a glass of killdevil. Kill the Devil, ay, that was what it was for, because it had been a Hell of a life while it lasted. The landlord looked open-mouthed in astonishment when I, a gentleman, ordered a slave drink, but gave it to me even so, and it tasted suitably infernal.

I thought about all that had happened: the failed mutiny on the *Carefree*, Scudamore's treachery, the activities on the slave deck with Jack, Butterworth's truncated prick, the scramble, the woman slave who was flogged for sleeping with me, the small malevolent eyes of the clergyman called Holt, my shot that freed the world of the very same. I was not a man to suffer from memories, but I have to admit they were not happy ones.

I walked inland and soon glimpsed the clergy's plantation through the trees. I crept a bit nearer to take a look. It was just as I would have feared, had I given it any thought. The stone church was still standing and a new dwelling-house had been built. I made my way through the undergrowth until I could see the sugar-cane fields. No change there either, except possibly for the worse, because now the priests had extended them to double their size, both in the number of slaves and the amount of cleared land. And they had engaged slave-masters and a white overseer. So that was all I had achieved. The priests were no longer relying on their God to give them the strength to handle their slaves themselves. So what had been gained? That they had learned a lesson and were not such complete numskulls as before?

I walked back to Charlotte Amalia and rowed out to the boat where Hands was strutting about in his fine clothes. Like most other gentle-men of fortune he was as excited as a child, tricking himself out in a ruff, cockade, brass buttons and whatever else he could find. They were like peacocks as soon as the opportunity arose, but they looked like nothing on earth, however much they might preen themselves and swagger. Hands was no exception, but he also had his personal appearance counting against him.

"Hands," said I, "you can stop your masquerade. There ain't no need to pretend any more, there'll be more on us tonight. I got us another twelve men."

Hands let out an expressive whistle.

"You've recruited men in this hole?" he exclaimed. "Damn me if that ain't bad, in these times. Who've they sailed with before? Taylor? Roberts? Kidd? Any o' the big names?"

"None o' those. They're landlubbers, every man jack on 'em."

"Landlubbers!" he snorted disdainfully.

And he had every right, I have to admit, since no gentleman of fortune with any self-respect would sign on landlubbers if it could be avoided. They could have any amount of credentials, have been thieves, robbers or worse, without it making any difference. It was easier to make pirates of sailors than to make landlubbers into seamen.

But if Hands sulked about that, it was nothing compared with the moment he saw the boat-load of men that were rowed out to us, under appropriate guard.

"Plantation niggers!" he hissed and spat. "What the Hell's got into you, John? What the Devil can we do with that lot aboard? They ain't never even seen a ship afore!"

"That they have," said I cheerfully. "Slave deck for two months, that ain't no little experience. They won't spew all over you and your fine costumes at the first puff o' wind. They're tough ol' rogues, I can vouch for that. I was with 'em when they was shipped over."

Hands looked at me wide-eyed, and that really meant something, because his were normally narrow slits, like loopholes.

"Besides," said I, waving the certificates under his nose, "they're mine, the whole lot on 'em. I've bought 'em."

Hands smiled. That was the sort of language he understood. But he changed his tune when the Governor's boat came alongside and he could see all the individual faces.

"A woman!" he cried, as if he'd seen a rattlesnake.

"Ay," said I, "I know what you're thinking, that women are naught but rabble that cause discord and enmity among real men, and make 'em soft in mind and body. Am I right?"

"Right!" he grunted. "Women ain't got no place aboard ship."

"And why, may I ask? Have you ever thought about it?"

"It ain't good. It just leads to jealousy and argument. And we got other things to think about. With women around the men get weak an' feeble. They can't fight an' stick together, that's just the way it is."

"But why, Hands? I'll tell you. Because most o' the men on board ship ain't naught but bloody whoremongers. They've nothin' but cunt in their heads the moment they sees a woman. And to get some cunt, they puts on airs, struts about like turkey-cocks, and roars like lions. They're like animals, Hands, on'y worse, because animals at least go for smell. I say to Hell with weaklings who can't stand on their own two feet when they catches sight of a skirt. That's for one. And for the second, this ain't no pirate ship, and you does as I says on board. Understood?"

Hands made no reply, but slunk off sullenly, as was his nature.

"Cap'n Johnson, ahoy there!" came a cry from the boat, and in no time at all one of the soldiers had transferred twelve branded slaves and one ditto woman, all of them my personal property for the moment.

I signed a receipt to say that I had taken the goods, and was given a salute and a case of rum from the Governor's own cellar. It was obvious that he did not know his real debt to me.

As soon as the soldier had started climbing down our puny rope ladder I gave Hands the order to weigh anchor, with the help of the blacks if he needed it, and hoisted some of the sails. We were already under way as the boat alongside pushed off, because Hands knew his stuff. Before we were out of earshot I turned round – I could not help myself – and shouted, "Give the Governor my greetings, and thank him for his gift. And tell him the thanks came from John Silver. John Silver, remember the name!"

But they must have done that long before, since up came two muskets. The bullets whined past my head and the next instant we were out of range. I laughed fit to burst. This was the life, thought I.

Only one person laughed with me, the woman Dolores. None of the others could see why nearly getting a bullet in the brain was so exciting. Not even Hands, who had certainly hit the nail on the head when he told Defoe there was no point in going to war if you could not die from it.

Thirty-five

E SAILED SOUTH all through the night, since I had asked Hands to find a sheltered bay behind the coral reef on the windward side where we would not be disturbed. I mostly stood at the helm, while Hands made a fair job of navigating, taking soundings, heaving the log, taking bearings by the Pole Star and writing his courses on the slate he had set up before we left. He was still sulking at our having landlubbers and a woman on board, but he did what was required of him. I, for once, was very content with myself and with matters in general.

It has not been often, when all's said and done, that I have had such peace of mind in the long life I've lived. No, I have been a restless soul, I can see that now, from start to finish. Not especially happy, either, for the most part, if memories are to be trusted.

How could Dolores always be so calm and unmoved? She stayed with me and stood by me for the remainder of her life, but it was seldom she spoke to me. It seemed as though she felt she had already said all she had to say this side of the grave. I never insisted, never pressed her to open her mouth, for what would I have gained by it? In her way she was a woman who made men more chaste than nuns, whether they wanted to be or not.

I remember how she reacted when I brought her the news that Scudamore had been hanged at Cape Corso, after being betrayed by the negroes on board his own ship. She let out her clear, rippling laugh that was enough to make anyone think life worth living. She laughed that laugh on and off for the whole of one day, clapping her hands in pure joy and dancing with excitement and gratitude. She had never forgotten that Scudamore had pawed her with his sticky fingers without her consent.

Ay, I was probably the only one who was permitted to touch her. And not even I was allowed inside her, except for once, that very first night on the island, as a token of thanks, I should think. After that I had to be satisfied with caressing her and being caressed, though nowhere was out of bounds. She was not prudish nor sanctimonious like fine folk, but she said that if I wanted her for the rest of our lives, then it would have to be without offspring. I went along with her conditions, which for the likes of me seemed quite natural. What child with any sense would have wanted the likes of me as a father, may I ask? And John Silver's posterity is what I am taking care of at this moment, myself, here and now, in black and white.

So, without grumbling, I let Dolores have her way. And my sap flowed at regular intervals, by her hand or my own, whichever it might be. But I was probably the only one of all the gentlemen of fortune who kept to one steady woman ashore, except for some who had settled down on Madagascar; but even they in most cases had a whole harem.

"You're a funny devil!" George Merry used to say to me when I had put forward an opinion or two to the fo'c's'le council and my words had become law.

I can see now, by this stage of my life, that this was not an empty phrase. I did not even belong among the motley and varied troops of the gentlemen of fortune.

Was that why Dolores stayed with me? I have no answer to that. Admittedly I bought her freedom, but is that everything in this world, for others than myself? Why did she take a fancy to the likes of me? Why did I never get to know what she was thinking?

She stood at my side all through the night as we sailed away from the island of St Thomas, where she had worked in the cane fields for four years; but as for speaking, not one word. Jack and the others slept on deck, directly on the boards, as their bodies were used to. Hands cursed and swore whenever he went for'ard to cast the plumb line and had to watch where he put his feet, but he left them in peace.

She stood at my side all night, naked as God created her, if it were possible to comprehend that God could create both the likes of her and the likes of Butterworth at the same time. Occasionally she touched me, as if to assure herself that everything was real, that her days as a slave were over. The water was so luminous that the sea sparkled as if we were sailing out in space. The night was so warm that the strong trade wind between the islands gave us just the freshness we needed. You can live a long time for such a night, I can warrant.

We anchored shortly after daybreak to Dolores' rippling laughter, the first sound she had uttered since leaving St Thomas. It awoke the others, and even made Hands smile before he became aware of what he was doing. He cooked breakfast – meat, bread and a glass of the Governor's rum for those who wanted it. When they had all eaten their fill, I addressed them, explaining the situation to them, that I had bought their freedom, once and for all, and I showed them the certificates.

"I'd like to tear 'em up," said I, "but being free in this world ain't that easy. Who would believe any of you if you went round on shore insisting you was free men? They would think you was liars and escaped slaves, with your brands an' all. If you wants to be free, you'll have to accept that you must sail with me as far as Jamaica. I can have papers issued there so you'll be human beings again. Without papers and c'tif'cates, you have to understand, you'll always be suspected o' the worst. That's one thing. The other thing to consider is what sort o' life you can live a'terwards on this side o' the Atlantic. If you asks me, it would be almost as before: plantations, house-boys, pack-horses in harbours, though with a miserable wage and no whips. You'll be going around the rest o' your lives on your knees if you stays here, however free you are."

I paused.

"What's your suggestion?" asked Jack, who could see I had something up my sleeve.

"'Tis this. We sails back to Jamaica and makes you free men and women. That's number one. Then I offers you a place on this ship for as long as you likes. Hands and I intend to join a gentleman o' fortune who's been ravaging the area for some time. In his comp'ny we could all become rich and buy our freedom for the rest of our lives; that's what we white men do. And fin'lly I promise you, on my honour and conscience, even though I ain't got much of either, to put you ashore on Madagascar as soon as we gets there, and we'll be there sooner or later."

The negroes' faces were shining like suns, naturally enough.

"We've not forgotten what you did for us on board the ship," said Jack, standing up and speaking on the others' behalf. "And now you've made us human beings again. The Sakalava will always be your brothers."

"Thank'ee kindly," said I, "but there ain't no cause to be so formal. Give an' take, that's my motto."

I glanced across at Dolores.

"John Silver," said she of a sudden, "why have you bought our freedom?"

"Why?"

She said nothing more, but waited for me.

"To have something in hand, in case I might need it one day," I said with some difficulty, endeavouring to tell the truth, I suppose, though I had not actually thought about it.

She smiled.

"Not out of pity?" she asked. "Not because you felt sorry for us poor slaves?"

"Not so far as I knows!" I replied.

"That's good!" was all she said.

But as for understanding what she meant, I'm damned if I did, though there was nothing wrong with the language or the words. She spoke English like a native, in a manner of speaking, and must have understood everything I had said up till then, even the first day when she had been hoisted aboard the *Carefree*.

We weighed anchor at about noon, and as soon as we were out on the open sea Hands came up to me and launched his attack.

"Have you gone mad, John? You're throwing away a small fortune, that's what you're a-doin'! Set 'em free! What'ud be the point o' that? And the woman too! You ain't stupid enough to think that the pirates we're looking for would take her on board? Ay, I know 'bout Anne Read and Mary Bonnet, and I've heard all the stories, but they were white, and behaved like real men. They wasn't any o' your usual bloody women. I'd never have believed this o' you, you who've been quartermaster with England and Taylor. Think o' your reputation, Silver. Honest folk like me would laugh you to scorn if you hove into view with a woman in tow."

I let him carry on for a while and warm to his theme. My silence fired him even more until in the end he was standing bawling his stupid and ignominious remarks right into my face. I had soon had enough. The negroes had also heard and Jack was all prepared to intervene. I gave him a nod, and in an instant Hands was held in a vice-like grip by three black men. I calmly lashed the helm, pulled out my gully, and let its point play over Hands' skin, tickling his neck and making him open his big mouth by placing the sharp edge against his lips.

"Hands," said I with a smile, "I don't run around telling you what to think and what to do. So you shouldn't give a damn what I do with my life, my money and my reputation. Is that plain enough for you?"

His staring, terrified eyes were rolling in their sockets and looking up to Heaven. He could not nod unless he wanted his mouth slit open to twice its size.

"And another thing: now mebbe you can see why it can be good to have a few negroes to hand."

Always wanting to please, he took it into his head to nod in any case, the blockhead, and if I had not eased off with the gully, it would have been questionable whether he would ever have uttered a single word again. As it was, the blade just made some superficial nicks at the corners of his mouth.

"I didn't mean no harm," said he, dribbling blood.

I gave Jack another nod and Hands was released.

"It were for your own sake," he bubbled.

"I knows that, me ol' messmate," said I. "But now you knows how to keep in with John Silver."

He understood it and never forgot it, except when he drank himself senseless. But as for understanding people, that he never did, neither before nor after. To think that he could take that tone with me when I had thirteen slaves that I had just freed! How stupid can you get? And he was grateful, too, that I had not just slit his throat. He had completely forgotten that I needed him to navigate us back to Port Royal. So he felt indebted to me, like the others: but it was good not to have to listen to his gibberish for a while, as he could scarce open his mouth for weeks afterwards.

We arrived at Port Royal without having encountered any pirates or other ships at all. I dressed up in my finest clothes, made contact with the Governor, and to his surprise and that of everybody else, made the slaves free men and women.

"May I enquire what you have in mind by this measure?" he asked. "You must be able to see that it's hardly a good example for the slaves here on the island."

"I can comprehend that very well, sir," I replied courteously. "But the fact is that I'm going to use them at sea. And on board ship you have to punish sailors if you're going to keep order. You know what they're like, unwilling, lazy, thick-skinned and obstinate. They have to be tamed, like unbroken horses. But punishing white men in front of slaves just isn't done. 'Tis an invitation to mutiny. So my idea is simple, but effective: I make the slaves free seamen so that I can treat all alike."

The Governor brightened up.

"Maybe that's not such a foolish notion" said he. "Well thought, Captain Johnson, and worth trying."

"Is it not, indeed?" I replied, and received the documents to certify that my slaves had their full rights to live an equally wretched life as almost everyone else.

I dressed the negroes up as sailors. I gave Hands the task of taking on provisions, with Jack's help. And the ship had to be painted, careened and the blacks taught seamanship. I left everything in Hands' hands, in a manner of speaking, not least because for a long time, with his sore mouth, he still could not curse and swear the way he usually did, but had to make do with pointing and showing.

Only then did I turn my attention to the woman. I brought her something to cover her nakedness with, for she had been stark naked ever since she came on board. Then I took her to a tavern where I bespoke the best food and drink there was. She did not demur. But all the time she had a mocking countenance that seemed to imply that she was not going to let me lead her by the nose. As if I had the slightest inclination to do so! But she was self-contained by nature, and that is a devilish tough shell to crack, as I for one should know.

Would you believe, I became bashful, stammered out my words in a jumble, and did not know which way to turn. Worst of all was the fact that she laughed in my face when I could not get my words out.

It was not funny for the likes of me, but I tried not to let it discompose me. I haltingly recounted my story and without beating about the bush told her what I reckoned, that she could be my woman ashore, look after my affairs, and be my fixed point here on earth.

"Most of my sort don't have anything like that," said I, "and don't fret themselves about it neither. They don't give a shit for the morrow and always forget about the day that's gone. They float around on the oceans like rudderless ships. But I takes care o' my skin and intends to do so till I dies – and not with a rope round my neck nor choking on vomit, neither. So I could make use o' someone like you, someone who can't be bought for all the gold in the world."

She looked at me seriously, for once.

"No demands or conditions," I went on, "not even that you should share my bed when I'm ashore. No gratitude for the fact that I bought your freedom. You would look after yourself and me as you see fit."

It was then that she opened her full lips for the longest speech I ever managed to get out of her.

"Yes," said she, "you, John Silver, are the sort that needs my sort, even though you look after yourself for the most part, like me. You're right to have seen that. I was brought up on the one hand among slaves and on the other among marines and their officers. I know more about you white men and your so-called civilisation than you yourself will ever understand. I can see that you're not like the others. You're like me, though you don't have my pride. You're submitting yourself to me because you need me and want me, but a man like you should keep away from love. You won't be able to endure it, and won't be made happy by it. Being free is the only thing that counts for you. Yes, I'll gladly be your woman, but I don't want to have you submitting yourself to me. That would be the death of you, and what would be gained?"

If I had been hesitant before, I was silenced now. When she saw how perplexed and taken aback I was she burst out laughing in her inimitable way that made you know you were alive.

"Don't take things so to heart!" said she, exactly as I had said to Jack and the others. "You're amazed by my words, or just by the fact that I've thought about it and have words to express it. Is that not right? It is not so strange. I was sent to school by my white father, a colonel in the army, was baptised, and was filled up with your God in Heaven and the truth of life. I went into service in the grandest houses in the Colonies. I grew up and was endowed with the beautiful, supple body that you've seen, and was the object of the wildest lusts and desires, even from my own father. My mother taught me the most important thing: pride, never to forget that I had been branded as a slave, and that the mark could never be hidden or cut away. One day when my father was taking me, I stuck a knife into him. After that I was sold on as a slave to another place, since no one dared touch me, not even to put a noose round my neck. So you see, John Silver, that I have nothing to envy you, and nothing to admire you for. But after everything I heard about the slave on the *Carefree*, saw at the auction in Charlotte Amalia, was told about the uprising on the clergy's plantation, and then now, I've understood enough to know that if I were going to stay with any one person to gain some respect and be left in peace, then that person would be John Silver."

That is what she said to me, did Dolores, as if it were a declaration, the longest I ever heard. A goddess of few words, was Dolores. She never said anything but what was absolutely essential, as far as I could judge.

She stayed with me for nineteen years before she went and died without a word. Even I can weep for that. I have tried to laugh instead, but it sticks in my throat. I have sometimes asked myself whether I would have survived and saved my skin for as long as I did if it had not been for her. Even as an enemy to mankind, you have to have somewhere to go and someone to depend upon, perhaps, when all's said and done, not in order to survive, but in order not to go mad, which also is a kind of death. I saw it when Flint's company was broken up, I saw it at other times and heard about hundreds of other occasions when pirates took to flight to escape pursuit or the gallows. They were empty-handed, as much at a loss as orphan children, as flustered and confused as chickens. There was nowhere they could feel secure after that. But rather than let themselves be hunted and pursued, they ran into the face of death. They became their own executioners. Anything was better than being completely alone in the world and at the same time being lawful prey to all and sundry.

Ah, Jim lad, it looks as if I'm getting sentimental in my old age. 'Tis a downhill slope for John Silver indeed. Writing about yourself, Jim, is one long-drawn-out blood-letting. It has turned me into a bloodless old devil, I can tell you. I can only hope that this other John Silver, the one I've put down on paper, has got something of the scintillating spark of life that I had in the old days. But not even that is certain, so the whole enterprise is totally meaningless. For if he is to have any prospects after this, he must have life and be of flesh and blood. That's the main thing. But how can I know whether he is alive? I can hardly stand up myself.

And to think that I was always against haste and skimped work! How many gentlemen of fortune went all round the world just because they could not control themselves and wait? They wanted everything in advance, life and death included. And here I sit fretting over whether I will be able to put a full stop to a life which is no more than what I write down, before the time comes to end my own.

It is a fortunate thing, I can tell you, that Dolores cannot see me now. She would have laughed right to my face. She did not bleed me of life, at any rate, you may lay to it. She did not give much either, but I had enough myself, and to spare.

I installed Dolores comfortably in Port Royal before we sailed out in search of Flint. In order not to arouse suspicion, I bought a tavern. There were three rooms on the first floor where Dolores settled herself in, with relief, I think, though she did not show any outward sign of it. She was far from being a restless soul like me, who could only sit still for any length of time if it were a question of life or death. But she did not need to keep looking over her shoulder all the time as I did.

For I'll tell you, Jim, there was nowhere I could feel safe by then, not even in Port Royal. Though Port Royal was just as it had been before the great earthquake that buried two thousand of the world's greatest riff-raff, if you can believe what's said – a throng of sailors, freed and unfreed slaves, smugglers, traders of all degrees of honesty, dock-workers, drunkards, beggars, discharged soldiers and other similarly unreliable sorts.

Yet the town no longer lived up to its reputation of being as sickly as a hospital, as dangerous as the plague, as hot as Hell and as sinful as the Devil himself. In the good old days there were free ports like Port Royal for the likes of me. Those days were over now. Port Royal was overflowing with the flotsam and jetsam of former companies who had accepted amnesty or who were in such a wretched state that it was not worth hanging them. In any case it would not have been a punishment, but rather an alleviation of their condition and a relief. On top of that, Taylor had sailed to the West Indies and every one of his old crew who was still alive would have happily turned in the likes of me to earn a crust.

But not only that. In the midst of Port Royal's gin palaces, brothels, seedy shops, hovels and a few grander stone houses for the upper classes and the Governor, the Admiralty had built one of its courthouses that were the gateway to Hell for me and my kind. There was a sign above the door bearing the words *The Naked Truth*! But what perversion of the law was this naked truth? Testimonies, informants, tattle, rumour and calumny, that was what they called the truth. And mark my words, according to the letter of the law one pitiful testimony was enough to bring down the likes of me. The only crime where more was demanded was treason. No, it is credibility, not the naked truth they profess, with which men regulate matters of life and death ashore. And for lack of it, it was easy to end your days in irons on Gallows Point, the newly created place of execution in Port Royal.

So it was a relief for me, too, to set off in search of Flint when everything was disposed to my full satisfaction. Dolores safe and secure, myself insecure and vulnerable. But that was the way I wanted it. What was risking your life from time to time on board a ship, compared with constantly, day in and day out, every single moment, having to fear for your skin and the gallows? No, I have never had a peaceful moment on land in the whole of my long life, as far as I can recall, whether or not I kept my hands unblemished and my back covered.

Thirty-six

WAS FLINT A real live person, do I hear you ask? Ay, to all appearances, must be my answer, even if it was hard to believe when the *Walrus* came suddenly upon us astern, towering over our pitiful little brig in the dawn of a damp, calm morning before the sun had had time to melt away the mist. Our sails had hung slack all night long, and the only noise on my night watch had been the snores of the crew, a squeak here and there from the blocks and the dripping of dew from sailcloth and yards.

Yet there she was, Flint's ship, like a phantom, with the Jolly Roger flying at her stern. The flag was hung from a crosspiece so that it could be seen in the windless calm. He had even thought of that, had Flint, conscientious captain that he was. But how had he found us in the mist and darkness? And how had he been able to come up with us when there was not a breath of air in the sails?

Slowly, as if guided by an invisible hand, the ghost ship drew alongside with all its cannon out. I saw some figures leaning over the rail, as unconcerned as if they were the crew of a peaceful merchantman. They were so sure of themselves and of their superiority that they were allowing some of the crew to stand and watch; there were probably even some still asleep, so quiet and tranquil did it seem on deck.

I, of course, was anxious to see the nameless pirate who had already made himself so notorious, yet could hardly be said to exist. He came up on to the poop deck at the same moment that all the ship's cannon were brought to bear on us. I saw him nod and immediately a few swift men were up in the rigging taking in the topsails so that the ship lay to alongside of us. I understood then that Flint was not supernatural, but of this world: he had managed to catch a current of air higher up with his topsails, while we with our shorter masts were becalmed. That is how it could be sometimes, a barely perceptible breeze would die away at surface level while continuing to blow as light as a feather higher up. But he was a seaman of devilish fine ability in any case, this captain.

Another nod from him and there came a shot across our bows. A skilful gunner it was, too, who shot off our bowsprit so that the foresail came down with a crash. Then Flint strolled across to the rail and asked us politely to strike our flag.

"With the greatest of pleasure!" I shouted back, just as a great commotion started on board because I had not thought to wake the others.

"There's no danger!" I cried as I hauled down the flag. "We've found what we were looking for."

They all had happy countenances, and happiest of the lot was Israel Hands, who had not had a single glass of the strong stuff in the four weeks we had been sailing to and fro between the islands. Nor much entertainment either, for that matter, since he was not a solitary man by nature.

"To sea! To sea!" he yelled, the pirates' watchword. "Put out a boat, in Hell's name! Do we have to wait all day to be boarded?"

This bewildered the fearsome pirates, and they looked at one another as if not knowing what to make of it. They were not used to being met with such wholehearted delight. A few years before – ay, when I was sailing with England – you could reckon on half the crew of any merchantman wanting nothing better than to join us. There were times when not even heavily armed men o' war dared attack, out of pure and simple fear that their own crew would mutiny. Ah, that was when we were the ones who could pick and choose.

Flint knew that, of course. Our cries of joy left him unmoved, but to be safe, he employed certain measures that I noted with respect. The boarding party he sent over was armed to the teeth and took no unnecessary risks, although even so they were not enough on their guard.

"I'd like to have a parley with your cap'n," said I, when they had climbed aboard and assured themselves we were no more than fourteen unarmed men. "If I may," I added politely.

"No, you mayn't," one of them said, as if that was his last word on the subject.

"I'm Long John Silver," said I, "quartermaster with England an' Taylor. The ugly devil over there is Israel Hands, Teach's first mate. The others are my body-guard, but free men for all that. And we've been a-sailin' round in this ol' tub for nigh on a month a-waitin' to be captured by you. So I'll be obliged if you'll take me to your cap'n!"

My words made some impression, that was plain, but they were suspicious devils, you may lay to it.

"How do we know you're telling the truth?" one of them asked.

"Telling the truth!" I screeched, enough to make him jump. "Do I have to show you papers to prove who I am? That I've sailed with England an' Taylor? I'm offering you a ship and fourteen men, and you starts talking about truth. Have I demanded to know who you are?"

This made some of them laugh out loud.

"What the Hell is so funny?" I asked.

"That the likes o' you should demand anything at all o' the likes of us," a third man replied. "If you ain't observed as much, you're lying beneath eighteen of our cannon."

"Are you a-threatenin' me?" I yelled, stressing the last word.

"Call it what you likes," said he, shrugging his shoulders. "Here 'tis us who decides and you who does what we says."

"Oh, I see," said I, as smooth as honey.

I took a few steps towards the big-mouthed man and one of his comrades who was standing next to him with a broad grin on his face. The former put his hand on his cutlass, but that was all. It did not occur to him until it was too late that there were things in this world that might take precedence over his cannon. In an instant I had smashed their skulls together with a horrendous crack, with hands that could have rivalled Captain Barlow's.

So now you know that too, Jim. 'Twas two I killed with my bare hands, not four as Israel Hands boasted and as you, Jim, wrote in your book. How would it have been done, a man banging four heads together at the same time? No, there has to be some limit, even for the likes of me.

But two crushed skulls were more than enough to change their tune. They went as silent as the grave, to be more precise.

"No one," I roared, "no one, mark you, tells John Silver what he can and cannot do."

The remaining pirates stood as if rooted to the deck. They had probably never seen a real madman who was not drunk. Ill at ease, they looked at each other uncertainly, no one daring to take the first step. Their minds were unprepared for this, none of them had thought they might meet their end on this calm, mild and mist-bound morning just seizing a wretched, defenceless brig. But there you are. Gentlemen of fortune lived for today because they might be dead on the morrow, but to imagine they could just as easily die today was rarely something they were capable of. If they were taken by surprise in bed, for instance, they would jump overboard and forget they could not swim. They would give up and strike their flag, forgetting that the gallows was the only thing that awaited them. They would flee into the jungle, forgetting that they had neither weapons nor water to keep body and soul together.

Flint's crew, however, were made of better stuff than most. When I had calmed down I could see the first signs of decisiveness returning, and saw that I had risked my own and the others' skins by my headlong and foolhardy ways.

"My offer stands," I said more ingratiatingly. "Two brutes less is still a cheap price to pay for fourteen first-class men, two of 'em who knows their jobs inside out."

But hardly had I finished speaking before I heard a yell behind me, a shot and a bullet hitting the rail. I turned. Now there was a third pirate lying on the deck stone dead, his neck snapped. It was Jack who had stepped in.

"Ah, well," said I, "three for fourteen ain't so bad neither. But hadn't we better be on our way across afore this turns into a blood-bath?"

At that very moment Flint's foghorn voice echoed over the water.

"Any more and I'll sink your damned hulk, men and all!" he screamed in a fury, the way he was when sailors died, gesticulating violently with his telescope.

There could be little doubt that he was in earnest.

"Come on, shift yourselves, and let's have the rabble over here!" he shouted to his men.

They recovered some of the colour in their faces when they heard their captain's voice; but that was about as much as they recovered. Hands, Jack and I were rowed over and taken up to the poop deck to come face to face with this pirate who still had no name.

One of the sailors with us did all he could to imbue us with fear. He promised us that it was far worse to burn in Hell than to be exposed to the wrath of their captain. He wished us a good journey to the other side, and hoped he would be one of the chosen few who would have the pleasure of torturing the life out of us. I was not to think I could get away with murthering good men just as I liked, he said.

I let him carry on, but made a mental note of him – which turned out to be waste of effort. When we came up on the poop deck, within earshot of the captain, the sailor spoke his final words with malicious glee, "Cap'n Flint will flay you alive!"

For a moment I thought he was not exaggerating in the slightest, because no sooner had he spoken than the said Flint gave an infernal bellow, drew his cutlass and came rushing towards us. Jack threw himself forward, the fool, to take the blow in my stead. He got nothing for his pains. The cutlass struck Flint's own man with terrible force and ended his life on the spot.

"The incompetent cur!" Flint cried, giving the limp body a kick as other sailors came running over in dismay.

In the end there was quite a gathering on deck. Flint blinked a few times, wiped his hand over his brow and seemed as if he were awakening from a trance. He looked down at the body first and then up at his men.

"I'm sorry," he said in a gloomy voice that as far as I could judge was genuine, "but how many times do I have to explain that no names are to be mentioned when outsiders are listening? Does it have to be so hard to get it into your thick heads that this ship and its crew have to be nameless if we're to survive? How many do I have to kill to no bloody avail before you all understand that I'm determined we ain't going to be captured just because some of you can't keep your mouths shut? Now go to Hell, all of you! But make sure you empty our prize and scuttle her!"

The crew ran off hither and thither as if they were being driven with a whip.

"And now, gentlemen," said Flint, turning to us, "who the Hell do you think you are? Murthering my crew after striking your flag!"

"The same manner of men as yourselves," I replied, to Flint's obvious surprise.

I told him who we were, what we wanted and why. I told him too that the twelve negroes would go to their deaths for my sake, of their own free will, lest he be thinking of doing away with me and then taking on the rest.

"John Silver," said he, cogitating. "I've heard of you. An awkward customer, so they say."

"It depends entirely on how I'm treated, sir. I can be a good shipmate too. There are plenty o' witnesses to that."

"And how," asked he, "do we go about fostering that side of you?"

"By not taking any liberties agin' me. Especially behind my back."

"Like the two you killed?"

"Something like that."

"All right, Silver. Welcome aboard."

"If the council agrees," I added.

"Naturally," said Flint, "I'd forgotten that. You're an advocate for the crew, as quartermaster, and speak their cause before God, Satan and all the captains on this earth."

"Not before God, sir. We ain't exactly on speaking terms, Him and me."

"I can imagine!" said Flint with a wry smile.

He seldom laughed, did Flint. It was not in his nature. No, he was a sad and gloomy devil through and through.

"For your sake," said he, "I'll call a meeting of the fo'c's'le council. There's always somebody who likes to express an opinion. But there's one thing I'd like you to remember, Silver: I've got my own principles and my own articles. And they'll only be changed over my dead body: just so's you know."

[348]

"And what are they, if I may ask, sir?"

"That no one is to jeopardise this ship's strength and safety. That we shouldn't, from either arrogance or stupidity, make the same mistakes that nearly all the others in our business have made. We're the last, Silver, and by the Devil we're going to keep ourselves in trim and stay alive to frighten the wits out of every merchant, shipowner and captain on this earth. Putting a stop to trade at sea for good, that's my aim. Putting a stop to the abuse of good seamen, Silver, that's why I'm here."

"And booty?" said I. "Prizes, money, gold?"

"That too. Because that's the underbelly of trade. That's where the kicks hit hardest."

He looked me straight in the eye to see what effect his words had made. I did not show it, obviously, but I had not expected Flint to be the principled kind. There had certainly been others who had put on an appearance of sailing for prize-money for a good cause. And I am not talking about Captain Misson, who was pure invention and wishful thinking on the part of Defoe. But Roberts and Davis both thought they had God and right on their side. When Roberts harangued governors and crew he invoked higher principles. He sought out lack of liberty both on land and at sea; he even had the impudence to offer a priest a place on board, but on that matter he was judiciously outvoted by the council. Flint was no thinker like Roberts or Davis. Flint hardly thought at all, if you ask me; he was an enthusiast. Trying to talk sense to him was a waste of time. No, you had to play on Flint like a musical instrument if you wanted to get anywhere with him, but it was not easy, because he was badly tuned and as changeable in mood as wind and weather. And to think that even he, the bloodthirsty devil, had good intentions, had aims and principles, and wanted to safeguard the lives of good seamen.

Well, he could do that for me.

"I'm your man," said I.

There was not much else to say. We fetched our chests and made them fast in a corner of the lower deck alongside the others. There were men everywhere, not to be wondered at with an hundred and thirty hands on board. A third of them were still slumbering in their ham- mocks. No more than that could sleep at any one time, because there was not enough space.

People everywhere, then, in every cranny. Men playing dice, sewing and splicing, hanging over the rail and staring at the empty horizon, singing and whistling, carving wood, old dried cheese, ivory, even beef that was hard as a rock. Some were telling stories, sorting out their chests for the hundredth time, playing with the ship's dogs and cats, hunting cockroaches or picking out lice. Some slept, some caulked or painted, and a few, believe it or not, sailed the ship, trimming the sails, navigating, acting as look-out. Others were cleaning their weapons, competing at arm-wrestling and marksmanship, or doing duty in the galley and stirring the pots. And then there were those, the great majority, who were doing absolutely nothing, as if they had never done aught else and as if there were naught else they would rather be doing.

I had almost forgotten how bad it was, and how to accustom myself to rubbing along with such a crowd that thronged everywhere. It was to our credit that we were able to leave one another in peace, but when all's said and done we had not signed on to sail in Hell. That was where we had come from, for the most part.

I asked someone about watches and stations.

"Well," said he, "we has our stations when we go into attack, that's plain enough. But otherwise 'tis just the galley that has a rota, because nobody wants to go there. You get little but curses for your pains. Oh, and berths, naturally. Everything else is done by whoever happens to be on deck."

"Does that work out?" I asked, remembering the mass of incompetents on board the *Fancy* who had never pulled their weight, and were hardly able to, either.

"We got first-class seamen here, the whole lot of 'em, I can vouch for that. They knows what they're a-doin' of. You wait an' see when we starts to manoeuvre prop'ly. 'Tis a treat to watch, I can tell you. You wouldn't believe it when you looks at 'em a-lyin' around on deck, would you?"

He laughed, proud of being one of them. And he was speaking the truth, for never have I seen such a well-sailed ship as the *Walrus*, and never a crew who could get their vessel to sing with joy as she did. But they were just as good at letting the time pass and doing almost nothing. After all, we rarely needed to sail at speed. We mostly just lay in wait, floating indolently around in some remote corner of the great ocean where we might expect an unescorted merchantman to turn up. Ay, the idleness and lounging were as precious as all the gold in the world. Gold burned a hole in their pockets when they got hold of it, but where free time was concerned, they made the most of it, and never wasted it. They never played dice for the galley rota, because they were all afraid of losing.

I wandered round on deck all that first morning while our old ship was emptied and scuttled. I wished to see and learn, study the mood, discover the men's dispositions and abilities. I found that we had several craftsmen on board: a surgeon with a diploma, three carpenters, two of whom were Scots and one a Finn, all from forested countries and thus among the best of their profession, as was well known, four musicians to inspire us with courage and console us in melancholy, and two pilots, one for the Antilles and one for the west coast of Africa. Flint had really managed to gather together all the skills he needed.

The sailors were all seasoned men, both in terms of their tanned skins and the length of their experience. There was a mere handful who had not sailed for prize-money before. Flint only wanted those who had a noose around their necks. He reckoned they were the only ones that could be depended upon. There was probably something in that, but Flint had nonetheless forgotten the most important fact of all, that most of them would not care whether they lived or died. They may have had the noose around their necks, but that did not necessarily make them the same as me. On the contrary. With the gallows hanging over their heads they would risk their lives for almost anything. No, they did not fight for their lives. They thought they would die soon enough in any case.

But it was a sweet crew, you may lay to it, with a captain such as Flint to put some spirit into them when it was needed, if the likes of him and me were to have things our way. And they had pride in their calling. To strike flag for just anyone would infringe their honour. They had some sense of shame after all.

I was surprised, on the other hand, to discover that Flint had taken on half a dozen Indians from the Mosquito Coast. These Indians had once allied themselves with the buccaneers out of hatred for the Spanish, and had sailed with us since then. They were the only people on land we could call our friends, and the young men of the tribe were sent out to serve with us for a few years. Partly to show their scorn for the Spaniards, their elders said, partly to get some experience of the world. It was always a good thing, they said, because young men needed to stimulate their minds in order to still the restlessness in their bodies. So they sailed with us gentlemen of fortune for a few years, and fought and risked their lives like the rest of us, before returning to their tribes. They took home with them a few iron tools, but wanted no part of the booty. They just laughed at our feverish hunt for gold and silver in every shape and form.

Why did they ally themselves with us? How could such people have any time for the likes of Flint and others in the same mould? For one reason, and one reason alone, if you ask me: because they were good at life and death.

Once a year the Indians sacrificed a living person, a prisoner saved for the purpose. For a whole year before the sacrifice took place the chosen man had his every wish granted, everything except freedom. He had slaves to tend him all day long, he was dressed in the most costly garments, was given the tastiest and most succulent food, did not have to lift a finger, and lived in all the comfort and luxury the tribe could muster. He was regarded as a demi-god, and people made an obeisance when he came in their path, even grovelling in the dirt for him. After a year of this homage he was burned alive on a pyre, and mourned like a dear friend or kinsman who had passed away.

But what has this to do with the likes of us? Well, I am not really sure. But think what happens when we are hanged, so that the rest of you can be at peace. We are mocked, ridiculed and despised. We are treated like rats, cockroaches or lice. We are hanged like scum and villains. No, you ordinary folk do not know how lives are taken, because you are not really concerned about life. You casually take the life of heathens, slaves, Jews, witches, criminals, pirates, Indians, enemies of all races, beggars – ay, even sailors. The Indians understood at least that lives should not be taken in random ways. I have sometimes thought we gentlemen of fortune were similar to the slaves that the Indians sacrificed once a year. The difference was that we offered ourselves of our own free will, deliberately, and without the slightest recognition of our service.

Later, when I had come to know Flint better, I asked him why he had taken these Indians on board.

"They watch over my life," replied he, and that was all I could get out of him.

But I felt I knew that Flint was not entirely to be believed on this matter. He was the sort who would die just to give life meaning, he was the slave to be sacrificed, no more and no less. The Indians became his friends for that very reason: because they knew how a human being should be sacrificed if necessity demanded.

While I was wandering around deep in thought, with all the time in the world, and looking and listening, who should heave in sight but that old trickster, Pew.

"Good day to you, Mr Silver!" said he respectfully, since I was one of those who had always used him as he deserved, like a dog. "Wonderful to meet you. Always a pleasure. An' you're a-goin' to be quartermaster again? No better man for the job, if you asks me. I seen how you put an end to Hipps and Lewis with your bare hands."

He laughed, and would have slapped me on the back had he dared.

"That's our ol' friend Silver, I told 'em on board. You won't find his like anywhere – exceptin' possibly for Flint. With Silver an' Flint, I said, I warrant we can take on the whole world. Ain't I right, Mr Silver?"

"It all depends," I replied, "on how many cowardly wretches of your ilk we're afflicted with."

"O' course, o' course," said he, withdrawing with a submissive bow.

That is the kind of man he was, I thought to myself, but I have to live with him and talk to him. He was one of the worthless ones, but even he had to have a voice in the company, nothing else was possible if we were to have peace on board and survive.

I went for'ard to the bowsprit and climbed out into the netting. There and in the look-out was one of the few places you could be alone with your thoughts. I lay listening to the surge of water round the bows, the sound of the rigging and the indeterminate voices on deck. Everything would be all right, thought I, when I had become used to the hurly-burly. I had found some peace at last, there was no haste or urgency for anything. Letting time pass by, with small tasks mostly, and larger ones occasionally, as pleasantly as possible, while increasing my wealth, and with Dolores waiting for me ashore – it was in truth far from being the worst way of spending your life, you may lay to that.

I fell asleep and was awoken by Flint's foghorn voice.

"All hands on deck!" he bawled. "All men to council!"

There was a bustle and a hubbub without compare, because this was something they were not used to. Those asleep below were called up on deck by their excited comrades. A buzz of anticipation spread like wildfire. If Flint was calling the council together, something big must be brewing, they thought. I sauntered up on deck and found myself right behind Flint. As if he had eyes in the back of his head he turned and nodded to me. Before us was the most motley collection of sea-farers I had ever seen.

"Men," Flint shouted, "most of you will have observed that we've taken on additional strength. 'Tis Long John Silver here, quartermaster with England and Taylor, who's joined us, with thirteen crew. I'm sure some of you know him already. If I'm not mistaken some of you sailed with England and Taylor. Is there anyone who has any objections? Shall we take on Silver and his company?"

"Take 'em on! Take 'em on!" several men shouted.

"He killed Hipps and Lewis for their insolence," said Flint drily.

"No harm done!"

That was Pew, and several others agreed with him.

"Silver's the man for us!" shouted Pew, and there were more sounds of approval.

[354]

But when the hum died down an unmistakable voice made itself heard.

"Not for me!" came the whining tones of Deval – who else? "John Silver defied the council an' Taylor an' spared the lives o' both England and Cap'n Mackra."

There was a hushed silence in the ranks of men. Everyone knew it was a serious allegation Deval had made, one that was a matter of life or death among gentlemen of fortune. Flint turned to me with a slight smile. He wanted to see if I could get myself out of this situation. It amused him, the devil!

And that louse Deval probably reckoned he would finally get his revenge. What was he doing here? He had hung on with the tattered remnants of Taylor's company, I had heard. Taylor, who had a blind spot for that sort of thing, had showered him with friendliness and made him his right-hand man. Deval had gone back to the West Indies with Taylor, lived on his booty for a while, and then managed to get taken on by the *Walrus* inadvertently. He had probably hoped that Flint would accord him the same esteem that Taylor had, but if there were anyone who needed no assistance in beating people to a pulp or worse, it was Flint. Leastways, one thing was certain, I thought as I stood in front of the *Walrus*'s expectant crew: if I had been Edward England's evil demon, then Deval was mine.

"Cap'n Mackra can burn in Hell for all I care," I began. "But ay, 'tis true enough, even if it comes from a swab like Deval here, I saved the life of Edward England. And mark my words, I'd do it again. England was an honourable man and a skilful cap'n. We took twenty-six ships under his command, and he never interfered in the decisions o' the fo'c's'le council. He thought too highly of himself to put on the airs an' graces of a cap'n appointed by the grace o' God, like so many other arrogant and loud-mouthed navigators that we happen to 'lect to lead our ships, for lack of anyone better."

Out of the corner of my eye I could see Flint's smile go rigid, but only for a brief moment. He was not too stupid to see that it was fair game to use the means at my disposal.

"True 'nough," I went on, "I defied Taylor, not just once but a hundred times. He was a cowardly and calculating devil who hadn't put his hand to a single day's work in his whole life."

This brought scattered laughter, since they all knew his hands were not up to much.

"Taylor," I roared, "would betray anyone for a shillin'. How many were it who met their end when Taylor sailed back to the West Indies to buy himself free passage? How many? Taylor was on'y interested in saving his own skin. He didn't give a fig about the likes o' you. And who d'you think he used as his executioner? Who were it he used to do his dirty work? – and that's the right word for it. Who were it who licked Taylor's arse to get a pat on the back? Who if not our excellent shipmate Deval, as'll do anythin' at all for a little friendliness, even from the likes o' Taylor. No wonder, says I. His mother was a whore who didn't want to know him. She sold him for money to a fornicator by the name o' Dunn whose child she'd had. An' Deval here thought he'd been a-taken in for his own sake! That's the truth, gen'lemen, and now you can decide how the Hell you please on the matter."

"It ain't true," Deval yelled, venting his spleen, humiliation and shame.

"It ain't for you to judge, damn you," I responded to him. "'Tis for the fo'c's'le council. If you wants to have it out with me in private, that's one thing, but if you wants to expose me in public I got a right to defend myself."

"Ay, true 'nough!" shouted somebody.

And so I took it upon myself to tell them Deval's story, and before I had even told the half of it, Deval had disappeared below deck, to the taunts and jeers of the crew. I looked Flint in the eye, with a wholly impassive countenance, and received a glance of recognition in return.

"Is John Silver taken on?" asked he.

A great cheer rose up. Ay, then, if not before, it was very plain to me how important it is to be able to tell yarns that are worthy of the belief of others, though in fact that time I had told the truth.

Learn from that, Jim – but I think you must be well aware of it already, judging by what you wrote about me. We had a boy on the *Walrus*, John by name, the one who was good to me when I lost my leg. I took note of him the very first day, because he was standing not far from me, with eyes as big as saucers. John was one who took me at my word and believed everything I said. He became attached to me, Jim, exactly as you did, because of my gift of the gab. That's the supreme thing, Jim, remember that as well: talking to folk, so that when all's said and done, 'tis not so damned lonely in this world.

Thirty-seven

ECOLLECTING AND WRITING about my first day on board the old *Walrus* put me suddenly in excellent spirits. I felt like a human being again. I had forgotten how it was to have a fair wind in your soul and to have put up as much sail as the old hulk can take. Ay, it was like rising from the grave again, after taking my leave of Snelgrave.

So there is life in the carcass yet. Dead one day and alive the next. I ate like a pack of wolves at dinner, which was served as if everything were as it used to be. Jack ate with me and I think he was pleased on my behalf. I asked him what he did during the day. I was well aware, I said, that I had cut a rather miserable figure of late, but that I would soon be finished and then he would see what the old dotard was still capable of.

"What do you do with your time?" I asked.

"Nothing," he replied. "I get the food on the table for the two of us, that's about all."

"I know. I don't like you looking a'ter me. But I'll soon have written my last word, and then, by thunder, we'll get out a-hunting again."

"There's no need," said Jack.

"No need?"

"No. Food comes every day, bread, fruit and meat. I fetch it from down below."

"Fine," said I. "I don't want my money to rot away doing nothing."

"It doesn't cost anything."

"Don't cost nothing?"

"No, 'tis a gift. To John Silver."

"Well, shiver my timbers," I exclaimed. "Why all this generosity all of a sudden? Oh, I know, the devils are showing compassion for me. They

[358]

feel sorry for me. Ain't that it? They think John Silver's wanting in his mind. They think I've gone mad. Ain't that so?"

"I don't know," said Jack.

"Don't know? Ain't you heard what's being said about me?"

"No, I've heard nothing."

"Don't you speak to your people?"

"They're not my people. I don't talk their language."

"And what about yours? Your Sakalava?"

"They've gone home. There's on'y me left here."

I must say that made me feel uneasy, though it did not dampen my good humour. So since the feast for Snelgrave's crew Jack could not have uttered a single word, save to me. How long ago was it that *The Delight of Bristol* sailed? A week? Two? A month? Two? And I'd had the impudence to ask Jack what he was doing with his time!

"When I've finished . . . " said I.

"I know," Jack interrupted, "we'll hunt pigs and make barbecues."

"Ay, like we used to. When we had all the time in the world."

"Haven't we now?"

"You know what I mean. When you don't think 'twill all come to an end one day. An unwritten page, Jack, that's life at its best. We were good at it, weren't we?"

Jack nodded.

"Do you remember the first day on the *Walrus*? I'll never forget it."

"Why?" he asked.

Looking at him now, it occurred to me that he and his fellow-tribesmen had not been part of my memories. From the moment I set foot on the deck of the *Walrus* I had forgotten them.

"What did you do that day?" I asked.

"We met two other Sakalava. Former slaves like us. We sat together."

"Sat together?"

"Ay. Waiting to come back here. To Madagascar."

"Waiting?"

"Ay," said Jack, "that's what we did on board."

"But you an' I sailed with Flint for three years."

"Ay. There were times when we thought we'd never come back. But you'd promised we'd be put ashore as soon as we got here."

Jack was not one to play games with the truth, but this was hard to swallow. The first part of the period with Flint was the best time of my life, and yet Jack and the others had just been sitting waiting for it to end. And to think that I had wanted to talk over old memories with him! There would be no point in it at all. What memories can you have if you are just sitting on your backside waiting?

"I thought you were happy on board."

"It was better than the plantation. But we're not like you."

"No," said I, managing a laugh, "there ain't many who are, I've come to understand."

"I mean Sakalava and gentlemen of fortune. We have a country and we're a people. You didn't give a damn for such things, as you used to say."

"Why didn't you get out if it was so hellish?"

"It wasn't Hell. It was nothing."

"Nothing?"

"No. No soul."

"No soul? What about liberty? Having all the time in the world before you? Being free from care, letting the days pass, with no hurry. Getting rich and being able to do what you want when 'tis over. Ain't that soul, or whatever you call it?"

"You can't have soul all on your own. Then you're nothing."

"We weren't alone on board. We were a hundred an' thirty men."

"Not together. We Sakalava fought for one another. You fought for yourselves. Every man for himself. How many died in those years? What were their names? Where did they come from? Where were they going? 'Tis all one, as you would say. The men who died were forgotten by the next day. They died for a good cause, you used to say. Yours! No, you were alone, all of you, never together. Where's the soul in that?"

"I don't know," said I good-naturedly, because I did not want to spoil the mood.

When all was said and done, Jack was the only one I had left to talk to, apart from John Silver.

"I've never been able to comprehend what it is you mean by soul," I went on.

"No," said Jack.

"And yet you've always called us brothers."

"Ay. We are brothers. You don't need me. I get by without you. But we need one another."

"That was what Dolores used to say."

I had a strange feeling in my chest, in the midst of my excellent humour.

"When I've finished," said I, "you must explain to me what soul is."

"Ay," said Jack.

"When I've done it, we'll have a feast. We'll invite everyone who's still alive and ever set foot on board the *Walrus*. At least we knew how to celebrate, you have to agree. We were together then, I reckon, say what you will."

"Ay, you were good at that, even together. You had soul then. But there weren't many who remembered it on the morrow."

I had to laugh at that, because he was right. Jack laughed too, which made me think he did indeed have some memories from the years with Flint.

All three years flashed past before me. I could see every single prize we took and the face of every man I had known, both dead and alive. I saw Sainte Marie, not far from here, where we gathered to enjoy the fruits of our short life with impunity, and I could hear the laughs and cries of pain and joy, our own and others'. I could smell the thousand smells and stenches from the ship and from the islands to windward, I could hear all the songs and yarns started up by first one and then another, and saw myself passing whole nights seated in the look-out, suspended in space. I admired the seamanship when we rode out a storm or made the ship ready. I chuckled at all our masquerades and impostures to deceive unsuspecting merchantmen, I heard myself get the better of quarrelsome trouble-makers, and prided myself on the times I had forced Flint to give way to my or the council's wishes, and I delighted in seeing an hundred and thirty men assembled in council, and hearing all the words exchanged so fervently before we came to a decision. Ay, I longed to go back to the golden times when we had taken a prize with precious stones in her cargo and I excitedly felt them flow through my fingers, or when I was lying for hours in the bowsprit net again and letting the time pass. All this and much more I saw and spoke of in as much detail as anyone could wish.

"Ah, shiver my timbers, it has been a long life!" I exclaimed and went to clasp Jack's arm.

It was not there. I became aware then that I had had my eyes closed the whole time. When I opened them I saw I was alone. Jack had gone. I could have no objection to that. I also would have tired of listening to someone who was just talking to himself. Jack was better off without me. There was no denying it. The only one who needed me in order to live was Long John Silver, and soon he too would be able to stand on his own one foot.

Thirty-eight

AH, JIM LAD, I'm forgetting you, of course, exactly as I forgot Defoe, forgot that it was him I was talking to. 'Tis not always easy keeping everything in your head when you've reached my venerable age.

I was going to tell you about Flint. I thought it might interest the likes of you. Ay, I wanted to tell you that we were human beings too, even me, we who were vermin and scum in the eyes of the world. I wanted at least to say that we could get along together, be considerate to each other and sail a ship for several years without wringing one another's necks. A hundred and thirty men in one old tub that was so small that we could not even bed down all at the same time! Maybe I said that already, I can no longer be sure.

Then I talked to Jack and discovered that I could actually spend another whole lifetime writing about my years with Flint. Would you believe it? But that life will not be granted to me. I have risen from the dead several times while I was alive, true enough, but all is up with me now, and that is as true as the Gospels and as true as my name is John Silver, which is more or less the same thing in the end.

Anyhow, I have already told Flint's whole story to Jack, even if he was not listening. I felt empty and hollow afterwards, I can tell you. It is no fun telling stories and discovering in the middle of it all that nobody is listening, not even the man closest to you. Perhaps a life such as mine can be too long, after all.

But then . . . You know I'm not a timid man. A lion's nothing along-side of old Long John, that's what they said, and it was quite right. Wasn't I the only one not in a mortal panic when Ben Gunn tried to affright us out of our wits with Flint's ghost? No, I was never afraid of Flint. He would never treacherously stab his own kind in the back. Straight to the point, that was his way. But last night was really something, Jim! In my dreams Flint walked again. He appeared as he had been at the end, when he had nigh on drunk himself to death, and had begun to see that he would never make any difference to trade or put fear into the world, no matter how many ships he plundered, how many worthy captains appointed by the grace of God he might slaughter, or how much booty he might seize. We had caused the prices of goods to double in our waters, but that was all. Flint could not patrol the whole world on his own. We were like vicious mosquitos, whose bite could create an itch for a day: but that was all we ever were, and no more. Ships sailed under increasingly stronger escort, and Flint obstinately refused to stake everything on one card as long as he remained in command of his senses. There was no point whatsoever in hazarding the *Walrus*, crew and all, to take a single prize, in terms of what Flint wanted to achieve.

There were some who tried to make him change his mind, putting forward the view that we should content ourselves with the riches we had already collected, and so dissolve the company. He could see for himself, they said, what little damage we were able to inflict.

Such sentiments put Flint into a rage, and a few men met their deaths on that account. That was also why Flint sailed to what you called Treasure Island and buried the treasure. Gentlemen of fortune were not usually foolish enough to bury their hard-won gains. How would they have had the time? Or the desire? No, it was probably only Kidd, as far as I know, apart from Flint, who took up the spade, and Kidd had his reasons, just as Flint had.

And something else you should know: the six men Flint took with him on to the island to dig, and whose lives he terminated with his own hands – ay, you heard what Flint looked like when he came back – they were the very men who had threatened to summon the fo'c's'le council if Flint would not shift his views. They did not understand that a man like Flint would never in his life change his opinion.

Anyhow, as time went on his mind became darker and more demented. In the end I was almost the only one who could make him see sense and keep him under control, myself and Darby M'Graw, who looked after his rum. That was a new article in Flint's rule book, that no one but M'Graw could touch his rum.

"They all want to do for me!" Flint would roar when I went into his cabin. "The bloody cowards. They want me dead, they want to give up and throw away their lives on whores and good living ashore. It'll be over my dead body, Silver, you mind that. We'll fight to the last. We'll ruin every single damned shipowner. D'you hear, Silver!"

"The way you bawl an' go on, Cap'n, I should think it'd be heard all the way to London."

"A bloody good job too!" he raved. "Damned if I won't let 'em know they're alive."

He glared at me with his rheumy eyes, as red as rotting tomatoes. His scar from Treasure Island gleamed white on his swollen and tallowy face. One hand held his cutlass in a clamp-like grip, as if the two were one.

It was in that guise he came to me in my dream, Jim, armed to the teeth. I was sitting at my desk writing these last few sighs of my life. Flint took up position behind me, reading over my shoulder. And then he started to laugh. A mocking laugh, the devil, that made him shake all over. There was a malicious glint in his eyes, that made me think my time had come to burn in Hell. I put my hands over my ears so as not to hear, and closed my eyes in order not to see, but it was as if I had neither hands nor eyelids. And when Flint saw me cowering in fear of him, his jeers grew until he was nothing but one enormous gaping grin.

I was exceeding fearful, I have to admit, and wondering how I could put a stop to the devilry. Was I to give in to the likes of Flint? said I to myself. Wasn't I a better man than him in every way? Why should I be so unnerved? Letting him stand there sneering at me! What do I care what he thinks about a life like mine? It makes no difference to me.

So I picked up my pen, dipped it in the inkwell, set it to paper and wrote the first words of my story of Flint. But when he saw his name on the paper he fell abruptly silent, and then let out a scream of rage that would have frighted the Devil himself out of his wits, if he had any. Then Flint raised his bloodstained cutlass and aimed a blow at me with all his might, multiplied by his frenzy.

"Nameless!" he screamed. "Nameless! No devil's going to lay hands on my name!"

And the cutlass came crashing down.

I woke up, Jim, in a cold sweat and shaking like a drunkard. Shiver my sides if Flint wasn't far worse to tussle with when dead than when alive, you may lay to it. Ay, I admit I feared I was about to die, and I was terror-stricken. I've been in fear for my skin all my life, but never had I been filled with such utter dread as at that moment, when I thought it was at an end. Again and again I saw Flint's cutlass whipping through the air. Awake as I was, I still expected to feel its sharp blade slice into the back of my neck.

But nothing happened. Then I understood that it was not me Flint was after, and not my neck his cutlass was aimed at. It was the other John Silver's head he was trying to shear off. It was the John Silver on paper, in black and white, the one of us twain who had some life to talk about, that Flint wanted to put an end to for all eternity.

It was unpleasant trying to write about Flint after that. Every time I took up my pen I could see the cutlass before my eyes. I could live with the mocking laughter if I had to, but the cutlass, and the oblivion afterwards, that was unbearable to imagine.

But now I have found the courage to do just that, to write about Flint and to say this one last thing, in a low voice: that I had some good years with Flint on the *Walrus*. We sailed first in the West Indies, then on the triangular route. It must have been in the third year that we came to Madagascar, and I put Jack and his Sakalava ashore as promised, to the bitter resentment of Flint and the others, because it was Flint's law on the *Walrus* that no one could leave unless the whole company was dissolved. But by that time there was no one who dared oppose me, not even Flint, and certainly not such petty folk as George Merry, Dick Anderson or the fawning Ben Gunn. Jack and the others took with them my share of the booty that was not in stones or ready money, and they settled on the cliff in Ranter Bay, as happy as children, to attend my return.

It was on the way back to the West Indies that I got my hands on Deval and did something about him. I was tired of his sidelong glances, filled with hatred, and had made up my mind to silence him, for good and all if need be. The last straw came on the day we sighted Barbados. Deval, like all the others, had heard the story of my freed slaves and my woman ashore, from Israel Hands' now healed but still equally big mouth. I was standing leaning over the rail, and damn me if I wasn't thinking about Dolores, when I heard Deval's whining voice start up a song:

Once I had an Irish girl, she was fat and lazy;
Now I've got a negro one, she drives me almost crazy.

Before I had time to do anything about it, the whole crew, in their excitement at seeing land, joined in, and were roaring out the same two lines over and over again, so that even the gulls were silenced. I turned round, and there stood Deval, leering at me with the most self-satisfied grin imaginable. But, by gum, when he saw the look on my face the grin disappeared in an instant.

First I put a stop to the song with a terrifying bellow, then I took Deval by the neck and throttled him till he was half dead. Slacking my grip, I told him in front of everyone what a wretched louse and cockroach he was. And in my over-enthusiasm I told him in the end what a shit his hero Dunn had been, how he had tried to take my life, and that it was me who had slain him as he deserved.

"He was mad," I yelled, unable longer to contain myself, "why else would he have dragged around a lubberly swab like you?"

Deval went as white as chalk, and I might have seen what I had done, and been able to nip it in the bud, had the look-out not at that very moment shouted that there was a sail ahead. So things took the course they did, we captured the *Rose*, I lost a leg, Deval did likewise, and I acquired a new name, Barbecue, which was not to be taken lightly.

After that we must have sailed in the West Indies for about a year, before Flint drank himself to death in Savannah. It was during that year that he lost his reason, the little amount he had ever had, and made his reputation as the cruellest and bloodiest pirate ever to have infested the oceans. If you ask me, he was out to get himself killed in battle rather than admit defeat. He really was the sort who would have to die before his life had any meaning. But did it help him? Like Hell it did!

He would throw caution to the winds, and cry out for all the world to hear that he was the formidable pirate Flint, the last of them all, who had the intellect and repute to strike mortal fear into the whole human race. And so it was: you cannot present yourself as cruel and implacable in the long term without becoming so, not even with aims as worthy as Flint's. And what is there then to choose from, other than madness or sudden death, if it is to have any meaning while it lasts?

Ay, had it not been for me we would certainly have been captured, killed or hanged, the whole lot of us. Was I to give up, I who had sailed my whole life in gloves to leave myself unmarked, I who had arranged everything so well with Dolores ashore and a body-guard at sea, just so that Flint could cause the ruination of us all with his sick and rum-soaked brain? It was not likely, to put it mildly! I made sure the *Walrus* changed her shape before every attack as always. I made sure the crew kept their mouths shut in front of strangers and on land. I took care that we continued to be a ghost ship that emerged from the void and disappeared again, leaving only fear and terror in our wake. I held Flint in check when he wanted to attack ships where the outcome was uncertain. Ay, if anyone was counting, I must have saved many hundreds from a painful death that year, my own included.

So we remained a nameless and frightening rumour until after Flint's death. So well had we hidden our activities that no one had any firm evidence that we existed at all. I took the risk of returning to Bristol and buying myself the Spy-glass to get hold of Billy Bones and that accursed map. I sent for Dolores, and for a while I'm damned if we weren't respectable folk just like any number of others in Bristol.

Occasionally, Jim, I've felt sorry for Flint, just as you felt sorry for me. Flint really did reckon he could save the lives of wretched sailors and improve conditions for them. He hated shipowners and captains from the bottom of his heart, which must in that case have been a good one, despite everything. No, what was wrong with him was his head. Though he had a few lucid moments towards the end, between bouts of rage and intoxication.

On a mild and clear night, somewhere in the Atlantic, where we were waiting while the *Walrus* rocked gently in a powerful swell, her backed sails billowing in a light breeze, Flint sent for me. He was sitting in his cabin at his one and only table. The oil lamp, the very same that hangs in my study now, cast strange shadows over his ravaged face.

"Sit down, Silver!" said he. "Join me for a glass of rum."

I sat down opposite him and he filled two glasses to the brim with a steady hand.

"You're the only fellow who's worth a damn on board this ship," said he. "Including myself."

He paused, as if he wanted me to agree, but what could I say to that?

"Why did you never let yourself be made cap'n?" he asked.

"To cover my back," I replied.

"Ain't I got mine covered? What's wrong with my back?"

"You can be deposed. No one can depose John Silver."

He stared hard at me for some time. He was trying to work out whether I was threatening him with removal.

"Silver," said he after a while, "I can never make you out."

"No," I replied with a grin, "that's what I hope. That would be worse than death."

Flint peered into his rum glass as if it were a crystal ball.

"That's right, Silver," said he. "It's right, what I said. You're the only one who's worth a damn. You've got judgement. Tell me, Silver, am I losing my mind? Give me a frank answer! You know I'd never hurt a hair of your head."

"I don't know," said I, as the honest soul I could be. "I don't know how much you had to lose. But it sometimes seems as if you're out to take the lives of us all, and your own first, which would help neither the one nor the other."

"I know," said he in a cracked voice, taking a good swig of rum. "I know. I thought I knew what I wanted in life. To put to death as many villains as possible. Remove them from this earth. Avenge all dead seamen, that was my aim. But now I've come round to thinking that we ain't no more than fly-shit, whatever we do. I'm the dreaded pirate Flint, yet I can't even say it out loud if I want to stay alive. I've become nameless, and damn me, so are all of us. We don't count. In the eyes of the world we're nothing. What is an individual human being, Silver?

Nothing, absolutely nothing. Do you know – of course you do, you're an educated and well-read fellow – that that bastard Cromwell sent ten thousand Irish and Scottish convicts to Barbados? Not one poor devil survived. Not a single one, Silver. Who remembers them now, any of them, or what they thought or wanted? They're gone, evaporated like mist into thin air. D'you know what I heard from an old buccaneer? The Spaniards had sent a group of soldiers to exterminate some Indians. One of the soldiers forced an Indian up against a tree with his lance. The Indian only had his knife and was as good as dead. But what did he do? He threw himself forward and impaled himself on the lance, so that he could stick his own knife in the Spaniard. They both died in one another's arms. What's the point of it? What good does it do? None. 'Tis nothing but dust in the memory of the world. Or look at the monks that L'Olonnais forced to erect ladders against the walls of Cartagena. He thought the Spaniards wouldn't shoot their own clergy. But neither God nor the Spaniards gave a damn about a few wretched monks, however much they prayed for their lives. They were gunned down to the last cassock. Who cares, Silver? A few monks, a Spanish soldier, an Indian or ten thousand convicts more or less, it don't matter. And seamen, how many lose their lives, d'you reckon? A couple of thousand in English ships every year. And what do they get for it? Not a bloody thing, not even a decent funeral. We're fly-shit, Silver, and count for naught. Ay, 'tis true, 'tis just as well to put an end to our misery, that's probably the most rational thing to do. There's no reason to linger on in this world. An individual human being like me is totally dispensable, Silver. Totally dispensable."

"Not on board the *Walrus*," I replied. "No ship has had a better cap'n."

"I don't give a shit about the *Walrus*!" he cried. "A coffin, that's what she is, with a collection of Sybarites who only think of themselves. No more'n that."

He drained his glass.

"You're a good man, Silver," said he, wiping his mouth. "How the Hell do you manage to stand it? What keeps you going? Don't a man like you puzzle his head about the meaning of it all?"

"No," said I.

"Why not? Why don't you drown yourself in rum like the rest of us? Why don't you think about it all the time?"

"The Devil alone knows," I replied with a laugh. "Mebbe because I'd go mad if I did."

Flint stared at me uncomprehendingly.

"Like you," I added, just to square the count.

Then I got up and went out. A month later Flint was dead. But he is not forgotten, and it may be that the greatest thing he did in his life was to have a posthumous reputation. Like myself. He was right in one respect, at any rate: a life that does not live on after its death in some way, whether in print or in popular legend, is no more than fly-shit. Or mist evaporated into thin air.

Thirty-nine

T HIS MORNING, LIKE so many others, the darkness of night paled imperceptibly to grey, and black turned to blue, except in the east where the first rays of the sun rose like a flaming fire. Here on Madagascar you hardly know where you are before it is suddenly light or dark. Dusk and dawn are like the flashes of a cannon. In Bristol, as I remember, the sun would go down so slowly over the sea in the west that it looked as if it would hang on the horizon for ever. Here the light flooded in all at once and filled every tiny corner. The only memory of darkness was the sharply defined shadows.

The brown paper lay before me in the harsh light, naked, unwritten, as alluring as Eliza's sun-tanned body, as irresistible as Dolores' unyielding eyes, in readiness to receive any life, any story. It was just a question of picking and choosing.

Yet now the whole morning has gone and the paper is still untouched. I am beginning to feel that I have little more of any value to write. John Silver's life is over and done. The urge to write has run its course. Gone is the madness of wanting to write a log-book when the voyage is over. I am as empty as a drained bottle of rum.

Yet I cannot complain. I have thrown the bodies overboard, John Silver himself amongst them. I no longer need to associate myself with him or anyone else. Not even Flint will walk again, I am certain of that. Now they will be able to live undisturbed by my need to involve myself, if they can, and stand on what feet they still have.

Days have gone by. What confounded emptiness! What am I waiting for? Death? That is the worst wait of all, waiting for the void. It is shameful, but would it not be best to put a line through the whole bloody lot, through me, through Long John Silver, draw a skull and crossbones in the log-book, bring the dead reckoning to a conclusion? I have always thought it was sinful to lay a hand on yourself, not to dare to live the only life you have. But when life is at an end anyhow, and the only thing you have left is a rotting hulk with broken masts and yards that will not even bear a sail ... And who the Hell would be concerned whether I had sinned against myself and my articles when I am dead and gone? Not me, at any rate, and I would be the chief mourner in this case, after all.

Several days have passed. Weeks? Months? I am still alive. Today I went into my study for the first time since I finished. There it lay, the life of John Silver, as it all happened. I thumbed through it, dipping into it here and there, and suddenly felt a strange emotion. It was tenderness, pride, shame, uncertainty, wonder, distaste, all intermingled. Was this really what I had intended, that John Silver should lie here and rot away, like me?

And then I started thinking about you, Jim, and of my resolves. That John Silver should not live in disrepute, that he should not stand unchallenged, that he should have the last word – that was his mark – or at least that he should have a say in the matter and that people should know that he was also a human being of sorts, alone and his own man, with his damned back to watch, but nonetheless some kind of human being. And at that, Jim, I was moved to tears. I owe it to John Silver, in view of all he has given me, to make sure he has a chance to live on after his death. Shall he too, like so many in our profession, have lived in vain? No! He shall not evaporate into thin air.

So I intend to stay alive a while longer, I regret to say, until another ship puts in that can carry John Silver to you. You will have to take responsibility for him, Jim. I depend upon you. I have nobody else to entrust him to. I have written you a note to explain what it is you have in your hands.

That's all, Jim. I wish you a long and happy life. And I think you might join me in a toast to our old shipmate. Long live John Silver!

Forty

WELL, JIM, IT was too early to wish John Silver a long life after all. There was no point in trying to kill him off. But now finally I hope we can bring things to a conclusion, now at last I can be sure of my ground. Never take an advance on death, Jim, not even your own, that's what I've always said.

I hung on to what little life there was left for the sake of these pages that are cluttering up my desk, describing what it was really like to be Long John Silver, called Barbecue by his friends, if he had any, and by his foes, of which he had many. An end to foolery and fantasy. An end to humbug and deceit. Cards on the table for the first time. Nothing but the truth, straight to the point, without tricks or evasions. How it really was and nothing more. That was what was needed, though not to keep me sane for a while longer, as I had imagined, but just to keep me alive. For that is how it has turned out, whether I like it or not.

And now that I see the camp fires below the cliff, and hear the calls of the soldiers who have come to take me, alive rather than dead, it is this life that counts. I shall defend myself, there can be no doubt about that, to the last drop of blood if they will not accept my conditions. I shall take some of the lives of those who are ordered to lay hands on mine. Give and take, that was ever my course, and I pity neither them nor myself.

I have finally sent Jack away. It was not easy to make him go, the last one remaining. He insisted he wanted to give his life for me even though I would not hear of it. So pointless! How did he think I would benefit from his life when we were both dead, I roared at him in my former voice. There were more than an hundred men on the frigate that was lying so peacefully at anchor in Ranter Bay, together with marines and thirty-six cannon that could be put ashore. Of course half of the men would be killed when they stormed the cliff, and maybe more if there were two of us. But the result would be the same: an ignominious death for both him and myself.

Jack started talking about fetching reinforcements and gathering a band of natives to attack the Englishmen from the rear.

"Those are marines," said I. "It would be a blood-bath, no more an' no less."

I knew perfectly well how it would be if an hundred negroes with just a few muskets and pistols between them, and otherwise only bows and arrows, set upon several score well-drilled marines and twice the number of battle-hardened sailors of the Royal Navy. The natives would be slaughtered like cattle even before our turn came. But Jack would not listen, however much I shouted and however I expressed it.

"Are you deaf?" I screamed.

"I'm staying," said he.

"Like Hell you are!" I roared, and picked up the two pistols that were lying on the table. "If you don't get out of here I'll shoot you on the spot. So you'll get what you want in any case."

"Go ahead!" the devil said quite calmly, with a grin on his face to boot.

It enraged me so, that I put the pistol to my own head. That had its effect, and shiver my sides if in my agitation I was not in earnest. Now it was my turn to smile.

"You see," said I, reverting to my amicable tone, "there's naught to be done. You know as well as I do that I mean what I say. I've never led you by the nose. We might as well part friends."

"Indeed," said Jack despondently. "You and I are brothers, are we not?"

"As you like, Jack. We're brothers, but I'll stake my life we're bastards in that case, each of us in his own way. And don't look so damned miserable. It's all up with me now, you can see that. The old hulk is rotten and the cap'n's brains are addled. That's how it is, and nothin' to be done. You're not exactly a young man any more, neither, but you're strong and healthy. You've got a good few years left. Go back to your tribe, like the others: do whatever you please, but get away from here!"

I really wanted to rid myself of him because he was looking at me as if he cared for me above all else. And he had tears in his eyes. He took a step forward, embraced me and said that I always had talked nonsense. I freed myself from his grasp and pushed him out. He went into the weapon store and emerged with a cutlass and three pistols. He gave me a look which I shall not forget for a long time – or not until a day or two hence, when I am dead – and turned and disappeared without a word, as was his wont.

But who was it who had the wool pulled over his eyes in the end but me? Jack went straight down to the soldiers' camp, fired his three shots and struck out wildly around him until he himself fell to a well-aimed ball. He took fourteen men with him, as was assiduously pointed out to me on the morrow by an immaculate marine officer who came up to see me with a white flag to state his dirty business.

"Was that one of your men?" he asked with a look of abhorrence on his face.

"Ay," said I, for I was not going to deny Jack as the last thing I did this side of the grave. "But he was not obeying my orders. I sent him away so that he wouldn't die unnecessarily. I'm not so stupid that I don't know what business you're engaged on."

"We have orders to take a certain Long John Silver, known as Barbecue, to Bristol, where he is to be tried for crimes against human-ity. Is that you?"

"My good man," said I, laughing so much that tears ran down my face, "you bring a frigate with several hundred men from England to Ranter Bay, acting on orders, and meet a one-legged man of advanced years, and then you ask him who he is!"

"I have to be sure."

"Sure of what?"

"Sure that it is the right person."

"Ay, of course," said I, laughing again, to the officer's obvious discon-certion. "What would it look like if you turned up before Trelawney and his cronies with some poor devil who had nothing to do with the matter whatsoever!"

"Trelawney?" he exclaimed. "Do you know him?"

"Ay," said I, "we made a voyage together, he and I. I cooked his food, if I remember rightly, but I never had the chance to square the account."

"So you are . . . ?"

"Long John Silver, Barbecue. Just so, Cap'n, or whatever you are. That's me, no more an' no less, at your service, sir, as you see."

He looked at me and looked all around.

"I have orders . . ."

"Ay, we've heard that already. But how? – that's what I'd very much like to know. You want me alive, I understand. Nothing less will do for the gentlemen in Bristol."

The officer could do no more than nod rhythmically.

"It won't be as easy as you might have thought," I told him. "You can't shoot at me, in case a bullet hits me. You can't bombard my cliff, because the roof might fall in on me. You can only charge at me all together, so that those I don't manage to shoot dead can overpower me. Is it worth it? There'll be a blood-bath, sir. With that brass cannon that never overheats, I'd easily be able to kill fifty of you before you reached me. Is it really worth it, I ask?"

"I have my orders," said he obstinately.

"Is that the only thing you have to say? Try to think for yourself! It usually works if you push yourself like the Devil!"

But instead he clammed up completely. What was wrong with him, I wondered? Then I understood. He was afraid, scared out of his wits, no more and no less. Nothing strange in that, if you thought about it. He had obviously heard one horror story after another about my modest person and probably reckoned that I had a whole company of blood-thirsty pirates hidden in the bushes. He was expecting a shot in the back at any moment. Jack's frenzied attack had strengthened this conviction.

"I'm quite alone," said I.

"Alone?"

He looked at me incredulously.

"Ay," said I, "as alone as God our Father in Heaven. The crew and the rats have deserted the ship and there's only me left."

"Only . . . " he began, a little colour coming back into his cheeks.

"Only me, ay," I interrupted. "I know what you're thinking, that it won't be difficult to get some shackles on me. One man against an hundred and fifty, that's nothing, says you. Not so fast, sir, says I. Remember you have to take me alive, and that I can fire this cannon as well as any cannoneer in the Royal Navy; ay, better even. My terms remain at fifty of your men. And not even then can you be sure of taking me alive. I can always put a gun to my own head. Don't you think I would be capable of that? I can see you're in some doubt. Then you should just remember that I'm an old man, a sinking ship, that's what I am. Do you reckon I would let myself be clapped in irons and spend six months below deck, just to be brought before a judge and then hanged like a dog?"

He looked at me as if in two minds, not because he was afraid any more, but because he had at long last begun to think for himself.

"Them's my terms," I concluded. "I'll settle the hash of fifty of your rosy-cheeked marines and deliver myself blessedly departed and stone dead, a corpse that could never be preserved long enough to be hung up for public exhibition in Bristol. What d'you say?"

"What do you want?" he asked with reluctance and irritation, but not without a hint of interest.

"To do a deal!" said I.

"I cannot be bought," was his response.

"I thought as much. I assume your pay for taking on this commission is ample. And that you were selected for your incorruptible nature, since you were going to have to deal with me. No, I wasn't thinking of trying to buy you. I can recognise a man of principle when I see one, as sure as my name's Silver. Come inside with me and I'll show you something! You don't need to be afraid, I'm alone, and don't intend to attack you from behind. As I've said, you have everything to gain and nothing to lose from making a treaty with me. You won't get me back alive, you may lay to that. But I can offer you something at least as valuable, maybe even more so, than the wretched life that yet remains to me."

He was still hesitant, but followed me in all the same. His eyes opened wide when he caught sight of all my riches, especially the precious stones lying scattered loose over my desk. By coincidence a ray of sunlight fell right across the desk and made them sparkle for all they were worth:

there is nothing like the deep glitter and scintillating reflections of precious stones.

"You ain't regretting your position?" I asked playfully.

He shook his head.

"If we can reach an agreement," I went on, "you're welcome to take whatever's left of these when I'm dead. 'Tis all one to me."

I noted the glint of greed in his eyes.

"But here," said I, indicating the sheaves of paper in pride of place at the centre of the desk, "this is what I want to show you."

He looked at me with incomprehension, as if I was not in full command of my faculties. He was not exactly talkative, this dutiful servant of the Crown. Unless he were just afraid of falling into temptation and giving way to his conflicting desires.

"These pages," I explained, admittedly not without a certain measure of satisfaction, for it had been a minor form of torture compiling it all, "contain the life that was mine, the true history of Long John Silver, known as Barbecue. Don't look so astonished! I can both read and write. How else do you think I was able to lead so many by the nose in my time? You've read young Hawkins' yarn, I presume? To find out what sort of monster – what sort of enemy to mankind – you were being sent out to bring back home?"

It was crystal clear that the officer no longer knew whether he was coming or going, but he could still nod.

"I surprise you, don't I? I wasn't the sort you'd expected to meet? Not by a long shot! But it ain't so strange, when all's said an' done, as I used to say. The John Silver you came for is lying there on the table. That's a fact, though 'tis hard to believe. I'm afraid you won't be able to hang him from a gallows the way you could me, but he can do everything else. He can be put on trial and sentenced, not to death, but to oblivion, and that's a punishment as good as any. I'm offering you this instead of myself, and 'tis no bad exchange, if you ask me. You get a whole life, from beginning to end, including all my good deeds and evil acts, in black and white, without excuses or prevarications, just as it was, straight to the point."

"What do you mean by that?" he exclaimed.

"A life," said I, "flesh and blood, instead of an empty and leaky hulk like me. I'm prepared to hand this over to you. Trelawney and his friends wanted John Silver alive. So here you are, says I. There he is, for ever and ever if required. I want you to take him back with you, give him to young Jim Hawkins to read, and let him decide John Silver's further fortunes and adventures. Hawkins has already done his bit. But I'd like a receipt to show that you've taken possession of John Silver's life. It must be written in the log-book and witnessed by me and by yourself. In return I promise not to take fifty or so of your marines to the grave with me. And those are generous terms."

"I can't possibly go along with this," he objected, as stubborn as a mule, stupid as a cow and blind as a bat.

"Don't you understand a thing?" I yelled. "You won't get me to Bristol alive, whatever happens. That's the essence of it."

"You have to sleep and eat," said he self-confidently. "You can't hold out for ever."

"I'm damned if I intend to, either. Come with me and I'll show you something interesting."

I limped out to the yard with the officer in tow.

"Look at this!" said I, pointing to a fuse sticking out of a pipe in the ground. "As a soldier you must know what a fuse looks like. This one goes straight down to a powder-keg that probably has an hundred times more powder in it than you have aboard your frigate. I'm sure you're smart enough to be able to imagine what would happen if I lit it. The whole accursed cliff we're standing on would be blown sky-high. D'you understand now?"

To prove that I was serious I struck a light and held it an inch from the fuse. Beads of sweat broke out on the officer's steadfast brow.

"I thought so," said I, lit the fuse and let it burn for a couple of inches before putting it out again.

He had gone as stiff as a handspike, except for his knees that were knocking uncontrollably, much to my amusement.

"You don't need to feel ashamed," said I. "You ain't the first to have difficulties with John Silver. But you can think yourself lucky you're still alive. If you play your cards right, you'll not only stay alive, you'll get home with your honour intact. And that, sir, is something that not many men who've had dealings with me have been able to do. What d'you say?"

He looked for a few moments as if he needed to get his breath.

"I'll have to speak to the ship's captain," he finally managed to blurt out.

"Quite right too!" said I, and slapped him on the back in a friendly fashion. "The cap'n must lend us his log-book. And don't forget to tell 'em that everything up here is free for anyone to lay their hands on when I'm dead and buried. You've got the whole day ahead of you, but you'd do best to bring me an answer an hour before nightfall. If I'm going to manage to shoot fifty or so, I'd rather see what I'm a-doing. And another thing. You've probably observed that there's on'y one narrow path that comes up here. Explain to the cap'n that a single shot from my twelve pounder, loaded with grapeshot and case-shot, is enough to take the lives of half a dozen or more, and that I'll have time to reload before the next bunch appear. Ask him to think hard whether his conscience will allow him to pick a dozen of his men who will definitely have to forfeit their lives just to capture me."

The officer turned and went without a word, struck dumb with astonishment, presumably, if he had been using his brain at all. There was a risk that he was so benumbed and his pride so injured that he might have given up thinking altogether. He was certainly not far off it, at any rate.

But no more than an hour or two had passed before he was back, waving his white flag and with the log-book under his arm. He still said not a word. Having to strike his flag for the likes of me naturally offended against everything he held sacred in this life. I opened the log-book and wrote: "Herewith received on board *Long John Silver, The true and eventful History of my Life of Liberty and Adventure as a Gentleman of Fortune and Enemy to Mankind*, to be conveyed to Bristol and delivered to Jim Hawkins, Esquire." The officer signed in a sprawling hand, and I witnessed his signature with my most elegant flourishes.

"Tomorrow," said I, "you can come up and fetch the papers, including the end. I have a few more lines to add."

He closed the log-book.

"Just don't think you can take me by surprise in the night," I added. "The cannon is loaded, I'll light torches and there ain't nothing wrong with my hearing. And don't forget about the fuse!"

There was little risk of that, to judge by his face.

"Be of good cheer, my hearty!" said I. "John Silver, dead or alive, ain't everything in life."

And with that I was alone again, and sat down to complete my story. I am the only one left in the end. I should have foreseen long ago that it would finish like this. My life was an open log-book, but did I ever read it before it was too late? Not at all!

Alone, then, until death me do part. That was the price to be paid in this world, I have to assume, for keeping your back covered. Did I pay dear or come off easily, you may ask? Should we laugh or cry? The Devil alone knows! I did not grieve over it while I lived, anyhow. And there is no point in an inquisition at the very end. But you have to ask yourself whether liberty and loneliness do not go hand in hand in this world, or so it seems, if you want to be a human being.

Not that I suffered because of it. I managed to live all my life before I became aware of it. But I have come to see now that loneliness is the only sin here on earth, and the only real punishment for the likes of me. That, and possibly only that, is worse than death. But regrets? No, even I have some pride left in my soul. Besides, who should I repent to? I never promised anybody anything, not even myself, till death us did part. I never entered a marriage contract with the rest of humanity, and did indeed become its enemy. Ay, I was not even married to myself. Yet I survived unpunished, it seems, and who should I thank for that, if not myself? It would be too much to hope that God had His omnipotent finger in the pie. But if I were to wish for one thing this side of the grave it would be to be received into Heaven after all. Just imagine seeing the faces of all the faithful, and all those captains by the grace of God, when I turned up!

Well, I have lived, you may lay to that, as true as my name's John Silver, known as Long, known as Barbecue, though it did not last right to the end, and perhaps has not been much to boast about. On the other hand I have done what I could to outlive myself. That was not the intention, of course, but I had no idea what it meant to write down a life such as mine. Tomorrow a high-principled officer is coming to fetch this John Silver. What will Silver's life be after that, if he has any? To be honest, 'tis all the same to me on the other side. But I'll lay for certain that he won't go forth to set an example for marines, priests and ships' captains.

What is there left to say? I did as well as I could from the beginning to the end. I remained true to the self I became, and that's that. I may have had a noose around my neck, but I covered my back. If you ask me.

The Admiralty, by Hand

IR,

I write this letter in haste to advise you of the outcome of the
expedition with which I was encharged, to arrest the pirate
John Silver and bring him to England to receive his rightful
punishment. The official report will follow in a few days
when the ship has docked in London. This letter is being
despatched by courier from Plymouth.

Regrettably I am obliged to inform you that it was not
possible to bring back the said John Silver alive. I can however convey the gratifying intelligence that he is dead, with
absolute certainty, and that the world is thus freed from
one of the worst enemies to mankind. There is consequently
also every reason to believe that piracy has been eradicated
for the foreseeable future. Without John Silver and his like
to entice seamen into becoming what they called gentlemen
of fortune, it will be easier to prevent further depletion of
the ranks.

Before he died, John Silver handed over to me personally
a manuscript which contains, as far as I can judge, a full
account of his infamous life. He asked me to deliver this to
Jim Hawkins Esquire, who, as you will perhaps remember,
was the one who opened our eyes to the possibility of finding and punishing John Silver. I have of course given Jim
Hawkins to understand that he cannot make free use of
Silver's account without consulting the Admiralty, and he

declared himself willing to abide by this stipulation. Having read the account during the homeward voyage I would respectfully recommend that it not be published without substantial revision. It would, it is true, serve as an exemplary deterrent for our youth, but it also includes a number of sections of a compromising nature for the Kingdom, among them the rather ticklish affair of Governor Warrender at Fort Charles in Kinsale, and the captain's disregard of regulations pertaining to female slaves on board his ship. In addition there is the unacceptable fact that John Silver displays not the least remorse for his sinful and criminal existence. On the contrary, he seems to maintain that his life was right and proper for one such as himself, and he ended his days, moreover, as a man of some wealth, secure in his fortress, surrounded by slaves whose freedom he had purchased. This is hardly salutary reading, especially as Silver himself describes the life he has led as one of liberty, rather than of wrongdoing. It is a matter of profound regret that we could not punish him as he deserved, and hang him in chains for public exhibition while he yet lived.

I regarded myself, however, as having no choice. Firstly, we were surprised by a well-armed troop of his pirates in the middle of the night, and lost fourteen men before prevailing over them with great bravery and forcing their retreat. Silver asserts in his manuscript that the attack was the work of a single man, but what else can one expect from such a mendacious deceiver as he? Secondly, Silver threatened to kill fifty of our marines, and then take his own life, if we stormed his fortress. There can be no doubt that he was serious in his intent, and was fully capable of both acts. While we were negotiating, he even ignited the fuse to his powder store and extinguished it only at the last moment, in my presence. My judgement of the situation and of Silver's state of mind was proved correct in the clearest possible manner. Having taken possession of his written account, and having rejoined my men, a mighty explosion was heard as Silver blew himself, and the cliff which he had fortified, to pieces. Two of our men were killed by falling rocks, and several received minor wounds. Unfortunately very little remained of Silver's stolen goods collected over a lifetime: scarce sufficient, in my estimation, to reimburse the costs of the expedition. The profit which Sir John Trelawney predicted has thus not been realised. I enclose the letter which John Silver addressed to Jim Hawkins. It will be perfectly obvious from this that Silver's account should be treated with the utmost discretion, and possibly denominated secret, in accordance with the provision relating to threats to the security of the Realm.

Your humble and obedient servant
Captain William Cunningham

Jim Hawkins, by Hand

JIM,

I bequeath and entrust these pages to you. They are, you could say, my log-book. In my old age I amused myself by recollecting, as the aged do, and writing down what it was like to be Long John Silver. If I have one wish before I die, Jim, it is that you should read these pages. I know that I was not God's favourite child in the eyes of folk like you, but I was a human being at least, and a good shipmate. I saved your life, as I am sure you will remember. I do not demand that you in return should save mine as it is described in these pages. But I do ask you not to kill off the only life that John Silver had. Put him into safe-keeping. One day, perhaps, there will be someone who needs to know that he really existed and was some kind of human being after all. Then he will not have lived in vain, like so many others, and to no avail. This is my last wish.

John Silver

Postscript

Every literary work is in part the author's own and in large part borrowed plumage. I would therefore like to thank the following persons for their kind but involuntary assistance. Without them this book would have been fiction pure and simple.

Liars

Daniel Defoe, Robert Louis Stevenson, Sven Delblanc, Gabriel García Márquez, Albert Camus, William Golding, René Char, Dostoyevsky, R. F. Delderfield, John Goldsmith, Patrick O'Brian, Tobias Smollett, C. M. Bennett, Henry Fielding, Machiavelli, The Holy Spirit.

Truth-tellers

Captain Johnson (alias Daniel Defoe), Exquemelin, Thorkild Hansen, Michel Le Bris, Marcus Rediker, Gérard A. Jaeger, Gilles Lapouge, David Mitchell, William Dampier, Kåre Lauring, James Sutherland, Yves Kergof, Janne Flyghed, Thomas Anderberg, Erland Holmström.

Those who would still prefer not to believe that reality is stranger than fiction may be interested to know that as far as can be judged from the evidence suggests that the following, and much more besides, accord fully with the truth: Edward England's later life, Miss Warrender's tragic marriage and end, the buccaneers' *matelotage* and wife-sharing, the blinded ship *Rôdeur*, the clergy's treatment of slaves on the island of St Thomas, Defoe's lies, deceits and history of pirates, the negroes' chronic melancholy, the surgeon's mouth-opener, Taylor's withered hands, the Indians from the Mosquito Coast who sailed with the pirates,

Judge Jeffreys at the Angel Tavern, the tyranny of ships' captains appointed by the grace of God (with the exception of Snelgrave), the newly baptised slave with the amputated hands and feet who wrote to the mission to thank them for his redemption, the sudden and ugly deaths of Captains Rickets and Skinner on the *Fancy*, Roger Ball's attempt to blow himself up, the ban on women on pirate ships, the rise and fall of Captain Mackra, Matthews' punitive expedition to bring Plantain to the gallows, the reaction of captains to Snelgrave's book on the slave trade, the indomitable nature of the Sakalava tribe, the books in Snelgrave's ship's library, Blackbeard's game with his pistols at Israel Hands' expense, the Spanish soldier and the Indian who stabbed each other to death, the wild boar that ate apricots and had tasty flesh, Silver's tunnel through Old Head of Kinsale, the Isle of Sainte Marie in Madagascar as a short-lived Paradise for pirates, etc, etc.

A special note of thanks is also due to the pirates Thomas Roberts, John Cane and William Davison, whose confessions of sins before their imminent hanging have been reproduced here in unabridged form, in so far as one can rely on Daniel Defoe, in his *General History of the Pyrates*, having been true to the originals.

Finally, a note of gratitude to all the sailors whose intolerable lives must surpass the understanding of anyone who has the slightest ounce of humanity in him. Without all those seamen, upon whose dead bodies the modern welfare state was constructed, neither this book nor Long John Silver would ever have seen the light of day.

Björn Larsson,
on board the S/Y *Rustica*, Camariñas, 20 July 1994.